Alexandr's Cherished Submissive
A Submissive's Wish Novel

By: Ann Mayburn
Published by Fated Desires Publishing, LLC.
ISBN: 978-1-62322-157-7
© 2015 Ann Mayburn
Cover Art by Scott Carpenter

This ebook is licensed for your personal enjoyment only.
This ebook may not be re-sold or given away to other
people. If you would like to share this book with another
person, please purchase an additional copy for each person
or use proper retail channels to lend a copy. If you're
reading this book and did not purchase it, or it was not
purchased for your use only, then please return it and
purchase your own copy. Thank you for respecting the
hard work of this author. To obtain permission to excerpt
portions of the text, please contact the publisher at
admin@fateddesires.com.
All characters in this book are fiction and figments of the
author's imagination.

Alexandr's Cherished Submissive

7 years ago

From the moment Alexandr Novikov met the young auburn haired woman bartending at her uncle's pub in Ireland, he'd been fascinated by her delicate beauty and fiery spirit. Unfortunately, he is in no position to offer her the kind of safe, normal life she deserves so he attempts to put her from his mind for her own good. Something easier said then done when a deal is struck between the Novikov Bratva and the Irish Cleary Gang, an arrangement that includes Alex and his men being on twenty-four hour bodyguard duty with the object of his forbidden desires.

Jessica Venture came to Dublin to spend some time bonding with her birth mother's family, a connect she desperately needed after losing her adoptive parents within a year of each other back in the States. The last thing she expected was to fall in love with a handsome, mysterious, and sometimes scary man who was well known for his sexual appetite, but rejected her attempts to seduce him.

There are outside forces that will do anything to keep them apart, and Jessica will have to make a desperate choice that will change their lives forever.

Warning: *There is light bondage, domestic discipline, spanking, and a F/F scene that is a voyeuristic Doms delight.*

Author's Note: This is part One of Two for Alex and Jessica's story. In Alexandr's Cherished Submissive we get a look into the past and the events that shaped Alex and Jessica into the people they are today. Part Two, Alexandr's Reluctant Submissive, is present day on, and the expected release date is August 2015.

Dear Beloved Readers,

Thank you, as always, for giving me the chance to entertain you and welcome back to the world of the Novikov *Bratva*. Alex and Jessica's story is a long, complex one with many things happening in the past that will have a ripple effect on the future. Because of this, Alex's story has been split into two gigantic parts. Part 1, Alexandr's Cherished Submissive, is about Alex and Jessica's past, while Part 2, Alexandr's Reluctant Submissive, is present day on. Now, for those that have read the previous books in the series(which I would HIGHLY suggest) you know 'something bad' is going to happen to Alex and Jessica. It does, it'll rip your heart out, but I don't end the book on a negative note, so keep reading even though you feel like rending your clothing and pulling out your hair. Or you throw your eReader against the wall. Either way, don't. ;)

I would also like to thank my Beta readers for helping me whip Alex into shape, Karah Belseth, April Renee Symes, Ashley Haines, Leann Mallow, Jennifer Severino, Tammy McGowan, Barb Evans, and the ever so lovely Dianne Sandvik. Thank you ladies so much for your suggestions and sharp eyes, you really helped me smooth Alex's story out and went above and beyond the call of duty to battle your way through my unedited crap. I mean raw masterpiece. ;)

So grab your tissues and a cold drink, sit back, and I hope you enjoy Alex.

Ann Mayburn

Author Note

This is part One of Two for Alex and Jessica's story. In Alexandr's Cherished Submissive we get a look into the past and the events that shaped Alex and Jessica into the people they are today. Part Two, Alexandr's Reluctant Submissive, is present day on, and the expected release date is early Fall 2015.

Glossary

a mhuirnín- Irish for 'my darling'

bogger- An Irish term for someone outside the city, a farmer, someone country/redneck

Bratva- The Russian Mafia, more specifically it's often used to denote the different organizations. For example, the Novikov *Bratva*, or the Sokolov *Bratva*.

Devushka milaya- Russian for 'Sweet girl'.

dorogoya- Russian for dear/darling

Gobshite- A variation of <u>shit</u>, especially in Ireland and the United Kingdom

Krasavitsa- Russian for beautiful

Laskovaya- Russian for Sweetie

Lyublyu tebya vsem sertsem, vsey dushyu- Russian for 'I love you with all my heart, with all my soul'.

Malyshka- affectionate form of 'little girl' in Russian

Pizda- Russian for pussy.

prinsessa moya- Russian for 'My princess'.

Radost moya. Moya krasivaya. Ya lyubb-lyu tebya vsem sertsem, vsey dushoyu. Ya budu vsegda lyubit tebya. Vsegda- Russian for 'My joy, my beauty. I love you with all of my heart and soul. I will always love you, always.'

Sinn Féin- is an Irish republican political party active in both the Republic of Ireland and Northern Ireland.

Sladkaya moya- Russian for 'My sweet'.

Sovietnik- ("Councilor"), is the advisor and most close trusted individuals to the *Pakhan*, similar to the Consigliere in Italian-American Mafia crime families and Sicilian Mafia clans.

to, chto ty delayesh' so mnoy- Russian for 'What are you doing to me?'

Ti takaya krasivaya- Russian for 'You are so beautiful to me."

Ya palyubIl tebyas pervava vzglyada- Russian for 'I have loved you since the first moment I saw you'.

Chapter One

7 years ago
Dublin, Ireland

Alexandr Novikov lounged in a not-so-well-lit back corner of a cavernous room, relaxing in the boisterous atmosphere. Rain had dampened the wool of his jacket, releasing the musk of the fabric every time he shifted. A hint of the sweet scent of pipe tobacco had seeped into the bones of the building, which, on damp nights like this, released the ghostly smell of phantom smoke. In a neat twist of fate, the place he found himself in tonight was a high-end working man's bar that had seen more than its fair share of violence but still managed to retain its weathered glory. One of his favorite places on Earth to visit, even if he was here for *Bratva* business.

The pub had been around since the 1700s and was controlled by the Irish mafia for almost as long. In spite of the frequent fights and roughhousing, the bar itself was crafted of rock-solid, aged wood that had taken on a rich patina over the years, giving the thick planks an almost silky look. The mullioned windows and stained glass, which looked out into a bleary view of the street, were either original or excellent reproductions. Carefully trimmed ivy grew over portions of the intricate brickwork on the exterior of the building and well maintained flower boxes on the upper level windows allowed the bar to blend in nicely with its upscale neighborhood.

Regardless of the fact that the pub was often filled with clientele of a rougher sort, there were rarely any conflicts. Anyone who came here for a drink knew better than to make any trouble. Peter

Cleary, the owner of this establishment and a good portion of Dublin, didn't suffer fools gladly. Probably one of the reasons Alex got along with him so well, and nothing that was about to happen tonight would endanger their friendship. While he would do everything he could to minimize any disturbance, the man he was hunting was at the top of a long list of assassinations he'd been assigned. As powerful as Peter was, the Novikov *Bratva* was a deadly leviathan lurking in the criminal depths that sharks like the Cleary mafia could only begin to imagine. Still, that didn't mean Alex liked creating problems for one of the few men he considered more than a business acquaintance.

Alex had been coming to this bar for over ten years for work and pleasure, and even though it almost felt like home, he was on high alert. Without being conspicuous, he constantly scanned the crowd while sipping his pint of dark lager, knowing that he blended in perfectly. When he traveled abroad on family business, to dress like a local and not draw attention to himself. And even if he hadn't, no one would have been stupid enough to try and pick a fight with him. He'd grown up in a landscape saturated with violence and it had marked his soul.

Despite being in a heightened state of readiness, he kept his mask of indifference in place, a carefully nondescript indifference that could be interpreted by people in many ways.

Most of those assumptions would be wrong.

As he scanned over the crowd again, his gaze invariably honed in on the pretty, auburn-haired young woman tending the bar at his end of the long room. She was new. During his frequent visits, Alex had bedded most of the waitstaff who worked here, but he had an unusually powerful desire to be balls-deep in the oddly beguiling young woman. He'd been with some great beauties, females so amazing they'd won prizes for their attractiveness, and none of them had drawn his attention like this. The redhead was attractive, in a sweet way, but she didn't hold any of the exotic, sultry promise he preferred in his conquests...but he was unable to stop watching her. As he stared at her, he tried to puzzle out why he couldn't keep his eyes off of her and focus on his hunt.

Being distracted by a female while on assignment never happened. He was calm, cool, analytical, and focused. Even when he was a boy, he could concentrate to the point where he was impossible to distract. Yet here he was, daydreaming about long, dark cherry red hair wrapped around a pale, slender body. She reminded him of a dancer, all grace and flowing motions.

Then she grinned, and his heart gave a hard thud. In that one second, she transformed from merely pretty to stunning. He'd never seen anyone smile with such open happiness before. It lit her from within, making her pale skin seem almost luminescent in the dim golden lighting of the pub. Her teeth revealed by her parted pink lips were perfect, lovely. She must have been some dentist's pride and joy. Alex imagined her smiling at him, and something funny twisted in his stomach, a craving to know her in a very intimate way that only grew stronger as he observed her.

The first time he'd seen her, three days ago when he arrived in Ireland, he'd made note of her. He'd been fascinated by the tall, graceful woman with the most beautiful hair he'd ever seen. It was natural— her red eyebrows and fair lashes along with freckles attested to that—and when she happened to look his way, he sucked in a breath at the sight of her feline— like, bright blue eyes. Exotic eyes that would haunt

3

the man lucky enough to see them. The dazzling gaze of an enchantress in the face of an innocent.

When she grew into her unusual beauty, she would breathtaking.

He hoped she'd notice him, but she seemed to be ignoring his part of the room. The more he studied her out of the corner of his eye, the more he realized she was avoiding looking at him on purpose, doing everything she could to keep from turning her face in his direction. Right now, she was talking to a customer who was getting a good eyeful of her bare belly while she reached for a glass from the rack above the bar. The skin of her slender torso was pure, creamy perfection, and he wondered where her freckles stopped.

The purple silk blouse she wore with its artful draping complimented her lean form, and he knew her small, firm tits would fill his mouth perfectly. When she bent and reached a certain way, a sliver of the delicate curve of her breast was revealed by the loose armhole of her shirt. Overhead speakers hidden among the scrolling crown molding piped out Sarah McLachlan singing some song about being happy. His breath caught as the slender woman unconsciously danced to the beat, a flowing movement that reminded him of the way the women of the Russian ballet moved. Her breasts swayed while she shifted her arms in time to the music, even her graceful fingers becoming part of the dance. His mind drifted to thoughts of slipping up behind her, of filling his hands with her warmth while he buried his face in all that fabulous hair and ground his erection into her pert bottom.

Shifting uncomfortably as his dick began to harden, he tore his eyes from the new bartender and returned to scanning the crowd while nursing his beer. She distracted him far too easily, and he needed to focus. This was not a vacation. This was work. There was a man here, Jake, who Alex needed to follow home then dispose of. Jake had crossed the wrong people in Russia, and Alex's unique skill set had been called into action. So far, the man had proven hard to track down, but Alex had cashed in a favor with a female business associate, and she had managed to lure Jake here tonight.

He should be focusing on his hunt, not hoping for another glimpse of the bartender's bright smile.

Jake's bellowing laugh rang across the room, drawing Alex's attention back to his target. He was a red-faced, sweaty, wasted-off-his-middle-aged-ass mess, and Alex couldn't wait to be done with this assignment. Damn that stupid fuck for being so greedy. Jake lived well but, like so many, was never satisfied with what he had. He always wanted more, and he thought he could get it by stealing from Jorg Novikov. Thought that because the head of the Novikov *Bratva* was old, he was also weak.

Jake was about to find out how wrong he was.

The drugs Alex had slipped into Jake's drink should have been kicking in so his mark was probably only minimally aware of his surroundings. Alex wished he had more time to make the man pay, but he needed this job to be over with. The disgusting pig of a man was now pawing at the woman he'd come in with, his meaty, sweaty hands leaving invisible trails of slime on her. He could see the disgust on her face from across the room. Alex would have to throw a couple extra thousand Euros her way for enduring the fat man's touch.

Watching his mark, Alex tried to get the taste of anger out of his mouth by taking a long drink. The fucker had left behind a young son in Russia who was now living with his grandparents, his mother already dead and his father about to be. A child who could have been used to punish Jake, could have been killed for his father's sins, while this waste of humanity sat in a pub in Ireland, getting drunk with stolen money. Alex curled his lip in disgust and stood, cursing the stupid fuck for making him fly all the way out here to get rid of him. There was nowhere, nowhere on Earth the fat man could run and hide. Nowhere that the Novikov *Bratva* didn't have eyes, ears, and friends willing to die for them, and powerful people who owed them favors. Even if Jake went to the Arctic Circle, Alex would be there with a rifle waiting behind a snowdrift to finish his pathetic life.

Then again, Jake fleeing to Ireland did give Alex the excuse to be away from the craziness of Moscow. They'd just taken over another *Bratva's* prostitution business, and there had been many...replacements made with management. Meaning he'd had to end the lives of a couple dozen abusive, monstrous pimps. A necessary evil that had been assigned to him, and a task he hadn't minded doing. A year ago, the old leader of the Sokolov *Bratva* had been overthrown, and the new man in charge didn't give a shit about the women working for him. As a result, the prostitutes decided to leave the Sokolov *Bratva's* protection for the Novikov Bratva, which took care of those who worked for them. A few of the pimps had tried to reclaim their girls, but Alex had taken great pleasure in helping Dimitri send a brutal message of what would happen if anyone hurt the women. This time, in the form of the tortured body of one of the pimps dumped in the alley behind one of the Sokolov's brothels.

Thankfully, Dimitri was slipping into his role as head of the prostitution arm of the Novikov Bratva nicely, a heavy responsibility for any twenty-two-year-old, but Dimitri was passionate about the safety of the women working for them and took his job seriously. This allowed Alex to focus on the more legitimate businesses of the Novikov Empire, to be the public face of the organization. An odd job for someone who was also his father's favorite assassin.

Over on the other side of the lengthy, antique bar, which took up the far wall, two balding old men threw their arms around each other's shoulders and sang an off-key Celtic song with their eyes closed and faces tipped to the ceiling. Other men laughed and held their drinks up, singing along with gusto. Even the bartenders got into it, and he found himself and the young redhead were the only people in the bar not singing. Their eyes met through the crowd, and he had a moment of feeling a deep connection. Her gaze held his and her lips parted and her hard nipples pressed against her top. He needed to kiss her until the taste of her filled his mouth and suck on those unbelievably puffy, pink lips. She turned away first, her eyes lowered and then looked up and laughed as the old men finished their song, clapping and giving them a smile that put roses in her cheeks.

Irish beauty through and through. Something he'd developed a taste for over the last few years. Not that he didn't think Russian women weren't the most stunning women in the world—he did—but he'd been spending more and more time in Western Europe at his father, Jorg's, command. It was no secret Alex was the favored son for inheriting control of the Novikov *Bratva* after the old man passed. Jorg wanted Alex to spend time with the various organizations, criminal and otherwise, that supported the Novikovs to remind them that the Novikov *Bratva* was something to be feared. But Alex spent more time forming bonds of friendship than he did menacing their allies, much to his father's aggravation and reluctant admiration.

Ruling wasn't just about violence and intimidation. A wise man valued willing loyalty more than fearful service.

Or, at least, Alex tried to.

Jorg was perfectly fine with being one of the most dreaded men in the deadly world of the Russian mafia, the boogeyman criminals warned each other about. He believed might made right and expected his sons to feel the same way. Unfortunately for Jorg, Alex and his brother Dimitri had been heavily influenced in their upbringing by their Uncle Petrov, a man just as powerful as Jorg but with a devoted following of men and women who would die for the Dubinski *Bratva*.

Petrov Dubinski was Alex's mother's brother, and successfully ran a powerful *Bratva* of his own. Uncle Petrov offered not only power and money to the people who worked for him, he also offered peace and safety for them and their families, as well as prosperity. Something more valuable than gold and diamonds, something his men would do anything to protect without hesitation.

Alex found his gaze wandering back to the girl smiling at a customer as she filled his mug with dark beer. When her slender, pale fingers gripped the old brass spigot, he couldn't help but imagine what it would be like to have her hand wrapped around his cock. He wanted to fuck that delicate redhead until she turned pink all over. His erection started to get harder, and he tried to calm himself down. This rampant, almost uncontrollable arousal irritated him. He wasn't ruled by his dick. He had better self-control than this. He could sit in a sniper blind for days without moving more than an inch in any direction, and he'd never lost his head over a female.

Because of who he was, he could have hundreds of the most desirable women in the world on their knees begging for him if he wanted. Back home in Moscow, he had over a dozen women, gorgeous, refined, experienced, and all eagerly waiting for his phone call. Of course, he never seriously dated any of them, but he did shower the one he was currently fucking with expensive gifts before he set her aside. And when he was done, he was done. The women he picked were aware of the reality of their situation and were fine with how things worked. Perhaps he should see if the lovely bartender would be open to such an arrangement.

Across the room, Jake pushed back from his table on unsteady legs and headed in the direction of the bathroom, occasionally bumping into someone with a muttered apology.

With his empty glass in hand, Alex approached the bar, his view of the windowless bathroom and hall perfect, so if his drunk mark tried to leave out the back Alex would know without hovering too close and tipping Jake off.

The redhead behind the bar ignored him until he cleared his throat. Three times. When she finally turned around, it was with a sour twist to her lovely, Cupid's bow lips. Up this close, he marveled at how ethereal she appeared, how delicate. Like she was a princess out of one of the illustrated fairy tales his mother had read to him when he was young. Her eyes were captivating, the brightest cornflower blue he'd ever seen rimmed in a thin line of navy and framed with long red-gold lashes.

She snapped him out of his silent appreciation when she spoke with a terse American accent. "Can I help you?"

He raised a brow, and a slight blush pinked her cheeks. He enjoyed that color on her. Porcelain skin like hers would show her every emotion and every spank of his hand. He forced his voice to remain calm even though desire tightened his gut. "Another dark lager."

When he gave her his most charming smile, her frown grew even more pronounced. Either his charisma was gone, or this woman did not like him for some reason. Without another word, she turned and got his drink as quickly as she could. He kept his gaze on the bathroom, which now had a line forming, while waiting for Jake to come out. The slam of his beer on the bar accompanied by a small splash of liquid onto his hand drew his gaze back to her instantly.

Her eyes darted to his wet hand, and she sighed then said in a softer voice, "Sorry about that. Let me get something to clean you up with."

When she looked up at him through her lashes, the need for her touch overwhelmed him, but he had a feeling she'd bolt if he attempted to so much as caress her cheek. "Is all right."

She blinked at him, some of her ire melting away as curiosity took its place. He held her gaze and found himself unable to look away, drawn to her obvious inquisitiveness like a moth to the flame. A tingle of electricity moved through him and he rubbed the suddenly sensitive tips of his fingers against the smooth edge of the glass holding his beer. Even though she was pretty with her high cheekbones and pouty, pink lips, it was the spirit shining in her unguarded gaze that captured him. It had been a long, long time since he'd been around a woman who had so few barriers between herself and the world. He wondered who this American girl was and what she was doing here in Peter Cleary's pub. Usually Peter's girls were more experienced, many of them happily entertained Peter's men, but this woman did not strike him as the type to spread her legs for a bunch of thugs.

When she continued to stare at him, he cleared his throat. "Towel?"

"What? Oh, yeah...right."

He had to hide his smile as she fetched a clean towel and returned to the bar with pink cheeks. Jake had yet to appear, but Alex could care less about the two hundred and fifty thousand dollar hit at the moment. The only thing he could focus on was how soft and good her slender fingers felt against his hand, even if she was wiping him down as quickly as possible. More of that unusual, but not unpleasant, electricity arced between them as she quickly cleaned him. If this rare chemistry between them carried over into the bedroom, fucking her would be a once-in-a-lifetime experience.

Desire clouded his mind, and his accent thickened. "What is your name?"

Her voice came out quiet, but firm. "None of your business."

"My name is Alex Gorev." It was actually Alex Novikov, but he strictly went by aliases while in Western Europe and was known in this area of the world as Gorev.

She arched a delicate brow at him then snorted. "I've been warned about you."

She had such an adorable scowl when she said that, and his cock thickened.

If she was his submissive, he'd be fucking her sassy little mouth right now.

"Warned?"

"Yep." She glowered at him, her fingers tapping on her arm, the thick silver ring she wore on her thumb flashing in the warm light.

He wondered if she'd been warned about his darker carnal habits or his being a high-ranking member of the Novikov *Bratva*. It was hard to contain his anger, something unusual for him, as he

11

spoke louder than he intended, "Who warned you? What did they say?"

She seemed taken aback, her jaded expression slipping, leaving one of alarm as he snarled at her. Evidently, the young woman had not been around many men who raised their voices if her wide eyes were any indication. He would have to keep the fact that she was unused to dealing with a man like him in mind in the future.

Gentling his tone as much as he could, his voice still came out unusually low as he said, "Tell me, what has been said about me? I deserve to know."

While they were talking, the wait at the bar for a drink had built up, leaving the other bartender giving the beautiful redhead some pointed looks. With a sigh, the woman he was strangely obsessed with crossed her arms beneath her small breasts, pressing the fabric against them, giving Alex a great view of her thick, stiff nipples.

He watched her succulent lips part to speak, and imagined kissing her while she whispered her naughty secrets to him, in the dark, of all the things she wanted him to do with her.

"Look, buddy, you have the reputation of going through women like toilet paper. So please spare me your attempts at being charming. I don't care to have you wipe your ass with me then toss me away as I've been shit on enough by the world in general these last few years. So move along. This"—she waved her hand in his direction—"ain't happening."

He inwardly winced at her analogy. Evidently, the women he'd bedded here had been talking, not that he should be surprised. Not many women were happy when they discovered he had no interest in them for anything other than sex and friendly companionship. He'd never dated a woman, never saw a need to. He wasn't ready to settle down, and no woman had interested him for more than a month or two, at most, unless they were fine with just fucking.

A glance showed the line for the bathroom was longer than ever, but he barely paid attention. His focus was on this mysterious American who was resisting him, not something he was used to with a woman. The situation would be amusing if it wasn't happening to him.

It only made him want her all the more.

Adding a touch of seduction to his gaze, he watched her closely, now only dimly aware of the line for the bathroom growing. "Do you believe everything that is told to you?"

She laughed, the melody of her joy immediately bringing a smile to his face and everyone's within hearing distance. She might not physically turn heads, but her merriment made her irresistible. It even made him smile, which he rarely did in public. He was sure he'd smiled more during this conversation at a crowded bar than he had in months. If Dimitri could see him right now, he'd be laughing his ass off at how foolish Alex was behaving as he pursued the bartender.

The Novikov brothers didn't chase women. Women chased them. Or at least they usually did.

Tossing her hair over her shoulder, the warm red highlights glinting beneath the brighter lights behind the bar, she held up her finger to the other bartender indicating she'd only be a minute then turned back to him with an impatient expression making a furrow between her eyebrows. "I'm sure you know you're amazingly hot for an old guy—"

If he'd been drinking his lager, he would have choked. "Old guy? I am twenty-nine."

She held up her hands, silver bangles glinting on her slender arms. "Hey, whatever. To a twenty year old that's like...ancient."

Had she just called him ancient?

A growl escaped him, but instead of being scared, she laughed again. "Like I said, as good looking as you are, I bet women are throwing their panties at you everywhere you go. So why don't you bother one of them? I'm not trying to slut-shame you, you do what you have to do, but I don't like people who break hearts, and I'm not interested in a one-night-stand."

Instead of acknowledging that women did indeed throw themselves at him everywhere he went and that he broke hearts, he shrugged, deciding silence was the best option—although he was curious as to what 'slut shaming' was.

She smirked when he didn't say anything. "I'll let you know right now that I have absolutely no time for players. In fact, they disgust me. You, buddy, are barking up the wrong tree. Now, if you'll excuse me, I have a job to do."

With that, she lifted her pert nose and turned, her waist-length hair swishing behind her in a way that reminded him of how a cat would flick its tail, as she stalked away with an irritated twitch of her hips.

Bemused, he watched her huff around the bar for a moment, her stiff movements making her perfect breasts bounce as she pointedly ignored him. His cock twitched again in interest. She was a sassy little thing and would need a firm hand in bed. Might be fun to spend some time with a woman who had some spirit to her instead of his usual companions who indulged his every whim.

Tearing his gaze from her, he turned his attention back to the bathroom where a long line had formed and a guy was knocking on the door, loudly. Abandoning his beer, he signaled for the bouncer to go get Peter.

Alex's senses were tingling in a way that let him

know something was about to happen. His sixth sense had saved his ass more times than he could count, and he instantly fell back on a lifetime of training. As the son of a powerful *Bratva* lord, Alex had spent his entire life immersed in a world where men created their own, often violent and bloody rules. His instincts had been honed to such a fine edge that he could often feel trouble before anything actually happened. It had earned him an almost mythical reputation, and he liked it that way.

Still, he didn't want any unnecessary attention drawn to Peter Cleary's pub. Not that the local police would ever do anything. They were paid off by Peter and scared of incurring his ire, but Alex did try to not offend his allies. With them as friendly as they could be considering the circumstances, he'd rather not have Peter pissing and moaning at him about a corpse on his property. The bathroom had no windows, only brick walls, and that drunk motherfucker had not come out of the small room. So, unless Fat Fuck Jake had somehow slithered down the drain, something was wrong.

He brushed aside the man knocking on the door. "Move."

With that, he kicked the door in and it bounced off something on the floor. It took some force, but he nudged the door open enough to stick his head through and stared. For the first time in a long time, he was surprised. There, lying on the floor, was Jake. Dead. Apparently, either from falling down and hitting his head—there was a large pool of blood around his head and some on the edge of the toilet— or passing out and choking on his own vomit.

Laughter threatened, but Alex needed to blend in, not stick out, and he would definitely stick out if he started chuckling at the sight of a corpse. His wry amusement continued to grow, and he really had to

15

struggle to choke back his mirth. Closing his expression down, he rubbed his neatly trimmed goatee and looked at the hulking bouncer hovering nearby. "I need Peter."

Before the bouncer could move, Peter, along with two of his brawny enforcers, strode down the hall. The burly, middle-aged man was shirtless, his thickly muscled chest covered with hair as red as the hair on his head and as equally smattered with white. Tattoos spread from shoulder to shoulder and across his upper back in a colorful display of Celtic knot work. When his gaze met Alex's, the head of the Cleary gang's solid jaw was set at a no-bullshit angle before he barked out, "Get yer arses back. All a'ya."

The customers left in spite of their blatant, and in some cases, drunken curiosity, the threat of getting beat bloody a good motivator. When Peter Cleary said move, a person moved.

His pale, freckled face was flushed, and he ran an agitated hand through his dark red, curly hair. "What the fuck, Alex? Mary was suckin' my dick, and I gotta stop that bliss to come out here and see a fuckin' bathroom? Do y'know how often that woman is in a mood good enough t'give head?"

Laughing, Alex rubbed his face with both hands. "Open the door."

Of course, the bodyguards held the door open for Peter, and a second after he looked around the corner, he started laughing as well. When he turned back, Peter shook his head with a disbelieving grin twitching his thick lips. "You lucky asshole. Yer fucking mark did himself in. Unbelievable."

"What can I say? Lady Luck loves me."

Snorting back a laugh, Peter shut the door then sighed. "Ain't that the truth."

Alex merely chuckled while he sent a text to his father that the job had been done.

After ordering his enforcers to clean up the mess, Peter turned to Alex and clapped him on the shoulder. "Well, now that yer finished, I have something I'd like to discuss with you. A business proposition I think will benefit us all."

Chapter Two

Letting out a tired sigh as the adrenaline slowly drained from his system, Alex followed Peter, texting a few of his men to update them before returning his attention to his surroundings. Together, they made their way down the hall, and when they entered the main area of the pub, most of the crowd avoided looking at them. They passed the bar heading to the stairs that would take them to the second level, and Alex caught the auburn-haired bartender's eye. She was watching him and Peter with a suspicious frown he wanted to kiss off her lips. Their gazes met, and he swore the room faded until it was just the two of them, bound together by a connection stronger than anything he'd ever felt.

"Who is new bartender? The redhead in purple shirt."

To his surprise, Peter froze in place and gave Alex a dark, menacing look. "Her name is Jessica, and you'll do well to stay away from her."

Peter had never given a shit before if Alex seduced every waitress and bartender in the building, so his aggressive response brought Alex's attention to razor sharp focus on the other man. "Why?"

"Later."

Alex followed a silent Peter upstairs, past the offices on the second floor and up to the third floor, which he'd turned into his private residence. The eight thousand square foot space somehow managed to be comfortable and cozy, thanks to Mary's feminine touch. After nodding to the armed men guarding his home, Peter led Alex into his private office. With the windows looking out over the busy streets of Dublin, Peter's office was a relaxing space

19

cluttered with the mementos of a man who'd lived a full life. Alex scanned the various awards and certificates of merit lining the walls that Peter had accumulated during his political career.

Alex's friend sat back with a sigh. "The woman at the bar, that's Jessica, my niece. Keep your filthy hands off'a her."

Alex looked away from a framed magazine article featuring a picture of Peter smiling with Prince Charles and stared at his friend in shock. "Your niece? Your sister died long ago, no?"

One of the things that had cemented Peter and Alex's friendship was that they had both lost their sisters to the violence that saturated their world, but in different ways. While Alex's mother and half-sister had been assassinated by a rival *Bratva*, Peter's older sister had fled to America with a member of an Irish gang that was the Cleary's sworn enemy. For years, Peter had searched for her. Unfortunately, she covered her tracks well, and he'd been unable to find her.

"Much has changed since we spoke last, my friend."

Peter made his way to Alex with two crystal tumblers, each glass containing a rich amber liquid. As usual, in private he lost a bit of his deep Irish brogue that he used in certain areas of his public life. Peter was a smart man and knew the people loyal to him related better to someone who talked like them. On the flip side of that he could also sound like the highly educated man he was while talking with his fellow politicians.

"Is good or bad change?"

"Both. My private investigator found a misfiled police report about a Jane Doe, later identified as Katie, being found dead of a brain hemorrhage. The second page of the report detailed there was a sixteen-month-old child found with Katie. A girl, who was put into the American foster care system."

Alex accepted his glass when Peter handed it to him, then took a sip. "When did you find this out?"

"Ten months ago. It took me another few months to find the girl, Jessica. From what we've been able to piece together, Katie and that piece o' shit she ran off with split up not long after they arrived in the United States. He died a few months after Katie in a shootout with the local police, never known' he'd had a daughter who was almost two years old."

Alex let out a low sigh as he witnessed Peter struggling to contain his emotions. Men did not cry in front of other men, but even among the monsters he dealt with, the grief over loss of family was understood all too well. With this in mind, Alex looked away, pretending to scan Peter's cluttered bookshelf as he sipped his drink. "I am sorry for your hardship."

After a few moments, Peter spoke again, his voice under control now and his emotions locked down tight. "Fortune was smiling on my niece 'cause she'd been adopted by a good, lovin' family and was raised on a farm in rural America. They adored her, and Jessica never felt anything but loved."

Thinking of how many children ended up on the street without parents, Alex nodded. "She was very lucky. Must have strong guardian angels."

Peter raised his glass in a toast then took a drink before answering. "Unfortunately, her adoptive parents died of unrelated illnesses a year or two before I found her. As soon as I had a DNA confirmation of who she was—I didn't want to disrupt her life if we had the wrong girl—I contacted her, hoping she'd at least hear me out. I didn't have anything to worry about. Jessica was ecstatic to learn she had blood relatives and I... well, fuck, I felt like I

21

had a piece of Katie back with me. Jessica has her mother's joy, and when she smiles, it reminds me of the way Katie would smile at me when she was Jessica's age, right before Katie took off with that sod. Never thought I'd get a chance to see anything that beautiful again."

Inwardly, Alex sighed over the fact that Jessica was Peter's niece, which meant Alex wouldn't get to experience the pleasure of having her slender thighs wrapped around his hips. There was no way in hell his friend would let him near his niece and with good reason. Peter knew about Alex, knew about his reputation with women, and Alex could respect the man's desire that he stay away from the lovely Jessica.

If he had a niece, he sure as hell wouldn't want a man nine years older than she, an assassin at that, perusing her. Now he just needed his body to realize she would never happen and move on to another pair of long legs to dream about. Unfortunately, some primitive instinct that couldn't be ignored shouted that she belonged to him and wouldn't allow him to put her in the mental 'hands-off' box.

He realized Peter had said something and forced himself to pay attention. "What was that?"

"I said she's a sweet girl with a gentle heart."

Chuckling, Alex raised his glass to his lips and took a drink. "Do not worry. She already told me I do not have a chance in hell with her. It seems your other waitresses warned her about me."

Grinning with no small amount of relief, Peter sat back and crossed his arms over his bare chest. "You can't expect to fuck your way through my staff and have them not talk. Women are bitchy, territorial creatures, and your dick and wallet are big enough that they all piss and moan at each other about who you're gonna fuck on any given night. If you weren't so damn handy to have around, I'd have banned you from my pub for putting my girls in a snit."

Alex sighed and tried to get his friend off the subject of Alex's rather robust sex life. "You said you wanted to talk some business?"

"I do." The laughter dropped from his face, and Peter sat forward then placed his empty glass on the desk with a resounding thud, his work-reddened hands curving around the smooth surface. "It's an election year."

"And?"

He moved out of his chair and grabbed a blue button down shirt hanging off a brass hook on the wall. Shrugging it on, he studied Alex before once again taking his seat. "Any election is full of bullshit and backstabbin', but things have stepped up a notch. One of my informants has told me there are some new players, backed by a powerful organization, that want me out of power. They have no chance of gettin' rid of me, so they must try to weaken my hold in other ways."

"Does that not happen every election? Politics are nothing if not full of bullshit and backstabbing. Is way of world."

"This is different."

"How?"

Peter leaned back in his chair, his thick fingers tapping on the desk as he looked out the window. "The *Sinn Féin* are gaining strength, and their leader, Martin Keeler, has been a thorn in my side over the last few years, but he's an honest man and fair. Or at least he was until he was killed in a car bombing six months ago."

"Do you know who did it?"

"No, I have my suspicions, but that's all they are right now. There are three men who are running for his spot as leader of the *Sinn Féin,* and all three of them are as dirty as the bottom of a coal mine."

"You think they are responsible for his death?"

"One of them is." Peter sighed heavily. "Nathan Clarke, not the nicest of men, but a strong leader, would be my choice of the three to head the party. He drives me *gobshite*, but he knows how to keep his nose clean and avoid drawing attention. While I haven't publicly given him my support, he knows he has it, as do his opponents."

"Who are they?"

"Ryan White and Liam Sweeny."

Alex frowned, something tickling his memory about those names. "They are familiar to me, why?"

"Both have ties to different *Bratvas*. Ryan is the grandson of Nicolai Gilyov."

That made Alex go on alert. "And Liam?"

"Is married to the daughter of Gleb Tepov."

Alex let out a long string of swear words. The Tepov and Gilyov *Bratvas* were both rivals of the Novikovs. If either Liam or Ryan became the heads of one of Ireland's largest political parties, it would not be good for the Clearys and their allies, like the Novikov *Bratva*. It would also give the rival *Bratvas* more power back in Russia, maybe enough to weaken the Novikov *Bratva* and take away some territory. The Novikov *Bratva* needed Peter and his political connections not only to secure their interests in Ireland, but because Ireland was part of one of the main European smuggling routes.

If Peter's power base was eroded away, that would mean the Novikovs would either have to form new alliances with the Gilyov and Tepov *Bratvas*, which would never happen, or they would suffer major losses in both profit and mobility. Ireland was a secure, protected country where they could store merchandise that wouldn't be safe anywhere in Russia. Plus, Peter was the absolute best in the world at forging documents, a skill worth more than gold and was more sought after than diamonds. One of the reasons Alex saw Peter so much was that he was always seeking Peter out for one set of papers or another.

Peter must have seen the realization on Alex's face because he nodded. "It's a tight race, but as long as Nathan has my support, he should be able to beat Liam and Ryan."

Things began to fall into place for Alex. "So they will target you, distract you, hope you will withdraw your support."

"They already have. An anonymous tip almost had a business of mine raided last week. Thankfully, one of my men inside the police department found out and alerted me in time to move the drugs out and legal stock in. Later, I received a message that if I don't withdraw my support from Nathan there will be *dire* consequences for those I love. I'm not worried about Mary. She can handle herself and was raised by a man meaner than anyone I've ever met. Her security detail has been with her for twenty years, and they do their job well. No, my enemies have a much easier target to go after."

Peter's last few words were filled with a rage that Alex easily understood. "Jessica."

"Yes, Jessica."

The thought of anyone harming her made his muscles tighten as an unusually strong protective feeling settled into his bones with an angry burn. "Does she know?"

"That I'm one of the biggest criminal lords in Ireland? No." He stared at a framed photo on the wall that Alex knew was a picture of Peter and Katie together when they were kids. Her face was narrower than Peter's, like Jessica's, but she didn't have her daughter's almond-shaped eyes. "I wanted to protect

Jessica, to get to know her without the shadow of my life tainting our relationship. Now, I'm even more hesitant to tell her. She loves me, Alex, me and Mary both. Hell, Mary looks at her like the daughter we never had, and it would break her heart to have Jessica turn her back on us out of fear or disgust."

"You cannot keep it from her forever. Especially if she is in danger. How long will she be here?"

"She's thinkin' about movin' here permanently, but will be livin' here in Ireland for the next year, studyin' abroad and attendin' school. Smart lass, top of her class. While she's in Ireland, I can protect her. Over in America, she'd be an easy target." He met Alex's gaze. "This is where you come in."

"What do you mean?"

Peter hesitated then said in a low voice, "Your father and I have made a deal. He has agreed to have you, Oleg, Maks, and Luka stay in Ireland until the election is over and guard Jessica."

"He what?" Alex grit his teeth. He had plans, meetings he had to attend and territories to defend. His father knew this, yet he expected Alex to drop everything to attend to his whims. Typical. If he didn't love the old man so much, he might end his life with a bullet to the head someday. "Jorg did not consult me on this."

Peter nodded. "I figured as much. But before you lose yer head, you need to listen to what I'm offering in return. I think you'll see why 'ol Jorg would be willing to lose his *Sovietnik* fer so long."

Taking a deep breath then letting it out, Alex nodded. "What is it?"

"I'm gonna teach you all I know about forgery and introduce you to my connections in exchange for you and your men keeping Jessica alive and happy."

Alex stared at Peter, totally knocked out of his anger. What Peter was offering him was unheard of.

No one knew all of Peter's secrets, and the other man liked to keep it that way. Being one of a kind kept him alive. For him to offer to teach Alex his tricks was priceless. Certainly more than worth the headache that would come from rearranging his schedule to stay in Ireland until the election was over. It was almost too good to be true, so Alex tried to look for a hidden trap. He trusted no one completely, except for his brother Dimitri.

"This is beyond generous. Why?"

"I'm gonna assume you mean why would I teach you in exchange for you protecting Jessica. First, you are one of the best assassins in the world, Alex. I don't say that as flattery, but because you know the tricks for taking someone out. You have the instincts to spot trouble before it happens. Second, with the Novikov *Bratva* givin' their obvious support, my enemies will think twice before they touch Jessica. Third, I know you will not hesitate to eliminate a threat, and you won't be stupid about it. When you want someone to disappear, they disappear. And everyone knows what happens if they go after someone under your protection. The last example you made of a would-be assassin still makes people think twice."

He shrugged, unable to argue with the fact he'd done something brutal to make sure his enemies knew he would not hesitate to eliminate any threat to his client. "Makes sense, but is unbalanced trade. What more do you want that you not telling me?"

"All I want is for you to keep my niece alive, to protect her, and let the sweet lass lead a life oblivious to the danger that surrounds her. She should not have to pay for my sins. My men understand and would give their lives for her, but they are limited in where they can go. You are more of a neutral third party than they are, able to enter territories in Dublin

that would cause a war if one of my men trespassed."
He looked at the picture of his sister again, and pain
swam in the depths of his distant gaze. "Yer father
gets it."

"What?"

"He knows this trade isn't unbalanced. He knows
what Jessica's death would do to me, to my strong
Mary. I know you don't understand, but someday,
when you fall in love and have a family of your own,
you will know that you'll do anything, *anything* to
keep them alive because they are your heart and soul.
Jessica, she's my kin. Only descendent I've got. My
bloodline ends with her. You know Mary and I can't
have children, and even though we're trying to adopt
and we will love that child like our own. I owe Jessica
a good life because my sister isn't here to give it to
her. I owe Katie that, and I will do everything I can to
keep Jessica happy because she's a good girl and I
love her."

Alex's thoughts turned to his own mother, his
stepmother, and his beautiful half-sister and how
their deaths had indeed killed his father's heart and
soul, leaving a void in him that he filled with death
and violence. Oh, his father loved Dimitri and Alex,
but it was a cold, hard love, now without mercy,
without joy. When he was younger, Alex had often
thought of how different his life would have been if
those women had lived, what kind of man his father
could have been instead of the ruthless monster he'd
become. Unfortunately, he was still Alex's father, and
no matter how much he tried to harden his heart
against the old man, he couldn't make himself stop
loving him. At one time, Jorg had been the best father
a child could ask for, doting and loving, their home
filled with feminine laughter and soft voices.

Jorg adored his family, and the loss of two wives
and a daughter had slowly destroyed any compassion

28

he'd possessed, leaving him with a heart encased in ice and a paranoia that could get out of control if he wasn't on his stabilizing medicines.

Peter's voice interrupted Alex's dark deliberations. "My men will be guardin' her as well, of course, but you and yer men will be doing the majority of the protection. I'm settin' you up in a room across the hall from Jessica's apartment in one of the buildings I own. Yer men'll have places on the floors below and above. The only way to access her apartment is through her front door."

"Or scale wall of building."

"Her apartment faces the street. It's too visible for anyone to scale without drawing unwanted attention. The windows are bulletproof, and no one is getting in without having to get through my men and yours. I realize there will be some business you'll have to attend to personally, but your father has assured me Oleg and Maks will watch over her. Luka will also be stopping by from time to time to cover for you when needed."

"They are good men." He shifted in his chair, excitement beginning to build at the thought of his unusual assignment. At the very least, it would be nice to spend the next six months in relative comfort instead of at his father's training camp in Siberia. "How do you explain to Jessica my presence?"

"I'm going to tell her you're part of my personal security that I've assigned to guard her. I'll tell her you'll be working in the United States next year, and having you watching over her will help you and your men with your American English. She's used to political figures having what they call the Secret Service in the States, so she will know you're there as her bodyguards. She just won't know how serious your duty actually is. You'll be going by yer Gorev alias to keep her from doin' an Internet search and figurin' out who you are."

Knowing his father had arranged this behind his back irritated him, but he forced those thoughts away. Alex had been given a job, and he would fulfill it. Thankfully, this would not be an unpleasant job, and he wouldn't be out stalking someone in order to end their life. Though the idea of babysitting some young woman wasn't exactly at the top of his list of things he enjoyed, especially when he couldn't fuck her, he had a feeling this assignment was going to be a good one. "When do I start?"

"In a week. That should give you time enough to make a trip home and get what you need."

He'd have to find time to visit with Dimitri, but he should be able to set things up for his absence. "Then I will see you in a week."

Chapter Three

J essica Venture slumped over the end of the bar after her busy shift, savoring a beer. Sighing in delight, she got off her aching feet, which throbbed to the beat of her heart. She'd waitressed back in Iowa at a busy family diner, especially on Sunday after church, but being a bartender in a popular bar in the heart of Dublin was a totally new experience, and not just because she was still learning the local dialect. Thankfully, she was a quick study, and everyone she worked with was at least passingly nice to her. She didn't get along with a few of the younger bartenders but not to the point where it was an issue. More like a mutual distaste than actual anger. The vast majority of people she'd met through her job and her newfound family had been really cool and welcoming.

Her family had deeply rooted history in this area, and her return to the city of her mother's birth had been celebrated. Evidently she was the last descendant of a long line of some pretty amazing people. Her Uncle Peter and Aunt Mary couldn't have children, so there'd been some hints she needed to settle down and have some kids so the Cleary line could continue. She wasn't offended, no one meant any harm when they said it, and she chose to find it funny instead of getting upset.

Ireland didn't feel like home yet, but there was no denying she'd felt a certain resonance in her soul the first time she drove to Dublin from the airport with her aunt and uncle. The whole place had a different vibe from anywhere she'd been in America, and it had taken her a bit to get used to it. Her aunt had really helped a lot in getting her familiar with the city and Ireland in general. They'd hit it off right away and had become good friends.

This was Jessica's third week on the job, and she'd finally gotten a handle on how to work as quickly as possible to keep up with high demand and keep her head above water. Unfortunately, she kept screwing up tonight because of a certain irritating man who'd thrown a wrench in her ability to focus on the task at hand. He distracted her to the point that she forgot where she was, and instead of making drinks, she thought about how she longed to touch his lips surrounded by his goatee and see if the rough hair made the skin feel softer by contrast. With his deep gray eyes and classic good looks, he'd robbed her of her sanity with a glance. Usually, she could ignore guys hitting on her or trying to pick her up, but this man's intense gaze affected her like a physical touch. And his accented voice... Her nipples tightened at the memory of the way he said her name. It wasn't the traditional Jessica. No, he turned her name into something exotic that sounded like Jez-E-kah. Now her pussy tingled as well, and she cursed her body, which obviously didn't know lusting after Alex was a bad idea.

Yep, despite the fact that he was older and in an entirely different league, they had serious chemistry between them.

Unfortunately, he was the kind of guy Jessica would never date.

When she'd asked about the sexy-as-sin man with the thick black hair and piercing gray eyes, the women she worked with had gone right the fuck off about how big a player he was— all of them, not just the bitchy ones. Evidently, he viewed the servers at the pub as his personal harem, and he had the charm of the devil. Rumor had it that no woman had more than two dates with him before they were ready to fuck his kinky brains out and have his babies.

She'd thought it was all exaggerated bullshit. Then she saw him, and every hair on her body stood up as if a mild electrical shock radiated through her nervous system. Add to that his penetrating, hooded gaze when he stared at her, and she'd been unable to stop her body from responding. This was a man who oozed sex appeal, and he'd been directing all that lust straight at her, making her panties damp without even touching her. She regretted wearing the camisole instead of a bra beneath her shirt. As small as her breasts were, that wasn't usually an issue, but tonight, her nipples had been rock-hard and had drawn leering stares from more than one drunk.

Until she reminded them that Peter was her uncle, and suddenly, they became as polite as could be.

Her body still buzzed hours later as she recalled the change in Alex after she accidentally spilled beer on him. She wanted to say she was angry because she was morally outraged by Alex's heart-breaker behavior. The truth was she felt a pull to him so strong she felt like she should be able to see glowing strands connecting them together. His hands were big and rough, and she wondered what they would feel like sliding over her body.

The sight of his long, almost artistic fingers brought to mind breathy moans in the dark as he slowly sank them into her aching pussy.

"'Night, Jessica," one of the bartenders she worked with said with a smile and a wave.

Startled from her erotic daydreams, she sat up on her barstool and hoped she wasn't blushing. "'Night, Beth."

Since her apartment was in the building around the corner, Jessica liked to linger for a little while after closing and just absorb the silence. She'd never been in a city as old as Dublin, and sometimes it felt like the age of the city pressed down on her. From what Aunt Mary had said, this building used to be part of a nobleman's estate, but it had been sold to her great-great-great grandfather to pay off his gambling debts. Rumor had it that the pub had also been an upscale brothel back in the day, with the bar masquerading as a gentleman's club for cover, hiding the real reason the men of Dublin entered this building.

A man shifted across the room, one of the stone faced bouncers, and drew her wandering attention before she inwardly sighed. Uncle Peter had insanely good security because he was a politician, and he always had at least one of his men near Jessica. Not enough to be invasive, but everywhere she went, she knew someone was watching over her. Even if she was just grocery shopping with Aunt Mary, a man or two would discreetly follow them. She had to admit it was kind of nice to have that protection as she explored a city ten times the size of the small town where she'd grown up. Then again, their constant, watchful presence also hampered her ability to freely explore places on a whim. And it certainly screwed up any plans she had to buy a new vibrator at the elegant lingerie and adult toy store she always passed on the way to her favorite bakery.

Right now, her oversized babysitter for the evening lurked in the far corner, the same area where Alex had sat earlier, and was talking with one of the bartenders. Both of them were flirting with each other heavily enough that Jessica was sure someone was going to get laid tonight. Too bad it wouldn't be her. She'd been going through a dating dry spell since moving here to spend some time in Ireland getting to know her roots. While there were plenty of cute guys around, and she had flirted with a few, nothing ever happened beyond the initial encounter.

She was also looking into going to a college in Dublin instead of returning to the University of Iowa. There was just something about Ireland and the people that called to her, and she wasn't ready to leave yet. Hopefully, she'd find a nice Irish guy who would treat her the way her father treated her mother, with kindness, respect, and endless love. Her biological father, on the other hand, was a dick who'd left his pregnant woman stranded in a foreign country while he ran off with a neighbor. If her biological dad was the perfect example of being a world-class asshole, her adoptive father was the polar opposite. He was like a living, breathing John Wayne, country-tough and about as masculine as a man could get with a no-drama, no-bullshit attitude. He'd taken care of Jessica and her mother, spoiling and protecting them in his own quiet way, giving his love freely with both deeds and words. She was totally her Daddy's little girl, and his death had rocked her to the core, making her realize how much she'd depended on him and her mom for everything. Then, when her mother died later, she'd thought for sure she'd slipped into such a deep depression that she'd never get out.

It was during the darkest time that a bit of light came into her life in the form of a phone call from a man who'd identified himself as Peter Cleary, her uncle. After the revelation that she did indeed have living blood relatives, she'd cried until she passed out, relieved that she would get a chance to know who she was and what kind of history she had flowing in her veins, who she looked like. That she wasn't alone. She later learned that her birth mother, Katie fled to The United States with a boy her family did not approve of. Jessica's biological father had also died, and she wondered how she had the bad luck to end up with two sets of dead parents. Her biological father had been an only child, and there were no other living relatives left on her father's side.

Her uncle's voice came from the stairway, and someone laughed in a deep rumbling tone. She watched the stairs, interested to see if the man's face matched his sexy chuckle. Maybe she just needed some good, old-fashioned down-and-dirty sex to get her out of her rut. It would be nice to have a man at her side as she wandered around and explored the city. Someone who was smart and could entertain her with tales of the different historic buildings. A man with big hands and an even bigger cock was just what the doctor ordered.

Sheesh, she needed to get laid.

At the sight of Alex smiling at her uncle, she inwardly groaned and wanted to bang her head on the bar. When he was out of sight, it was easy to dismiss just how mesmerizing he was, how tempting. Why hadn't she gone home when she had the chance? The more she thought about Alex, the more she wanted him, and that could not happen. She loathed womanizers. Her first serious boyfriend had cheated on her, and the fact that her birth father had abandoned her mother for another woman only deepened her disgust with men who treated women like objects to use and discard at whim.

Casual sex was all good and fun as long as both parties knew not to involve their hearts. Heck, she'd had her fair share of casual hookups in school and on spring break. She'd heard Alex had no heart, and he loved to make women fall in love with him then leave them high and dry, breaking up with them for no reason other than he was done playing his games.

What a sick asshole.

A shiver of revulsion chased back the desire that had flared at the sight of Alex, and she turned back to the bar, wondering if she should just chug her beer and make a run for it before he noticed her.

"Jessica," her uncle called out in a loud voice, "I'd like you to meet an old friend of mine, Alexandr Gorev."

She tried to assume a polite, bored expression then turned around. At the sight of Alex's smirking lips—lips she wanted to suck and nibble on—her determination not to like him flared to life. No, she would not be turned on by the mere sight of Alex. Unacceptable. Her hormones would just have to go back to sleep until she found a suitable man. She'd finally come to a place in her life where she'd found a peaceful port in the storm after her parents' deaths. She wasn't going to sacrifice it for anyone, especially a man who was sure to break her heart. Better that she let Alex know right now that she'd never spread her legs for him and he should move on to easier prey.

Inclining her head to Alex, she said in a smooth voice, "Well, you got the old part right. We've already met."

Oh, how she loved the annoyance that filled Alex's handsome face. She had no idea why he was so uptight about his age. He was, unfairly, one of those men who would only get better looking with time. Before she could help it, a giggle escaped at the sight of Alex's offended expression. Then Peter began to laugh.

"Ouch. Alex, you're slipping."

Alex muttered something to Peter in a language she didn't recognize then returned his attention to her. "I will have plenty of time to change her mind in the next six months, yes?"

She turned to her uncle, praying she didn't just hear that. "What?"

Giving Alex a warning look, Peter nodded. "Alex

and his men are your new bodyguards."

"Pardon me?"

Alex had an irritating smirk twitching his lips that made her want to smack him. "We will be seeing much of each other, Jessica."

The way he said her name with a slight purr made her pussy clench, and she hated herself for reacting so easily to him.

"Uh-uh. No way. You are both out of your damn minds if you think he's going anywhere near my body. I don't need to see a constant stream of women parading into his apartment. Gah, I hope the walls are thick." Alex arched a brow, having the gall to look offended, and she glared at him. "You're a manwhore, plain and simple."

Peter tsked. "Jessica, mind yer manners. You know nothin' about Alex, only rumors, and you're bein' impolite to my guest."

She flushed and dropped her eyes to the ground before muttering, "Yes, sir."

There wasn't a doubt in her mind that Uncle Peter loved her, but he was a stickler for manners. He'd tried to explain to her that Dublin wasn't like the States, that women conducted themselves differently, that the men had pride, sometimes in excessive amounts. He'd gone on and on about a man's reputation being important, and if she was blatantly disrespectful, it could get her in a world of trouble, but she hadn't really understood what he was talking about. Their conversation had been odd, and he kept hesitating, like he wanted to say something but couldn't. Finally, to ease the worried look on his face, she'd agreed to watch her normally sarcastic mouth and not make any problems for him.

Alex's gray eyes sparkled with suppressed mirth as he arched a brow in Jessica's direction. "Do not worry. You will hardly know we are here."

Before she could respond, Peter returned and shook Alex's hand. "I'll see you next week. Give my regards to your father, and tell Dimitri that it's been too long since he's come to visit us."

"I will." Alex gave Jessica that almost-smile of his that was beginning to drive her crazy and walked out the bar without a backward glance.

After Alex left, her uncle sat next to her and stole a sip of her beer, ignoring her glare. "Don't be angry, lass. Alex is a trustworthy man, and more importantly, he is very good at his job. I know he can be a bit of a prick, but I just want you to be safe. I thought long and hard about who to assign to you, and he's the best man for the job. Let me have this, Jessica. I need to know yer being taken care of when I'm not around."

She was all set to argue with Peter, but his obvious need to protect her pricked the balloon of her anger. Shit, she was acting like a brat and not considering his feelings, only hers. Jessica's father had been overprotective like Uncle Peter, and she had to admit that, in an odd way, her uncle's overbearing manner made her feel loved. It reminded her of home, and she found herself giving Peter a quick, one-armed hug before returning to her stool. "It's okay. I understand. I don't like it, but I understand."

Her uncle didn't say anything for a moment then smiled at her, the familiar light of his love returning to his eyes. "How was work tonight?"

"Good. How was yours?"

"Busy, lass," he said with a deep sigh. "Always busy."

She smiled at him and he winked. She liked the fact that her uncle seemed to go out of his way to spend time with her. He was always dealing with his business and political crud, but he made sure he had downtime with her whenever he could. With a thud,

39

the entrance door shut and snicked as the lock was turned. Then they were alone.

Leaning against the bar, she studied his tired expression while he absently examined the racks holding the various glasses behind the bar. "You work too hard."

"Better to be busy than bored."

"Good point." She cracked her neck, the strain of the long night pressing down on her and making her eager for her bed. "Having a not-working bathroom for a half-hour sucked. Glad they were able to repair it quickly. I was afraid I was going to have guys asking me for a pitcher to piss in."

Peter laughed then yawned. Dark bags had formed beneath his eyes, and she was glad she hadn't inherited that physical trait from the Cleary side of her gene pool. When she was tired, her eyes got a bit red rimmed, but it made her look more stoned than anything else. She hoped Uncle Peter was taking care of his health and made a mental note to talk to Aunt Mary about his diet.

Thumping his fist on the bar, he stood and sighed while looking down at her with an affectionate smile that warmed her heart. "I'm gonna go turn in before my beautiful Mary sends out a search team for me. Paul will walk you home whenever you're ready."

She yawned as well and muttered, "Tomorrow's my day off so I'm gonna sleep in."

"Wish I could get a day off," Peter said with a teasing smile and gave her hair a gentle ruffle.

"Yeah, it's tough being the king of Dublin," she said, referring to the way people seemed to kiss his ass everywhere they went. All she had to do was mention that she was Peter Cleary's niece and things would go smoothly.

"Maybe not the king, more like a duke."

Shaking her head, she gathered up her purse

with a smile and a mock curtsey. "Goodnight, your lordship."

"Goodnight, sweetheart. Oh, and Jessica?"

"Yeah?"

"Don't get yer sights set on Alex."

"Alex?"

He gave her a narrow-eyed look, his cheeks puffing as he huffed out a laugh. "Lass, I saw how you stared at him. I may be old, but I'm not so blind that I can't see a pretty girl makin' eyes at a handsome fella. I'd just advise you to cast your sights on someone else."

Flushing a no-doubt bright red, she started to walk to the front door while trying to keep her stride unhurried and casual. "I wasn't making eyes at him. I was staring at him in disgust."

Peter sighed and threw up his hands in defeat "What you said earlier? You were right. I can't tell you who you can or cannot see. My family made that mistake with your mother, and I'm not gonna repeat it. I will say, however, that there are a billion men I'd rather see you with than Alexandr. You deserve a good, safe man. Someone you can grow old with. He's not the man for you, my darlin' lass."

Slightly puzzled by his words, but too tired to dissect them now, she called over her shoulder, "You have nothing to worry about, Uncle Peter. Seriously. I have no interest in him. He's way too old for me and acts like he's the King Turd of Shit Mountain. No thanks."

That made Peter burst into laughter, and she left the pub with a smile on her face and a bodyguard watching her back.

A few days later, she'd almost managed to forget about the mysterious Alexandr when there was a commotion outside of her apartment. Men were yelling in a language she didn't understand, and she wondered if she should call Peter and let him know about the noise. Moving quietly, she tiptoed over to the peephole on her massive door and looked through. The door itself was made of a bulletproof material so she was as safe behind it as she could be. When Peter had informed her of that, she'd been a little curious at the level of security in this building, but then realized that being family to a politician came with an inherently heightened level of danger. There were whack-jobs out there who would want to hurt her merely to get at her uncle.

A quick peek revealed two unfamiliar, but attractive in an intimidating way, guys dressed in black pants and dark leather jackets. The one with the deep reddish-blonde hair and green eyes wore a deep blue button down shirt that stretched out over his wide shoulders. The other man wore a crisp white dress shirt and had dark-blonde hair with a deep cleft in his chin. When they moved away from the keyhole, she sucked in a quick breath as her nipples tightened at the sight of a very familiar man standing in front of the door across the hall from hers. Firm lips, square jaw, and a dark goatee all gave Alex Gorev a sinister, yet oh so tempting, edge. Sin in its most delicious form. A woman could look at him and know he'd push her limits, make her taste forbidden fruit.

And his hands...holy moly she'd never see such big hands on a guy.

To her disgust, she'd spent much of her free time lately fantasizing about what it would feel like to be kissed by a man with facial hair who just happened to look like Alex. Would it feel silky or rough against her face? And what if he dined down south? What would *that* feel like? She could imagine, but she'd bet the real thing was much better than her hand and vibrator. Adding to his good looks were his intense gray eyes, ringed with the thinnest band of black, a muscular body, and his killer smile. He was a feast for all the female senses, wrapped up in a body made for brutal pleasure. Since he was attractive and had solid self-confidence bordering on arrogance, he was like her sexual catnip. Catnip she now masturbated to on a nightly basis despite her anger at herself for dreaming about him.

Humiliation mixed with excitement burned her cheeks, and she let out a muffled squeak when Alex looked directly at her, almost as if he could see her peering through the peephole. He blew her a kiss then said something in whatever language they spoke that made the other men laugh. Alex opened the apartment door across the hall and flicked the lights on before saying loudly, "Jessica, I know you are watching me. I can feel it. Your uncle told me that you have a set of keys that I will need. When you are done spying, bring them to me."

Her body flushed with embarrassment while her brain came up with inventive ways to wipe that smug smirk off his face. That arrogant, good-looking, insanely sexy, older man made her react in a way no one ever had, certainly not the boys she'd dated back home—and the guys she'd previously dated definitely seemed like immature boys in the face of Alex's refined sexuality. No, she needed to keep her distance.

As long as she remained professional and polite with him, he'd just be a harmless fantasy. After all, he was her bodyguard. That meant she'd have to get used to him being around in the background. Hell, she barely even knew the guys her uncle had following her around. It would be no big deal. She would just grab the keys, chuck them at him, and then calmly and coolly stroll back into her place where she would throw every lock on the door she had.

Then she'd go play with herself with the shower massager for a couple hours.

Appalled with her out-of-control libido, she moved away from the door, heading into her big—by Irish standards—kitchen. It always did her heart good when she saw the appliances from the States that Aunt Mary had installed for her, brands she was familiar with that couldn't be found in Ireland and that would ease the homesickness of being in a strange place. Peter had also left framed pictures of their family all over the house, each with a descriptive tag saying who that person was and how they were related to her. Tears prickled her eyes as she realized how much her mother had left behind to run off to America with her loser birth father.

Blinking rapidly while fanning herself, she fought back the burn in her nose until she was sure she wasn't going to cry. She caught her reflection in the vast silver framed mirror in the foyer and paused, giving her image a critical eye. She wanted to look good for her encounter with Alexandr, though she would never admit it out loud. Her gray yoga pants would have to suffice, along with the overly large pink socks she wore to combat the damp chill that sometimes crept up on her. She ditched the gray hoodie jacket then quickly checked her pink t-shirt for any stains.

As she took her hair out of her bun, she glanced behind her and spied a bottle of whiskey someone had given her as a gift. She chewed on her lower lip for a moment, trying to figure out if giving him a welcome gift was a good idea, then decided to say fuck it. There was no reason they couldn't both be mature adults about the situation. Starting off on the right foot by being polite was important. Grabbing the bottle, along with the keys Peter had left for Alex, she opened her door and took the four steps necessary to reach Alexandr's door.

Men's deep voices came from inside Alex's apartment, their unfamiliar language sounding almost melodic in a rough way, and she hesitated before knocking loudly. The murmurs cut off, and she strained to hear if anyone was coming to the door and wondered if she should knock again. Before she could raise her fist, the door opened and revealed Alexandr, his gray-eyed gaze capturing her and making her whole body light up.

He was even more handsome up close than she remembered, and her lower abdomen began to tighten and warm. Tingles radiated from her scalp down to her toes, and she drank in the sight of him. Dressed in a pair of dark tailored pants that fit his muscular legs well and an off-white button down shirt with the sleeves rolled up to reveal powerful forearms dusted with dark hair, he took her breath away. A few buttons at the top of his shirt were also undone, showing the curve of his well-defined neck and some soft-looking chest hair. Crap, he was even hotter than she remembered.

For a long, tension-filled moment, they merely stared at each other. She tried to read his expression, but he was good at masking his feelings. The only thing he couldn't control were his pupils, which dilated as he stared at her. She'd learned in a psychology class last year that humans were hard wired to react to that pupil dilation as a mating signal on a primitive level. So even though Alexandr might appear bored while he assessed her, as if he were opening the door to a pesky Jehovah's Witness, his body's reaction to her told a different story.

She wanted to smirk about his sexual interest in her, to let him know that she felt nothing but disdain for him, but her sex was getting wet from just his mesmerizing gaze, like he was telepathically whispering to her all the raw, nasty things he was going to indulge in with her. She loved a man who could talk dirty, and with Alexandr's rough, accented voice it would be the cherry on the top of her lust-filled cake. The light glinted in his gaze as he took the smallest of steps forward, now close enough that she swore he could feel his heat pressing against her. The tips of her nipples grew hypersensitive, and she desperately tried to regain control of her body, which seemed intent on fucking this annoying man. He was as handsome as ever, as arrogant as ever, and while they stared at each other, she wanted to smack the arrogance out of him then throw him down in the middle of the hallway and fuck the hell out of him just to get him out of her system.

For someone determined to not fall under his sexual spell, that was a rather alarming thought, which made her voice come out tight as she said, "Here, keys and a housewarming present."

He barely caught in one hand the whisky she thrust at him then the keys she pressed into his other hand.

Another man appeared behind Alexandr, the husky blond babe, and he gave her a very flirtatious smile as his gaze took a blatant and leisurely journey down her body. "Alex, who is beauty?"

Before she could respond, Alexandr said something in a low, tight voice that held the edge of a snarl. Whatever he said shocked the blond man if the blood draining from his face was any indication. The blond man quickly backed away with his hands in the air, speaking in a hushed rush before spinning on his heel and leaving them alone. The man's fear had been so palpable she wondered what the heck he was afraid of. Alex wasn't that scary...was he?

The only information she'd been able to get on

Alexandr was that he grew up in Belarus and ran his own personal protection company. Said company was supposed to be one of the best in the world for personal security, but there wasn't much information on it other than the fact that they handled some famous people as clients. There were no pictures of him and only a mention here and there of being in different society pages with various lovely model types in fabulous dresses and dripping in jewels. Those images sent a pang through her stomach, and she tried to tell herself it was anger, not jealousy.

She wasn't surprised to see so many beautiful women hanging all over him. Evidently, from what she'd heard at work, Alexandr had a very thick cock, and the women loved it, but he was never with a woman for long. All five of the bartenders who had been with him, and a couple of the waitresses as well, had all agreed on that. He was lovely. He was charming. He was good for some fantastic sex and pricey gifts, but that was about it.

Alexandr Gorev was booty call material, and she was no longer a booty call kind of girl. Been there, done that, and had discovered the hard way she couldn't do casual sex. With that thought in mind, she turned around and walked back into her apartment, slamming her door shut before she did anything stupid.

But she had a feeling it was too late for that.

With a low groan, she slid down the door after her drama queen exit, thunking her head against it while softly calling herself every name in the book. Why was she so awkward around Alex? She could normally shoot down guys with no problem, but if she was actually attracted to a man, she turned into a tongue-tied fool. It was beyond embarrassing, and she was pretty sure Alexandr thought she was a nut job. He was older, incredibly handsome, and so charismatic he could sell a ketchup Popsicle to a lady wearing white gloves. Other than for sex, there was no reason he would want anything to do with her. She was just a girl who was tending bar for her uncle with no clear direction in life and not an ounce of sophistication.

Before her mind could spiral deeper into a pity party, she heard a series of sharp knocks on her door. Without even looking through the peephole, she opened the door and stared at his shoes. "Hello, Alexandr."

"Jessica," he said in a soft, coaxing tone, "look at me."

When she finally raised her gaze to his, she met his worried eyes. He studied her for a moment then gave her a small smile. "Are you all right? I did not mean to anger you."

"No." She sighed, sucking it up and just getting on with the humiliation. "I was mad at myself. For some reason, I find it hard to speak around you."

He laughed, and she couldn't help but smile in response. She noticed he held the bottle of whiskey in one big hand. Damn, his hands were so sexy, large enough grip her and hold her tight. Big enough to run over her body and bring her the kind of pleasure she'd only dreamed about. And they looked as strong as the rest of him. An odd symbol was tattooed on the webbing between his pointer finger and thumb, and she wondered what it meant. She also wondered why she wanted to lick it then suck on his thumb.

Oblivious to her internal battle with her hormones, he tilted his head and gave her a look she couldn't quite decipher. "Why do you find it hard to speak around me?"

Not wanting to admit her insecurities to this roughly beautiful man, she gestured to the whiskey. "Are you returning this? If you don't like the brand, I have lots of others to choose from. I don't know if it's the custom here or what, but when I moved in, I got a ton of booze as housewarming presents."

He quirked a brow at her. "No, is very good, high quality. I was hoping you would drink with me. Is tradition in my country to celebrate new beginnings with a...what is word...cheer—no, a toast."

Then he gave her a small, soft smile that took all the fight out of her and replaced it with hunger.

Blah, she was so weak.

Giving him an exasperated look, and her overly eager body a stern mental talking to, she opened the door then waved him in. "If you want me to drink with you, I'm afraid you'll have to settle for Tequila. And if you're supposed to be my bodyguard, shouldn't you be guarding me instead of getting wasted?"

"Maks and Gleb are watching your apartment. They wanted to come meet you, but I did not want to overwhelm you. Come, let us welcome each other as neighbors properly. Would be rude to refuse."

She cocked her head to the side, brushing her hair out of her face before tucking it behind her ear. A lifetime of having polite Midwestern manners drilled into her head by her mother had a pang of guilt hitting her when she mentally replayed her words and realized how discourteous she was being. It wasn't his fault she got all flustered around him, and if he was trying to smooth things over between them, she could at the very least act in a civilized manner toward him.

"You're right, I am being rude, please forgive me. Would you like to join me for a drink, neighbor?"

Chapter Four

A lex admired Jessica's heart-shaped ass as she walked in front of him, and the deep red of her hair burning like embers in the dim lighting of her cozy home. The sight of her long legs clad in those deliciously tight pants had him fighting an erection. He didn't want to scare her off, and regardless of his body's reaction to her, this young woman could be nothing more than a job. She was skittish, but he needed her to feel safe enough around him to trust him and his men with her life. There might be a time where her obeying him without question could save her, and he couldn't let his attraction to her get in the way of keeping her alive and well.

He tried to argue with himself that his loyalty to his *Bratva* was the only reason he was feeling so zealous about her protection, but that was not true. There was something about Jessica that brought him a peace like he'd never experienced, but her inner fire challenged him as well. He'd bet that beneath her quick temper lay a sweet soul that was easily wounded, therefore well protected against anyone trying to gain access. Not that he didn't like her sass. It got him hard as fuck, but the knowledge that he could probably make her submit to him in the bedroom teased him without mercy. Tempting him to take just a small taste of her.

He imagined her riding him, her amazing silky, straight hair swaying across his thighs as he brought her to a back-bending orgasm. Dreaming about Jessica in such a carnal state was not helping his determination to keep from pulling her into his arms and giving her the kiss he knew she wanted. The need trembled along her skin, evident in the way she pressed her thighs together, in how she stole quick glances as if unable to help herself from checking him out. The way her gaze lingered on his crotch was not helping the situation.

Need suffused her expression when she allowed herself to look at him.

Before he could stop himself, he asked, "Did you ever dance ballet?"

That brought her eyes back to his, wide with puzzlement and making her look adorable in her confusion. "No, why?"

"Because you are very graceful."

She walked over to a set of light wood cabinets, opened a door, and pulled down a cut crystal bottle filled with clear liquid. When she glanced at him, she smiled a real smile, and it warmed his blood. When she wasn't busy trying to be a bitch, she was actually rather gentle by nature. He usually liked tough women who knew how to keep their emotions safe, but something about her openness appealed to him.

He watched her pink lips move as she talked, wanting to taste them. "I was too much of a tomboy to do ballet."

"What is tomboy?"

"It means...a girl who acts more like a boy than a girl. So instead of doing ballet and beauty pageants like my mom would have liked, I did horseback riding and played sports. You know, boy stuff."

"You like horses?"

"Yeah, we had four of them at my parents' farm. I grew up around horses and love going camping and horseback riding. There is something really comforting about having a horse with you when you're out there beneath the stars." She looked longingly out the small, dark window in her kitchen. "If it ever stops raining, I want to see if I can find stables around here."

"I will arrange it."

She blinked at him. "Hmmm?"

"You wish to ride. I will make that happen."

Her lips curved into a smile he wanted to kiss. "Are you my bodyguard or my genie?"

"What is genie?"

"You know, a spirit that grants three wishes. From Middle Eastern fairy tales."

"Ahhh, this I know. I am not genie, but if you desire something, tell me and you will have it. Is my job to take care of you. Is privilege for the men in your life to provide for you even if we are merely your bodyguards. Gives us purpose, pride."

"Well, thanks, but I can take care of myself." She sighed then glanced up at him through her pale lashes. "Sorry, that was kind of rude. What I meant to say was thank you, but if I want something, I can get it for myself or do it. You don't need to do it for me."

He'd run into this independent attitude in Western women before, so he tried to explain to her why it was his job to make sure she was content. He didn't normally give a shit if his clients were happy as long as they were safe, but Jessica was different. She wasn't some jaded politician or crime lord, and he was sure she didn't understand how things were in his country, or how he was raised to treat a woman of worth. And she was a woman of worth, not one of the spoiled socialites or models he usually dated.

Actually, she was the only woman of worth he'd ever been attracted to like this, so this need to make her understand him was a new experience for him as well.

Leaning against the edge of the counter, he looked into her eyes and said in a low voice, "Making you happy brings me pleasure."

"What?"

His English was good, thanks to years of tutoring and immersion, yet he still struggled to put his thoughts into words. "I am bodyguard, but I am also man. If something would make you happy, is my duty to provide for you. That makes me satisfied."

"Satisfied?"

"Yes."

"Huh, I never considered it that way, but you're right. My dad, well, my adoptive father, he took care of me and my mom, and you're right, it did make him happy and satisfied. We weren't super rich, but we were well off enough that my mom could stay home and raise me, and we still managed to take family vacations. I even got a decent used truck for my sixteenth birthday" She flushed and set the bottle down. "Though I'm sure, to you, we would be considered poor."

That offended him, even if it was probably true. "I think you were raised in love. That is without price."

Her eyes grew watery, and he sucked in a breath, wondering what he said to offend her. When she began to blink rapidly, she looked away, obviously struggling for composure. She fanned her face. "Yes, I was raised with love, and yes, I know how lucky I am to have had them in my life. Can we not talk about this right now, please?"

The need to comfort her consumed him, but he managed not to reach for her. Sometimes, he forgot how young she was compared to him, how fragile. Not just in years but also in experience. Taking pity on her, he changed the subject before she burst out into tears. "Yes, we can talk about how Maks refuses to go shopping more than two hours a week."

"Pardon me?"

"Maks is another of your bodyguards. He will be watching over you when I cannot along with your third primary bodyguard, Oleg. There will be other men coming and going to replace Maks and Oleg for two weeks at a time so they can go home and visit with their families."

"Oh, right. Three full-time bodyguards? Wow. That's...ummm...well, tell them I'm not huge shopper, more of a wanderer, so they should be okay."

"Oleg, he will shop with you without complaint, but is only because he has been trained by his wife and daughters to endure it."

That made Jessica burst out laughing. "Oh dear."

"Yes, but when you see Oleg, you will know why no one teases him about his devotion to his women. Is large man."

"I bet they don't." She smiled, her earlier happiness returning easily.

Alex was beginning to think she was one of those rare people who were easily pleased, and her default mode was cheerfulness. Not that he minded it. Her mood was contagious, and he found himself smiling more than he usually did. A soul as sweet as hers needed to be safeguarded against a world that would try to crush it like a butterfly. It would take a delicate touch to keep her safe without smothering her. Thankfully, he was here to do just that. A deep sense of expectation filled him, like he was about to embark on something important.

He leaned against the counter, watching as she searched around for the shot glasses, giving him a nice profile view of her perfect breast pressing against the soft cotton. A natural beauty who did not need makeup and jewels to shine. Alex had almost kicked Gleb's ass when he'd attempted to flirt with Jessica. Thankfully, Alex had kept his temper, because he had a feeling Jessica would not understand or condone them fighting until one of them was bloody.

Faint warning bells rang in his head that he was becoming infatuated with her in a way that was far from professional, but he ignored them.

She crossed the white tiles of the kitchen floor to him with two ruby shot glasses. Her lean hips swayed, and those fucking pants tormented him with hints of what she would look like naked. He wanted to rip the crotch open with his teeth and lick her pussy. He sucked in a slow breath through his nose and willed his erection to stand down. Just looking at her was as arousing as having his dick sucked by one of his random mistresses. The low lighting of her kitchen made her hair darken to almost a garnet tone, and her cornflower blue eyes mesmerized him.

He had a feeling there were many layers to Jessica, and he looked forward to getting to know her. After all, he would be here for the next six months, studying with Peter and strengthening the Novikov *Bratva's* presence in the British Isles. There was no reason he could not be friends with the girl.

She handed him a shot glass then raised hers in a toast. "May the wind be always at your back."

"To new neighbors," he replied, amused at the way she almost choked on her tequila.

"Yeah, neighbors." She fiddled with her glass, tension radiating from her.

The need to put her at ease had him softening his gaze for her in a way he'd never done with a woman before. "What part of America are you from?"

She looked up at him, and some of the shadows in her gaze dissipated as she studied his face then graced him with a wry smile that made the edges of his lips turn up in response. "The boring part. In the States, they call where I live 'flyover country'."

"What is flyover country?"

She looked at him then back at the glass in her

hands. "It's a place that's so dull all people do is fly over it, never landing. Like I said, boring."

Laughing, he took another sip from his tequila. "What is boring to you is exotic to me."

"Where are you from?"

He almost told her the truth, that his home was in Moscow, Russia, but instead, he said, "Minsk, in Belarus."

"Belarus, huh?" Leaning against the edge of her kitchen counter, she smiled at him. "I'm embarrassed to say I don't know much about your country. By 'much' I mean anything."

"Is boring," he replied with a teasing smile. "You tell me about your boring place, and I will tell you about mine."

She smiled at him, and his chest tightened. "Deal."

Motioning to him, she led them into her spacious living room done in shades of purple and gray. A thick, furry white rug lay beneath the small coffee table, and a few plants hung from hooks in front of the windows. She took a seat on the sofa and seemed a little surprised when he sat in the chair near her instead of next to her in an effort to make her comfortable. He obviously made her nervous, and he wanted to reassure her he meant her no harm.

They chatted about their homes and families, although Alex gave her an edited version of his. Telling her that his father was a ruthless monster who ruled one of the most powerful *Bratvas* in Russia with an iron fist and that he was one of the world's best assassins probably wouldn't be smart or the best way to get her to relax around him. Instead, he went with one of several background stories he had for his various aliases. But he didn't lie that much. He told her how his mother had passed away years ago, leaving out the part about them being assassinated, and how he had a younger half-brother he was very close with. He'd also once had a stepmother, a kind, sweet woman who had doted on Alex like her own, also assassinated. He said that she'd passed of an illness along with his much loved younger half-sister.

The cruel reminder of the reality of his life crashed down on him, and he felt like an asshole for even thinking of involving her in his world, yet he couldn't force himself to move. Her presence was like a balm to him, a soothing caress that seemed to wash clean some of the darkness clinging to him. The feeling left behind was so unusual that he couldn't really give it a name. He knew only that there was a warmth in his body, a relaxation that had the tension draining from his body.

Every time she smiled at him, that warmth grew more intense. It was a feeling that he could easily become addicted to, but he didn't like the loss of control over his normally carefully guarded emotions. He didn't know if it was her youth or her innocence, or both, but he found he genuinely liked her. She had a quick sense of humor and was bright. A pleasure to talk with. Damn, being here was making him think things about her he knew better than to even consider. Time to leave before he gave in to the forbidden temptation.

She was the kind of woman a man would be happy waking up next to for the rest of his life.

Alarmed by the direction of his thoughts, he set the glass down with a sigh. "I must go."

She stared at him, frowning slightly, her lower lip sticking out in a pout that he wanted to kiss so badly his cock ached. "Okay..."

Without another word, he went to her door, but her hand caught his shoulder. Right away, he stopped—her delicate touch was stronger than titanium. Then he slowly turned to face her. At the sight of the worry in her eyes, his gut clenched.

"Did I say something to offend you?"

"No." She gave him a disbelieving look, and there was no mistaking he'd hurt her feelings in some way so he tried to smooth it over. "It just occurred to me my men are in my apartment drinking as well and no doubt causing trouble. I need to go before they destroy."

Her giggle raced along his spine. "Yeah, you better get back."

The need to touch her swamped him, and he was helpless against his instincts around her. Looking into her eyes, he let the darkness he kept hidden from her rise to the surface. Her mouth parted, and she let out a soft breath, totally captured by his gaze and the desire he was having a hard time suppressing. He couldn't believe that at first he'd thought her merely pretty. Up close, her beauty captivated him. Women in his country would spend fortunes on plastic surgery trying to attain the perfection of her delicate, facial features, and her hair was the most gorgeous color he'd ever seen. Add to that her beautiful, tilted blue eyes, and she could slay a man with a glance.

All these emotions mixed with the sexual charge warming him, making it stronger until his cock ached. He'd meant to make a point and show Jessica how easily he could seduce her. Instead, he was the one who had a racing heart. Curving his hand behind her neck, he tugged her closer until less than a half-inch separated their bodies. The heat built between them as their gazes locked, drawn closer like iron filings to a magnet. Soon, she was pressed against him from breast to hip, and he wanted to fuck her more than he'd ever wanted a woman. She smelled so good, felt so good, and his heart cried out in protest at the thought of releasing her.

It took everything he had, but somehow he found the strength to let her go and take a step back, hoping she didn't see the tremors going through him. "I would have you, and it would be the most amazing experience of my life—perfection, but it is not right time."

A little bit of panic cleared the lust from her gaze, and she almost reached for him before lacing her hands behind her back and lifting her small, pointed chin. "Alex, I know that you're used to women offering to have your babies, but although you are attractive, you're also correct. We are not meant to be."

He wanted to scream at her that she was wrong and the potential for what they could have together was everything he wanted but couldn't have. "Yes."

A smile curved her lips, and she visibly relaxed. "But we can still be friends."

"Friends?"

"Yeah, you know, friends. If you're going to be around a lot, I'd rather things be comfortable between us."

The misery in his heart lightened as he clung to that idea, desperate to have some reason to spend time with her. "Yes, I would like to be friends."

"Strictly platonic friends."

"Of course."

Walking him to her door, she held her hand out. "Thanks for stopping by, friend."

He took it, but instead of shaking, he gave her knuckles a soft kiss, brushing his goatee against her creamy skin and taking her fresh scent in deep. "Thank you for good hospitality, friend."

When he left, she still hadn't responded, but she was cradling the hand he'd kissed to her chest with a stunned look. They would be friends, just friends, and he would treat her as nothing more than a client.

Surely he was strong enough to resist the innocent charms of a girl who was still learning how to be a woman.

Two weeks later, Alex had realized the futility of trying to see Jessica as nothing more than a client. His resolve to leave her alone had been quickly replaced by his need to see her as often as he could. Which wasn't as often as he'd like. In between learning forgery from Peter and dealing with *Bratva* issues, he'd been busy. In an effort to get his desires under control, he'd been to a local BDSM dungeon a couple times and had relieved himself with some willing and beautiful submissives, but none of them quenched the fire for Jessica that steadily grew inside of him.

Though it shamed him to admit it, when he was in his apartment in Dublin, he'd listen for her door opening into the communal hallway and dash for his, pretending to be leaving at the same time. He'd forgotten his jacket a couple times, and she'd given him odd looks, but made small talk with him. Every time he did see her, his obsession with her grew. Her enchanting blue eyes held more depth and wisdom than most grown women, yet she wasn't bitter. The world was a bright, exciting place for Jessica, an adventure, and he loved watching her experience it while he guarded her.

To say she brought out his protective instincts was like saying water was wet. He was obsessed with keeping her safe, something that had proven difficult. Not because of any outright attacks on her, but because Jessica liked to wander and didn't pay any attention to her surroundings, ignorant of the headaches she was creating for her bodyguards. A couple times, she'd been in real danger, but she never knew it. Luka, Oleg, and Maks were quick to neutralize any threat, but they'd told him Jessica seemed to attract trouble through no fault of her own because she believed the best in people. It never seemed to occur to her that someone would want to hurt her, and that made her very vulnerable to men who liked to prey on the innocent.

Alex had been with her more than once when she walked blindly into situations and places she had no business being, like stopping in a bar owned by rival Irish mafia family, the O'Doyles, before he could stop her. The blood feud between Peter's people and the O'Doyles went back centuries, but when Jessica walked up to the bar, fearless in her ignorance, and asked for directions, Alex had been a heartbeat away from reaching for his gun and shooting his way out.

Oblivious of the tension her presence was causing in the pub, she'd complimented the bartender on the huge stained glass window behind him and had asked him about it. The young O'Doyle man working at the bar stared at her then answered her questions about the stained glass that used to be in a church. The bartender had given Alex a baffled look, plainly thrown off by Jessica's friendliness, but Alex merely shrugged. By the time she left, the bartender was telling her about other spots in Dublin and where she could find more historical buildings that might interest her with a genuine smile.

Things like that happened all the time around his girl. She needed someone to protect her, someone to fight off the wolves that would be drawn to her. More than one predator had tried to apprehend Jessica when Alex and his men trailed behind her, attempting to give her some semblance of privacy as she took in the world around her. It was not safe for a woman to walk alone in certain parts of Dublin, and poor Luka had come home repeatedly with scraped up knuckles, shaking his head and regaling Alex about another night spent guarding the fairy princess who seemed to float her way through the world in a fragile bubble of ignorant bliss.

If she wasn't so damn sweet and adorable, he'd have strangled her by now.

When Alex mentioned his men didn't speak English as well as she did, she immediately volunteered to tutor them any way she could. She'd embraced the role eagerly, spending a great deal of her free time with the men, talking and hanging out with them until she became a part of their lives. To Alex's amusement, Oleg, his mentor and a man he thought of as a surrogate uncle, and Maks, Alex's right-hand man and fellow assassin, had grown rather fond of Jessica during those talks. She was very open and told them much about her life, all of which they repeated to Alex. He was sure all of his men knew his interest in Jessica went far beyond a professional one, but so far, none of them had said anything.

Alex wandered into the pub, knowing Jessica was there. Maks had said Jessica was withdrawn and quiet, not her usual self at all. He was worried about her, but she pretended nothing was wrong. It bothered Alex more than he cared to admit that someone or something might have hurt her, but he'd been tied up with one of Peter's men all day learning how to forge passports.

Now it was late, and the bar was closing, but no one paid him any mind. It wasn't unusual to see him here when Jessica was working, and when he spotted her sitting in a booth at the back of the large room, he was glad he had come instead of Maks. Dressed in a tight navy shirt and worn jeans, she looked tired, almost ill, and the luster was gone from her gaze. She had an open bottle of vodka in front of her and a shot glass.

Without asking, he grabbed the bottle from her hands and slid into the booth next to her. A slow jazz melody was playing low, and the atmosphere was relaxed. Unfortunately, his girl was not. Tension radiated from her, and when he touched her, she was as stiff as stone. When her lower lip trembled he clenched his hands into fists. Something, or someone had hurt her, badly, and he had to tamp down on the urge to order her to tell him who had done this to her so he could go end their life.

Her voice came out thick as she continued to stare at the shot glass she was toying with. "Hello, friend."

When she didn't say anything else, he took a long drink before handing the bottle back to her. If there was one thing he understood, it was the need to drown emotion in alcohol. Sometimes it was the only way life seemed bearable. The thought of Jessica feeling that way hurt him inside, in a place in his soul he'd never felt before.

"Hello, friend." He brushed her hair back, revealing a few tear tracks. "Why are you sad? Has someone upset you?"

She took in a deep, watery breath and let it out slowly. "No. I'm sorry. You might not want to hang out with me right now. I'm afraid I won't be very good company."

"Jessica," he said in a soothing tone that made her turn her wounded gaze in his direction. "What is wrong?"

Her lower lip trembled, and she blinked back tears. "It's the anniversary of my mom's death. Well, my adoptive mom. My birth mother died not long after I was born. But I've heard so many good things about her from Peter that I feel like I know her. Makes me wish more than ever she'd stuck around long enough for me to remember how it felt to hug

64

her."

It took a great deal of effort for Alex to hide his emotional reaction to her words. Having lost not just his mother but the stepmother he'd loved as well to mafia violence gave him an insight into her pain that made his chest hurt. He hated the thought of her suffering, but didn't know how to make it any better.

"I am sorry for your loss. How long ago?"

"Two years." She gave a watery sigh and glanced over at him. The blue of her irises glowed like neon because of her red, swollen eyes. "I was hoping this year would be better, but it's not."

Without thought, he pulled her into his embrace, tucking her head beneath his chin. She fit against him perfectly, her body molding to his as if they'd found solace in each other's arms for years. She felt divine and his entire body lit up at her touch.

Her breath came out in a shuddering sigh. "You smell good."

He smiled against the top of her head. "I glad you approve."

Jessica nodded, her arms wrapping around his waist as she wiggled closer. Taking the silent hint, he gently pulled her into his arms until she was cradled on his lap. Holding her like this made him realize how tiny she was. He'd look like a dark beast rutting on a fairy princess if they ever had sex.

No, no thinking about that right now.

Unable to reply, he merely nodded. Realizing the pub was almost empty except for the cleaning people who were watching them curiously, he brushed her hair back again. "Come, is time to go home."

"Yeah, home," she said in a wistful voice.

Their trip back to their apartment was silent, her gait a little unsteady from the alcohol, and he missed her normal, happy chatter.

When they reached the hallway separating their

apartments, she looked up at him. "Can I ask you a favor?"

"What is it?"

"Will you come up to the roof with me?"

"Why?"

"I have something I have to do, and I'd rather not be alone while I do it, if that's okay with you."

He needed to take the wounded look out of her eyes. "Anything you need, Jessica, I will do."

Her voice thickened as she whispered, "Thanks. Wait here, I'll be right back."

When she came out into the hallway, he frowned at the sight of a big, white, helium-filled balloon with what appeared to be a bunch of writing on it in black marker.

"What is that?"

She flushed, closed her door, and started toward the stairway at the end of the hall that led to the roof. "It's...well, it's a way of grieving."

"I do not understand."

As they made their way up the stairs, she explained. "My friend told me about this, and the idea kinda stuck with me. Her younger brother died of cancer, and every year on the anniversary of his death, she writes him a letter on a balloon then sets it free. She said it was her way of communicating with him. At first, I thought it was kind of a silly idea, but like I said, the more I thought about it the more sense it made. So...I...uh went and got a balloon today and wrote a letter on it to my mom. When something hurts this bad, you'll do anything to relieve the agony, even send up a balloon with the hopes of it reaching heaven."

The ambient light from the city dimly illuminated her face as she opened the door to the rooftop, the chilly breeze making her hair flair about her. When she looked over at him with the balloon in

66

her hand, he was struck dumb by her beauty, his breath literally taken away. He didn't know if it was the lighting or the grief blanketing her, but he had a glimpse of the woman she would one day become. He reached out without thought and brushed a tear from her cheek, relishing the feel of her soft, damp skin.

"I do not think is silly."

Her weak smile made him want to gather her into his arms, but instead, he led her a little farther out onto the roof. The night was cloudy, and the wind was brisk enough that it cut through his thick coat and gloves. Jessica didn't seem to be bothered by it, but he didn't know if that was because of the alcohol or her emotions. Reaching out, she grasped his hand and held it tight enough that it hurt, but he didn't pull away. She could jerk his arm off if it would make her feel better, and he would gladly let her do it.

For a long moment, she stared up at the balloon whipping back and forth in the wind. Then slowly, with great reluctance, she raised her hand and let it go. Together, they watched the balloon rise into the sky, flying over the rooftops as it continued to climb until they lost sight of it. She shivered, and he drew her into his arms then gently pressed her head against his chest. He held her while she cried, her muffled sobs tearing through him.

His chest hurt, and he struggled to reign in his emotions, but she'd totally overwhelmed him. When she pulled back, her gaze fastened on his lips. "I'm so tired of hurting, Alex," she whispered. "I don't want to feel this terrible loss anymore. Kiss me and make it go away."

A hard tremor went through him that had nothing to do with the cold. He was dying to kiss her, to take her hard, to bury himself in her and give her nothing but pleasure, which was exactly the reason he could not indulge in any type of physical intimacy with her. One kiss and there would be no going back. Plus, she was drunk and grieving right now. She had no idea what she was asking for.

He gently pulled out of her arms and set her away from him. "I can think of another way to distract you."

She gave him a puzzled look, her eyes glassy from the alcohol and her tears. "And what would that be?"

"Do you play chess?"

Chapter Five

Jessica blinked up at him like an adorable owl, and he couldn't help but laugh at her stunned expression. "I offer sex and you want to play chess?"

"You did not offer sex, because you are drunk. *Nyet, prinsessa moya.* Now if you make the same offer tomorrow when you are sober..."

"What did you just say?"

"*Nyet* means no."

"And the other part?"

Not ready to explain why he called her his princess, he tried to distract her. "Are you trying to...what is the phrase...back out? To not play because you are scared? Is okay, I understand. You do not want embarrassment of losing."

She glared at him. If she'd been a cat, her fur would have been standing up. Then her expression cleared, and the first hint of the vibrant young woman he'd come to know peeking through her veil of mourning. "Tell you what. If I win at chess, I get an orgasm. If you win, I'll owe you some future favor."

Dirty images galore exploded in his thoughts as he imagined all the things he could request as a favor. The need to take her was so strong for a moment that he took a step closer to her then stopped. Goddamn it, his body wasn't even remotely under his control anymore. The savage part of him kept rising to the surface, demanding he take her, make her his. He'd never felt this way about a woman before, this duality of caring for Jessica in the gentlest of ways combined with an almost psychotic need to destroy anything that threatened her in the most violent manner possible.

He was so fucked.

"Agreed." He almost bit his tongue, intending to say he was going to bed, but somehow that word slipped out instead. "Do you have board?"

Fluttering her lashes at him, she motioned for him to follow her as she headed back to the stairs. "I may have one or two."

When they were in her warm, inviting apartment, she led him into the cozy living room and flipped on the lights, revealing a new piece of pottery on the coffee table he hadn't seen before. Little by little, Jessica was putting her stamp on the apartment, and he was glad she was making it her home instead of just a place to sleep. It was decorated with furniture similar to his place across the hall, and he realized Jessica probably didn't have much of anything of her own here in Ireland. His gut tightened when he considered the fact that all of Jessica's things were in the US because that's where she lived.

He did not like the idea of her returning to the United States at all. His gaze cut over to another wall, his memory triggering that something new had been added over there as well. There were three new, framed photographs sitting on the shelves that flanked the big screen TV, and he wanted to go look at them, but Jessica motioned him to follow her in the opposite direction.

As soon as she turned on the dim brass lamp over the chessboard, he couldn't help but smile. Then he wondered if the elaborate, detailed fantasy chessboard had come with the apartment or if it was one of Jessica's personal possessions. The board featured an elfin maiden as the queen, and she reminded him of Jessica with her delicate beauty. For a moment, he was disgusted with himself for getting this soft over a woman, but she'd shared something deep with him tonight by allowing him to witness her ritual to deal with her family members' deaths. It was a much healthier tradition than drinking into oblivion, which is how Alex and Dimitri coped with their losses. Then again, Jessica had been drinking heavily earlier in the night and was probably still pretty drunk right now.

She was a bit unsteady as she took her seat. Then she had to use the bathroom. Then she was thirsty and needed some water. Then she wanted a sandwich—and made him one as well—before they finally sat down to play. Her delay had allowed her time to sober up, and he wondered if that was a calculated move or if she was just drunk and hungry. She'd consumed a fair amount of strong alcohol, and he felt slightly guilty that he was playing with an inebriated woman for a favor, but all was fair in love and war.

His guilt lasted about three rounds until he realized he'd been suckered by a girl barely old enough to drink. Alex prided himself on being a methodical, ruthless chess player, impossible to ruffle, always cool and composed. After all, he'd learned to play chess from his father, and the head of the Novikov *Bratva* was famous for his brilliant strategies in chess and life. Yet, Alex found himself losing, badly, to a girl who was playing chess with one hand and eating chips out of a huge ceramic bowl with the other. Even worse, she seemed more interested in her food than the game, which meant beating him had been easy for her.

Alex's distress might have been a bit obvious as he ran a hand through his hair repeatedly, staring at the board. Jessica was either crazy, or a genius. She'd managed to get him in checkmate without him even being aware of her plan. She was a ruthless player, sacrificing with abandon. She'd shut him down in a perfectly executed series of moves he'd been unable to predict. Normally, he'd be irritated—he wasn't a good loser—but her glee at managing to trap him brought a smile to her face and light back to her eyes.

Her lips pressed together as she tried to hold back her laughter. "What? Did you think that just because I have tits and a pussy I couldn't play chess?"

That was right along the lines of what he'd been thinking, much to his chagrin, and he gave her his warmest smile, adoring the way she blushed. In an impulsive moment, he decided to be honest with her. "You are brilliant. I have played many, many crafty players...but you...you take my breath away. So sweet, so pure, but such a dirty, cutthroat strategist. Brilliant."

If he thought he'd seen her happy before, it was nothing compared to her smile right now. It positively stunned him, and he had to resist the urge to reach across the table and pull her to him for a kiss. "Thanks. My dad taught me how to play as well. He may have been a farmer, but that didn't mean he wasn't smart. My mom used to say that he could have been anything he wanted, a doctor, a lawyer, President of the United States, but instead, he'd chosen to be happy."

Her voice broke on the last word, and tears filled her eyes. The pain that radiated from her felt like his own, but he had no idea how to ease her. It sounded callous, cruel even, but he never really cared about a woman's emotions enough to offer her comfort. Oh, he'd soothed female friends when they were hurt or troubled, but this was different. More personal somehow.

"Every summer when blueberry season rolled around, he'd take us out to this huge, old patch that lined our road for miles. Sweetest berries ever if you could get them before the birds did. He told me one day when I was younger and my mom and some friends were with us picking berries, that he was the happiest man in the world, and it was all because of 'his girls'." She stopped eating and sighed. "It made me proud to know that. To know that my mom and I were so special to him that we made him the happiest man in the world. I can still remember that moment perfectly. Shit...I...shit...gimme a sec', okay?"

"Of course."

As he watched Jessica fight back her tears, his need to make her his grew. He wanted to protect her and fill her life with nothing but happiness, to keep the bright light of her spirit burning, undimmed by sorrow. She deserved to know nothing but happiness, to have a man who would worship her and treat her like the princess she was. If she was his woman, he would do just that, and he knew his life with her would be bliss. The mental image of waking up every morning to see her glorious hair spread over his pillow, to see those beautiful blue eyes warmed with love felt so right that the temptation of keeping her sank deep into his soul and settled there.

But his world wasn't ready for her yet, so he would have to keep his distance until he could rectify certain delicate situations.

She must have sensed his shift in mood because she dashed a tear off her cheek and forced a smile. "You're awfully quiet. Are you butt hurt about losing to a girl?"

What she said was so absurd, so *not* what he was thinking, that he couldn't help but laugh. "I assure you, my pride, and ass, are intact."

Something shifted in her gaze as they grinned at each other, a spark of heat that made her pupils dilate. Her gaze was on his mouth, and she bit her lower lip. He couldn't help but wonder if she was thinking about kissing him, or him kissing her...in more intimate places. The thought of tasting her *pizda* made his mouth water, and his cock pressed against his pants in an uncomfortable manner. She'd caused him to become achingly hard at just the thought of what she would look like when she was coming on his tongue.

She slowly stood from her chair, her hair falling around her like silk. He watched her gather her courage, her shoulders squaring and a determined, possibly dangerous look heating her gaze. He should leave, but he remained where he was, spellbound by the gentle creature approaching him. Without a doubt, for all of her sexual aggression, she was skittish. Her gaze darted about before finally settling somewhere in the region of his lips. A gentle rain had begun to fall outside, and he found it to be the perfect backdrop for his Jessica.

She was a daughter of Ireland, and he admired her pale, perfect beauty that housed such a strong spirit.

After swallowing hard and unclenching her fists, she tentatively reached out and placed her faintly trembling fingertip against his lips. "I want these." She ran the tips of her fingers over her mouth. "Here. Please."

Raw, carnal need blasted through him, but he tried to keep it in check. He wanted to devour her. Instead, he kissed the tip of her finger, tasting the salt on her skin, to give her one last chance to run. Still sitting, he looked up at her, now inundated by the faint smell of her musky, aroused sex. He'd never endured such torture as he maintained his calm with a perfect bounty waiting for his touch. Too bad he had to be strong for both their sakes.

"Jessica, this is not good idea. I do not want to harm friendship."

"Please, Alex. I need to feel alive. Be my

friend...kiss me."

His control deserted him, and without thought, he gripped her hips and nuzzled his face against her flat belly. She smelled so good, and when he lifted her top with his nose so he could kiss her hip, she shivered against him. Soft, so very, very soft. The way she responded to his touch was intoxicating. Vast amounts of hormones flooded his system while the need to have her roared through him. He wanted her more than he'd ever wanted anyone, and if she touched him, he wouldn't be able to stop until he was inside her with her nails digging into his back hard enough to draw blood.

Her breath came out in shallow pants, and when he looked up at her, the absolute trust in her eyes was like a harsh slap of reality.

"We cannot do this. Is mistake."

A hot blush filled her face, and he didn't like how easily her feelings got hurt. Shit, he hadn't meant to sound so harsh, but she couldn't know his plans for her yet, know he'd made a dangerous decision that would change the course of both their lives. Better to let her remain ignorant and free of worry. He would complicate her world soon enough.

Her face paled even as her cheeks remained red. "I see."

Jessica swayed so hard her hip bumped the table, and the chess pieces rolled to the floor. She flinched and rubbed her hip, immediately triggering his need to care for her. The tears were back in her eyes, and he cursed himself for being such a fool, for engaging in play like this with her when she was at her most vulnerable. The way she winced when she touched her hip made him flinch, and he knew that it was at least one thing he could take care of for her.

He pulled her gray pants down to reveal her reddened skin. Ignoring her attempt to push him away—she obviously had no idea how to fight—he gently rubbed the mark, relishing how soft her skin was. She relaxed beneath his touch, her body swaying into his as he caressed her. Her swearing at him finally penetrated his concern, and he couldn't help but smile.

His princess had a dirty mouth.

"I said, get your motherfucking hands off of me, you big, perverted bastard. You don't want me. I get that loud and clear so let me go. I'll be damned if I'll be any man's pity fuck."

He wasn't sure what a pity fuck was, but he knew he didn't like the pain in her voice. Instead of fighting with her, he merely stood then held her close and gently stroked her back with long, soothing sweeps of his hand. She fought his hold for a few more moments, token wiggles that did nothing to dislodge him, before she melted against him. Good, she needed to know his touch, to become comfortable with him. It was going to be a long, slow seduction to win Jessica's heart, but he was known for his patience. If he could wait three days in a tree to get the perfect shot on a mark, he could wait for Jessica to become more comfortable with him.

"Shhh, *dorogoya*. Let me hold you."

Her entire body seemed to conform to his, and her lighter weight easily settled against his much taller, solid frame. When her arms went around his waist, he sighed against the top of her head before placing a gentle kiss there. She smelled sweet, edible, almost like an apple pie. It was such an unusual scent to him. The women he was intimate with usually wore expensive perfumes and lotions, but he found the crisp, spicy scent highly erotic on her.

After standing there for several long minutes, cuddling with each other, Jessica stiffened in his arms, then leaned back and softened slightly. "I'm

76

not usually like this."

"I know." He understood her pride, the need to appear strong.

She met his gaze, and some of the shame left her expression. "Thanks...for tonight...for everything."

"Is honor," he murmured, then brushed a strand of her brilliant hair back from her cheek.

She searched his face before she spoke. "Would you sleep with me tonight?"

Oh, how she tempted him. "Jessica, I told you I would not take advantage."

She rolled her eyes. "I'm not talking about sex. Calm down, Casanova. Your virtue is safe. I know I'll have a hard time falling asleep tonight and...and I'm lonely. Really, really lonely. When you hold me like this, I don't feel alone anymore. So just for tonight, can you help me not be lonely?"

His heart ached as he stared down at her, wanting to tell her he finally felt at peace with her in his arms, but he couldn't, so instead he took her hand and nodded.

Her bedroom was surprisingly feminine compared to the rest of the apartment, pale peach walls and a brass canopy bed with a jade floral silk comforter. A small fireplace with a large, grey-colored marble hearth took up the far wall, and framed photographs of people he recognized as different members of her family took up every inch of mantle space. There were some clothes scattered on the floor, but for the most part, Jessica kept her room clean. She turned off the light next to her bed before he could get a good look at the rest of the space.

"Take your shoes off," she whispered, then with a bit of her usual spirit returning, she added in a leering voice that ended up sounding like a giggle, "or anything else you want."

He laughed and shook his head. "Behave."

Normally, he slept nude, but he kept everything on except his shoes. He turned his back while Jessica put on a thick, green flannel nightgown that fell to her knees. The fact she chose that dowdy thing instead of some silky piece of lingerie let him know he'd made the right choice, that regardless of her words, she was not ready for him yet.

The sheets rustled as she scooted beneath them then wiggled around until she was comfortable. Instead of joining her, he lay down atop the sheets, needing that barrier between them. He had no intention of spending the night. The temptation of waking next to her and touching her would be too much for his sleep-softened brain to absorb, but he could be with her until she went to sleep.

So when she laid her head on his chest and cuddled against him, he gladly gathered her into his arms and lightly rubbed her slender back. He soaked into his dark soul her light and marveled at how right and perfect she felt against him, how she seemed to energize and renew him somehow. There was no more fighting the fact that she was meant for him. It would take time for his still-forming plans to work, but when he was ready, he was going to take Jessica Venture and make her his wife.

And there wasn't a man in the world who would be able to stop him.

Chapter Six

ive weeks later, Jessica found herself cleaning the bar in the slow time between lunch and dinner while looking forward to her chess game that evening with Alex and his men. Maks, Oleg, and Luka seemed to have adopted her as their little sister, and she didn't mind one bit. They were always around, and she had to admit, as odd as it was, a group of older, scary bodyguards were her best friends in Ireland. Even when they weren't on duty, they would stop by to check on her and hang out. She'd also discovered that big, burly Oleg had a rather odd and secret fondness for the American dance shows featuring celebrities past their prime, and they'd spent many a night watching the shows while Oleg yelled at the judges.

Since the night of the anniversary of her mother's death, she'd rarely been alone with Alex, almost like he was avoiding it. Not that she could blame him after the way she'd drunkenly thrown herself at him. Those memories still made her burn with embarrassment when she thought about him repeatedly turning down her request for a kiss, but luckily, Alex pretended it never happened. For that, she was eternally grateful.

Disappointed, but grateful.

After that night, she knew she was firmly in the 'friend zone' box with Alex, a fact that was emphasized when she overheard one of the other bartenders talking about how good Alex had been in bed the night before. The woman, a big breasted brunette named Millie, had gone on and on about it, bragging to her friend about how many times she'd come. The only consolation Jessica had was that, when Alex was at the pub, he ignored Millie so she must not have been that great in the sack.

Oh, but the knowledge that Millie had sex with Alex burned like acid, knowing he'd fucked another woman when he could have easily had Jessica, but she managed to swallow back her pain. It wasn't his fault she'd developed a stupid crush on him. Since that night, he'd been nothing but kind to her. Once he let his guard down, she'd found that he had a great sense of humor, if a bit dry, and they shared many things in common. Like their love of chess. Their matches had become a regular thing, and she looked forward to pitting herself against him. Sometimes he won, most of the time she won, but it was always a challenge.

Whoever hosted the match that night would also prepare some food, and she thoroughly enjoyed having people over. Alex never came alone, always bringing a friend or two with him. She'd enjoyed getting to know them and loved the fact that these scary, stoic men relaxed enough around her in private to laugh and joke with her. Maks was a very handsome man with thick reddish-blond hair, and on the rare occasions when he did allow himself to smile, it was full of warmth. She'd learned that he was Alex's right-hand man and had grown up with Alex in Minsk. Then there was Oleg, a big, bald giant with a crocked nose who rarely smiled and spoke only the most rudimentary English, but had a wry sense of humor that always made her laugh. He was patient with her, and once she found out that he had two young daughters, she knew why he put up with her. Even when Alex wasn't around, Oleg would stop by to see if she wanted to go walk around the town or go to a pub.

Oleg would seek her out at work, and during slow times, she'd discuss philosophy and politics with him, fascinated by how different his Eastern European mindset was from her American one. Sometimes his practical view of life was almost brutal, but she could see his point in many ways, even if she found it odd. Then again, he found her unflinching optimism weird, and they would often descend into glass-half-full/half-empty discussions.

Then there was Luka with his golden brown hair and seductive gaze, the flirt of the bunch. He was a few years younger than Alex, closer to her age, and his eyes always seemed to twinkle with mischief. Luka wasn't around as much as the other two, but when it was his turn to guard her, he made sure she had fun. A couple times, she thought she'd caught him checking her out, but he never hit on her, so she just dismissed it as her imagination. To the men, she was nothing more than a friend, a client, and she sometimes wondered if they even noticed she was female. Not that she wanted them trying to make a move on her—none of them appealed to her like Alex—but she had to admit, now that she was comfortable in Ireland, it would be nice to have someone special to share her life with. Someone who would hold her hand, take her dancing, and kiss her until she couldn't breathe.

Someone to love.

"Hey, beautiful," a man said from behind her in a rich Irish brogue.

A happy smile already tugged at her mouth as she turned around to find John, one her uncle's men, leaning against the bar in his battered leather jacket, drops of rain gleaming in his light brown hair beneath the warm lights of the pub. He was a couple years older than she, good-looking in a boy-next-door way with warm, dark eyes. John worked for Peter as pretty much an errand boy, so he was always at the pub or with her uncle, and she saw him in passing a lot. His parents were both into politics like Peter, and they'd been at a dinner party her uncle had thrown one night. Nice people, friendly, if a little intimidating at first with their obviously top-of-the-line designer clothes and upper crust manners.

Wiping her hands on the clean bar towel before setting it aside, she did a quick glance up and down the bar to make sure no one needed anything before leaning against it and smiling at John. She was glad she'd taken a little extra time with her appearance tonight, curling her hair and going heavier on the makeup than usual in an effort to feel attractive. When his gaze warmed as it roamed her face, she fought a flush. "Hello, handsome."

They always greeted each other like this, and she enjoyed flirting with him. It was nice to have the attention of a man who was clearly into her, even if he didn't set her body aflame like Alex. As much fun as it was to hang out with Alex and his crew, she missed having someone to go on dates with. And if she was being honest, she was sexually starved as well. She'd never been without for this long since she started having sex when she was seventeen, and John looked like he'd know how to show a girl a good time. Still, a small part of her had held back from John in the stupid hope that maybe Alex would see her as something more than a friend, but after the last six weeks, she didn't think that was going to happen. That realization hurt, but not as much as having a crush on a man she knew was sleeping with other women.

That shit burned, hurt so badly that even thinking about it made the smile fall from her lips.

It was time to let her fantasies of Alex go and focus on reality.

John, ever attentive to her mood, reached across the counter and brushed a strand of hair back from her cheek that had escaped her silver barrette. "Why the sad eyes, *a mhuirnín*?"

She felt a soft, warm tingle where his fingertips brushed over the shell of her ear and down her jaw. Then the tingle settled into the neglected space between her legs. It wasn't the bone-clenching desire she felt whenever Alex touched her, but still, it was a nice sensation. Not wanting to discuss Alex with John, she looked away from John's steady gaze and out the mullioned windows facing the street. "I wish it would snow. It doesn't feel like Christmas without the snow."

"We may not have snow, but give it a few days, and everyone'll have their decorations up. That should lift your spirits. Dublin really is beautiful during the holidays, but probably different from the States." His gaze went gentle. "Must be hard being in a new place at Christmas."

"It is."

"Well, we're glad to have you here, and I know your aunt and uncle are overjoyed to have you with them. I hope you'll give us a chance to show you how good it can be here for you, Jessica."

The sincerity in his gaze touched her, and she patted his hand while she tried to not think about the fact that, if her parents were still alive, they'd be getting ready for their annual trip to the Milson's tree farm. Her extended relatives had invited her back to the States, but Uncle Peter and Aunt Mary were going all out for her this year, and she knew it would hurt their feelings if she left. They were having a big Christmas party next week and made sure to include her in the planning, doing their best to show her how pleased they were that she was spending the holidays with them instead of going home.

She wondered what Alex was going to do for Christmas and which lucky woman he was going to

83

celebrate the holidays with.

Angry at herself for caring, she forced a smile at John. "Can I get you anything to drink?"

"Nah." He studied her with enough intensity that she had to fight the urge to squirm. "I wanted to ask you something, though."

There was something in his intent expression that made her nervous. "What's that?"

"Would you like to come to the tree lighting with me?" When she didn't respond right away, his cheeks grew pink, and he said in a hurried torrent, "It's a big affair with music, and food, and all kinds of things to do and see. I figured since it was your first year here, you should see it right, like a local and not a tourist. That is if you want. Me and some of my friends are gonna go pub-hopping afterward, and I'd like you to come with us."

A bit of warmth traveled through her as he blathered on, and she couldn't help but smile at how tense he was beneath his usual cockiness. "I'd love to."

The way his tight shoulders dropped and the happy light in his eyes made her smile as he said in obvious surprise, "Really?"

"Sure, when is it?"

"Tomorrow. I already asked your Uncle Peter, and he said you could go."

"Umm, what? I didn't realize that I needed my uncle's permission to go anywhere."

He must have caught her peeved expression, because he grabbed one of her hands in his and ran his thumb over her knuckles in a soothing manner. "Easy there, Jessica. He's just tryin' to look out for you. Being who he is and all that, he has to be careful."

"Who he is?"

His gaze darted away. "You know, a politician

and a wealthy businessman."

She stiffened and lifted her chin. "Well, for future reference, I'm an adult who is capable of making her own decisions on who I do and don't go out with."

"Ahhh, lass, don't be mad. Lovely as you are, you know Peter's just looking out for you. God save me if I have daughters as beautiful as you. Turn my hair gray with worry before they're out of the cradle." He winked with a rakish grin, and she swore one of the nearby servers sighed.

That mollified her somewhat, but she still shot a glare in the direction of the stairs leading to her uncle's home, only to find Oleg sitting at a table nearby and watching them with a decidedly unhappy expression. She blinked, wondering what had her friend upset, but before she could give it any further thought, John drew her attention back to him by gently tugging at her hand.

"Jessica."

His expression was unexpectedly grave, and she frowned at him. "Yes?"

"Are you involved with Alex Gorev?"

"What? No, no. He's my bodyguard."

He raised an eyebrow and tilted his head in Oleg's direction. "Then why does one of his men look like he's thinkin' about cuttin' my throat?"

Oleg had indeed been looking at John like he was thinking about violent things. She shrugged, used to the men's overprotective nature with her. "That's just Oleg. He's a friend of mine, and my bodyguard, but he's also kinda overprotective. Says I remind him of his daughters. But don't worry, he's not mad at you. He always looks like that."

"He's your bodyguard and your friend?"

"Well, yeah. Why wouldn't we be friends? Alex lives across the hall from me, and they come over and hang out a lot. They're really nice guys once you get to know them and get past the language barrier."

John's expression became serious. "Jessica, you don't need to be around the likes of them. Let them guard you, but do not get personally involved with any of them. I know your uncle has his reasons for them being here, but I don't want you getting hurt by Alexandr...Gorev."

"He's been nothing but nice to me."

His lips twitched like he wanted to say something, but he finally shook his head. "Just trust me when I say Alex isn't the kind of man that's nice to a woman without wantin' something."

She tried to pull her hand away, but he held tight. "What are you trying to say?"

"I just worry about you is all. I like you. You're sweet, the sweetest girl I've ever met, and I don't want anyone to take advantage of your good nature. No offense, but you aren't used to men like Alex."

Irritated now, she jerked her hand. "Look, I'm not stupid, okay? I know how to take care of myself, and Alex and his men have been nothing but polite with me. Is it so hard to believe that someone would want to be my friend?"

"No, that's not hard to believe at all. Any man would consider himself lucky to have you smile at him, but he'd want you as more than a friend."

"Well, I can assure you that Alex and his buddies don't think of me that way."

"Yes, they do."

She snorted, and his expression softened. That little thrill of warmth stirred in her belly again.

"Ahhh, I see it now. You have no idea how lovely you are, do you? A man can't help but look at you and wonder what it would feel like to have your soft lips pressed to his, your cheeks pink from his kiss."

Heat suffused her face with her blush. She knew

she was pretty, though she wouldn't go so far as beautiful, and totally did not see herself as the kind of woman guys would fantasize about. They sure as shit hadn't in high school. For one thing, her body type wasn't the curvy kind men seemed to go gaga for, and for another, she certainly didn't draw attention like Gwen, the stunning bartender who had slept with Alex. Whatever that woman had, Jessica obviously didn't. If she did, Alex would be in her bed instead of Gwen's.

"Thanks for the kind words, but you don't have to blow smoke up my ass."

He laughed, then reached across the bar, and cupped her chin in his hand. With desire darkening his gaze, he leaned in close enough that she could feel the warmth of his breath on her face as he whispered, "In case you haven't noticed, lass, I think you're gorgeous."

The pleasant flutter in her stomach was stronger this time, but before she could respond, Uncle Peter's voice rang out over the pub in a teasing shout, "John, get your filthy hands off my niece."

Startled, she jerked away and blushed furiously while the other patrons laughed. John merely smiled at her then turned to face her uncle with an arrogant tilt to his chin. When John did, he tensed, and all the humor disappeared from his face, replaced with a challenging look. Startled by his reaction, she turned to look at her uncle and gripped the edge of the bar when she saw a very pissed off Alex standing next to Peter and glaring at John. Oleg was now at Alex's side, and his glower was equally fierce.

Puzzled by their reaction, she kept quiet as John replied, "Hey, Peter. I'm takin' Jessica to the tree lighting tomorrow. Gonna meet mam and da' there."

Uncle Peter gave John a small smile then turned his gaze on her. "You sure you want to go with this *bogger*?"

She wasn't sure what *bogger* meant, but by the way John grinned, it was obvious he didn't find the term offensive. Aware of the blistering cold fury Alex now directed at her, she ignored him and spoke to Peter. "Yes."

A pleased look suffused her uncle's reddened face, but he shook his finger in warning at John. "Have her back by midnight, and keep yer hands to yerself, or I'll have them cut off and shoved up yer arse."

The men in the pub laughed again, and she knew her face must be bright red with embarrassment. "Nice, Uncle Peter. Very subtle. Now, if you'll excuse me, I have a job to do."

Before she could move, John caught her wrist lightly. "I'll see you tomorrow night at seven, yeah?"

"Yeah," she whispered back, trying to summon a smile and ignore the fact that Alex now appeared to be pissed off at her.

The weight of his gaze stung, and she walked away without looking at him. She was all too aware of Alex's anger burning into her as she moved to the other end of the bar and began filling a couple orders that had come in while she was talking with John. Fuck Alex. He had no right to be pissy with her.

The afternoon seemed to drag on into the evening as the day blended into night. The pub was busy enough that she didn't have a chance to take much of a break at all. By the time she was done for the night, her feet and back hurt, and she really regretted taking a double shift, but one of the other bartenders' kids was having a birthday so Jessica picked it up for her.

Once she was done for the night, as usual, Oleg followed her out the door. The roar of the pub was quickly muffled by the thick oak door and replaced by the hum of the busy street. The air was cold enough that she shoved her hands into the pockets of her thick wool coat and tucked her chin down into the green cashmere scarf her uncle had given her. They naturally fell in step with each other as they walked the familiar route back to her place. Oleg was a tall, big man so she found herself taking two strides for his every one just to keep up with him as he constantly scanned the crowd. Unable to stop her mouth, she tried to get some information out of him about Alex's earlier angry mood.

"So, uh, what crawled up his majesty's ass and died?"

Oleg grunted, his version of a chuckle. "You would do well to be careful with Alex tonight, *prinsessa*."

"Why? What happened? Is he okay?"

All too aware that she'd once again betrayed her excessive interest in Alex, she stared ahead as they navigated the busy street, the damp pavement scenting the air and mixing with the delicious aromas of various foods. Laughter rang out here and there, adding to the energy filling the sidewalk. She tried to ignore Oleg's all-too-knowing gaze on her face and concentrate on people-watching as they walked.

When he finally spoke, it was in a soft, chiding voice that Oleg seemed to use only with her or when he was talking to his daughters on the phone. Gentle, but firm. "Jessica, you think he would react well to you going on date with other man?"

She chewed her lower lip then frowned. "Did he really think I was going to react well when he continues to have sex with the other bartenders? He's made it abundantly clear that he sees me as nothing more than a friend. And trust me, the fact that he's regularly screwing one of my co-workers grinds that point home."

89

Oleg stopped abruptly, and a couple people stumbled around them, but no one bumped into him or her. The big man was not the kind of guy someone wanted to accidentally touch. People were always aware and wary of her friend. "Who told you these things?"

Little prickles ran over her skin as Oleg's gaze turned murky...cold. It was totally creepy, and even though she knew he would never hurt her, he was really angry. Torn between the need to confess everything he wanted to know just so he'd stop looking at her like that and shutting the fuck up, she froze, the indecision leaving her paralyzed. Her heart raced, and she wondered for the first time what she had gotten herself into by becoming friends with these dark men. She was definitely out of her depth, but up until this point, they'd been nothing but kind, understanding, and funny, Oleg in particular. The memory of her time spent with him talking about his oldest daughter and a dog he'd gotten her for Christmas had made Jessica laugh so hard she was reduced to tears, and her apprehension eased. Concentrating on that mental image, her fear drained away, replaced by irritation.

Before she could stop herself, she blurted out in a torrent of angry words, "He flirts with women right in front of me, Oleg. In. My. Face. It doesn't take a rocket scientist to figure it out. That's fine. He does his thing, whatever. But that does not mean he has some kind of claim on me! I am my own damn woman, living my life, *alone*, and I don't need anyone. Especially not a pompous asshole who likes to play mind games with women and seems determined to fuck his way through Dublin!"

There was a moment of silence, and a couple people walking past chuckled. A guy up the street yelled something about how he wanted to fuck his way through her or some dumb, drunk stuff. That broke her staring contest with Oleg as he turned his glare on the loud man who was stumbling away with a group of his friends urging him on. Humiliation filled her when she realized she'd just screeched like a harpy in the middle of a crowded street.

Awesome.

Eager to end this embarrassing freak show, she quickly pushed her way through the crowd and reached the double front doors of her apartment building in record time despite wearing brown leather boots with two-inch heels. Those inches didn't seem like a lot, until she'd worked a double in them and her calves ached. Oleg trailed her the whole way, and she wanted to yell at him to give her some damn space, but she was done entertaining the drunks for the night. After going through the outer safety doors, past a guard, and through another set of doors to a guarded lobby, Jessica let out a low sigh as the muffled silence of the building soothed her.

She knew the security of this building was crazy high because Uncle Peter wanted to keep her as safe as he could. She understood his paranoia, even if it made her uncomfortable. He'd lost his sister, and Jessica knew she looked like a delicate version of her mother. It didn't take a psychiatrist to figure out why he worried so much about her.

Most nights, she took the stairs, but the thought of climbing three flights made her feet throb in protest. So instead, she stood there with Oleg, waiting in uncomfortable silence for the elevator. She hated it when people were mad at her so, as usual, she found herself apologizing. "I'm sorry I yelled at you."

"Is all right. At least you did not throw things. My wife would have heaved knife at me by now."

Unsure if he was kidding or not—it would take a hell of a woman to be married to Oleg—she gave him a weak smile. "I'll keep that in mind."

The elevator finally arrived, and they both stepped inside. She leaned against the wall and yawned, tired yet oddly keyed up. Tense. It must have been apparent because Oleg rested a hand on her shoulder and gave it a gentle squeeze. "Jessica, be calm."

"I am calm," she snapped. "Is he home?"

Oleg frowned. "Alex?"

"Yes, Alex."

They reached her floor, and Oleg followed her out. "Why?"

"Because we need to sort some shit out."

"He is, but he has company."

A horrible thought occurred to her. "Female company? Does he have some skank in there right now?"

Wrong thing to say.

Oleg stepped closer until he was almost within touching distance, his displeasure obvious. "If he was entertaining a woman, as his friend it would be none of your business, Jessica, and you would have no right to question him."

That stung and she stumbled back a step. "Right."

"However, that is not what he is doing. Is anniversary of his stepmother and half-sister's death. His brother, Dimitri, is here with him. Is not good time for them."

The blow of his words struck her so deeply, the air in her lungs escaped with a hard rush. She was a terrible, self-absorbed person and felt like such a bitch. An ache filled her throat as she said, "Oh, no, oh, God. I feel horrible. Is there anything I can do for them?"

He studied her for a long moment, his dark gaze unreadable. "Can you cook?"

"Well, yes. My mother taught me. It's nothing fancy, but they're farm recipes that have been handed down over the generations through my family." She swallowed hard, her selfish mind turning to the loss of her mother before she forced herself to focus. "I think I have the stuff I need in my kitchen for biscuits and gravy. It's good, belly-filling comfort food."

Oleg's gaze had warmed by this point, and he tilted his head to her door. "Go. Change into something nice. It is important in my country that a woman looks good for the first meeting with people."

"Uh...what?"

He sighed. "Give the men something beautiful to look at, yes? You be surprised how much lovely girl can lift man's spirits. My wife will put extra effort into her appearance when I come home from work. It makes time away from her worth it. She is smart woman. You do same for Alex, and it will make him proud for Dimitri to meet you."

See, just when she thought she had Oleg figured out, he'd do something that would totally change her view on him. "Okay, and thanks for letting me know. Are you sure they won't mind company? I mean I can just give them the food at the door. That might be better. I don't want to interrupt their private time."

Gripping her shoulders lightly, he turned her in the direction of her door and gave her a little push. "Go."

At the authoritative tone in his voice, she began moving before her mind caught up with her body. "Thanks again, my friend."

"You are welcome, *prinsessa*."

Chapter Seven

Rage exploded from Alex as he listened to Oleg tell him someone had been filling Jessica's head with shit about him.

"What fucking bitch's tongue do I have to cut out for this? I haven't been with a woman in months. Not since the night Jessica and I first played chess."

"Trust me, I'm aware of your unusual restraint. It's made you irritable." Oleg frowned. "Jessica would not say who was spreading rumors about you, but I have my theories and will find out."

Dimitri gave a dry laugh, drawing Alex's gaze to his little brother who was not so little anymore. They may have had different mothers, but they shared the black-ringed, gray Novikov eyes, and both had Jorg's dark hair, though Dimitri's had more red in it from his mother. His hair was longer than Alex remembered seeing it, the tips now reaching almost to his collar. Dressed in black pants and a deep burgundy dress shirt opened at the throat to expose a thick gold chain, he looked tired.

The past few months had been busy for both of them. Their father had been on a tear lately, making some irrational decisions that were having a widespread impact on the Novikov *Bratva*. Alex had done what he could from Ireland and had gone home as much as possible to smooth things over with various allies, but Dimitri had to bear the brunt of damage control. His brother seemed to have hardened in their time apart and Alex wondered if that was a good or bad thing.

Giving him a considering look, Dimitri leaned back and extended his arms over the back of the sleek leather couch. "Is this the Jessica you've been talking about? I was hoping to meet her while I was here."

Torn between the need to protect Jessica from his world and the desire for his brother to meet her, he shrugged. "It sounds like she is angry with me. Perhaps another time."

Oleg cleared his throat. "She will be coming over in a little bit with what she calls comfort food that she is making for you both."

At the mention of food, Dimitri sat all the way up. "Home cooked?"

"Yes. It is something called biscuits and gravy. She said her mother taught her how to make it. An old American family recipe."

Dimitri grinned at Alex. "This girl sounds wonderful, Alex. Marry her."

Shaking his head, he smiled at his brother. Dimitri had just turned twenty-two a few months ago but still had the appetite of a teenager. Then again, Dimitri never seemed to stop growing, so his endless hunger was justifiable.

Oleg cracked his neck. "I need to check with some contacts about the Sokolov and Gilyov situations. I will leave you for the evening. Dimitri, it is good to see you again."

Dimitri stood and came over to Oleg, giving the older man a brief, back smacking hug. "Keep safe, my friend."

The door clicked shut behind Oleg, and Alex watched Dimitri wander over to the dark window with his drink then look down at the busy street below. "Your women are asking about you back home. They miss your cock. This celibacy thing you are doing is foolish. I've never known you to go this long without a woman. Are you ill? Your dick no longer work? Nico has pills for that."

Shaking his head, not ready to tell his brother how serious he was about his future with Jessica,

Alex gladly took the distraction of talking about their mutual friend. "How are Nico and his exquisite sub?"

"In love, disgustingly so. Catrin asked me to remind you she expects to see you in Rome at Laz Stefano's manor." He gave a soft laugh filled with sexual undertones. "Are you going to take one of your girls or will you be inviting this Jessica to one of the Stefano's hedonistic parties?"

His gut clenched, but he forced his voice to remain steady. "I do not know if Jessica is into the BDSM scene."

Dimitri merely nodded, still looking down to the street below. "Nico has been talking lately about proposing to Catrin."

That surprised a smile out of him. "Good. She will make a wonderful wife."

"They are very happy together." He turned and made his way back to the couch where Alex sat. "Do you think she will say yes?

"Why wouldn't she?"

"You know Catrin. She is not one for commitment."

"Nico lets her play with anyone she wants."

"Yes, he lets his girlfriend play with whoever she wants, but his wife? He may not be so willing to share." Outside, a car horn beeped loud enough to penetrate the thick glass of the bulletproof windows. "This Jessica, are you willing to share her?"

"Keep your hands off of her."

Raising his eyebrows, Dimitri gave him a mock-surprised look. "So defensive. Don't tell me this girl means something to you."

It didn't take Alex long to realize Dimitri was baiting him and fishing for information. Obviously, he'd been more transparent about his feelings than he thought. Eventually he would tell his brother, but the time wasn't right yet. "She is just a girl."

"Hmm. A girl that you talk about every time we speak. A girl that has you suddenly celibate." Dimitri grunted then carefully set his glass on the coaster on the small, dark wood coffee table. "Maks tells me this Jessica of yours is very sweet, very innocent. That when she looks at you, it is like the sun and moon rise and set on your command. He says he would have been in her bed long ago, but you forbid it."

"She is Peter's niece. I am merely strengthening the ties between our families by watching out for her." It took all his self-control to keep from going and hunting down Maks. "It would not help for Maks to bed her and break her heart."

"Do not bullshit me, Alex. You never get possessive over a woman, yet the mere mention of Maks fucking her has you enraged. While you may be able to hide it from others, I know you so do not lie to me."

Knowing Dimitri was right, he said nothing.

"And when I say your women miss you, I mean your women are complaining that you are ignoring them. Last time you were in Moscow, you didn't visit a single one or the Club. You know people will notice these things, and before long, someone will become curious about what, or who, has drawn your attention."

He forced himself to remain calm, knowing his brother was only speaking the truth, but hating that he was right. "I was busy last time I was in Moscow, trying to soothe tempers after our father decided to intercept a shipment of heroin meant for the Kumarin *Bratva*. Stopping a war between the families was more important than pussy."

Dimitri gave a dry laugh. "I've seen you get a blow job while performing a hit. Again, do not lie to me, Alex. Lie to everyone else, but not to me."

His brother's words stung, but he was right. No

matter what, they were always honest with each other. Dimitri was the one person in this fucked up world he trusted completely. Even so, he struggled to open up. "She is different."

"What do you mean?"

"I mean, I can feel her when she walks into a room without even seeing her. It is like my body is attuned to her in a way I've never experienced. And she is so full of life. Her spirit shines in her eyes, and it is a beautiful thing. Life is an adventure to Jessica." He sighed and ran his fingers through his hair. "And she's smart, funny, and so very kind. If she sees someone who needs help, anyone, she will stop and assist them with no thought to her own self or safety."

"Maks told me she has helped ease tensions with the O'Doyle gang's blood feud with Peter."

He couldn't help the small smile of remembrance curving his lips. "They own her favorite bakery."

"What?"

"One day, while Maks was with her, Jessica saw an old woman stuck on the side of the road in a delivery van with a flat tire. Maks saw the name on the van and knew who it was, but before he could stop her, Jessica was changing the woman's tire, regardless of Margo O'Doyle's protests."

Dimitri gave a low whistle. "The matriarch of the O'Doyle clan?"

"The very same. Maks said Margo seemed taken aback, and Maks tried to get Jessica to leave, but she refused to budge until they'd changed the tire for the helpless old woman."

"Helpless? That 'helpless' old woman single-handedly took out six armed men back in the fifties during the Green Street massacre. The story is still legend." Dimitri frowned. "Did Margo know who Jessica was?"

"*Everyone* knows who Jessica is. Peter made

99

sure to spread the word far and wide that if anyone harmed her there would be hell to pay. And even if they didn't know, all you have to do is take one look at Jessica to know who she is. Her mother was well-known by the O'Doyle gang—she went to a private school with some of their girls—and only a blind man could miss the resemblance."

"Hmm, would have been the perfect opportunity to kidnap her."

"Yes, it would have, but evidently, Jessica made such an impression on Margo that she declared Jessica off limits. Now Jessica goes to the bakery often and stays for tea with Margo. This forced Peter to thank Margo personally for protecting his niece and opened a line of communication between the gangs. They are by no means allies, but at least they've stopped killing and sabotaging each other."

"Maybe she can work the same magic with the Boldin *Bratva*, eh?"

Before Alex could respond, there was a knock on the door. Dimitri gave him a shit-eating grin, leaped from the couch, and ran to the small foyer of the apartment. Alex cursed inwardly, knowing his brother could be a little...overwhelming when he was in the mood and that Dimitri loved to fuck with him. Then again, it was nice to give Dimitri something to think about other than the morbid anniversary they had gathered together for.

Jessica's nervous voice came from beyond Dimitri's broad shoulders. "Uh...hi. Is Alex home?"

The purr in Dimitri's voice alerted Alex to the fact that his brother was in full-on charming mode. "You must be Jessica. I am Dimitri, Alex's brother."

"I can tell. You both have the same amazing eyes." She let out a nervous giggle, and Alex glared in the direction of the foyer.

"Here, beautiful lady, let me carry for you."

"Thanks."

A moment later, Jessica stepped into the living room. His heart gave the solid thud it always did when he saw her, and his nervous system lit up. Tonight, her gorgeous red hair was pulled back into a thick braid and small gold hoops glittered in her ears. She wore a dark green tank top with a cream cardigan along with a pair of khaki pants that fit her long legs perfectly. Her gaze darted to him, and she gave him an unsure smile. A blush put some pink in her cheeks, only adding to her appeal. Without a second thought, he stood and moved to her side, taking in a deep breath of her apples and spice scent.

He'd missed her.

"Oleg told me your brother was visiting so I...uh...made this for you guys. If you've already had dinner, I can put it in the fridge, and you can warm it up for breakfast or whatever."

Dimitri was already on his way into the kitchen with the large blue pot. "We eat now."

She nervously shifted and began to edge back toward the foyer. "Well, have a good night."

Alex tilted his head. "You are leaving?"

"I don't want to interrupt your time with your brother." She lowered her voice, and her gaze darted to Dimitri in the kitchen. "Oleg told me what today is. I totally understand if you want to be alone."

"Stay." The soft word came out more like a command than a request. She still looked ready to bolt so he gently took her small hand in his, a shock moving through his system at that simple touch. Her lips parted, and she stared up at him, allowing him to draw her closer until they were separated by less than a foot.

"Are...are you sure?"

"Yes, *prinsessa moya*, I am sure. We could use your light tonight."

"My light?"

"Your soul shines so bright it...what is right word...pushes away shadows."

A pink flush flooded her cheeks, and her grip tightened on his hand. Then she gave him a shy look from beneath her strawberry-blonde lashes always made him smile. He wasn't lying. The warmth she gave off while she was happy affected everyone around her, lifting their spirits as well. It wasn't magic or any mystical bullshit. It was simply the natural reaction of being around a genuinely good, sweet person. A rare commodity in his evil world.

She looked away, but not before he saw a pleased smile curve her pink lips. "Thank you. Are you sure Dimitri won't mind?"

"Stay," came Dimitri's muffled shout, and Alex looked over to see Dimitri eating right from the pot. "Food is good."

He sighed and led Jessica into the living room, not releasing her hand even as Dimitri gave him a pointed look then grinned when Alex sat on the couch with Jessica at his side. She fidgeted for a moment, gently trying to extract her hand, but he wasn't letting her go. With his thumb stroking her palm, he shook his head at his brother.

Speaking quickly in Russian, Alex said, "Jessica knows nothing about the *Bratva* or Peter's gang. She thinks he is a politician and that I'm a professional bodyguard from Belarus."

Dimitri's words came out garbled as he continued to shove the food into his mouth. "Understood. Are you sure she hasn't figured out Peter? She works at his headquarters, right?"

"Jessica was raised in a small town in America, an idyllic place where people do not lock their doors at night and everyone knows everyone. It would never occur to her to even suspect something like that, and Peter has made it well-known what will happen if someone were to tell her."

"How long do you plan on hiding this?"

His gut churned. He knew about the hard decisions he would eventually have to make. He was sure Jessica would feel betrayed by his keeping it from her, but the less she knew the safer she would be. Someday, he would tell her the whole truth, but he hoped to have her so in love and happy with him by then that she wouldn't leave him.

"I do not want our world to touch hers yet."

Dimitri's gaze went to Jessica's hand entwined with Alex's. "You know she will find out eventually. Would be best if you are honest with her if you truly want a future with this girl."

"Be honest and tell her what? That I've killed dozens of men? That I run drugs, guns, and just about everything else illegal for a criminal organization? That her uncle who she loves, is equally corrupt? How exactly would I do that without destroying any chance with her?"

Instead of being upset, Dimitri shrugged. "Don't ask me. I only fuck whores. I don't have to explain myself to them. Look, you haven't even slept with her yet. Maybe she is terrible in bed or will only do vanilla sex. I say fuck her, find out if she can handle our lifestyle, and—if she can—marry her, and have a dozen babies."

"It is more complicated than that."

Dimitri set his empty plate down with a sigh. "Then don't fuck her. Either way, stop whining like a little bitch about it and do something."

"Fuck you."

Grinning, Dimitri switched to English. "Sweet Jessica, you like vodka?"

Five hours later, Alex had a very drunk Jessica

sitting next to him, fucking *gossiping* with his little brother about sex. She was talking to Dimitri like they'd been friends for years, laughing over the same crude humor, turning a normally dour and depressing evening into something else entirely. She giggled into her cupped hands, her sparkling blue eyes meeting his as Dimitri told her about the time he'd been caught by a girl's father sneaking out of her bedroom when he was sixteen. Normally, he would have been laughing as well, but his mind was stills stuck on Jessica describing the time she got caught skinny dipping with her high school boyfriend in his pool by his parents.

Jessica slumped against him as she fell back, laughing so hard tears were trailing down her face while Dimitri told an elaborate story about trying to run and put his pants on at the same time while an angry father chased him with a butcher knife, threatening to unman him. He loved seeing her like this, happy and full of life. Being around her made him happy, and not only him, but his men as well. They all enjoyed spending time with the bright and kind young woman. Her silken hair brushed over the edge of his chin, sending a tingle along his body.

"Tell me, Jessica," Dimitri said with a leer. "What is the wildest thing you have ever done?"

All Alex's efforts to remain unaffected were blown to smithereens when Jessica confessed to having made out heavily with a girl. She'd whispered a short story about the girls being drunk together after a concert, how she'd danced with her friend and then made out with her while they were dancing with everyone at the party watching them and cheering them on. Dimitri's eyes were so wide it was comical, and Jessica's gleeful snort of laughter made Alex grin even as his dick ached.

"You should see your face." Jessica heaved in a

breath, but remained relaxed against him. "I thought there was no way I could shock you."

Chuckling, Alex couldn't stop himself from smoothing his fingers over her cheek on the pretense of tucking her hair behind her ear. "It is because you are so innocent looking."

Dimitri cleared his throat and gave Alex a pointed look. "You like people watching you?"

Her slight weight pressed into Alex as she rested against him. "I do. Not, like, all the time or anything super crazy, but knowing that someone is getting off on what I'm doing? It's hot."

"Is hot," Dimitri agreed with a shit-eating grin thrown at Alex. His younger brother was a voyeur and loved to watch people fuck, and he knew Alex was both a voyeur and an exhibitionist. "Very hot. I did not know American women were so...kinky? Is right word?"

"Yeah, kinky is the right word." She snorted a laugh again while Alex grappled with his intense fantasies of fucking her at his home BDSM club in Moscow. "I don't know how things are where you're from, but most of my friends aren't as hung up on sex as our parents. And we don't slut shame each other."

"Slut shame?"

"Yeah, how if a guy has a one night stand, it's okay, but if a girl does, she's a slut. I don't believe in that shit. If you're both consenting adults, get your freak on. That said, I can't abide cheating. Ever. If a guy bullshits the girl and tells her that if she has sex with him it'll be with the intent of forming a relationship..."—she rubbed her eyes and yawned— "then he's a manwhore, and I can't stand men like that. I would never, ever cheat on a man, and I expect the same from him."

Dimitri looked up at Alex, winked, and said in Russian, "You lucky, lucky son of a bitch. If you don't want her, I'll marry her tomorrow. Sweet, kinky, loyal, and she can cook."

A sour tang of unusual jealousy made Alex's gut clench, and he slipped a possessive arm around Jessica before responding back in Russian, "Stay away from her."

Instead of cowering from Alex's anger as most men would, Dimitri wiggled his eyebrows. "Aww, come on. You heard her, one of her fantasies is two men at once...and another couple. Imagine watching Jessica eat another woman's pussy while you fuck her. Like I said, you lucky son of a bitch."

Shaking his head, Alex couldn't help but laugh even as he wanted to yell at his brother to stop thinking about Jessica like that. Dimitri was too charming for his own good, but Alex liked to see his brother happy like this, especially tonight. What was normally an evening spent drinking until they passed out had instead become one of the best nights Alex could remember having in a long time.

Jessica turned in his arms, then glanced up at him, and smiled, her beauty devouring his heart. She reached up and traced his lips with her fingertip, the velvety rasp of her skin against his lips making his cock throb. When her eyes crinkled as she giggled over something, he sighed, knowing she was going to feel like shit in the morning. Funny that it was usually him and Dimitri who passed out drunk on this grim anniversary. Instead, for the first time in many years, they were a little buzzed, but not smashed into an alcohol-fueled oblivion.

"Alex," Jessica murmured while petting his goatee. "Did you know, when you talk in Russian, it makes me wet?"

Dimitri choked on his Scotch.

Alex blinked down at her, wondering what the hell he was getting himself into. "My voice makes your pussy wet?"

She nodded slowly, her eyelids growing heavy. With a sleepy grumble, she moved until she was curled up in his lap, her body resting heavily enough against his that he realized she would pass out soon. Then she nuzzled her face against his throat, her nose and lips brushing his skin and leaving a burning path of sparks everywhere they touched.

"You smell so good. I want to rub myself all over you so I can smell you on me." His skin beneath her lips grew sensitive, and the heat of her breath tested the limits of his self-control. Her husky voice was the distilled essence of debauchery as she whispered, "Wanna to know a secret?"

"*Da*. I mean yes."

"I think you're the most amazing man I've ever met, and I want you so damn bad, dream about you constantly, but you don't want me and that sucks."

His heart gave an odd thump, and his chest actually hurt. Knowing she probably wouldn't remember their conversation tomorrow, he brushed her hair back from her face. Her smile was beautiful, but sleepy, as she beamed at him. "I tell you secret. I do want you."

All too aware of Dimitri watching them closely, his expression unexpectedly grave, Alex had to keep his gaze on Jessica as she blinked slowly up at him. "Then why don't you take me?"

"*Prinsessa moya*, you deserve better than me."

"But I don't want better. I want you."

"I cannot have you."

"But don't you understand? You could if you wanted me as badly as I want you. I'd be so happy to be your girlfriend, Alex, even though I know you don't do girlfriends, only fuck buddies." Her voice slurred as she weakly thumped him on the shoulder. "Hell, I'd be happy just to be your fuck buddy. You'd be my own personal sex toy."

Ignoring Dimitri's laughter, he shook his head. "You are drunk, would not be right."

She leaned up and gave him a somewhat sloppy kiss on the cheek. "See, always an excuse. If you really wanted me, you wouldn't let anything stop you."

Alex sighed then placed a long kiss on Jessica's forehead, relishing the feel of her in his arms. He pulled back, and she smiled, her lips eventually softening into a lush, pink bow. Her eyes closed, and she rubbed her cheek against his chest like an affectionate cat. Staring at her plump lips, he imagined how they would feel against his. He wondered how she would kiss, what she would like, and how she tasted.

Dimitri gave a sarcastic sigh. "You are screwed."

"What?" Alex whispered, not wanting to wake Jessica. She was so cuddled into him there wasn't a part of her body that wasn't pressed against his. The urge to sleep with her gripped him, and he gritted his teeth. That could potentially be very bad, but he was finding it hard to give a shit about what he shouldn't do anymore. Especially when she was begging for him and he wanted to give in to her so badly.

The need to take her had almost overwhelmed him, but he was not sure he could keep her safe yet. The Novikov curse had ravaged his family for two generations, and it would take more than a few weeks to make sure the curse would never touch Jessica. Then again, he and Dimitri had made great strides with the Boldin family, agreeing to leave each other's women alone despite their shared bloody past. Hell, the head of the Boldin *Bratva* had two daughters and a wife. Why shouldn't he and Dimitri have the same chance at happiness? Having her in his arms, sleeping against him, had to be one of the best feelings he'd ever experienced. He could only imagine how wonderful it would feel to have it every night for the rest of his life.

He was turned from his deep thoughts by Jessica snoring lightly. The sound was so...dainty that it made him laugh. "She even snores cute."

Dimitri raised a brow as Alex stood with Jessica cradled against him. "I am taking her to bed."

"To her apartment?"

He didn't hesitate when he said, "No, to my room."

Giving him a shit-eating grin, Dimitri sat back and tilted his chin up, "Lucky bastard."

Alex resisted the urge to roll his eyes before he started back to his room with Jessica held against him. He honestly did not want to touch her when she was this drunk. First, because he didn't want her to use alcohol as an excuse to push him away. Second, because he wanted her in the right frame of mind when he told her how things were going to be from now on. Third, because he would never want to have sex for the first time with a wasted woman. Not that he had any problem screwing a woman when she was really drunk. If that's what she liked, he was more than happy to oblige. Drunk sex was fun, but not when they hadn't spoken of it sober and made plans.

He nudged the door open then turned on the light switch with his elbow. The dim room was illuminated by golden sconces, giving the cozy space a warm glow, and the hunter green accents complemented the dark wood of his dresser and massive bed. As he lowered her to the bed, he couldn't help but notice the freckles on the bridge of her nose and dusting the tops of her high cheekbones. He could have stood there and watched her forever, but he forced himself to move away and close the thick, white velvet curtains.

After using the bathroom, he came back out with a wet washcloth and placed it on the back of Jessica's neck, waking her up.

He dodged her attempts to smack him away. "Can you use bathroom on own or do you need me to help you?"

She muttered something, then pushed off the bed, and staggered into the bathroom. Evidently, she was awake enough to take care of business and wash up, because when she zigzagged back to bed, she flopped onto his pillow and mumbled, "Used your toothbrush. Don't have cooties. Need water."

Laughing to himself, he did as she asked and added a couple ibuprofen to the mix. He helped her sit up enough to drink. She pushed him back when he was done. "Close your eyes."

"What?"

She didn't wait for him to comply, instead falling on her back while clumsily kicking off her shoes, sending them sailing across the room, one almost hitting him in the head. Before he knew it, she'd slipped out of her khakis, leaving him staring at her tiny, pale yellow panties. They looked like cotton and had pink bows at the hips. He'd seen far sexier underwear in his life, but damned if his dick wasn't twitching at the erotic temptation of the high cut panties against her creamy skin. A moment later, she started fidgeting then managed to take her bra off without removing her shirt. Once this was done, she let out a long sigh and curled up on his bed, her long legs spread out, revealing the slit of her pussy covered by yellow cotton fabric. She grabbed a pillow and cuddled it close, frowning in irritation as she tried unsuccessfully to reach the comforter to pull it up.

With a sigh, he lifted the thick down comforter over her then smoothed her hair back from her face. She captivated him, and he looked forward to spending many hours just watching her. The complex feelings he had for her were sometimes so intense he was afraid to give them a name. One thing was certain, she would soon be his and only his.

Every delicate inch of her.

He fought his arousal at the thought of owning her in every way, of her wearing his collar and his ring, even as he scolded himself for moving too fast. Shit. It was those sweet, cotton panties. They killed him. Made him want to defile her in the worst way. His dick, not used to being denied a woman's touch for this long, twitched at the thought of sucking her arousal from the crotch of her panties.

Shit.

After turning off the lights and making sure his gun was easily accessible, but not easily seen, he changed into a pair of sleep pants and got into his bed with a smile. She rolled closer to him, gravity pulling her body against his. Once she pressed against him, he almost held his breath, unsure for once of what he should do. If she was any other woman, he'd be fucking her by now, but Jessica's trust was something he would cherish, not violate. He rolled onto his back and moved her so that her head was resting on his chest, her long, smooth legs tangling with his. Her fresh scent teased him, and his cock was so hard it ached, but he did nothing to relieve himself.

Life had given him enough experience to appreciate Jessica, to savor her as he taught her about all the pleasures the world had to offer. He liked taking care of her like this—a lot. It satisfied some urge he'd never had before, some basic need to protect and provide for this young woman. He kept far enough away that they had space between them, but he couldn't resist repeatedly running his fingers through her hair. Satisfaction filled him along with a faint sense of foreboding as he thought about the dangerous world into which he was going to bring her.

He must have fallen asleep, because he was slowly awakened by the feeling of a woman's lips brushing against his own and a warm, soft body wrapped around his tall frame. His mind drifted as his lips parted, and he returned her kiss, the taste of her sizzling along his nerves, lighting him up from within. Plush and full, her lips pillowed his, and he groaned softly, the sensation of her legs rubbing over his making his dick harden. She was practically panting with desire, so aroused that he wondered how long she'd been seducing him awake.

Whoever this woman was, she *really* knew how to kiss.

He cupped her tight ass and pulled her groin against his, gasping into her mouth when she threw her leg over his hip, opening her core to him. The moment her pussy rubbed against his cloth-covered cock, he growled again, the desire to be inside of this woman driving him mad. She moaned deeply when he flexed his hips against her, rubbing his long shaft over her mound.

"Alex," she whispered against his mouth. "You feel so good."

Her voice triggered the memory of an exquisitely beautiful face, and he broke their kiss, his body trembling with the need to take her, to fuck her, to pound her so hard she would never be the same.

"Jessica, *to, chto ty delayesh' so mnoy.*"

"Oh shit," she shuddered and ground harder over his dick, the scent of her need filling his nostrils. "I swear you could make me come just by talking."

"We should not be doing. Is not right."

All of his good intentions went right out the

window when she grabbed his hand then shoved it down the front of her panties. "Feel how wet I am for you?"

As if he had no control over his own body, his fingers stroked down over the soft curls covering her mound, to her shaved pussy lips, which were glazed with her need. And puffy. Shit, she had one of his favorite kinds of pussy. Thick outer lips that begged to hug his cock as he fucked her. He could just imagine sliding his dick into her like he was sliding his finger in. Tight, blissfully tight. It didn't help that he could now smell her arousal, the musk calling to him and inviting him to take a taste of her need.

To lick her where she was sweet and wet.

Her sheath squeezed his finger while she moaned, and he swore he ejaculated a little bit. She had a very strong cunt. The kind that would wring his come out in bone-wrenching sucks. A deep shudder wracked his spine, making his balls tingle before his cock throbbed even harder. Just the friction of her body against his made him crazy with the need to fuck her.

Sliding his finger in and out, he let her pull him down to kiss him again, her tongue stroking against his as the bed sheets rustled with their movements. He couldn't believe he was actually touching Jessica, had his finger inside of the slickest, tightest pussy he'd ever had the pleasure of playing with. With his thumb, he quickly found her clit, erect and poking out, easy to caress and manipulate. She must have been sensitive because he had to use a light touch to keep her from flinching away.

It took skill to get a woman like Jessica off, and he loved how she responded to his delicate strokes. She kissed her way over his jaw to his ear, lightly sucking on the lobe while she whispered, "Why won't you touch me like this when I'm awake? I need you.

Please fuck me."

He froze, a little mewl of need coming from her as she rocked her hips against his hand, obviously close to orgasm. "I will not have sex with you tonight."

She sighed in obvious disappointment, but didn't stop riding his fingers. "You never do. Not even in my dreams."

He couldn't leave her like this, couldn't let her return to her dreams filled with frustration. "I will take care of you, *prinsessa moya*. Take off your panties and spread your legs for your Master."

She responded instantly and stripped then leaned back, her legs going wide and her hips going up, moving against his hand when he resumed touching her. There was something about her that was shameless, unapologetic as she rode his fingers, grasping at him with her tight cunt. She was confident about her desires, and he wondered how far he could push her boundaries, how far she'd want him to push.

Who knew that beneath her sweet exterior lay a dirty little sex vixen.

The things he could show her...sins so sweet they were worth going to hell over.

Her voice was rough when she spoke. "I'm getting close. Can you feel it?"

He could feel it, could even see it by the tremble in her thighs. Knowing he was going to make her orgasm, hard, sent a surge of strong male pride through him. It made him feel powerful and in control, two things he craved.

He leaned down and gently licked her clit, groaning deep in his throat, "*Ti takaya krasivaya.*"

The bed creaked as he sucked her swollen bud gently, softly, and her back arched when she screamed his name. "Alex!"

114

He nearly ripped down his sleep pants as he began to stroke his cock. His spine tingled as a hard and fast orgasm rushed through him. Holy Mother of God, she turned him on so much that feeling her come apart beneath him was enough to get him off. Coming into his fist, he groaned and plunged his tongue into her along with the fingers of his other hand. The taste of her filled him as he eased her down from her orgasm, eventually removing his fingers while she moaned low and deep. After rolling away from her, he staggered out of bed on weak legs and got a towel, then washed up, his whole body humming with pleasure. He returned to the bed with a clean washcloth and a towel then cleaned her gently while she sighed. He studied her face in the faint light coming through the windows, loving the mysterious smile that curved her lips while she relaxed into his touch. He laid a towel over the damp spot on the sheets, then retrieved her panties, and helped her slip them back on. Her sleepy smile was adorable, and he stole another kiss from her delicious lips. When she reached up to gently caress his cheek, an unfamiliar pain raced through him.

He laid back and pulled her onto his chest again, their combined musk filling the room. His whole body rioted with sensations he'd never experienced before, an intense emotion growing in him that threatened to overwhelm him. It took him a moment to realize that among other things, he was happy, truly content in a way he'd never experienced before.

She shifted until her head was beside his, then settled and became an enjoyable weight on him. He pressed his face into her hair, inhaling the mingled scents of apples and Jessica mixed with him. A warm buzz filled his body, and a bliss he'd never experienced before lightened his heart until he was grinning to himself in the darkness.

This night had changed everything, but he couldn't bring himself to care. Whatever he had to go through to keep Jessica at his side was worth it a thousand times over if he could have the pleasure of falling asleep with her in his arms, curled trustingly into his body while her taste lingered on his tongue.

Chapter Eight

J essica was so warm and comfortable, even if her mouth was as dry as a desert. Floating, her mind drifted in serenity, a deep relaxation tempting her to go back to sleep, but there was something odd teasing at the edges of her mind. She lay there for a few moments, her brain slowly waking up as she realized someone was spooning her, someone with a strong body that smelled wonderful, a heady mixture of citrus and sandalwood that made her feel safe. His breath warmed the top of her head as he slept deeply behind her, his body completely relaxed against hers. Whoever he was, he must be massive because he dwarfed her, and she was tall for a girl. Crisp chest hair brushed her back. Then facial hair tickled the side of her neck as he nuzzled closer in his sleep. The pieces of the puzzle all clicked together, and when she realized who the man holding her so tenderly was, she tensed, and panic made her heart thump hard as she opened her eyes.

Sure enough, she was in Alex's bedroom.

Shit.

What was she doing in Alex's room?

And where were her pants?

A quick scan of her body reassured her that she still wore her panties and shirt, but her pants and bra were definitely missing. When she shifted her legs slightly, trying desperately not to wake Alex, she was relieved to feel that he wore what felt like soft sleep pants, but the hairy arm around her was bare as was the warm, furry chest behind her. One of her favorite daydreams lately was to imagine Alex nude, or at least shirtless, but now that he actually was, she was afraid to move, let alone breathe. That didn't stop a

117

tingle of excitement tightening her belly at the thought of a half-naked Alex holding her, but she forced her hormones to calm the hell down as she tried to think.

How did she get here?

Concentrating, she tried to remember everything she could about the previous night. In spite of the evening's somber nature, Dimitri broke out the vodka after dinner and proceeded to teach her how to drink it 'properly'. That was when her recollections became blurry before fading completely. She knew they'd laughed, a lot. She remembered at one point Dimitri and Alex had thrown their arms around each other while they bellowed out some songs in Russian, and she could remember sitting between them, almost cuddling them, as they told her amusing stories about each other. Then another memory came clear as day, and she fervently wished she could die of embarrassment to save herself the future humiliation of having to look Alex and Dimitri in the eye.

At some point, they'd started talking about sex and Jessica, being completely wasted, was pretty sure she'd let it all hang out. And there was *a lot* to hang out.

Kisha, Jessica's best friend back home, had a cool mom who had hundreds of romance novels lining the bookshelves of her house. When she and Kisha were teenagers, they would 'borrow' from her mom's library. They read all about the steamy adventures of amazing men and women doing some rather kinky things and giggled over the sex parts. She'd only had one serious boyfriend in high school, but she'd given him her virginity, and afterward, they'd gone at it like rabbits. Then there were her sexual escapades in college and on spring break. Oh, God, had she told them about having sex in the ocean off of Cancun with that hot Brazilian guy?

An image of Dimitri staring at her in shock flitted through her aching brain, and she stifled a groan.

Double crap. If she'd shocked Dimitri, then whatever she said must have been bad. They probably thought she was some kind of mega skank now. The kind of woman that would sleep with men while not wearing pants. Or a bra.

The soft flesh between her legs felt sensitive, and she bit her lip, trying to remember if she'd done anything with Alex. Her fragmented dream came to mind, but she had dirty dreams about Alex almost every night. In this dream, as in the others, he wouldn't fuck her, but he did make her orgasm—hard. Her nipples tightened almost uncomfortably fast, and she shifted against Alex. God, he was so strong, so warm. He moved and pressed his groin into her bottom, cuddling her so close that she felt enveloped by him.

If only he would hold her like this when they were awake.

The sheets were warmed by their bodies, and the wonderful heat had seeped into her bones on this chilly December morning. The sun was already up, and she closed her eyes, taking in a deep breath and trying to commit the memory of being in Alex's bed to mind since it was probably never going to happen again. The urgent need to use the bathroom battled with her desire to stay still and not wake Alex, but her bladder won out eventually.

Moving as carefully as possible, she tried to ease out of Alex's arms, but he tugged her back against him.

"*Ostavat'sya*," he murmured against the top of her head.

She pushed against his steely arm, trying to ignore how silky his skin felt stretched tight over his impressive muscles. "I have to use the bathroom."

He grumbled, but released her. The moment she was out of his arms, she gathered up her pants from the floor next to the bed, but she couldn't find her bra. Not daring to stay any longer, and certainly not daring to look at Alex, she darted out into the hallway then shoved her legs into her pants. Her shoes were around here somewhere, but thankfully, the key to her apartment was still in the pocket of her khakis.

Moving as quietly as possible, she crept across the bare wood floors of the apartment, squinting at the glare of the bright sunlight streaming through the windows and burning her eyes.

When a man's deep voice came from somewhere to her left, she let out a little squeak of surprise and flinched. "You have no goodbye for me, sweet Jessica?"

She turned to find a shirtless Dimitri lounging on the couch with his laptop and a cup of tea steaming on the coffee table. Both Gorev brothers had lucked out in the genetic lottery because his wide chest was almost as impressive as Alex's, and probably would be once Dimitri had fully grown into the man he would someday be. His knowing grin heated her face, and she hated how easily she blushed. He was dressed in a pair of deep brown trousers and scratched leisurely at his chest. That movement drew her gaze to the eight pointed star tattoos on either of his shoulders. Dimitri still held traces of the teenage boy he'd been not too long ago, his body not as bulky as his brother's, but Dimitri was quicker to smile. She met his smirking gaze then quickly looked away.

Keeping her voice low, she moved closer to the couch with her eyes focused on the table. "That's right. You're leaving today for Paris."

"I will be back next week, and we spend time together, yes?"

"Uh...sure." She started to inch toward the door,

wanting to make her getaway. "It was nice meeting you, Dimitri."

"Stop." His tone was so authoritative she froze in place. "Come here."

Chewing her lip, wishing she'd just made a run for it instead of stopping to be polite, she moved closer to the couch, extremely uncomfortable. "Yes?"

"Why do you sneak?"

"What?"

"You move quiet, like mouse."

"I-uh, didn't want to wake up Alex."

The lie was so bold that it practically screamed in her every word, and Dimitri must have picked up on it because he frowned. "Why will you not meet eyes?"

He appeared genuinely upset, and she winced. "I'm sorry, I don't usually get that drunk."

"Ahhh, you are embarrassed. No need."

"Right, so I'll just be going now."

"Wait."

Once again, she froze in place. "Dimitri, I have to work, so I need to do some stuff."

"My memory of last night is not so good. Yes? Too much vodka."

She was sure Dimitri was going to tease her. He'd done it a lot last night, so his understanding eased her embarrassment a bit. "Yeah, way too much vodka."

"I need to thank you."

"For what?"

He studied her for a long moment, the amusement draining from his gaze and leaving behind a young man with eyes too old for his face. "My brother is hard man, filled with much responsibility. Has been long time since I see him laugh like he laugh with you. Is nice to see him happy. You are good friend. He likes you very much, and so do I."

That damn blush came back, and she tried to hide her smile. "Thanks."

The sound of movement came from Alex's room, and she darted for the foyer, throwing a quick "Travel safe" to Dimitri before she ran out the door and into her apartment.

After she shut the door and locked it, she sprinted to her bathroom and took care of her full to bursting bladder. Then she dragged herself into the kitchen and took some aspirin before grabbing a muffin and eating half of it in an effort to ease her hangover. The light on her phone was blinking, so she listened to a message from one of her aunts back in the States, then another from one of her friends back home. The last message was from John, reminding her that they had a date tonight and to dress warm. Guilt raced through her as she thought about the fact that she woke up in one man's arms and would be going out with another guy tonight.

Not that she'd done anything sexual with Alex...at least she didn't think she had. She knew Alex well enough to know he wasn't the kind of guy to take advantage of a drunk girl, and she was also well aware that she wasn't his type. The thought that maybe her dream wasn't a dream was too much to bear, and she shook her head, trying to block it out even as the motion made her brain hurt.

With a groan, she stumbled into her bedroom then headed for the shower, wondering if she'd thrown herself at him. The lack of bra and pants indicated that she might have tried, or she'd just taken them off because she usually slept in panties and an old, oversized T-shirt. God, what if she'd been so drunk she'd stripped in front of Alex? The hot water was doing wonders for her headache, but it did nothing to wash away the mortification filling her. A vague mental image of her kissing Alex, sucking on his tongue, in the soft darkness of his bedroom began to form, but she quickly banished the thought.

Last night, for the first time in a long time, she'd allowed herself to completely relax and let loose. Hell, the last time she'd gotten drunk that hadn't involved a pity party over being homesick was back in college in Iowa. Oh, she'd gotten tipsy a time or two at one of her Uncle Pat's parties and while sharing a bottle of wine with her Aunt Mary, but not shit faced, blacked out, smashed. It was all Dimitri's fault. That man was a bad influence in the best of ways, and with every shot she'd done with him, she relaxed more and more until it felt like she was hanging out with old friends. Despite the dark nature of the previous night, both men had gone out of their way to include her in conversations, to put her at ease and make her feel welcome. Actually, they made her feel more than welcome. They made her feel safe. Dimitri had proven to be funny with a dry wit, and his obvious, over-the-top flirting pissed Alex off, which Jessica found amusing and kind of sweet.

Truth be told, she enjoyed Alex's jealous reaction, or what her drunken mind had told her was him being jealous.

Toweling off, she brushed her teeth then studied her pink-cheeked face. She could always ask Alex if she'd gotten horny and tried to hump his leg, but she'd rather jump off Ha'Penny Bridge than talk about what a loser she was. He'd made it more than clear that he viewed her as a friend, and she was sure his handholding last night had been more for comfort than romance. Hell, she'd done everything but strip naked and spread her legs for him when he'd been there for her on the anniversary of her adopted mother's passing, and he flat out wasn't interested.

He obviously had a type, and an unsophisticated, skinny redhead wasn't it.

When she met her bloodshot gaze in the mirror, she didn't like the sadness and defeat she saw there. She wasn't the kind of woman who enjoyed mind games, and she certainly didn't want to waste her time with a man who would never return her affection as anything other than friendship. Yes, Alex was an amazing man, probably an amazing lover, and he made her feel more alive than she'd felt in a long time, but she was lonely. She wanted someone who would see her as a woman, someone she could fall in love with and maybe start to build something long-term. She wanted the kind of marriage her parents had rather than the constant heartache of wondering who Alex was fucking when he wasn't with her.

Really, she needed to pull her tattered self-respect together and forget Alexandr Gorev.

Giving herself a stern glare before she turned from the mirror to grab her hair dryer, she vowed that she wouldn't think about Alex tonight. She'd go out with John, enjoy Dublin, enjoy being alive and young, and maybe start to fall in love. Those thoughts fragmented when she picked up her clothes and caught a whiff of her handsome bodyguard's unique citrus and sandalwood scent. She held up her shirt and buried her nose in the cloth, her heart aching as she tried to convince herself that she didn't want Alex anymore.

Seven hours later, Jessica stepped back from the mirror and took a critical look at herself. The makeup managed to hide most of the dark circles under her eyes, and the blush added some color to her pale cheeks. All day, she'd swung between the need to go over to Alex's place and pretend nothing was wrong like any mature, urbane woman would and wanting to do everything she could to avoid ever seeing him again. Maks had stopped by earlier to see if she would like to go get some coffee and was concerned by her appearance. She begged off saying she was hung over. He obviously didn't believe her, and she had to practically shut the door in his face when he tried to come in so he could make her soup. When he asked her if Alex knew she was sick, she pretended that she was going to throw up in order to avoid talking about it.

She was such a coward.

Tugging at the edge of her black silk tunic shirt with its boat-neck collar, she turned this way and that in the mirror, making sure her dark green leggings fit perfectly where they disappeared into her black, calf-high boots. She'd curled her hair so it fell in ringlets down her back, and she wore the small diamond studs her parents had given her for her high school graduation. The outfit flattered her lean frame, but once again, she wished God had been a little more generous in the tits and ass department.

Maybe she should look into some padded underwear that would at least give her the illusion of having hips, instead of looking like a twelve-year-old boy. Or some of those bras that had built in supports. Then again, nothing would be more humiliating than getting naked with a man for the first time only to have him wonder where the hell all her curves went. Or copping a feel and getting a handful of foam padding.

With a sigh, she went out into her living room, trying to psych herself up about the night. John was a nice, good-looking guy, and he was really into her. If she was back home, her girlfriends would be over right now, helping her get ready for her date and giggling with her. Instead, she was alone, and a wave of homesickness swamped her. She had just picked her purse up from the couch to call her best friend Kisha when there was a knock on the front door.

Taking a peek through the peephole, she was glad to see it was John, looking as handsome as ever in his leather jacket now paired with a dark wool flat cap that brought out the golden tones in his brown hair. He held a bouquet of pink roses in his arms, and that terrible hollowness of being homesick eased a little bit as she opened the door.

His dark eyes lit up at the sight of her, and his smile was genuine. "Jessica, you look amazing. Here. These are for you. I wasn't sure what kind of flowers you liked, but my mam said you can't go wrong with roses."

She took the flowers, inhaling their slightly spicy scent with a smile. "These are lovely, thank you. Come on in and let me put them in some water."

After she cut the stems, she arranged the roses in a crystal vase. John wandered around her small living room, studying the pictures above her mantle. Inside of her cozy apartment he seemed bigger than she remembered, and she watched him as he stopped before a large, silver framed picture.

"This your mam and da?'"

She placed the roses on the small coffee table and moved to his side where he looked at a picture of her parents standing in front of their barn with Jessica sitting proudly on her first horse. It had been a beautiful summer day and the land stretching out into the horizon behind them was full of vibrant green corn stalks. For a moment, she could almost smell the fresh scent of the fields on a late summer evening, and her throat tightened. Her dad, a strong, tall man with dark hair and an easy smile, held her palomino horse's reigns while her petite, blonde mother was snuggled into his side. It was her seventh birthday that day. She was wearing her best party dress and a purple, plastic, princess crown. A grin from ear to ear revealed that she was missing her two front teeth. For a moment, the memory of her father's rich cologne filled her, and she ached to feel his strong arms around her, always ready to give her a hug.

Her parents adored her, and the feeling was entirely mutual.

God, she missed them.

"Yes, these are my parents." She traced her fingers lightly over the glass, blinking back tears.

He glanced down at her placing the picture back after making a small, distressed sound. "I'm sorry, I didn't mean to make you sad."

She touched her fingers to her lips then to the glass. "It's okay. I just miss them. Kind of sneaks up on me every once in a while that they're gone."

John gently stroked her cheek and gave her a kind smile. "Whenever my sister is sad, she demands large quantities of chocolate. Let's get going, and we can grab some hot chocolate from a place I know along the way. Then we'll head over for the tree lighting."

His obvious efforts to make her feel better did help, so she tried to shove her personal shit aside and enjoy her first date in almost a year. "Deal."

Jessica stood outside of her apartment door in the communal hallway at some time after midnight, laughing quietly as John teased her. For once, she was actually all alone with a handsome young man. Peter had promised to not send any bodyguards with her tonight and it seemed like he'd kept his word. No doubt there'd been someone following her, but she hadn't seen them. Feeling free for the first time in a long time, she'd had a great time walking the streets of Dublin with him and some of his friends, feeling normal for the first time in a long time. Dublin certainly had a different vibe than back home, but she was beginning to get used to the urban atmosphere. Plus, being around people her own age was something she'd been missing.

Oleg, Maks, and Alex were all fascinating in their own way, and they made her laugh, but there was a seriousness to them that never really left. John and his friends were the opposite—carefree, fun-loving, immature in the way only college boys could be. And it was nice to hang out with their girlfriends and talk about normal girl stuff. She'd even agreed to meet up with a few of them next week to go shopping, another activity she missed. Oh, she went with her Aunt Mary and had a great time, but it was different than having girlfriends to laugh with.

Her cheeks hurt from smiling so much, and from drinking a few too many beers, as she smacked John on the arm. "I did not make that face!"

"Yes, you did. I thought your eyes were going to pop out of your head."

"I can't believe they were having sex right there in the alley!"

A frisson of heat went through her, and she resisted the urge to press her thighs together. The sight of the couple, the woman facing the brick wall, her hands braced and legs spread with her skirt lifted over her pale hips while her man thrust into her, made Jessica incredibly aroused. With harsh thrusts of his hips, the man had fucked that mystery woman hard enough that she gave a helpless whimper every time he buried himself deep. Even though Jessica had only gotten a glimpse in the dim lighting, watching them made her pussy wet and her nipples as hard as diamonds. She didn't know what it was about public sex and the idea of being seen and caught, but something about it had always been one of her favorite fantasies.

She'd only done something like that once, well

twice if she counted having sex in the ocean, but it had been one of the best sexual experiences of her life. Last year, she'd been at a Halloween party off campus with her roommates and had gotten way too drunk and hooked up with a really cute guy dressed up like a pirate. They'd gone at it hot and heavy. Her costume disguised her, giving her the drunken courage to have sex with him in a place that was isolated, but where other people could see. They'd been alone on the balcony, and she knew that there were a couple guys below watching them and cheering them on. Knowing those strangers were getting turned on by looking at her had led to some good orgasms. Of course, the next day she was totally embarrassed, but the memory was still one of her favorite masturbation fantasies.

John stepped closer, and she was all too aware of how his brown eyes had darkened further. His laughter faded, and the tension grew between them. The scent of the beer he'd had and his woodsy cologne reached her, and she knew he was going to kiss her. She darted a glance at Alex's door, and a pang of stupid guilt went through her, like she was somehow cheating on him even though they didn't have a sexual or romantic relationship in any way. Then again, she woke up in his bed this morning with his body wrapped around hers.

And that dream...so intense it almost felt real.

"Jessica," John spoke softly, drawing her gaze from Alex's door and back to him. "I had a really good time with you tonight."

"Me too," she replied with a small smile. She was determined to live in the moment and told her misplaced guilt to take a hike.

He stroked his hand along her jaw then cupped her neck, gently tilting her head up with his thumb. She didn't resist his touch, and when he brushed his

129

lips over hers, a warm tingle rushed through her. Pulling back a bit, he studied her face. Whatever he saw there seemed to reassure him because he went back for a second kiss, this one much deeper. His tongue brushed over her lips, and she opened for him, sliding her arms up over his broad shoulders, tasting the lingering bitterness of the dark stout he drank earlier in the night, losing herself in his touch. He was a good kisser, gentle and seductive, slowly building her arousal until she was kissing him back while he pressed her against her door. He began to inch his other hand up the front of her shirt, his obvious destination her breast even as she raised her hand to halt his progress.

She heard sound of a door opening and pulled away. Her heart sank when Alex stood framed in the doorway of his apartment, his face a mask of cold fury. He was wearing a dark wool coat over a black suit that fit him perfectly and carrying a large, oddly long suitcase. As always he looked good enough to eat, but oh man, she'd never seen him so angry before, and she found herself pressing up against her door in an effort to put more distance between them.

Maks followed Alex out, and they both glared at John, who still had his arm wrapped around her waist. All the arousal she felt for John vanished, replaced by shame when Alex's gaze moved to her. She felt like she should apologize to him. She'd never seen him so pissed off, and it scared her. His ire filled the small space of the hallway like an electrical storm, and John moved into a protective stance in front of her.

Keeping a firm grip on her, John lifted his chin. "Alex, Maks."

Maks lifted his chin back, but Alex's jaw clenched as though he was grinding his teeth. "I thought you were better, Jessica."

"What?"

His burning gaze came to her, and she shrank back. "Letting this *dolboeb* grope you like a common whore. I thought you had more class, not to go from one man's bed to straight to another's."

She gasped, his words a slap in her face. John started to say something, his tone aggressive, but she cut him off. "I can't believe you just said that!"

"Is truth."

John growled something in Gaelic that didn't sound complimentary, but Jessica yelled at the glowering Russian man first. "Who the fuck do you think you are, Alex Gorev? You...you of all people are going to try and pull a morality card on me? Are you for fucking real?"

Maks stepped in between them. "Enough."

"Oh no, Maks, it isn't enough. I don't know what fucking planet you live on, Alex, but you don't get any say in who I kiss and where." Her voice broke. "I can't believe you just called me a whore. I thought you were my friend."

"You sleep with me last night. Now you kissing other man. Is actions of whore."

"Alex," Maks snapped in a disapproving voice, but her temper flared to life.

John gave her a hard look, and she felt the need to defend herself.

"I passed out drunk with his brother there! We didn't do anything!"

Alex blinked at her, his gaze clearing for a moment before John tried to step in front of her again. "You do not remember?"

"Remember what?" Her cheeks burned as she recalled her dream that may not have been a dream. "I was passed out, wasted, I don't remember anything."

John looked down at her. "You got drunk with

him last night?"

"Him and his brother, but nothing happened!"

"I did not know you are such a good liar, Jessica," Alex growled out. "You know exactly what happened, how you woke me with your kisses, begged me to pleasure you."

"Shut up!" She whirled to face Alex full on, meeting his furious gaze with one of her own. Her temper was blazing, white hot, and without even thinking, she closed the distance between them and pushed her hands into his chest and shoved, surprising him enough that he went back a step. "God, why are you being such an asshole? What is wrong with you? Why can't you just leave me alone? Why did you have to ruin a good night? You don't want me—you've made that abundantly clear—so stop being such a dick! You've probably fucked dozens of women in the past few months, but you don't see me trying to mess up your dates with them!"

A hint of regret broke through Alex's cold expression, but she turned away before he could see the tears filling her eyes.

His voice was gentle as he said, "Jessica—"

"Maks, get him the fuck out of here." She turned to John, who looked ready to beat the hell out of Alex and not at all happy with her. "I'm sorry for this asshole. I really did have a very good time with you and your friends."

John looked down at her, displeasure darkening his features. "You kissed him?"

"We didn't do anything." She ignored Maks speaking to Alex in a low voice in Russian and held John's gaze. "You're the first man I've kissed in months, John. I haven't even been on a date since before I came to Ireland."

John gave Alex a smug, pointed look then turned

to Jessica and grabbed her, giving her a kiss that was a lot harder than his earlier one. She wasn't stupid. She knew John was trying to prove some kind of point by kissing her like this, and she didn't appreciate that so she ended it quickly by slipping out of his grip then fumbled for her keys with shaking hands. Maks shouted something at Alex, who was growling—fucking *growling*—as if he was somehow the offended party here.

"Goodnight," she told John then turned her gaze on Alex. "And I don't want to talk to you ever again. Friends don't treat each other like this, Alex. Just leave me the fuck alone! I'll tell Peter if he wants someone to watch over me, it won't be you. You...you asshole!"

She slammed the door shut behind her.

Male voices rose on the other side, and she gave a frustrated scream before throwing her purse on the couch and stomping to her bedroom. She knew Maks wouldn't let Alex do anything stupid, but she still worried about John as she threw herself onto her bed and let out another angry scream. *Damn him!* Damn that man for fucking with her head like this! Damn him for playing games with her, and damn him for not wanting her and getting all pissy when someone else did. She knew better than to get involved with him, knew that something like this would happen. She'd trusted him. Tears began to trail down her cheeks, and she curled up on her bed with her arms wrapped around herself.

Someone pounded on her front door, but she ignored it, pulling her pillow over her head to drown out the sounds of Alex's demands that she let him, that he needed to talk to her. Nothing he could say would take those words back or erase the memory of the disgust on his face as he called her a whore. With every second that passed, she built up walls around her wounded heart to harden it against his pleas. He sounded sorry and upset, but she didn't give a shit. The banging and yelling went on for some time before silence finally returned to her apartment, and she lay there in the dark for a long time, wishing she'd never met Alexandr Gorev and vowing that she would never speak to that prick again.

Chapter Nine

Oleg shuffled around in Alex's kitchen the next morning, tossing away two empty fifths of vodka. "You must be one of the stupidest assholes in the world."

"Fuck you," he snapped in a sullen mutter. Alex would have roared if the very idea of his loud voice ringing in his ears didn't hurt his head so much. "She was letting him maul her, touch her right in front of my fucking door, after she spent the night in my bed."

"So what? Why shouldn't she go on a date with a young man her age? Did you think that with as beautiful as she is no man would ask her out? That she'd be content with your friendship? You know she wants more, and she tried to get it from you, but you turned her away."

"Not because I don't want her."

"But she does not know that." Oleg shook his head, his rough face grim. "And she obviously did not remember whatever you did in bed with her."

"Fuck you," Alex mumbled again, his head aching almost as much as his heart. "She remembered. I could see it in her eyes."

Oleg snorted. "And you, of course, were patient and understanding with her. Knowing that she thinks her love for you is completely unreturned. Knowing that she was very, very drunk. You, of course, handled it gently and with great tact, making her understand that she is more than a friend to you."

"She knows we are more than friends," he muttered, feeling like shit both inside and outside.

With a sigh, Oleg looked to the ceiling then back at Alex. "You are going to screw this up if you don't make things right between you soon. Not to mention

Mary slitting your throat for hurting Jessica. You know John is going to go tattle to her."

"Fuck," Alex muttered then sighed at the memory of Jessica's silken hair flowing through his fingers. He wanted to touch her again, to lick the salt off the skin over her sensitive collarbone. But more than that, he wanted her gaze to light up at the sight of him and watch her soft lips curve into a smile that was only for him. Then the mental image of John kissing those lips made him see red.

"She was kissing him, Oleg. I almost killed that little shit."

"Instead, you lashed out at her, insulted her, and reminded her of the fact she doesn't have the pleasure of remembering your touch. This girl has been watching you with hungry eyes for months. Do you not think she may be just the littlest bit upset that she finally gets to kiss you and she cannot remember it? Such a smart man, yet such an idiot." Oleg shook his head as he looked at Alex sprawled out over his couch in the same clothes as last night. "She isn't answering my calls or Maks'. Luka is in Germany right now, so he emailed her asking if she wanted him to pick anything up for her while he's over there. She hasn't responded to him, either. You must have really pissed her off because she always asks Luka to bring her something."

"She's not answering mine, either," he said in a low voice, wishing he wasn't so hung over so he could get up and grab another bottle of alcohol to drown his sorrows in.

"Are you surprised? She loves you, Alex, and you crushed her."

He didn't like the shame filling him that had him looking away. He was Alexandr Novikov. He did not feel guilt over a woman—ever—yet his gut was burning with it, and he was practically jumping out of his skin with the need to see Jessica to make things right between them. "If she did before, she does not now."

"You're not an idiot. Stop acting like one. You know very well that she had strong feelings for you. The little girl wears her emotions plain to see, and only a fool could miss the way she pines over you. When you entered a room, she would automatically seek you out, and you do the same. The first thing you both look for is each other. I do not know what you said to her that was so harsh. Maks would only tell me you acted like a complete bastard, but you probably crushed her. She is not like us, Alex. She has lived a sheltered life. If you roared at her like you usually do when you're pissed off, you know you hurt her deeply. Like I said, do not pretend to be an idiot. Own your mistakes. It is what men do."

Oleg, as usual, was correct. Men did not whine and make excuses. They fixed their mistakes. He'd taken the precious gift of Jessica's trust and damaged it in a jealous rage. The memory of looking out his door and seeing Jessica and that idiot John kissing hit him in the chest like a well-aimed punch.

There was a series of coded knocks on the front door before it opened. Maks came in, looking a little worse for the wear. His blue eyes were bloodshot, and his reddish-blond hair mussed up. After Alex had been a royal asshole to Jessica, they'd gone and completed a hit that went off without a hitch, but Maks wouldn't talk to him. Alex knew his friend was pissed. He just didn't know how pissed until Maks spotted him sitting on the couch.

"You know, I've seen you be a vindictive dick before, but last night, I was ashamed to have you as a friend. You lashed out at Jessica like she was one of your whores." Before Alex could respond, Maks added, "If you do not want her, I will take her. It will not be easy to erase you from her heart, but I will be patient with her. She is a treasure, the kind of woman who would warm a man's cock and home for the rest of his life, and she is wasted on you."

Without thinking Alex was across the room, choking Maks and yelling, "You will not touch her!"

Oleg pried him off, leaving Alex slumped on the couch holding his pounding head in his hands. Rounding on him, Oleg glowered at Alex while Maks rubbed his throat. "Why? Why shouldn't he touch her? You obviously don't care about her."

"I do care. I care too much." He shot Maks an apologetic look while his friend glared at him.

"You're falling in love with her," Oleg stated in a low voice.

Unable to deny it, Alex shook his head. "It does not matter what I feel. You know our world isn't safe enough for me to be with her openly yet. I need more time."

"Your father is getting old," Maks ground out in a raspy voice as he massaged his throat with a grimace. "And Gedeon Boldin has agreed to a truce between the Novikov and Boldin *Bratvas*, a truce made behind your father's back, but one that has held strong for the last five years. Gedeon loves his family. He is like you. He wants peace between the *Bratvas*. The man lives in constant fear his wife and twin daughters will be taken from him, along with his son. Everyone is tired of suffering for the sins of your fathers."

Alex stared down at his clenched fists. He'd been going over and over this in his own head, so it was good to be able to discuss it with his men. "And what if my father found out about this truce? He lost both his wives and his only daughter. He is not a man who forgives and forgets."

"Your father," Oleg said in a low voice, "is an old,

old man who wishes for you and Dimitri to have a better life than the one he led. In the not too distant future, you will be the head of the Novikov *Bratva*. Perhaps it is time to start forming alliances for the future. Perhaps it is time for a new era to start. You have already begun with Gedeon. Use this time your father has given you to speak with your friends in Western Europe, and let them discreetly know that you personally hold no grudges against the Boldin *Bratva* and want peace."

What Oleg was saying amounted to treason, and Alex gave him a sharp look. "What are you suggesting? That I betray my father?"

"No. I suggest you continue what you have been doing, forming alliances, making friends. Do not think I have not seen what you have been up to, carefully building a wall of protection for Jessica. I've watched you slowly stalking her and have said nothing, but it is time for you to pull your head out of your ass with this girl. If you want her, take her. She will not remain without a man in her life forever."

"I can't risk it, risk her, yet. My father thought he built such a shield—twice—and look what happened." A hard shudder worked through him at the thought of some sniper's bullet ending Jessica's life. "I could not bear it if I caused Jessica's death."

"You are not your father," Maks said as he stared at Alex. "And you would not just be building a shield for your and Dimitri's future wives, but also for women like Oleg's wife and my sister. It wasn't just your mother, stepmother, and half-sister who were lost, but also the wives and daughters of some of your father's and grandfather's top men. This slaughter has to stop. We all know it, and it is only those insane old bastards your father has surrounded himself with that feel any different. This feud is weakening us, all of us, Boldin and Novikov alike. Our enemies glory in

139

that fact. But, despite your father's cruelty, you and your brother have proven yourselves, over and over again, to be fair and honest men. You have friends, powerful friends, who will support you in whatever you choose to do. They owe you, and they are not the kind of people who like to have markers out on them."

Alex glared at his friends. "What if it was your wife's life, Oleg? Your girls? Would you be so quick to risk them?"

Oleg crossed his arms. "I've known you since you were a boy, Alex, held you at your mother's funeral, and I want what is best for you and the Novikov *Bratva*. A good woman is essential to a man's health, to his heart. She keeps him humble, questions him, and gives him the strength to deal with difficult shit. Besides, they are already at risk, just as your Jessica is in danger thanks to her association with Peter."

Maks stood and studied Alex. "All of this is may be a moot point as far as Jessica is concerned." He spoke in a quiet voice. "You did not see how deeply he injured her last night. She is not like your usual women, Alex. She cannot take such harsh words without being wounded. Especially from you."

"She was kissing him right in front of my door," Alex said through grit teeth as shame and anger tightened his muscles.

"Yes, she was. Why shouldn't she? You give her no indication you want anything but friendship from her."

"She slept with me the night before. I tasted her pussy, buried my fingers in her tight, hot cunt. Made her scream my name. She *knows* she belongs to me."

Both men stared at him before Oleg said, "You had sex with her?"

"No. She was too drunk, but I couldn't deny her some relief when she begged for it. What she needs I want to give to her, whatever it may be."

The memory of waking up in the night to find Jessica cuddled up to him sent the sweetest ache through his soul. His contentment had been so complete that every muscle in his body relaxed, and his dreams were good for once. He usually had nightmares about death and torture, things he'd witnessed and heard of, or done himself. That night he'd dreamed of walking with his mother along the lake next to the Summer Palace on his family's estate. They used to do that when he was young whenever the weather was warm enough, talking about anything and everything. It had been nice to relive those moments in his sleep. Then he woke alone and hoping she was still in his apartment, but he knew she was gone.

When he found out from Dimitri that Jessica had left at the crack of dawn, he was looking forward to seeing her, but he had a delicate situation to handle for Peter as soon as possible. He was going to tell her he wanted her in his bed again that night, to have the unequaled pleasure of smelling her spiced apple scented hair, of her delicate body curved trustingly into his. He was also going to inform her that she belonged to him now, and he wasn't going to let her go over a kiss with a stupid boy.

Instead, he'd lashed out at her like a jealous fool.

He was done being a fool, and a wise man listened to his advisors so he asked Oleg, "You have more experience with keeping a woman happy. What should I do?"

"Give her some time to lick her wounds. If you approach her right now, she is still too hurt to listen to you. Let her know she is important to you, that you want more than friendship with her. She will try to protect herself from further pain by guarding her heart against you. It is human nature." Oleg started to head to the door. "You could call your Uncle Petrov for advice. He is very good with how a woman's mind works and would be more than happy to help."

Alex couldn't help but chuckle. Uncle Petrov, his late mother's older brother, had a strong-willed wife and three stubborn daughters he somehow managed to keep happy. Although it would be helpful to talk to him, Alex wasn't ready to tip off anyone that he was interested in a woman for something more than companionship and fucking. He trusted his uncle to keep the information to himself, but he also knew Petrov would be curious about Jessica, and he wasn't ready to bring her to the attention of anyone outside of his immediate circle yet.

Especially when he wasn't sure he could salvage the situation with Jessica.

He stood then stretched, his head aching with his sudden movement. "We have to take care of the warehouse situation, so the time for gossiping like women is over. It is time to work."

Chapter Ten

The pub was super busy with people gearing up for the holiday season and in the mood to celebrate. Laughter rang through the air, and everywhere she looked, people were smiling. Jessica welcomed the distraction of being in constant motion filling all the drink orders. Even her bad mood had lifted somewhat in the boisterous atmosphere. Her smile would be real for a few moments, but every time she thought about Alex yelling at her, a sour ball would form in her stomach, and her smile would vanish.

Oleg stopped by earlier and tried to apologize for Alex, but she refused to listen. She let Oleg know she would continue to be friends with him, but she didn't want to talk about Alex—at all. She'd managed to avoid the asshole so far, but he kept leaving messages on her phone she didn't listen to and texts she didn't read. Heck, even Luka had emailed her asking her to put Alex out of his misery and talk to him, but she ignored Luka as well. Yeah, eventually she'd have to deal with him. Alex wouldn't just go away, but she needed some time away from him to let her temper cool and her hurt feelings heal...and time to figure out how to deal with this mess.

John had also stopped by the pub, but he treated her differently now, and she knew Alex had ruined whatever she might've had with the handsome Irish man. She knew John wasn't happy to learn that she spent so much time with Alex, and she could tell that he didn't believe her when she said there was nothing going on with them. Hell, she didn't even believe herself. The more she thought about it, the more details of her time spent in Alex's bed came to her.

143

She was now sure they'd fooled around, and that it had been spectacular.

That only made her even more pissed. Of course Alex would be fantastic in bed. He had lots of experience. Hell, three of the six women working tonight had screwed him. Her smile was completely gone by this point, and she couldn't force herself to pretend, so she quickly cleaned up the bar and made sure everything was topped off. Peter had tried to get her to open up about her foul mood, as had Mary, but she claimed she was just going through a bout of insomnia. Peter wasn't stupid. He knew something had happened with Alex, but he seemed almost relieved that things had soured between them.

She filled an order for a group of rough looking men over on the far side of the room who were leering at her. She'd never seen them here before, but she kept an eye on their small group. Something about them had set her on alert. There usually wasn't trouble in the pub—the bouncers nipped that shit in the bud—but the place was filled to capacity. This was also Friday night of a payday weekend, and people were getting shit faced. That meant good tips for her, but it also meant the bouncers were busier than usual removing people when they got too wasted, or calling cabs for those who needed them.

She was nodding at something one of the patrons sitting at the bar had said when she thought she caught sight of Alex across the room, but when she took a closer look, she didn't see him. That didn't stop her stupid heart from beating faster as she simultaneously hoped he was and wasn't here. They needed to talk, but she was afraid of what he would say. To be honest, she was surprised it had taken him this long to approach her. His incessant phone calls and texts made it clear he wasn't giving up easily. The crowd parted again, and this time, she saw Alex, and he was looking directly at her. He wore his usual black suit with a subdued blue button-down shirt, the color bringing out his gorgeous eyes, which were now narrowed in either anger or determination. Her mouth became dry, and her heart raced as she remembered the skin-tingling sensation of his goatee brushing her face when they kissed.

And, if her memory was true, that man could kiss.

Fuck, he was coming her way.

Before he could get through the crowd, she practically ran to the end of the bar where Tilly, the manager for the night, stood emptying the dishwasher and stacking mugs.

"I have to use the bathroom. Can you cover for me for a minute?"

"Sure. Mind takin' out a couple bags of garbage while you're back there? It's piling up quick tonight 'cause of how busy we are, not that I'm sad about that. Good tips, yeah?"

"Yep."

She ducked through the back doors, not daring to look and see if Alex noticed that she'd fled. Wiping her sweaty palms against her bar apron, she tried to figure out what to do. The adult, practical part of her mind told her that Alex wouldn't cause a scene here, and she shouldn't be running and leaving the other bartenders short staffed. The irrational part of her mind was relieved that she'd managed to put off the eventual confrontation with Alex for at least a few more minutes.

She grabbed a couple bags full of trash and went out one of the backdoors of the pub to the alley behind. As soon as the cold air hit her, it cleared her head, even if it did hold the funk of ancient beer and sour milk. Sodium security lights illuminated the garbage bins and cast deep shadows in the alley as she tossed the bags inside. Movement out of the corner of her eye caught her attention, and she sucked in a harsh breath when she saw two big, intimidating men in dark clothing stalking toward her.

They didn't say a word, but menace radiated from them, and her lungs burned as she sucked in a harsh breath. Fear-driven adrenaline slammed through her veins, and she stumbled a step back, dropping the garbage bags on the ground. The two men didn't stop, the lights revealing them to be nondescript but huge and wore dark knit caps pulled down low on their brows. The man on the left had short dark hair, and the man on the right had a deep scar on his chin. All these details skipped through her panicked mind as she tried to figure out what to do.

She turned to the door, only to find she hadn't left it propped open behind her. It had shut and automatically locked. Now she felt like a complete dumbass, soon to be raped and dead, as she stood here and debated if she should scream or run. Neither option looked very good, and the men closed in on her rapidly. The thought of one of them touching her made her skin crawl. One of them lunged for her, and she tried to dart away but lost her footing. The solid, cold mass of the dumpster hit her butt as she drew in a deep breath to scream. She'd barely gotten a sound out before they were on her.

The one on the left clamped his big hand over her mouth, and she shuddered with revulsion at the bitter taste of his flesh against her mouth. The dark-haired man in the brown corduroy jacket captured one of her wrists and twisted it until it hurt, making her scream all the louder as her bones nearly snapped in a tidal wave of white-hot pain. The lessons she'd learned in a self-defense class fled, leaving her mind oddly spinning, terror filling her along with a strange sense of disbelief. This couldn't be happening to her. This couldn't be real. The agony shooting from her wrist disagreed with this thought, and she shook as adrenaline flooded her system.

"Keep yer mouth shut, or I'll fuckin' break every bone in yer hand."

Her knees went weak, but she nodded, and he eased up the pressure on her wrist.

The guy with the scar glanced up and down the alley then pulled out a knife. "Hold her still. We need 'ta leave a present for Peter. I think an ear'll do it."

Those harsh words broke her paralysis, and she started to fight them. The man in corduroy jacket grabbed her by the hair, slapped her three times hard enough that her ears rang, and her lip was cut against her teeth. Her panic-dazed thoughts grew disjointed by the force of the blows, and she tried to push away, to get their hands off of her, but they totally ignored her attempts to shove their hands away. They were talking to each other in some lyrical language she didn't understand, and the man who'd slapped her produced a pair of zip ties.

The world took on a surreal quality as nausea bubbled in her stomach, and she tried to get her legs to work, to kick out at them, but the man with his hand over her mouth suddenly pinched her nose shut, cutting off her air. Oh God, they were going to slice her ear off, and there was nothing she could do to stop them. With her lungs burning, she tried to claw at them, only to have the bald man grab her wrists and easily pin her while the man in the corduroy jacket called someone to pick them up.

Her vision was fading when suddenly the pressure holding her up was removed, and she slumped to the ground, sucking air into her burning lungs. A terrible, chilling roar echoed down the brick alleyway, and even in her stupor, it made her

147

whimper, and she tried to push away with her numb legs. Now with the men's weight off of her, she could breathe. With each ragged inhalation, her vision began to clear, the numbness fading to be quickly replaced by pain. Blinking, she tried clear away the tears blurring her vision in the odd lighting of the alley. She squinted at the sight of her attackers fighting someone in the deep shadows, as her mind tried to make sense of what she was seeing.

Something warm trickled down her face. She touched her aching cheek where she'd been struck and then looked at her fingertips stained red with blood.

Fuck, that asshole hit hard.

The noise stopped abruptly, and a moment later, she was being carefully lifted from the filthy ground. Bright light and voices came from behind them, and her head throbbed as shudders wracked her body. She had a brief glimpse of Alex's rage-filled eyes before he turned and began to speak rapidly in a language she couldn't understand. The fear began to leave her as he cradled her to his chest, and she buried her aching face against his shirt. She took in deep breaths laced with his masculine scent, the fabric of his shirt soft against her face. A sob tore from her, and she clung to him, dimly aware that she was also bleeding on him and probably stunk like garbage.

Someone tried to take her from Alex, and she shook her head in protest and wound her arms around his neck.

Alex let out a low, rumbling growl. "I will take her upstairs. Find out who they are."

A voice she recognized as her Uncle Peter spoke from right next to her. "Give her to me."

"You are too angry right now. You will frighten her."

"And you won't? You're fuckin' covered in blood."

"It does not matter to her, because she knows I would never harm her."

"What the fuck are—"

"Please," she whispered in a rough voice. "I need to wash their stink off me, get the taste of them out of my mouth. Take me to a bathroom."

Without another word, Alex turned and walked her back into the pub, using the private entrance to Peter's home above the bar. It was an odd place for her aunt and uncle to live, but it was also huge and good for entertaining. There were always people going in and out of his house, so she was surprised when she found they were alone except for guards stationed at every door who watched her with open anger mixed with concern. Alex made a soft, almost crooning sound as he carried her into the gleaming black marble master bathroom.

"Jessica, I put you down. I can turn on the water and clean you." His English wasn't coming to him as easily as it usually did, and she dimly noted that fact.

The only word that really got through to her fuzzy mind was clean. She wanted clean and pure right now, needed it. She was drowning in the stink of that alley, and she had to get it off. When she lifted her dirty hand to remove the stained remnants of her cream blouse, Alex made a soft hissing sound and gently held her arm still while he examined her wrist. With her free hand, she reached up and touched both her ears to reassure herself they were still there.

Alex shushed her softly when she cried out as he manipulated her hand. "This might be sprained. Let me tend you. Once endorphins wear off, will be pain. I swear to you I do nothing inappropriate."

Instead of answering, she merely held still while he deftly removed her clothes, leaving her in her

149

green bra and panties, before he turned the shower on. Steam soon filled the air, her ragged breathing drowned out beneath the rush of falling water. A quick glance down showed scratches marring her torso and red spots on her arms that she knew would eventually turn into bruises. Right then, she should have been totally embarrassed by her semi-naked state, but her mind seemed to be swaddled in cotton. She was beginning to process the incident, and she started to shake, her teeth chattering with each full body tremble.

A weird, keening noise filled the room, and it took her a moment to realize she was the one making that sound.

Alex spoke in the soft, soothing, crooning murmurs she loved as he led her into the shower. His fingers were gentle when he began to take her hair out of her mangled bun, and she turned her face gratefully to the water, opening her mouth and spitting the coppery taste of blood away. She gently probed her lip where it had been split, wincing at the sharp sting from her light touch. As her shudders subsided, the pain set in, and she whimpered when Alex gently turned her face to examine her cheek.

"Is not too bad, will not need stitches. How is vision, Jessica?"

With those words, he drew her out of her stupor enough for her to wonder if he was naked as well. Turning around, she found that he was standing in the shower with her, still wearing everything except his jacket, belt, socks, and shoes. Amusement crept in on the edges of her fading adrenaline rush, and a rather mad sounding giggle escaped her. Hands down, Alex would win any wet-shirt contest he entered.

Instead of fearing for his life at the creepy titter that had just come from her, he grabbed the soap and a washcloth from the shelf. "I will clean you quickly and will not touch intimate areas."

Even in the warmth of the shower, she began to shiver again, and by the time she was clean to Alex's satisfaction, the tears had restarted.

He set the soap aside then wrapped her in his arms, whispering things to her in Russian she didn't understand while she clung to him. Alex had saved her life. If he hadn't come...

She didn't realize she'd said those words aloud until Alex murmured, "I will always be there to save you, Jessica. Always. I swear it."

If she'd been a little more with it, she would have argued that he couldn't always be with her, but instead, she just absorbed his words and let them soothe her.

He helped her out of the shower, wrapped her up in a towel, and began to dry her hair with another. It was only when he unlocked and opened the door to the bathroom that she realized someone had been knocking on it. Aunt Mary stood in the doorway, along with Uncle Peter and several people behind them. Still dressed in a dark mink fur jacket, Aunt Mary pushed past a soaking wet Alex and swept Jessica into her arms.

"Oh my sweet girl," she murmured. "My sweet, sweet girl."

Jessica was vaguely aware that men were talking in loud voices, but she clung to her Aunt Mary, now sobbing again as her overwhelmed mind tried to find some release for her lingering terror. The adrenaline was wearing off, and her whole body ached and stung, her wrist throbbing almost as bad as her cheek. A moment later, Uncle Peter and Alex stood next to her while Alex began to go over her injuries that he'd seen while she was in the shower. Aunt Mary made shushing noises, rubbing her back until

151

the shudders slowed.

"My head hurts," she whispered.

"The doctor's on his way, Jessica," Uncle Peter growled out in a tight voice, his face flushed red and his eyes glittering with emotion.

Too overwhelmed to be embarrassed at her total breakdown, she nodded. The soft fur of Aunt Mary's jacket was now damp with her tears, and it rubbed against her face. The soft, tactile sensation that cut through the muzzy haze of fear and helped ground her in the present. She reached out to her uncle and was soon completely enveloped by her family, each of them holding her tight enough that it hurt, but she didn't protest. She needed their warmth, their love.

"Jessica," Peter whispered against her head.

"I'm okay," she whispered back while her Aunt Mary silently cried, placing the occasional kiss on Jessica's head and cheek. "I'm okay."

She had no idea how long they stood huddled together, but eventually, their hold on her loosened enough that she could step back and scrub a trembling hand over her blotchy face. They helped her to the room she'd stayed in when she first arrived in Ireland, and the familiar surroundings soothed her. The large room was decorated in soft tones of rose and white with a massive canopy bed fit for a princess. The lights were turned down low, lending to the comforting atmosphere.

A brass-framed photo of a young teenage Peter and her birth mother sat on the table next to the bed, and her already fragile emotions took another hit. Aunt Mary took Jessica into the adjacent bathroom and helped her dress in some sweatpants and a loose T-shirt before bundling her up in a thick, royal blue terry cloth robe that smelled of her Aunt's subtle perfume. When they returned to the bedroom where the men were huddled together, she clutched the robe to herself as she sat on the bed with her arms wrapped around her knees. Her mind slowly came back online and she looked for Alex.

"Where is he?"

"Who, darling?" Aunt Mary asked as she gently finished drying Jessica's long hair with a towel.

Her voice came out rough when she said in a much louder, slightly hysterical, voice, "Alex, where is Alex?"

"Shhh, he's talking with Peter."

"Please, I want Alex," she whispered and hugged her knees harder, trying to control the trembling that had begun to start up again.

Peter came into the room with another, older man with salt and pepper hair and kind blue eyes. When she didn't see Alex, she repeated in a stronger voice, "I want Alex."

With a sigh, Peter stood next to the bed. Reaching down, he gently cupped her cheek. "He'll be here in a few minutes, lass. He's getting some dry clothes on. Let's get you checked over real quick."

"Promise?"

"Yes, love, we promise," Aunt Mary murmured and ran a soothing hand over Jessica's back. "Anything you need, darling, just let us know, and we'll get it for you."

"Okay."

She zoned out while the doctor looked her over, answering his questions as best she could. When she described what had happened, how she'd been struck and how they were going to cut her ear off and leave it in the alley as morbid gift for Peter, she could practically feel the rage coming off her uncle. Aunt Mary held her good hand as the doctor manipulated her hurt one. An occasional tear rolled down Mary's pale cheek, but she tried to brush them away without Jessica noticing. They asked her a few more questions, but her mind was drifting again, and she refused to think about what had happened in an effort to shield herself from it.

The doctor was handing out some painkillers when Alex came back into the room, his presence filling it with harsh, masculine energy. Like her uncle had said, he'd changed into a dry pair of black trousers and a white button down shirt, but his hair was still damp. When his worry-filled, dark gray eyes met hers, she could feel her lower lip wobbling, and she tried to stop it by firming her mouth.

For a moment, what looked like helpless rage and pain twisted his features, but his expression smoothed out into his usual emotionless mask. "Jessica," he said in a soothing voice, "you are all right. We keep you safe. Never let harm near you again."

Her breath hitched, and she held her arms out to him, silently pleading with him to hold her. He was there in an instant, sitting on her bed and pulling her onto his lap, the scent of his laundry soap on his clean clothes surrounding her while she clung to him. He was so big, so strong, and he'd saved her. He held her and placed his lips against her temple while he whispered to her in Russian. She didn't understand the meaning of what he said, but there was no mistaking the profound relief in his voice.

When her latest crying jag was over, her head hurt more than ever. She looked up to find that the doctor was no longer there, and she was alone with her family and Alex. Mary was watching them carefully with a worried expression that would normally have caught Jessica's attention, but she was so mentally exhausted it was impossible to do anything more than exist in the moment. Uncle Peter was talking quietly on his phone as he watched her closely, his gaze darting between her and Alex with a decidedly unhappy frown deepening the lines around his mouth.

He caught her looking at him, and he gave her a grim smile that held no mirth. "Are you hurting?"

She nodded, her face rubbing against Alex's tear-dampened shirt beneath her cheek. "My head hurts."

"Here, love, take these." Aunt Mary handed her two pills and a glass of water.

She moved away from Alex just enough to take the medicine before clinging to him once more. He didn't seem to mind and continued to hold her close. His strong heart beat beneath her cheek, and the sound lulled her. The thought of what those men would have done to her if Alex hadn't followed her began to take root in her mind, but she refused to think about it right now.

Alex spoke in a low murmur, his chest rumbling beneath her ear. "Jessica, tell me what happened."

She went over what she could remember, her voice breaking now and again, the tremors returning as she relived it. When she got to the part about the ear, Alex went stiff. His grip on her grew almost punishing so she shoved at his chest. "Ow."

His grip loosened right away, and he smoothed her hair back from each ear. His expression was closed down, but she could see his pain. The thought of her being hurt seemed to truly upset him, and she gave a watery sigh before she reached up and held his cheek. She needed to give him something to let him know how much he meant to her. The memory of what it felt like to think she was going die still haunted her. He placed a kiss on her forehead then leaned back again. There was a tenderness in his gaze she'd never seen before mixing with remorse. Though he hid it well, he was obviously very upset.

With this in mind, she tugged gently on his hair, pulling him down so she could whisper as softly as she could in his ear, "I'm sorry. I remember now what happened that night in your bed, not all of it, but enough. You had the right to be angry with me. Just please don't call me names. It hurts."

Alex buried his face against her neck, a faint shudder working through him. She curled her fingers into his silken hair, stroking the back of his head, comforting him. The bed creaked as he shifted then looked up at her, that tenderness she'd briefly glimpsed even stronger. He studied her face then pressed another soft kiss to her forehead.

Aunt Mary returned from the bathroom and ran a soothing hand over Jessica's shoulder. "Let's get you in bed, darling."

When Alex tried to put her down, she dug her hands into his shirt and held tight, too afraid to worry about looking like a crazy woman. "Please, don't go."

His expression was uncompromising as he gently put her beneath the heavy covers. "I will not be gone long."

"Please, please stay. Don't go. Don't leave me alone. I need you."

He closed his eyes then blew out a harsh breath. "Mary, tell Peter I will be there in a few minutes."

With an obviously troubled look, Aunt Mary chewed her lower lip before saying, "Alex...are you sure?"

Alex replied in a voice that brooked no argument. "Go. I will attend to Jessica. I assure you that I will die before I let anything or anyone harm her. You have my word."

The pain pills must have been pretty potent because she was already beginning to feel a dulling sensation stealing over her body, over her thoughts. When Alex lay next to her, she gratefully curved into his solid warmth, burrowing into him until she was as close as physically possible. Alex didn't seem to mind as he held her tight, whispering against her hair in Russian and placing tender kisses on her face where it wasn't bruised. Drinking up his affection, she tried to fight the pills so she could cherish the feeling of him finally holding her like she'd wanted for so long.

She tried, but in spite of her best efforts, she was almost asleep when Oleg and Maks came into the room. They took one look at her and let out almost identical growls that would have been funny if they didn't look so furious. It was too much of a struggle to lift her hand so she merely whispered, "Hi, guys. Don't freak out. I'm okay. Really. I'm just a little tired."

Oleg clenched his fists, the veins on his burly forearms standing out in sharp relief. He didn't say anything to her, but began to speak to Alex in rapid Russian while Maks took out a cell phone and moved over to the corner of the room to make his call. Her gaze met Maks' deep green eyes, and she flinched at how scary he looked right now. He must have realized he was freaking her out because he turned away. When he looked back a moment later, his familiar warmth had dissipated the scary vibes, but the tension remained.

She gave him a weak smile that pulled at her sore lips in an attempt to reassure him, but he didn't return it.

Alex distracted her by growling something as he tensed behind her, but his big hands never stopping their slow caress of her back and shoulders.

With the red in his hair glinting in the dull light, Maks crossed the room and handed her his phone. "Jessica, Dimitri wishes to speak."

Alex grew silent behind her as she held the cell up and said in a thick voice, "Hello?"

"*Devushka milaya* ," Dimitri growled. "We make this right."

157

"What? Dimitri, I'm okay. Please don't worry about me. I-I survived." Her brain was starting to shut down thanks to the drugs, and she struggled to focus.

Alex took the phone from her and began to speak in rapid-fire Russian again. Oleg and Maks talked together, their faces tight and their body language aggressive. She wanted to tell them again that they didn't need to be so worried, that Alex saved her, but talking took way too much effort. It was a struggle to keep her eyes open anymore, so she gave up the fight and nuzzled her face into Alex's neck. Letting out a long sigh, she fell easily into a drugged, blessedly dreamless sleep.

Chapter Eleven

lex waited until he was sure Jessica was out before he eased her off of him and removed the robe before tucking her in. The sight of the creamy perfection of her cheek and temple already darkening with a deep bruise sent rage spinning through him. Her lips were swollen as well, the lower one split. With a soft touch, he smoothed the hair back from her forehead and placed a kiss there before standing and facing Oleg and Maks.

All tenderness fled as he locked his gaze on his men.

"Bring me to those bastards."

Oleg grimaced. "I am afraid it is too late. They had cyanide capsules in their mouths. We think they took the poison as soon as you interrupted them."

"Fuck." That was a clear indication these men were not only professionals, but loyal to the bone to someone.

"They had guns with the serial numbers scratched off, but nothing else to identify them and no tattoos. However, they knew enough about Peter's security setup to avoid being seen on the exterior cameras. With as busy as the sidewalks are right now, the men were able to blend in and get to the alley without anyone being the wiser. Peter's contacting his associates to see if any of the police cameras in the area caught anything."

"How did they know she would be out there?"

Maks looked down at his phone. "Someone must have been watching her from inside and tipped them off."

"Do you think anyone that works for Peter was in on it?"

Maks shook his head. "We questioned all of them. They were genuinely shocked and saddened by what happened to Jessica. None of their reactions were staged, but we are having them followed home to make sure."

Alex spared one more glance at a sleeping Jessica before looking back at Maks. "Stay here with her."

He nodded and stopped talking into his phone. "Luka says there has been no chatter that they've intercepted back home about Jessica. Everyone is too busy trying to deal with your father's sudden need to push for more territory."

Alex gritted his teeth, unable to deal with thinking about the mess his father, Jorg, was creating back home which Dimitri was trying to clean up. Jorg was on a tear to expand their western flank, territory that was held by the Boldin and Lerche *Bratvas*, while the rest of his advisors were attempting to talk him out of it. Most of them were good men, but they'd become his father's advisors because of their extreme loyalty. They would do anything for Jorg, and eventually, if Jorg wanted more territory, they would support him.

Alex knew he'd have to go home at some point to try and make his father see reason, but right now, his only concern was Jessica. The memory of following her out into the alley next to the pub with the intention of making her talk to him, only to see her delicate body being abused by two big men as she struggled, sent another burst of adrenaline through him. He wished those bastards were still alive so he could show them what true suffering was.

"Come on," Oleg said in a low voice. "Peter is waiting for us."

With one last look at a sleeping Jessica, Alex followed Oleg past the two men guarding the door and down the hall. They waited for one of Peter's men to key in the code for a solid steel door with no handle. They were ushered into a large, windowless room with a massive circular dark wood table in the middle and enormous flat screen TVs on three of the walls.

Peter's war room.

Alex approached the table where Peter was thumping his fist against the aged and scarred wood, his face red as he shouted about finding out who the fuck these men were. Mary stood behind his chair, her hands clutching the back as she watched Alex and Oleg, her blank face giving nothing away. Dressed in an elegant pale ivory blouse and tailored gray slacks, she looked like she should be running some business empire, not one of the most feared gangs in Europe. Mary was a sweet armful of a woman with an easy smile, but she was just as ruthless as her husband, and Alex never forgot that in his dealings with her.

Peter took a deep breath and turned to Alex, his face grim. Three of his men bustled about the room, talking quietly in the background. He glanced behind him. "All of you, out."

They waited for Peter's men to clear the room, but before the other man could speak, Alex asked, "Who did this to her?"

"Take yer fuckin' pick. I've got enough enemies to choose from." Peter growled and thumped his fist again. "Someone came into my territory, my fuckin' *home*, and almost took my niece!"

After giving Peter's shoulder a squeeze, Mary studied Alex. "What we need to think about is what they hoped to accomplish by takin' her and why. If we can figure that out, we can narrow down a list of possible suspects. While the kidnapping could be the work of one man, I don't think it is. This is too organized, too precise."

Alex's thoughts spun as he turned the situation

161

over in his mind. Normally, with his years of training in espionage and tactics, he was able to view things from an objective angle. Right now, however, his main concern was Jessica, and that was interfering with his ability to stick to pure logic. If there was an open power play being made for Peter's territory, it would mean this place could soon be a war zone.

"Attacking family is personal, insulting." Oleg said from behind him.

Peter nodded, closed his eyes and let out a long breath, then opened them again. "I want ta' send Jessica back home to the States, ta' keep her out of this, but I'm afraid it is already too late. It will be even easier for them to hit her there, and she can't very well live with one of my men guardin' her twenty-four/seven without attracting attention. Plus the American police might get involved, and that is the bloody last thing we need."

"I will take care of her," Alex declared before he was even aware the thought was in his head.

Mary stiffened. "No."

Peter glanced up at his wife, "Mary..."

"No," she repeated in a heated voice. "I'm not stupid, Alex. I see the way my niece looks at you, how you are around each other. That little girl adores you, or at least the man she thinks you are, and you're going to break her heart. She needs a nice, normal husband who can give her a family and a safe home."

Ignoring the fact that Mary was right and Jessica did deserve the kind of life he could never provide, Alex snorted. "You took her away from normal and safe when you brought her here. Is late now to be worried."

"How dare you—"

Peter held up his hand. "Enough, Mary. We knew the risk when we invited Jessica ta' stay with us. We knew it might make her a target for our enemies, but we took the chance because we both needed to see her, to spend time with her. I know you care for her, deeply, but she is not a child, and I won't drive her away by trying to control her life. You'd have to be blind not to see that Alex cares for her, and even though I can think of a million men I would rather see my niece fall in love with, Alex'll be able to keep her safe until we deal with this and neutralize the threat."

"He may keep her body safe"—Mary glared at Alex—"but her heart is another matter. I know your reputation with women, Alexandr, both here and in Russia. I mean no disrespect, but you have no business messing around with an innocent child like her, playing games with her emotions she's ill equipped to handle. She deserves better than to be the toy of a man who will leave her without a second thought once he decides their time is up."

Alex leaned forward, anger tightening his muscles. "*Nyet.* I play no games with Jessica."

She rolled her eyes, and her tone was biting. "Please." she hissed. "I heard from John what you did, what you said. You won't let Jessica date someone else, but it's okay for you to go around fuckin' everything that moves. And let's not forget the Novikov Curse."

This time Peter stopped his wife. "Enough, Mary."

"But, Peter, you know—"

"I said enough!"

Mary let out a little gasp, her eyes wide, obviously unused to Peter yelling at her.

Every word she said was true, yet Alex already knew what his course of action was. His time to get his world as ready for her as possible was up. Jessica was his, and he would do whatever was necessary to keep her safe. The sooner Peter and Mary realized

163

that, the better.

His thoughts cleared, and his indecision fled, the plans forming and falling into place, not just for keeping her safe now, but forever.

"I will be taking Jessica to Rome with me in a few days while I take care of some things. She will have around-the-clock protection, and I will introduce her to some of my business partners. Men who owe me and will help me keep her safe."

"Excuse me?" Mary shrieked, but Alex cut her off.

"Know this, I plan on marrying Jessica one day and making her my wife."

"But-but..." Mary stuttered and looked to Peter, who was watching Alex with a grim expression. "You hardly know her!"

"I know her better than you think. All this time I have spent with her has shown me a woman who is a treasure for right man. I am that man." He gave Mary a level look. "It was not you she begged to stay with her; it was me."

"You arrogant-"

Mary looked ready to totally lose her temper, but before she could continue, Peter interrupted, "Enough, Mary. It's done. We've known from the first time they saw each other that Jessica was taken with Alex and hoped it would fade, but we both know she's in love with him. I won't make the mistake of history repeating itself, tryin' to keep them apart." He sighed and rubbed his face. "Take care of her, Alex. She's one of the last family members I have left, and even though I haven't known her long, we love her very much want only the best for her."

"Nothing is more important to me than Jessica. I will guard her with my life."

They discussed some strategy and began to go over contingency plans. After this was done, Alex didn't bother returning to his home to change. Instead, he went straight back to Jessica's room. Maks was on the door, and to Alex's surprise, Luka was there as well. His friend looked tired, and his thick, normally well-styled, light brown hair was mussed, but his hazel eyes were deadly serious when they met Alex's.

"Your woman is safe, sleeping inside."

He was itching to get to Jessica, but it was important to let Luka know Alex appreciated his support. "How did you get here so fast, my old friend?"

Luka shifted and leaned against the door, his black suit wrinkled and a red silk tie loose around his neck. "I was in Berlin. Dimitri contacted me, and I got here as soon as I could. Your brother would have come as well, but things are not good back home."

Alex sucked in a harsh breath, hating how conflicted he felt. On the one hand, he wanted to return to Moscow to help Dimitri and the men loyal to them in staving off whatever disaster their father was cooking up, but he needed to go to Rome with Jessica to start weaving a web of protection around her that couldn't be broken. For the first time in his life, his loyalty was divided between his family and his woman, and he didn't know what to do about it.

"What did Dimitri say?"

With a grimace, Luka nodded. "That your father is...acting odd. Irrational. Yesterday he talked to Dimitri briefly about taking a hit out on Vili Boldin, who has been dead for seven years. Are you sure your father is taking his medication?"

"Yes, we have a private nurse with him at all times, and everyone in our inner circle is aware of how dangerous it would be if he isn't medicated. She will put the drugs in his food so he is forced to take them just in case he decides he no longer wants them.

He is acting irrationally now, but nowhere near as bad if he was off his medication." He exchanged a glance with Maks. "I cannot leave Jessica alone, but Moscow is not secure enough for her yet, and she is definitely not ready to meet my father."

"I understand," Luka murmured. "One of the reasons I do not have a girlfriend is because eventually I would have to introduce her to my mother."

That drew a tired chuckle from Alex. Luka's mother was as mean as a bear with a sore paw and loved to spread her misery around. Growing up, Luka had spent a great deal of time at Alex's home, and he thought of the man as more a brother than a friend.

Maks interrupted. "We have reinforcements on the way."

"Who?"

"I have three more men coming to join us in Rome, all Black Tier. Jessica will not know they are here, but they will be watching you."

Alex nodded, relieved his best men would be there to help guard her. Since he was in charge of the muscle side of the *Bratva,* he'd devised a level system for his men. At the bottom of the pyramid, there were the foot soldiers, and at the very top were the Black Tier, the most elite killers and fighters Alex and Luka had personally trained. These were men he trusted with his life, proven friends and staunch allies.

"I will see you in the morning. Have breakfast delivered at eight. Jessica likes french toast with strawberries and clotted cream from the restaurant down the street. Bring that with a pot of coffee."

"Got it," Maks said with a small smile. "Want me to get some milk with that? She usually drinks a glass with her morning meal."

He wasn't sure if Maks was being a smart-ass or not, but he didn't care. Finally, he got to be exactly

166

where he wanted, with Jessica, even if the situation was less than ideal. Mentally, he berated himself that he should have taken this step with her sooner, should have admitted his feelings for her, but he promised himself he wouldn't hold back anymore. Eventually, he would tell her the truth about his world, but first, he needed to woo her, to make her fall so deeply in love with him that even when she found out he was a demon among men she would gladly stay in hell with him rather than try to run.

Turning the door handle, he eased through then nodded at the men before closing and locking the door behind him. Jessica was a lump among the white pillows with one clasped tightly in her arms. She would never need a pillow to hug again. She would have him to cling to and to hold. He quickly used the bathroom and brushed his teeth then shed his clothes as he approached the bed. His cock started to fill until he caught sight of the bruise swelling her cheek, and his gut clenched.

The need to comfort her consumed him, and he slid beneath the soft sheets, the cotton smooth and cool against his skin. Though he turned off the lights, they were in the city, and it was never truly dark. The dim glow of streetlights reflected around the edges of the curtains. He gently shifted Jessica into his arms, pressed his face to her hair, and inhaled her clean scent. She felt so small, so defenseless in his arms, and his chest hurt, an unfamiliar pain that seemed to settle into his heart as he thought about how close he'd come to losing her. If he'd come out the back door one minute later, it might have been too late.

Never, never again would he allow her to be exposed to danger like that.

Her breathing was slow and even, her body a dead weight on his as he cuddled her against him. He'd been with many women, yet he'd never had the urge to simply hold one of his lovers and sleep with her curled into his side for anything other than the convenience of waking up with a warm body to fuck. He'd certainly never felt the heat that suffused him as her body melted into his.

Tomorrow, he'd have to start setting things up for Jessica's arrival in Rome. Even though he hated it, he would see to things personally, including briefing his men. He knew Peter and Mary would keep Jessica safe while he was gone. That didn't mean he didn't wish he could stay with her, but her safety was more important. He'd do some investigating on his own, contact some sources, and see if he could help steer Peter in the right direction toward finding whoever had ordered her kidnapping. It would also give him time to calm down and, he hoped, give Jessica a chance to heal before he whisked her away to Rome.

Sighing up at the ceiling, he closed his eyes and held her, sweeping his hand beneath her shirt over the small of her back, soothing himself with the fact that she was alive and in his arms. He knew she was his woman, made for him, meant for him, just like he'd been made for her. There wasn't a doubt in his mind she would be his wife, the mother to his children, the one bit of softness and light in his dark world. Now, he just needed to make her feel as loved as possible, to fill her life with joy, and bind her so tightly to him she'd never want to leave.

Chapter Twelve

Two days later, Jessica tried not to stare at the newest addition to her ever growing army of bodyguards, a gigantic man with a tattoo of a dagger piercing the side of his neck and shoulders so broad she was surprised he made it through the door without turning sideways. But what really caught her eye, other than his bulk, tattoos, and general scariness, were his sideburns that were so long they bordered on being mutton chops. It kind of made him look like Wolverine, if Wolverine was a serial killer. His name was Krom. No last name. Most of them were Russian, and throughout the past few days, Maks and Luka had introduced various new men to her.

All the new guys she met were very professional in their well-made dark suits and polite, but they made her anxious. She'd become used to the warmth and friendship she had with her bodyguards, not the chilling and professional distance the new guys displayed. When they looked at her, they studied her closely, almost as if they could read her mind, but they did not smile. Inevitably, their gaze would fall on the ugly bruises standing out like a beacon on her cheekbone, then down to her split lip, and they'd become even scarier as an almost offended anger filled them. Like they took the marks on her face personally.

Maks, bless his heart, knew the men freaked her out, so he would introduce her to each one, and she'd give them as much of a smile as she could without pulling too hard at her lower lip. After that, she would shake the new man's hand and thank him for coming—usually much to his surprise for some odd reason. She would then mumble out a quick apology for her troubles having pulled him to Dublin. At this point, Maks would groan and tell her there was nothing to be sorry about, and the new man would stare at her even harder.

By the time the latest guy arrived, she was tired, stressed out, and her head ached. The quiet of the small blue and white study with its comfortable gray chairs and reading nook had soothed her, making it easy to ignore Maks standing guard at the door. She pretended to read, but in reality, her mind was just kind of in heavy daydream mode. Her eyes had closed, and she was almost asleep on the oversized sofa when Maks appeared, yet again, with yet another stranger. If she'd met this latest guy, Krom, first, she might have been intimidated by his scarred face. He had a wicked slash going over his forehead and into his hairline, but after the parade of deadly predators/bodyguards who'd come through Uncle Peter's home, she was over being afraid. Heck, in a way, she was glad they were so intimidating. Hopefully, they'd scare off whoever was trying to hurt her, and she could move on with her life.

Maybe even want to leave the safety of her uncle's place eventually.

It wasn't like she'd been a total shut-in. She'd visited her apartment with her Aunt Mary under Maks and Luka's watchful gaze, but only long enough to pack up some things. Hell, she'd even showered at her place today...with an armed guard right outside and another in the hallway. And another in the stairway. Yeah. Overkill to the extreme, but she was also grateful for their presence because, without it, her paranoia might take her over and send her running to hide in a closet.

Almost getting kidnapped might have something to do with that new personality quirk.

She grimaced as her head throbbed harder, and she sat up. She pressed her hand to her forehead and tried not to fidget beneath their intense gaze. Since the...incident...any move she made was scrutinized. It was sweet that they were worried about her, but she was being suffocated by their concern. Yeah, it sucked. Yeah, it was scary. Yeah, she'd had some wicked nightmares, and yes, her paranoia had ramped up, but that didn't mean she was going to go into hysterics. She'd survived the death of both her parents, and those horrible times in her life had given her a new sense of what 'bad' was. Surviving an attempted kidnapping wasn't anywhere near having to bury the people she loved more than anything in the world. That didn't mean she wasn't crapping-her-pants scared when she allowed herself to dwell on her situation, but she wasn't going to let her fear rule her life.

With a tired sigh, she rubbed her hands on her black yoga pants and wondered how she was going to have a normal existence with all these behemoths breathing down her neck. They would not blend. Especially Krom. The guy could squish people with one mighty, tattooed hand.

Totally freaking out now, but trying to hold it in, she turned and smiled sweetly. "Maks, is Alex building an army around me?"

Krom frowned and looked to Maks who, she assumed, translated. Then Maks looked back at her with a tight expression. "We will do what is necessary to protect."

She nodded, then pushed herself from the couch, and moved to stand in front of the brute. She was tall for a woman at five foot ten, but this guy dwarfed her. She had to crane her neck to look up at him and force a smile. She needed to remember that he was a fellow human being and his crazy boss had put him on her already overstaffed babysitter/bodyguard detail. It wasn't Krom's fault he got dragged here, and he probably had a ton of things he'd rather be doing, so she tried to be as gracious as possible and launched into the speech she'd given close to a dozen times now.

"Hi, welcome to the family. You're going to be spending the next few days watching me sit around and twiddle my thumbs. Let Alex know what you like to eat, and we'll do our best to keep you fed and happy. If you like beer, Peter's pub has some excellent choices, and I highly recommend the restaurant on the corner with the blue pepper sign. They serve, oddly enough, a Tex-Mex that is to die for."

Maks shook his head and translated, leaving the other man frowning down at her again. He gave a short reply in Russian while he studied her. Tired beyond reason, she returned his stern look and yawned.

"Krom is old friend of Alex's." Maks' voice was unexpectedly serious.

"Aren't they all?" she muttered.

"He understands English and speaks English, but is not familiar with slang so please keep in mind. He will be in charge of your advance security. That means he will be scouting out locations of places you may go for any potential weaknesses. He will go over your security detail every morning with you and asks that, before you go anywhere, to please let him know so he does not have to hunt you down."

Her throat closed up as the reality of her world came crashing in, breaking through the fragile blanket of indifference in which she tried to smother her fear. Since the incident she'd been on an emotional roller coaster, fine one moment and sobbing the next. She hated it, hated the pitying looks she received like she was some broken doll. Her cheek ached as her pulse sped up, and the thickness in her throat became a burning in her nose. Grasping the cuffs of her pale gray, wool cardigan, she sat up straight and willed herself not to cry.

Maks always grew agitated when she cried, and she didn't need him hovering over her any more than he already was. It seemed like the moment she was awake he was waiting for her. The handsome man barely let her out of his sight, and she had to fight to keep him out of her room while she was getting dressed.

"Jessica, are you not feeling well?"

Her neck sagged as the pain in her head overwhelmed her pride, and she closed her eyes. "Headache."

She sensed movement in front of her, and she bit back a yelp when she opened her eyes and found Krom squatting down a bit so she was looking him in the face. He was all up in her personal space, but the intensity of his light brown gaze held her. There was no inflection in his voice as he spoke in Russian, and when he was done, he stayed where he was, watching her carefully.

"Krom says that there is no reason for tears. He is here now, and you will be protected and safe. So no crying. It irritates him. Makes him want to hurt those that make such a pretty woman sad. No more tears, okay?"

She blinked rapidly, then nodded and winced as her headache intensified.

Abruptly, Krom straightened and said something to Maks, then gently gripped her by the back of her neck and spun her around.

Fear caused her to twist in Krom's grasp, and she let out a startled, "What the hell?"

"Relax," Krom said in a deep voice that fair

shook her bones. "Will remove poison."

She stiffened further, wincing when pain exploded behind her eyes with a hard pound.

Maks made a soothing noise and moved around into her line of sight. "Krom is skilled with...what is word...touching muscle to make it feel better. To help whole body. Knows how to soothe head."

Jessica knew the answer as soon as Krom wrapped his big fingers and palms around her skull then squeezed. Almost instantly, the pain lessened then eased to the point that it was just an annoying background hum. She was putty in his hands. Krom knew pressure points, and he was now her new best friend. As his long fingers manipulated her scalp then her neck, she relaxed and let out a sigh of relief as the aching tightness slowly left her muscles. He was an angel, a side-burn-sporting, tattooed angel with a blessed touch. He began to press and massage her tight shoulders, taking away further tension until she was in danger of slumping over.

Krom spoke again, and Maks translated. "You need to drink more water and sleep."

She didn't bother to reply, only let out a languid sigh when Krom took a step back, and she collapsed onto the couch. She pulled a comfy teal throw pillow beneath her head and grabbed a furry, cranberry-colored one to hold against her before she mumbled an apology to the men and gave in to sleep.

A few hours after her long nap, she found herself in her Uncle Peter's study with him, her Aunt Mary, Alex, Maks, and Krom. Jessica had just been informed that she would be leaving the country. Told she was going like she was a little girl being sent off to stay with a relative. She stared at her Uncle Peter then glanced over at her Aunt Mary, today wearing a loose red knit dress with a pretty leather belt. The older woman was clearly not a fan of Alex's crazy plan, but she kept her lips pressed firmly together, her displeasure with the blank faced man sitting next to Jessica was obvious. Alex didn't care. He continued to ignore everyone but Peter.

She woke up alone after that horrible night and hadn't seen Alex again until earlier today when he'd given her a chin lift before leaving the room with a group of men she didn't recognize, all speaking in Russian. That had hurt. She thought they had something, but once again, he'd pulled back, and she was left with the wounded heart. Jesus, would she never learn?

Narrowing her eyes, she frowned at Alex, trying not to notice how handsome he was, how the familiar scent of his cologne soothed and aroused her. No, she needed to pay attention to one thing and one thing only. *She* would decide where she went and with whom. And most certainly, Mr. Alexandr Gorev did *not* get to tell her what to do. "You want to take me to Rome?"

"Yes." He replied like it was the most normal thing in the world, his attention now on his phone as he texted someone.

Irritated at his rude behavior, she turned her glare on him then regretted the action when it made her neck pinch. The day she'd gotten beat up, she hurt, but it was the days after, when pains in places she didn't even know she had surfaced, that she was really miserable. Days when she could have used a hug from a certain man she thought was into her. Or at the very least gave a shit enough to check on her the next day. He confused the hell out of her, and she didn't like it. And she certainly didn't want to have to deal with his bipolar ass in Rome of all places.

"I'm not going anywhere with you."

"You are going. End of discussion."

"Jessica," Peter said in a low voice, his face heavy and somber. "You are going."

"But..." She looked at him. "Why?"

"It's not safe for you here right now, lass. Until the authorities find out who did this, they could try it again. It's not likely, but I don't want to take any chances."

"You don't have to go with Alex," her aunt added. "We can send you anywhere you want."

Alex's anger prickled her skin in little stings, and when she turned back, she found him glaring at Mary. There were undercurrents here that she didn't understand, things she'd been left out of. She needed the truth, and she wanted it now.

Struggling to remain calm, she spoke in a measured tone. "Can I talk to Alex alone, please?"

Aunt Mary started to protest, but Uncle Peter stood and went over to his wife. "We'll give you a few minutes."

Jessica scarcely paid any attention to the door shutting as they left. Her gaze was focused on Alex, who was staring back at her. "What is going on? Have you lost your mind?"

"You are in danger. We make you safe."

Her nostrils flared, and she tried to remain calm as he glanced at his phone again. "I'm aware of that, but danger from who? Why am I being targeted?"

"Because you are loved."

"What?"

He tilted his head slightly. "Do you not want to go to Rome with me?"

"No, I don't."

For the first time since she'd entered the room, he focused entirely on her. "No?"

"No," she said in a firm voice.

"Then we will stay here, but it will put a strain on your uncle."

"What the hell are you talking about? God, for once can you just give me a clear answer?"

His gaze snapped with anger, as did his brisk voice. "You are target. And like any target, people will be tempted to take shots at you. If we stay in Ireland where is easy for them to get to you, there will be more attempts. When we go to Rome, is much safer. You will be untouchable."

The thought of having to live through another attempt on her life was more than she could bear right now. "Untouchable."

"*Prinsessa moya*, do not be scared. Trust me."

"I-I don't know. This is all happening so fast." Her lower lip trembled, and she gave him an imploring look. "Help me understand what's going on."

His lips softened, and he came over and kneeled before her chair, placing his warm palms on her thighs. It felt almost as if he was touching her bare skin. A warmth filled her belly, and her breath caught when he moved closer, forcing her thighs apart. Once his solid mass was between her legs, he slid his hands up slowly, glancing the sides of her breasts, until he'd ran his fingers into the thick hair at the back of her skull. He leaned closer, enveloping her in his scent, and rubbed his cheek against her uninjured one. Without even thinking about it, she wrapped her arms around his neck, holding him close and let out a long, heartfelt sigh.

"Is better?" he asked in a low voice while tenderly kissing her neck with soft rubs of his damp lips.

She nodded, unable to answer, relief filling her at being in his arms.

It was all kinds of better. Maybe the best.

His breath warmed her ear as he whispered, "I want to take you to Rome, not just to keep you safe, but to have you all to myself. Never in my life have I wanted a woman the way I want you. I am greedy for you in way you could not understand. I promise you that you will enjoy yourself. You will love the city, and it will love you. Come with me."

Trying to rally her brain, she pulled away a bit. He'd been a real jerk. "I don't understand. You vanished, and when I saw you earlier today, you totally ignored me. Those are not the actions of a man who desires me. You don't seem to be attracted to me at all. Then you say these nice things that make me think you really do want me."

"I have always wanted you, from the moment I saw you, but I had to make sure certain things were in place before I made you mine."

"What?"

He sighed, his warm breath ghosting over her. "We will discuss this later, in Rome."

"I don't want to discuss it later in Rome. If I'm even going with you, I want to discuss it now."

"Is not right time or place with your aunt and uncle hovering outside of door. I promise you, Jessica, that I will tell you, but not now. Trust that everything I do for you I do because you are special, important to me. Can you give me time to explain?"

He was being so nice, so charming and affectionate, that she found herself nodding. "I can give you time, but I want answers, Alex. I mean it."

"And you will get them." He stroked her inner thighs by her knees with his thumbs. "Does this mean you will come with me?"

Now it was her turn to rub her cheek against his, enjoying the tickle of his goatee. "I have always wanted to see the Roman ruins, and I've heard Italy is amazing. How long will I be there?"

He pulled back enough to place a delicate kiss on her lips. "A month or less, enough time for your uncle, I mean authorities, to find whoever targeted you."

It was impossible to say no when he looked at her with such warmth that it made her body light up and her brain turn to mush. "Okay, I'll come with you."

He grinned. "Okay."

"You know I'm placing a lot of trust in you, right?"

"I do. And you must know that your trust means much to me, is greatest gift. I will protect you. I will never let anyone harm you. From now on, Jessica, I devote myself to your happiness."

The sincerity in his voice undid her, and she drew in a watery breath and pressed her face to his neck as she whispered, "Thank you."

When Alex had said he was taking her to Rome, she had no idea he meant right that moment. He'd given her enough time to pack two suitcases, kiss her aunt and uncle goodbye, and whisked her off to the airport for a first class flight to Rome with Maks and Luka riding in coach. Oleg was home visiting with his family, but he would meet them in Rome, at some point, for a week to give one of the other guys a break.

The entire time they were in the airport, Alex had doted on her, holding her hand while she tried to ignore the people staring at her bruised face. It was better than it had been two days before, and she'd managed to conceal the discoloration a little bit with makeup, but thanks to her pale skin, it still was glaringly obvious. They'd stare at her face then give Alex a look that made her aware they thought he was the one who hurt her. By the fifth time this happened, she wanted to scream that he didn't abuse her, but Alex seemed oblivious to those narrow-eyed glares so it helped her keep her temper in check. She was usually so mellow and calm, but Alex seemed to magnify her emotions, and she found herself feeling very protective—and possessive—of him.

She was dressed in comfortable pants and a cute, navy top with lacy, capped sleeves and a high neckline, while he wore his usual suit, deep gray this time, along with a silver and navy tie that complimented her top. She would have thought it was a coincidence, but he'd gotten dressed after he'd seen what she was going to wear. It's like he wanted them to match.

Odd man.

Freshly shaved, he was in full on badass mode, and she found it interesting the way people seemed to avoid meeting his eyes. Then again, the women were too busy ogling all that was Alex in a suit to notice he had eyes. There was something about a dangerously sexy, well dressed man that flat out did it for her. So contained and in control, yet she knew the barely civilized man who hid below the public mask he wore. He rubbed his thumb gently on her hand as they moved through the crowd, his touch soothing her while he constantly scanned the busy crowd. She took that opportunity to study his face, and her heart fluttered. Just looking at him made her happy, and the fact that he seemed equally pleased to have her on his arm was almost surreal.

During their flight, they kept the talk light and easy, but there was a sexual tension building between them she couldn't miss. His every touch seemed to burn along her skin, and soon, she found herself completely under his control, relaxing as he took charge of her every need. Yeah, his bossiness with other people, like the poor flight attendant who'd annoyed him in some way, was irritating, but she couldn't get too mad since it was on her behalf.

Plus, in an odd way he, he made her feel safe. Cherished. It was in the way he watched her, how he paid attention to her silent moods, how he took care of her, and how he used any excuse to touch her. At all times, he made sure that she was comfortable, that she had everything she could possibly need. She wasn't used to a man fussing over her like this, and his attention was a soothing balm to her frazzled nerves.

Being spoiled was nice, and not something she'd ever experienced. Her parents had loved her to death, but they'd been financially conservative. She'd had to work on the farm for an allowance or get a job whenever she wanted something that her parents viewed as unnecessary while she was growing up. Like her senior year spring break trip to Cancun. Waitressing all those tables had provided enough money for her to have a good time, and her mother slipped her an extra two hundred dollars before she'd left along with a box of condoms, which made Jessica want to crawl beneath her bed and die as her mom lectured her on safe sex.

She let that memory play out, smiling a little bit as she remembered her dad also slipped her two hundred dollars, and told her not to get arrested because he would not be happy to have to fly down to Mexico to bail her out. In fact, he just might leave her there. He'd been smiling when he said it, but she wasn't entirely sure he was joking.

Alex shifted next to her as he took his jacket off, the scent of his cologne teasing her. Because they were in first class, the flight attendant was there almost instantly, taking his jacket and hanging it up before offering them a blanket in a low voice. Their flight was a late night one, and in the subdued atmosphere of the plane, she fell asleep on Alex's shoulder not long after their meal. When she woke up

181

a few hours later, they were in Rome, and when Alex led her out of the airport, a thrill raced through her. Everyone around them was speaking Italian, and she couldn't help but marvel at the fact that she was in Italy, of all places, with Alexandr Gorev, of all people.

As soon as they stepped out of the airport, she had to brace herself. The bright light pierced her eyes, and a wave of noise from the early morning rush of beeping cars, whistles, and people shouting hit her like a smack in the face, waking her fully as the rising sun warmed her skin. Her mouth was dry and her eyes gritty, but she couldn't help her huge smile as she got her bearings. However she'd gotten here, she was in Italy now, with an amazingly awesome man and a pack of scary ass bodyguards. When Alex smiled down at her, she marveled about how life had certainly changed in the last couple months. Back in Iowa, she never imagined anything like this could actually happen to her. She was so normal, so average, just another college girl whose greatest aspiration had been to figure out her major. And she never would have imagined that a man like Alexandr Gorev existed, let alone seemed to care deeply for her.

Alex noticed her watching him and leaned down to give her another soft kiss. "Why you smile?"

"How could I not? I'm in motherfucking Rome! This is awesome!"

She must have said that louder than she intended because a few people within hearing distance chuckled while an elegantly dressed woman curled her lip in distaste.

Turning away from that woman, she allowed Alex to guide her to a cream-colored Jaguar sedan that had pulled up to the curb.

A handsome driver in a black suit stepped out of the car and held the door open for her, smiling and speaking to Alex in rapid Italian. To her shock, Alex responded in what sounded to her like perfect Italian, and she stared up at him. He noticed her staring and frowned slightly.

"What is wrong?"

"You speak Italian?"

His lips twitched in a smile, and his gaze warmed. "Yes, along with French and German. Is good to know different languages for conducting business."

"Wow."

He cupped her cheek for a moment, then placed a kiss on her forehead, his goatee tickling her. "Get in the car, *prinsessa moya*. I want to check into our hotel, try to get some sleep, then show you Rome."

"Where are we staying?"

"The Hotel Hassler. Very exclusive, very beautiful. But if you do not like it, we will stay somewhere else."

Laughing, she slid into the luxury car and turned to Alex when he sat next to her. "I'm sure it will be wonderful."

The door closed, and he took her hand in his again, studying her as the driver pulled out into the busy traffic leaving the airport. He rubbed his thumb over the back of her hand, his lips barely moved when he spoke. "Jessica, I am making my intentions known to you."

"What?"

When he looked up, his gaze was intense and his expression stern and unforgiving. "I want you as my woman, Jessica. I am serious about you. More serious than I think you know."

"Your woman, what does that mean?"

He hesitated. "It means I want to make you mine in all ways."

"You mean like date me?"

"That, and more."

"More?"

"Everything."

"Oh." She leaned her head against the soft leather seat and looked at him. "Why?"

His eyes widened, the light catching the silver and making them gleam. "What you mean, why?"

"Alex, you don't date, you said so yourself. And to be honest, I wasn't really sure you would ever see me as more than a friend. I mean is that what we're doing now, being more than friends?"

Instead of being angry, he smiled. "You have always been more than a friend, Jessica. From the moment we met, I felt a connection with you like nothing I have ever experienced. I have never wanted to simply spend time with a woman. To always have her around me, to care about her every need. The careful rules of how I must live my life never applied to you. Do you not feel this between us? How powerful it is?"

Taken aback by his sincerity, she nodded then ran her fingertips down his cheek. "I know I've never met anyone like you before, Alex. You're not the man I first thought you were."

"For you, I am different." He held her hand and brought her fingertips to his lips, kissing them and tickling her with the soft brush of his facial hair. "You are only person that gets this part of me. To most, I am someone to be feared, but you...you, my *prinsessa* were never afraid."

"You intimidated me and made me nervous, pissed me off, but,"—grinning, she leaned forward and gave him a soft kiss on his lips just because she could—"I was never afraid of you."

He went to touch her cheek and brushed her bruise, making her flinch.

Hissing, he jerked back like he was the one who

184

had been struck. "Did I hurt you?"

Hating that the tender moment between them had been broken, she shook her head. "I'm okay."

He didn't say anything for a bit, only stared pensively out the window.

In an effort to lighten the mood, she laced her fingers with his. "So Peter mentioned that you have to do some work while you're here. Anything fun?"

His cold gaze snapped to hers, and she blinked hard at the darkness she saw there. "What I do is none of your business, Jessica."

"Um-I'm sorry...I didn't...that is...never mind." She tried to slip her hand away, but he wouldn't let her go.

With a sigh, he shook his head. "No, is I who am sorry. I work with some dangerous people, and I do not want you caught up in their mess."

"Dangerous people?" She frowned, nodding to herself. "I guess that makes sense. I mean, why would they hire a bodyguard service if they weren't in any kind of danger?"

His expression closed down again, and he didn't respond.

As they drove into the city of Rome itself, she forgot about Alex's odd mood and stared through the tinted windows of the Jaguar, and watched the city come alive as the sun rose higher in the sky. The buildings weren't massively tall, but they were packed together. Some districts looked old enough to have been around in the days of the Caesars, while others were as modern as could be. It was so different from America and had an even older feel than Dublin. Some of the side roads they passed were narrow to the point where she doubted even one of the tiny, compact European cars could go down them, and there were mopeds everywhere. It was pure vehicular chaos, and she was so happy she didn't have to try to navigate these crowded streets.

They passed monuments, stores, and cafes everywhere, each space capturing her attention as she made mental notes to come back here at some point. And the fountains, she'd never seen so many fountains situated in gorgeous plazas in one place. Each was unique, and they added an elegant charm to the city unlike anything she'd ever experienced. Alex gave her a bemused, indulgent smile as he watched her twist and turn in her seat to get a better view of the things they passed.

Jessica had inherited a sizable amount of money from her birth mother that Peter had given her— something about her mother's share of some business stocks—and she wouldn't mind spending some of it on the dazzling clothes she saw in the windows of some of the shops. It would certainly help her blend in with the endless parade of stylish, chic women who strolled through the city with such confidence. Goodness, it was like she'd been transported to the land of beautiful people.

Their car pulled up to a curb, and the driver got out then opened her door in a smooth, practiced move. As he helped Jessica out, her earlier excitement returned. She was practically bouncing at Alex's side while he talked with the driver. Once he was finished, he smiled down at her and held out his hand. She immediately wound her fingers through his, trying to look everywhere at once and soak up the beauty of this place.

Giving her knuckles a kiss, his goatee tickled her skin. "You like?"

"Oh, Alex, I love!" She gave him an impulsive hug, laughing when he grunted at how hard she squeezed him in her excitement.

They stood at the top of a huge set of old, marble stairs that led down to a plaza below with what looked like a big, very old fountain in the center. Behind them stood a tall, creamy beige building with some beautiful towers, and there was a large, dark stone obelisk. The tourists were easy to spot, not only because of their posing and picture taking, but because they were dressed far more casually than the residents of Rome. It made her self-consciously look down at her own outfit of leggings with black ballet flats and wish she'd dressed up a little more.

Glancing around from beneath her lashes, she released Alex when she noticed people watching them, and she hoped Alex wasn't ashamed of her lack of style and sophistication.

Unlike Jessica, he blended right in with the stylish crowd in his perfectly cut suit and more than one woman gave him a lingering look. Jessica couldn't blame them for eating up the eye-candy, but it did send a niggle of doubt through her that she would be able to keep Alex's attention. She couldn't help but feel like he'd soon realize he'd made a mistake, that she wasn't anything special at all.

Shit, she was borrowing trouble, as her mom liked to say, and she needed to calm down, go with the flow and all of that. As if she'd summoned her, Jessica's mother spoke in her head, repeating the same words she'd told Jessica on her first day of high school. It was a Dr. Seuss quotation, but it stuck with her, and she could almost feel her mom's hands on her shoulders, squeezing gently.

Be who you are and say what you feel, because those who mind don't matter and those who matter don't mind.

She turned her face to the sun, refusing to cry on such a beautiful day, in such a beautiful place, with such a beautiful man.

Tugging her hand, Alex broke her melancholy thoughts and began walking toward a building with

187

the words 'Hotel Hassler' on the roof in giant letters. A steady stream of obviously wealthy people walked in and out of the front of the hotel, and she tried to adopt their urbane, slightly bored expression. She didn't want these refined people to think she was some dumb tourist…even though she was. Déjà vu struck her, and she paused, glancing around her while she tried to figure out this odd feeling like she'd been here before. Something about the area she was in seemed familiar, and she slowed further, looking behind her. A memory tickled at her, and she stopped all together, trying to figure out why she knew those stairs.

Alex looked down at her. "What is it?"

"That place back there looks familiar." She studied the creamy building with the two towers, then the steps, then moved a couple paces closer to the street, and looked again. "Oh, my God! It's the Spanish Steps from *Roman Holiday*!"

"What is that?"

"It's an old American movie with Audrey Hepburn. My grandparents used to love classic movies, and *Roman Holiday* was one of their favorites. Whenever I slept over at their house, we'd always have movie night, and I've seen it at least a half dozen times."

"Would you like me to bring them here?"

"What?"

"Your grandparents. If it would make you happy, I will bring them to Rome with us someday."

She blinked back tears, her throat suddenly thick at the kindness of his gesture. "Thank you, but they passed away when I was in junior high. I'm sure they're watching me right now with my mom and dad, totally jealous. Actually, no, they're probably not jealous. They probably pulled some strings in heaven to get me here…with you."

The rare public smile he gave her was gentle, and he looped an arm around her waist and pulled her to his hard body. "I am glad you like."

"No, I don't like. I love." She beamed up at him, enjoying how the tension around his mouth relaxed. "Thank you."

He jerked his head up abruptly, and his grip pinned her to his side. Thrown off by his odd response, she looked around, but didn't see anything that would have set him off. Her heart raced, but she only saw people going about their business on a beautiful and unexpectedly warm December morning. Nothing nefarious to her untrained eyes, but maybe he saw something she didn't.

When he growled and pulled her closer, she gave him a poke in the ribs. "Alex, what's going on?"

"Fucking paparazzi," he muttered then turned them both and began to walk briskly to the hotel.

She went to look over her shoulder, but Alex held her tighter. "No, give them no attention."

"Are they going to hurt us?"

"No, but our picture may now be in gossip magazines."

"Gossip magazines? Why would they want a picture of me in a magazine?"

He cast her a sideways glance. "Is not you, is me."

"Okay, why the hell would they want a picture of you in a gossip magazine?"

"I am...a well-known businessman back home. My father is even more well-known."

"I thought you ran a security company?"

"I do, among other things. I will discuss with you later. Now is not time. Do not look back, Jessica. Keep walking. Maks is taking care of problem. Do not worry. Is merely...what is word...a minor irritation."

She wanted to ask him what the hell he was

talking about, but they were at the entrance to the Hotel Hassler, and she slowed down to take in the magnificent building with its enormous black wrought iron lamps. The elegant marble slab over the entrance with the words 'Hassler Villa Medici' embossed in gold gleamed in the sunlight. It was impressive, and she tried to smooth down her hair with her free hand while Alex led them inside through the spinning glass door. Once they were in the foyer, she took a couple steps and stopped to take in the huge space filled with marble columns, gold-gilded lights, and gorgeous classic furniture set against a rich red carpet. A few people meandered around, all the men wearing slacks and button down shirts, some in full suits, and the women looking as crisp and posh as could be.

In the comfortable ballet flats that she wore for traveling and discount rack shirt she was pretty sure she stood out like a sore thumb. Alex, on the other hand, seemed like he belonged here. While he led them across the lobby to the front desk, she tried to keep from fidgeting beneath the notice they'd drawn. A beautiful blonde woman working the desk smiled at them, but kept most of her attention on Alex after giving Jessica a brief glance. She said something in Italian, calling him by his first name, and he chuckled then replied in Italian. The woman's demeanor was obviously flirtatious, all batting eyes and pouty lips, and Jessica hated how her possessiveness flared to life.

Jealousy tightened her stomach as the woman outright ignored her now, practically fawning over Alex, who seemed to be oblivious. After a few moments of conversation with the woman, he looked down at Jessica and said in English, "This is my woman, Jessica. She is to have whatever she desires. If she wants a Ferrari, you will get it for her in the color she desires. Open an unlimited account for her in my name for the hotel shops and restaurant. My personal shopper will be arriving tomorrow, but I want something sent up from the boutique for her so we can go out for dinner tonight. Something in purple, I think, that will show off her beautiful body. And you will speak English so she understands."

The hotel worker's smile remained professional, but it held none of the warmth it had a few minutes ago, and her voice was stiff when she replied in lightly accented English, "Of course, Mr. Gorev. You are in the penthouse suite. If you need anything at all, please contact your usual personal concierge,"—her blue eyes flicked to Jessica in a slightly catty way then back to Alex—"Isabella."

Alex's hand holding hers flexed, and he said something in rapid-fire Italian. The woman paled, then nodded, and wrote something down. When she looked up again, her smile was definitely strained, and her face pasty beneath her makeup. "My mistake. Your personal concierge is Piero, and he will be happy to assist you with anything you need. Would you like him to take you to your room?"

"I know way," Alex said in a cold voice, and the woman blanched further.

"Of course. Have a wonderful stay."

After taking the key cards, Alex led Jessica to a bank of elevators and pressed the button. Normally, she would have been gaping at their surroundings, but her attention was solely on Alex, trying to read him. His reaction to this Isabella and the weighted looks the blonde had given him made her take notice. "Alex, who is Isabella?"

"No one important."

He didn't even look at her as he said that or when they were in the elevator and he pressed the button for their floor after sliding in his key card.

Suspicious.

She waited until the elevator had started up before trying again. "Did you fuck her?"

Okay, that wasn't quite as smooth as she wanted.

His shoulders tightened, and she knew the answer even before he spoke. "Yes, was convenient."

Her skin heated with irritation, and she tried to shake his hand off. "Convenient?"

Gripping her hand tighter, he looked over at her, and she couldn't decipher his expression. "Convenient."

Her temper, fueled by jealousy, flared. "Will she be convenient while you're here with me? I mean I understand how things are between us..."

His gaze turned downright pissed as he growled out, "And what is it you understand?"

"That..." She looked away, forcing her gaze to remain on the buttons of the elevator. "That we're both adults and know what this situation is."

"And what, *prinsessa moya*, is situation?"

There was a dangerous purr to his voice now, and she swallowed, gathering her courage and steeling her heart before she whispered, "Convenient."

At that moment, thank God, the door opened, and she practically jumped out of the enclosed space. She'd only had a chance to glance around the elegant hallway with four doors before Alex had her body pressed facing against the wall. He said something in Russian before growling and thrusting his hard cock against her. His big frame totally surrounded her, and a shiver raced down her spine to her pelvis as he ground his thick erection against her ass. A gasp escaped her before she could stop it, and her desire to have him deep inside of her flared to life, even as she grew pissed at the way he was manhandling her. Pleasure flooded her, and she relished his possessive,

192

dominant touch.

He whispered into her ear, "You are not convenient. You actually make life difficult. Having you here is going to draw attention. I am making public statement with you at my side."

"A public statement? What kind of public statement?" Her voice came out soft and husky. The brush of his lips against the back of her ear made her panties damp.

"That you, Jessica Venture, are my woman. *Mine*. And I protect what is mine."

The anger in his tone helped her mind clear from the lust-induced fog he'd woven around her. "Does that make you mad?"

"What?"

"Well," she sucked in a breath and said in a shaky voice, "you sounded angry."

Abruptly, he softened behind her, his breath warming her neck. "*Nyet*, I not mad at you. I cherish you. Is world that would try to take you from me that I am mad at."

He allowed her to turn in his arms, backing up just the slightest bit so she could look at him, their hips still pressed together. The muscles in his jaw flexed, and restrained desire rolled off of him, tingling over her sensitive skin. Never had a man looked at her like this, as though he was going to eat her alive or fuck her to death. Or both. The urge to rub up against him, to have him sink into her, made her wild for him. She stared into his eyes while dirty, naughty thoughts raced through her. They were in a public hallway. True, there were only four doors, but someone could come out at any moment. They might catch her while she stroked Alex's cock, milking him into a hard, fast orgasm.

She actually watched his eyes darken, going from mist to gunmetal gray, his pupils expanding while his lips softened.

"What are you thinking about, *prinsessa moya*? What has you so flushed, has made your nipples hard, your *pizda* soft and wet? I can smell your arousal, and it makes me hungry. Such a sensitive"— he rubbed his cock along her cloth-covered sex, making her moan deep in her throat—"pussy. I cannot wait to have my cock in you. You do not know how many times I stroked myself thinking about you, how many times I dreamed of fucking you."

Feeling incredibly bold, and aroused, and in need of his touch, she slowly licked her lower lip, willing him to see how badly she needed him. "Fuck me. Right here, right now."

She'd half expected him to argue, but instead, he dropped to his knees then spread her legs apart with his firm grip. Without thought, she followed his silent demands and tilted her pelvis to his face. He gave a dirty chuckle, then leaned in, and took a deep inhalation of her sex. His scenting her was so dirty, yet erotic, that she couldn't help but squirm with need. She'd never been with someone as sexual as Alex. It had crossed her mind that she might be some kind of freak for liking the things she did, that she'd never find a man willing to indulge her, but Alex quickly disabused her of that notion. If she was a freak, he was an outright pervert and didn't give a fuck who saw them.

She knew this because he muttered it against her pussy before tearing out the crotch of her leggings with his teeth. That only left her sex covered by her white, silk thong, and he let out a long groan, sliding his finger beneath her panties and up to her sopping wet core. Instead of finger fucking her, he only muttered 'soaked' before standing. Without preamble, he started to unzip his pants, and she reached for him, eager to help him get his beautiful cock out and fuck her. When he took a condom from his suit pocket, she could only pant, stroking him as best she could. He was nice and thick and so hard it almost felt like she was holding warm stone in her hands.

An amazing, big, fat cock for her to fuck herself on.

It didn't dawn on her that she'd said that aloud until Alex swore and fumbled with the condom. "I see I have filthy girl on my hands. Very, very filthy."

"You do," she whispered without shame, knowing he meant it as a compliment.

Their gazes met, and he easily picked her up, urging her to wrap her legs around his waist. The lighting in the hallway wasn't bright, but it was more than enough to see by. Having sex like this, out in the open, so exposed, made her pulse race, but it was the fact that she was doing this with Alex that made it extraordinary. He was her friend, her confidant, and now he was going to be her lover. The hallway was silent except for their rapid breathing, and she let out a soft moan of need as he rubbed his erection against her aching clit.

"For so long I have wanted you, sweet girl."

Going crazy with the need to have him inside, she nipped his lower lip. "Then fuck me."

Without any urging, she reached between them and guided him to her entrance. He held her poised there, the tip of his cock pushing slightly into her, just enough to give her the tease of being filled by him. She tried to wiggle down, but he held her tight without any strain. His muscles bulged as he kept tormenting her, driving her wild. Sweat beaded on his brow, and his thick cock jerked.

"You are mine, Jessica. Say it."

She met his gaze full on, willing him to know she meant it as she whispered, "I'm yours."

Her back arched and a soft scream escaped her as he slid in, pushing his way past her clenching muscles, forcing her body to take him.

"Fuck," Alex groaned as he continued to press in. "You will make me come too soon if you do not relax. Your pussy is too good, and it has been too long since I last had sex."

Those words danced on the edge of her mind, and she almost snapped at him for talking about fucking another woman while he was deep inside of her, but he chose that moment to slam the last few inches in and fill her with his rock-hard shaft. He was stretching her almost beyond her limit, and her pussy stung a little bit. His lips met hers in a gentle kiss, his tongue teasing her, his cock flexing inside of her when she bit his lower lip. Tears prickled her eyes, but she buried her face against his neck and willed them back, overwhelmed by him in the best possible way.

All discomfort fled when he began to gently rock into her, his position grinding her sensitive clit with his stroke. Her hands relaxed, nails no longer digging into his suit covered shoulders. Instead, she laced her fingers through his hair and clung to him as he kissed her harder, his intensity matching the stronger thrusts of his hips. Their panting breaths and moans filled the quiet space around them, and as she imagined the door to the elevator opening and people catching them, her body tensed while her orgasm tightened her belly. A moment later, she was coming, hard, and Alex let out an almost surprised groan, his body jerking against hers while he buried his face into her neck.

Alex kept her pressed against the wall, still connected as he shuddered. "Your pussy is too good, too perfect. I cannot hold back when you grip me like that."

He twitched inside of her, and she reflexively squeezed him with her internal muscles, making him jolt. With her heart still thundering and her body crushed against his, she began to rain kisses over his face. She liked the way he stilled and closed his eyes, his expression almost reverent. She smiled happily, affectionately nibbling his ear before whispering, "Hi, Alex," followed by a giggle.

He pulled back enough to look at her with a gentle smile and kissed each of her eyelids. "Hello, my Jessica."

It surprised her that Alex was a cuddler, but he proceeded to nuzzle and pet her, making her feel...well...cherished.

All too soon he sighed, gently helping her off his still erect dick. He took the used condom off and secured it before wrapping it up in a linen handkerchief in his suit pocket. He tended himself while she straightened her clothes as best she could. A quick glance down confirmed her fear that the crotch of her pants had been torn beyond repair and barely hanging on.

"Crap, I hope our room is nearby."

"It is." He winked and gave her a lecherous grin. "Your pussy gets such a pretty, rose red when you are well-fucked."

A flush suffused her cheeks, something that shouldn't have been possible after their uninhibited, kinky, totally amazing sex, but she was satisfied for the moment, and her urge to get out of the hallway grew. "Room, please?"

He slipped off his suit jacket, draping it around her shoulders. It fell to just below her butt, and she hoped it covered her enough for the walk down the hall. Thankfully, Alex didn't dawdle, and he stopped at the door at the end of the hall, flanked on either side by beautiful, wood tables and enormous

197

arrangements of real flowers in giant, crystal vases. She didn't have time to admire this, because Alex had the door to the suite open, and a familiar, masculine laugh filled the air.

Then Dimitri said, "Is good to see Jessica is a true redhead."

Chapter Thirteen

Alex sighed as Jessica screeched then frantically tugged his jacket down, trying to hide behind his back. Glaring at a laughing Dimitri sprawled out on the elegant dark cinnamon, damask-covered sofa across the large room, Alex snarled out in Russian, "Shut the fuck up. You're embarrassing her."

Still laughing, Dimitri stood up and tugged a folded blanket from the end of the couch then tossed it to Alex. "Sorry, sorry. I was not expecting to see lovely red curls when she walked through door. Lucky bastard."

"I know," Alex said while trying to hide a smug grin then switched to Russian while Jessica glared around his shoulder at his brother, adorable in her embarrassment. "What are you doing here?"

Dimitri's smile disappeared. "Father sent me."

"Why? Does he know about Jessica?"

"Yes, but I convinced him you are playing a complicated political game to strengthen the *Bratva* by seducing her."

"Did he believe you?"

"Yes. It helped that Oleg said the same thing. Father might believe I am still a stupid young man, but he trusts Oleg, and it is no secret Peter and Mary adore their new-found niece. Father was also pleased with the forged documents you sent. He said they were so good they could 'fool a doctor into believing a whore was a virgin'. "

"Charming as ever."

Alex relaxed slightly. His father had given him the task of using the new forgery skills Peter had taught him to make some documents that would, hopefully, get a few of their men into the United States without being caught. Jessica shifted next to him, clearly trying to pull down his jacket to hide as much of her as possible. She smelled like sex, and him. It was an aphrodisiac he wanted to explore by burying his face between her slim thighs. Her pussy was so soft and sweet against his mouth and on his tongue.

"Give me that." Jessica snatched the blanket from his hands. Her cheeks were bright red as she clearly struggled to hold onto her dignity while wrapping the blanket around her waist. "Where's our room?"

She happened to glance down and caught his erection pressing against his pants. Since he was not a small man, it was rather obvious. Her breath came out in a gasp, and her eyes grew wide. He'd ridden her hard, and she was probably a bit tender. It would take some effort, but he would have to take things slow with her. They had the rest of their lives to explore each other.

Even knowing that, he still he wanted to bury himself in her right now as she stared at him with lust in her beautiful blue eyes.

"Come," Dimitri snickered. "I will show you to your room so you may get dressed before Alex defiles you in front of me without offering to share. Greedy bastard."

She glanced up at him with shocked laughter in her eyes, and Alex curved his arm around her in a possessive manner. He wanted to punch his brother in the face, but he was also pleased to see Dimitri put her at ease. "Is not necessary. I will show her."

Dimitri smoothed his black slacks, the gold bracelet on his wrist glinting in the light. "You have some business associates waiting for you in the guest suite, Laz Stefano and his wife."

It took some effort to ease the sudden tensing of his body. "I wasn't expecting him so soon."

Shrugging, Dimitri winked at Jessica. "Laz is business associate and old friend of your uncle Peter. It is not surprising he would want to meet you. His wife is American, interesting woman. She is smart. I think you will like."

He gave Jessica a quick kiss, regretting he couldn't take her to their room and fuck her properly until they both passed out. "Go, get changed. There is wardrobe for you in there. The jewelry is in the safe. Dimitri will help you pick out something appropriate to wear."

"Appropriate?"

"You are about to meet the Mayor of Rome and his wife."

She paled. "Seriously?"

Dimitri shook his head and slung an arm over her shoulders while she scowled at him. "Is no big deal. They nice people, and Melanie, Mayor's wife, will love you."

Alex had to hold back a laugh. Melanie was a gorgeous blonde in her late thirties who had a taste for willowy young women, especially redheads. He would have to make sure he mentioned to Laz and Melanie that Jessica was very, very new to the scene and to not scare her. All he needed was for Melanie to do shots with Jessica and then attempt to go down on his woman. It might be more than Jessica could handle, and the last thing he wanted to do was make her apprehensive about sex. Then again, Jessica could be far wilder than he gave her credit for. He was certain she kept that explosive passion bottled up inside, a gift just for him to unwrap and savor.

He glared at his brother. "Do not upset her."

The innocent look Dimitri gave him was so out of character that Jessica giggled while his brother protested with his hands up. "I am nothing but gentleman."

Jessica snorted. "Come on. Help me find something to wear so I can meet the Mayor of Rome. Holy shit balls, my life is crazy."

Walking away with Jessica, Dimitri looked down at her with a smile. "Crazy bad or crazy good?"

She glanced back over her shoulder at Alex for a long moment and replied, "Crazy good."

He loved the way her face glowed with happiness when she said that.

Alex waited until they'd entered the master bedroom of the suite before he went into the sitting room and watched Laz speaking quietly with Melanie over by the window looking out over Rome. The leggy blonde was dressed in a stylish pale blue suit that went well with her fashionable tan and her white, dangerously high heels. Wearing a tasteful amount of expensive diamonds, she was the epitome of elegant grace. Her husband, Laz, wore his customary black suit, but his red tie had hints of the blue in Melanie's dress. Together, they presented a power couple in every sense of the word, a Master and his Switch who were supremely self-confident and comfortable with who they were.

Laz approached him first, giving his customary hug of greeting. Melanie followed a moment later, softly kissing both of his cheeks, and he noted a hint of her floral perfume. She stepped back and linked her arm through her husband's.

Smiling at him warmly, she said, "Alex, it is always a great pleasure to see you."

Since she was an American, her Italian was accented, but it had much improved since he'd seen her last year. "It is always a pleasure to return to Rome."

"You've been away for far too long. What? I have

to be abducted for you to come visit?"

Sighing, he shook his head and laughed. She had him there. Last time he'd seen Melanie was after he rescued her from her kidnapper. Thankfully, the thug hadn't harmed Melanie, probably because her feminine charms were honed to a razor edge, but she'd been a terrified mess when Alex had found her bound and gagged in a dusty, hot attic.

"I have been busy."

"So I heard from Dimitri. Jessica, right? He adores her, says you're happier with her than he's ever seen you."

"He also said she is young," Laz added with a wry smile on his handsome, angular face. "Younger than him and very much the innocent. Is this true?"

"Why?"

With a laugh, Melanie leaned over and patted Alex's cheek. "So suspicious, relax."

Laz slid his arm around his wife's waist, fitting her neatly into his side while she spoke to Alex. "We wanted to personally invite you to a private party we are throwing this weekend, but didn't know if your woman would be interested. A hunt, but not a big one. Something smaller, a little more intimate. Would it be something that Jessica would like to attend? If not, we can certainly have dinner at our vineyard instead like nice, normal, vanilla people. She'd love it. Very romantic."

Alex's lips twitched as he imagined taking his unexpectedly bold, adventurous woman to one of the Stefano's infamous BDSM hunts. If someone had asked him six months ago, hell, just two months ago, if Jessica was anything but straight vanilla he'd have laughed. Her innocence had him fooled. To his delight, he discovered that behind those innocent, blue eyes was a mind filled with dirty thoughts. Her enthusiasm surprised him as well. He was used to more...cultured lovers, women who were as highly trained in the arts of pleasure and companionship as the courtesans of old, and were just as cynical.

Jessica, on the other hand, had a raw passion that fit him perfectly. She had a hunger for sex equal to his, and he looked forward to teaching her new things, protecting her, taking care of her every need so she could live a life of pure happiness. This time in Rome, these stolen days away from the chaos of his life, were his gift to her. It was unavoidable that he would have to work at some point, but the majority of his time was going to be spent with his woman, and the idea made him happier than he'd been in a long time.

"Alex?" Laz was amused.

Trying to hide his surprise at being caught daydreaming like a fucking woman, he straightened his back and nodded to Melanie. "I believe she would greatly enjoy the hunt."

"This will be so much fun." Melanie grinned and enthusiasm sparkled in her eyes. "Is she a submissive?"

"I do not know for certain, but I believe she leans that way. She is just beginning to embrace her sexuality."

"For all intents and purposes, an innocent." Laz shook his head and chuckled. "And you're taking her to one of our hunts. I hope, for your sake my friend, that she is made of stern stuff."

"My Jessica is a surprisingly adventurous woman, not shy of her pleasure, just young. Very young."

"How young?" Melanie frowned at him.

"She is legal, twenty years old, but you will see when you meet her. She was raised on a farm in Iowa. In...what did she call it?...yes, 'fly over' country. Small town with strict parents. She has been sheltered but is eager to explore. She enjoys exhibitionism."

Whistling, Melanie crossed her arms. "Yeah, I know exactly the kind of sweet country girl you're talking about. One of my roommates in college was from Kansas, a state nearby, and she went wild once she got out of her parents' home. If Jessica is anything like my friend, and she's kinky, no wonder you're tied in knots. A woman like that is hard to resist."

"Some of us prefer more...experienced women," Laz said to his wife in a low, husky voice.

"And some of us enjoy teaching a woman what her body can do," Alex added while Melanie laughed softly.

"Dimitri said she's a redhead, right? Catrin is going to love her." Melanie sighed then absently smoothed the lapels of her husband's jacket. "Poor Nico, he's going to have his hands full with that one. She's a spitfire when she's angry."

Excitement at the thought of his close friends meeting Jessica filled him. He'd decided long ago how he was going to ease Jessica into his world, and he thought that Rome would be a good place to start. She was here on a vacation of sorts, and vacations generally put people into better moods, so it would be the perfect time for her to meet his inner circle. He knew Ivan was already here—they texted each other earlier—and made plans to get together so he could meet Jessica.

He met Laz's amused dark eyes. "Dimitri mentioned something about them coming, but I did not know Catrin and Nico were already here."

"Yes. We believe he's going to propose to her. Dimitri came as Nico's moral support."

His jaw clenched, and he tried to keep from being offended about not knowing any of this. "I see."

Dimitri chose that moment to enter the room.

"Jessica is getting ready and will join us soon."

Fighting for calm, Alex turned to face his brother, watching the bright smile die on his face as he read Alex's expression. "Nico is getting engaged? Why didn't he tell me?"

Holding up his hands, Dimitri shook his head. "Hopefully. Don't jinx it. It's not a sure thing. You know how Catrin is, so paranoid, so hard for her to trust. He asked that I keep it quiet so if he gets turned down, he won't have to be humiliated in front of everyone. Besides, he knows how busy you've been."

Melanie smiled, ignorant of the guilt hitting Alex that he'd been so involved in his own world he'd ignored his friends. "We will make sure he has everything he needs to win her hand. No one can resist love in Rome."

Right before Dimitri spoke, he knew his brother was going to say something that would piss him off. Dimitri had that devilish gleam in his eyes that meant nothing but trouble. Sure enough, when he opened his mouth Alex wanted to choke him.

"I would have thought you would be in a better mood considering you screwed Jessica's brains out in the hallway. You're welcome, by the way, you lucky bastard. Her body is amazing. Those long, long legs were made to be wrapped around a man."

"Shut up," Alex muttered, though he agreed, Jessica's body was amazing.

While Alex had been fucking his woman, Dimitri had come out of their suite, leered at them, and made some obscene gestures, then let Alex know he was keeping the hallway private.

Melanie laughed then strolled over to her husband's side, slipping her arm into his. "Mmm, I think I like this girl. She sounds fun."

With a considering look on his handsome face, Laz studied his wife then murmured, "Interested?"

206

A woman cleared her throat behind him and Alex turned to find his woman in a lovely, black, jersey dress that hugged her hips then flowed out to mid-thigh. Her hair was swept back and held in place with a thin, cream leather headband that matched her heels. The shoes weren't terribly tall, but Jessica's legs were so gorgeous that the heels made her look spectacular. The dress left a great deal of the expanse of her creamy thighs bare, and he wanted to lick that sweet skin. He remembered how smooth she was beneath his touch, and it took a great deal of effort to force his gaze higher.

The top was sleeveless, and the collar was made up of fishnet and dipped low in the front, revealing a hint of cleavage, baring the lightly freckled skin between her obviously braless breasts. A little bit of naughty in all that elegant class. Then his eyes landed on the site of her bruise, covered up with makeup so it wasn't quite as noticeable, but still a dark shadow on her cheek and temple. She fidgeted a bit beneath his gaze, and his protective instincts, always so close to the surface around her, flared to life, demanding he relieve her of her unease. He wanted her to know they were all staring at her because she was exquisite to look at, and she should be proud of her beauty.

When he met her tilted blue eyes, he smiled at how anxious she was, though she was trying to hide it. Her gaze was wide and kept darting around the room. When she saw Dimitri, she smiled, her loveliness blinding him, and she gave his brother a cute little wave.

Laz blinked, then cleared his throat, and held out his hand, approaching Jessica slowly. "Miss Venture, it is so nice to meet you. My name is Laz, and this is my wife, Melanie. We are old friends of your aunt and uncle, and we are pleased to meet you."

"It's nice to meet you as well, sir."

Jessica smiled and shook their hands, freezing a bit when Melanie tugged her into a hug and kissed both of her cheeks. When she pulled back, her smile turned mischievous while Jessica blushed a soft pink. Melanie gave Jessica a blatant come hither look that made Jessica flush harder, now a light red from her chest to her eyebrows.

Looking at Alex, Melanie said in Italian, "Very pretty, and you are a lucky, lucky man."

He offered Jessica his hand, and she clung to it right away. The strength of her grip surprised him, and he realized meeting people like the Mayor of Rome and his wife might be a bit out of her comfort zone. He should have paid better attention. Taking care of her was his priority now.

With this in mind, he gave Melanie an arched brow, and she immediately started a conversation with Dimitri in Italian on the other side of the room and dragged her husband along. Once they were sitting in the comfortable chairs surrounding the fireplace, he turned his attention to Jessica. She was looking across the room to where Melanie sat while chewing on her lower lip.

"Jessica?"

She startled and met his gaze then blurted out in a low whisper, "Am I crazy or was wife of the Mayor of Rome hitting on me?"

Unable to hide his laugh, he slipped one of his arms around her slender waist, tugging her close. The scent of an unfamiliar, but very nice perfume reached him as her warmth pressed into his body, fitting against him perfectly. Dipping his head closer to the creamy expanse of her lightly freckled neck, he took another deep breath, drawing the crisp scent of her deep into his lungs. There was a definite hint of apples, and spice, but also some herb that brightened it. A lovely, unique scent. He nuzzled his face against the side of her neck and breathed deep.

"You smell nice."

She hummed low in her throat and leaned back so she could smile up at him. "Dimitri got it for me. Said it was custom made by the guy who does his cologne. I have to say, I really like it. Smells better than my cheap mall stuff, that's for sure. He said he felt so badly about what had...what had happened and wanted to cheer me up. "

For some reason, the thought of Dimitri buying her anything irritated him. "I like, but only I buy it for you from now on."

She fought the bemused smile that seemed to want to curve her lips. "Yes, sir."

His cock twitched when she said that, and he had her close enough that she could feel him pressed against her belly. "I like it when you speak those words, *prinsessa moya*. I would like even more when you call me Master."

The light in her eyes dimmed, as did her smile. "I heard that about you. Quite a few of the bartenders liked to talk about...serving you."

The fucking bitches Jessica worked with had been running their mouths. Instead of responding, he placed a gentle kiss on the tip of her nose and tried to diffuse the situation. "Look at you, hours on a plane, a hard night, a hard fuck, and you are fresh as spring rain."

"Uh...thank you." She looked down, and her hand fluttered up to her cheek, her voice going husky. "I-I tried to cover it up the best I could. I hate the way people look at you like you did this to me. It pisses me off."

He'd noticed that, of course, and didn't give a fuck less, but it angered him that it had bothered Jessica. "People like to make snap judgments, quick assumptions. Is the easy way of life. Just go with personal experiences and prejudices and you will never have to think, or notice things. The observant man would know that someone like me would never hurt you, only protect you."

"Still, I want to yell at them that you didn't do it."

Amused by the fierce tone of her voice, he ran his knuckles along the delicate column of her throat. "I appreciate your defense of my virtue, but I assure you is all right."

Giving him a light punch in the ribs, she then looked away and crossed her arms. "I don't like how they stared at me."

"They stare because you are the most striking woman they have ever seen. An exotic beauty."

"Alex…"—she groaned and looked up to meet his gaze again—"…the side of my face is black and blue. It's hideous."

"*Dorogoya*, you are divine. I would not lie. If you had spinach in teeth, I would tell."

Her startled laugh bubbled out of her, the tension draining away, proving once again that his Jessica was born happy. He caught Dimitri, Laz, and Melanie all turning to look at them. With a smile, he lifted his chin up to his friends. "Would you like to join us for brunch at the hotel?"

"Of course." Melanie responded in English, and Jessica startled next to him.

"Are you American?"

The charming smile Melanie gave Jessica made her husband grin as he watched his wife flirt. "I am. I'm from California, the San Diego area. Where are you from?"

"Iowa. One of the most boring places on earth."

With a low laugh, Melanie stood then walked over to them with a definite sway of her hips. She took Jessica's hands in hers and gave her a mischievous look. "Well, sweetheart, you're in Rome now, and I am going to make sure you have so much fun you'll never stop smiling. This city is fabulous, and I'm not just saying that because I'm married to the mayor."

Alex pulled Jessica back to his side and gave Melanie a stern look out of Jessica's line of sight. Really, the woman was practically drooling all over his girl. Dimitri joined them and looked pointedly at Melanie, who was talking with Jessica about shopping. She was smiling bright and seemed oblivious to the way Melanie kept giving her little touches. Laz was on the phone on the other side of the room, talking quietly but keeping an eye on his wife. Laz met Alex's gaze, and he raised his brows, his dirty grin indicating he'd noticed his wife's obvious flirting and Jessica's blushing response.

An hour later, they were sitting back and enjoying their drinks, surrounded by people talking and laughing at their tables on the huge patio. Jessica was seated in the shade of the building in deference to her fair skin, but the rest of them enjoyed the sun on this warm winter day. Hanging baskets full of red and white geraniums dangled off the decorative wrought iron railing that revealed an impressive view of Rome lying out before them. Because the hotel was seated higher than most of city, the view seemed to stretch on forever, and Alex took in the monuments scattered here and there, ancient buildings that were each amazing in their own right.

He could not wait to show Jessica the world that now belonged to her.

If he could pry her away from Melanie.

The blonde woman, now wearing a fashionable white and black hat that shaded her face from the sun, sipped her coffee, set it down, and grinned. "So we'll do shopping and a spa day? I know the most fabulous place where they give the best hot stone massages."

"I'd love to." Jessica hesitated, then bit her lip, and looked over at Alex, the uncertainty clear on her expressive face. "Is that okay with you?"

He'd be a fool to turn down Melanie's offer. No one, anywhere, would shoot at Jessica while she was with Melanie. Not after the horrible example Alex and Laz had made of the men who'd kidnapped her. The woman was a multi-millionaire in her own right with a father who was part of the Russian mafia and an uncle by marriage in the Yakuza. Not to mention her husband's political power and good standing with the Italian mafia.

Plus, Alex and Dimitri had a virtual meeting tomorrow with his father, and he didn't want Jessica there. Eventually he'd have to tell her the truth about his family, but not yet. He wanted to squeeze out as much time as possible with her before he revealed she'd fallen in love with a monster and pray their bond was strong enough at that point to withstand the blow.

"Is okay, *prinsessa moya*." He tucked a few silken strands of her hair behind her delicate ear. "Buy whatever you want. I have already contacted my credit card companies. You have full use."

"I have my own money."

Offended, he stared at her. "You will not use your money. You will use mine."

She glared at him before turning to Melanie and saying with a fake smile, "Fine, then I'll just go and do some window shopping."

"What is that? Window shopping?" Laz said while smiling and raising a hand in greeting to someone sitting across the patio.

Melanie laughed, the sun catching the huge diamond sparkling on her ring finger. "It's when a woman only looks through windows at things she likes and doesn't buy anything."

Shaking his head, Laz gave his wife a teasing smile. "I do not know that word, because my wife always buys."

Alex could see Jessica getting geared up to argue with him over this. They needed to have a discussion about money, but not in front of his friends. So he stood and placed his napkin on his chair, then held his hand out to Jessica.

"It has been so nice to see you again, but it has been a long day of traveling for us, and we both need to recuperate."

Taking the hint, Melanie stood, kissed his cheeks, and then did the same with Jessica. She whispered something in Jessica's ear, and his girl giggled then gave Melanie a decidedly naughty wink.

Adorable.

"I will see you sometime this week?"

Smiling, Jessica slipped her hand into his. "Absolutely. You have my cell phone number. Just text me the details."

After they made their goodbyes, their vacated seats were immediately taken by people wishing to talk to the mayor and his wife. Alex pulled Jessica to his side and placed a kiss atop her head. She looked up at him, and he found himself drowning in her exotic gaze.

"You did good."

She relaxed a little more as they made their way to the elevator. The hotel was busier now than when they'd checked in, and the noise level had increased due to the high ceilings. To her surprise, she noticed a larger variety of people now. Anyone who stayed here was wealthy, but that didn't mean they had class. A woman with obviously dyed red hair, dripping in tacky gold, and sporting a huge amount of cleavage sauntered up to wait for the elevator with them. She gave Alex a blatantly flirty smile, which he ignored. How she could possibly think he'd want her when he had Jessica baffled him.

Once they were in the elevator, Alex stood behind Jessica with his arms wrapped around her, basically using her body as a barrier to keep the other woman away. This didn't seem to dissuade her much, and she kept staring at him. Thankfully, the woman left after a few floors with a disappointed pout, and Alex finally relaxed. Jessica snickered and patted his arm.

"There, the bad lady is gone. You can let go of me now."

He laughed, glad she understood him so well, even if her perception was a little too good. It wouldn't be long before she'd start questioning him about things she would see or hear, things that would tip her off to the true nature of his world. The thought sobered him, and he silently led her out of the elevator. He worried about what he was going to say to her, but when she paused at the spot they'd made love earlier and gave him a shy smile, his mind was drawn back to the present. He'd never met anyone who could keep him grounded like this, and he found it to be extremely refreshing. Usually, he was thinking about the future, trying to prepare for every threat that could be headed his way, but with Jessica, he enjoyed being with her so much he couldn't do anything but live in the moment.

Especially when she was so close. So warm, alive, and his. Fuck, he was lost in her and couldn't bring himself to give a shit. He wondered if she knew how securely she had him wrapped around her finger. She didn't even know how special she was and had no idea yet of her power as a woman. She was young enough to still be curious and old enough to enjoy the intense pleasures he could offer her. A mental flash of her body writhing against him as he fucked her sizzled through him, and he his dick tingled as it started to harden.

Once they were in the foyer of their suite, she sighed then tugged on his jacket. "Hold still."

She braced her hand on him, leaned down, took off first one shoe, then the other with a low groan while she wiggled her toes in the thick red carpet. Her bare feet were so tiny next his, and he liked her rose red toenail polish. "Oh God, so much better."

"You do not like the shoes?"

"What? No, I love them. Are you kidding? Thanks to you, I now have seven pairs of the most beautiful, ridiculously expensive, amazing high heels and high heeled boots I've ever seen in my closet. Dior, Firmani, Giuseppe Zanotti, Prada. Basically the rock stars of women's shoes." She gave a sigh that was close to the sound she made while he was deep inside of her. "They're so pretty, Alex. I want to wear them all, which means I have to get used to high heels again."

He knew better than to argue with her. Even if he didn't have a lot of experience in having a girlfriend, he had been with a lot of women who considered themselves fashion divas. It seemed like women worldwide liked their footwear. He certainly liked the way it looked on her.

He looked down at her with a small smile. "Are you tired?"

"Very. Those drinks and all that good food knocked me out. Do you think we can take a nap?"

The gleam in her eyes clued him into the nature of the 'nap' she wanted, as did her hard nipples pressing against her dress. Such sweet little tits and such beautiful nipples. He loved how they got rose-red after he'd been rough with them. For a moment, he could taste her skin against his tongue, and his cock began to throb. The need to have her consumed him, but he refused to rush it again. This time, they had a big bed, and he was going to use it to explore the beautiful body that had been hidden from him and denied to him for so long. Time to revel in the spoils of his delicious victory.

Alex gently pushed her back. "Go, wash up, and put on one of your nightgowns. I will be back in a few minutes."

She stole a glance at him, and heat rushed through her when she saw the lusty gleam in his eyes. "Okay."

"And Jessica?"

"Yes?"

"Make sure you cleanse your ass well, because I will have my tongue and fingers up it later."

Chapter Fourteen

J essica reclined on the sumptuous, crimson watered silk sofa, looking out the wide windows of the master bedroom, which showed a skyline she could fall in love with. She couldn't wait to see the view tonight, all lit up and sparkling like a scene out of a fairy tale. Hell, she kind of felt like she was living in a fairy tale right now—a rather dirty one. She'd been taken from her normal, boring life and thrust into this world of class and elegance.

Rome, for god's sake.

With Alex.

Who seemed to adore her.

It was all very surreal.

She was still lazily musing about her situation when Alex came out of the bathroom dressed in only a pair of black suit pants with the top button undone. Her gaze ever so slowly devoured him from his dark, thick hair down to his firm lips, following the trail of hair on his chest, past the slabs of his pectorals, and down to where his dick strained against his pants. A rush of heat sizzled along her nerves, and she felt herself grow damp with want.

"Jessica," Alex said in a soft, chiding voice. "Look at me, *prinsessa moya*. We need to discuss how your life will be from now on."

That snapped her out of her erotic daydream, and she sat up straight, the silken lilac nightgown with its hip-high slits on either side sliding over her skin. And, because her lack of curves, the straps almost fell off. Alex watched with great interest as her breast was almost revealed, showing the faintest hint of pink from her nipple. His admiration made her forget herself, but she wasn't sure she liked what Alex had just implied.

Maybe it was a translation issue.

"What do you mean, how it will be? Do I get a choice in it?"

"Absolutely," he responded at once. "I will never take away your free will. I want you with me willingly, always. But you must know, you belong to me now."

"Uh...what?" She frowned and tugged her top back in place, feeling like she needed to be clothed for this conversation. "I don't belong to anyone."

"Wrong. He took a step closer, and her heart rate increased. "You belong to me now, and I will cherish you always, but you are mine."

Totally confused, she shook her head and looked down at the ground then let loose with all the questions that had been piling up in her mind. "I don't get it. How can I belong to you? Are we dating? What are we doing? Why am I here? Why did you bring me with you? What do you want from me?"

He crouched down in front of her at the edge of the sofa, sitting back on his haunches, his thigh muscles bulging. Unable to help it, she wrapped her legs around his waist and tugged him closer. Her pussy was in total control, and that little bitch had it bad for Alex. She also had to admit she felt so much better when touching him. Alex drew her like a magnet, and she couldn't be near him without wanting to feel him. All throughout brunch he'd held her hand or stroked the exposed skin of her thigh, shoulder, neck, or her inner wrist. He'd stolen a few kisses, and each time, she'd flushed so hard her ears burned, which only amused those watching them.

"You belong to me because I am claiming you as mine. The world I live in is different, not what you are used to. The rules different, also, like fact that once man like me claims woman like you, it means you belong to me alone, and no one will dispute that fact."

She went to ask him what the hell a man like him meant, but he cut her off by raising his hand.

"To answer next question, no, we are not dating. You are mine. Is more than being girlfriend, is being everything." He spoke louder as she opened her mouth. "We are in Rome because I have business to do here, and I wanted to share with you. To see this place through your eyes, your wonder. I have so much to show you, but only if is what you want. Never will I force you to do anything you do not wish. My greatest joy is for you to trust me enough to protect, to keep safe, and to let me take care of you. I want to give you everything you ever desire. Everything."

This time when he paused, she didn't interrupt him. Instead, she curled her fingers through his hair.

"And what I want in return"—he leaned closer so they were nearly kissing as he spoke—"is you. All of you, heart, soul, and body. I want wake up with you whenever possible and fall asleep with you cuddled to my chest like kitten. Never have I felt happiness like I have with you. I did not know was possible to feel like this."

Emotion threatened to overwhelm her, and she took in a quick breath, her mouth moving before her mind caught up. "Alex, what do you and Peter really do? You're asking for my trust, but I don't think you're telling me everything I need to know about you. You're obviously way more than a bodyguard."

He froze, but didn't move away. His breathing increasing against her lips, but he was otherwise calm. "I cannot tell you...yet."

Irritated, she leaned back so she could study his face in the strong afternoon light. "What? Why not?"

He closed his eyes and sat back, widening the gulf between them. "I will tell you, eventually, I promise, but not now. Things must be dealt with, things I do not wish for you to know."

"It's bad, isn't it?"

He hesitated. "To some is bad, to some is life."

"So I'm just supposed to sit back and twiddle my thumbs until you decide it's time for me to know?" She clenched her hands into fists and stared at him. "Really? You talk about how much you cherish me, but *you* don't trust me with your secrets. A little hypocritical, don't you think?"

"Jessica." The scary tone of his voice clued her in that she might have just pissed him off. His next words confirmed it. "I will tell you when I can. Not because I playing game, but to protect you. Is hard for you to understand, but ignorance could save life. You are smart, you will figure things out, but I can confirm nothing until...certain events happen. I swear, is for own protection. I do trust you, more than I have every trusted anyone outside of my family. Please trust me."

Blowing out a harsh breath, trying to ignore his scent clinging to her skin, she pushed up on her elbows then frowned while tugging her top back into place. "Whatever. Sounds like a total cop-out to me."

"What happened to you in alley? It will happen again if I do not keep you innocent." He leaned toward her then ran his fingers through her hair with a soothing touch, the sudden fear filling her probably easy to read. "I will do anything to protect you, but I need you to be patient with me. Can you do that?"

She debated for a moment then sighed. "For how long?"

"I do not know."

"Let me get this straight, you want us to basically move in together, for me to be your woman, but I don't get to know anything about you? Are you trying to hide me?" Her heart plummeted. "Oh shit, are you married? Is that why you didn't want the paparazzi taking pictures of us?"

"*Nyet*, I am no married. You are only woman I care for, only woman I ever care for." He ignored her snort of disbelief. "You know much about me, Jessica. Feel deep in heart. You met my brother, my friends, and we had public lunch in very public place with two people the paparazzi love to photograph. I would never be ashamed of you, am proud to have you on my arm, love to show world the beauty that is mine."

She tried to ignore the warm tingle his words gave her. "People took pictures of us?"

"No doubt there are images of you and I on Internet by now." He gave her a bitter smile. "I am not unknown."

"Great," she muttered, her gaze tracing over his tattoos, both new and old.

"Jessica, all I ask for is time in Rome be about us. To learn each other before I move you into my home."

"Home? What home? You mean move to Minsk with you?" Irritated, she frowned at him. "How do you know I want to live with you?"

"*Laskovaya*, I know you better than you know yourself, and no, not Minsk. We buy home in Ireland, or in America if is what you want. Jessica, you know what is between us is special. You know you want to be mine as much as I want to be yours."

"God, you can be such an arrogant prick sometimes," she huffed out, trying to ignore the warm, squishy feelings filling her at the tender tone in his voice.

The edges of his lips curved upward, and she had to bite back a sigh at the way his eyes grew heavy lidded. "I have studied you, what you like and what you do not."

"What?"

"We have talked great deal, and you have told me many things about you. Things I remember." He smiled and leaned in, giving her a kiss on the nose that increased the tingling buzz of happiness trying to spin through her. "And I told you more about myself than I have ever shared with another woman."

She snorted and had to bite back a smile. Okay, so she liked the fact that she was different from the other women he'd been with, and he trusted her with personal thoughts and feelings. She'd done the same with him. Damn, he did know a lot about her because they'd been friends for months before becoming lovers.

"You're my friend," she whispered, her heart threatening to burst with the intensity of her feelings.

Puzzled, he pursed his lips. "More than friend."

"No, no, I know that. What I meant is I do trust you, Alex, because you're right. I do know you...sort of. I know that you hate sunflower seeds because one of your tutors chewed them and constantly had the husk in his teeth. I know that your first dog was a Dalmatian, and you love the scent of apples."

He laughed unexpectedly. "I love the smell of apples because is what you wear. Your scent is like baked apples with spice."

She flushed. "Oh, yeah. It's just some cheap stuff I got at the mall."

To her surprise, he cupped her chin and made her look at him as he lowered himself onto her body, his weight pressing her into the cushions. "Nothing about you is cheap. Everything you touch, everything you wear, becomes exquisite because of you."

Her lower lip quivered while he gently ran his thumb over her bruised cheek. "Thanks."

"I think I should show you now how delicious you are. Your skin is so smooth I could spend all day petting you, stroking you. Sometime we will go to my

222

home in Siberia. I will lock us in my room with roaring fire to keep us warm then fuck you until you beg me to stop. I will give you so many orgasms your body will not be able to take it, and you will faint. This, I promise."

"Uhn..." Well, that wasn't the most eloquent response, but he'd struck her dumb with his carnal words.

The faint lines around his eyes deepened. "Relax, Jessica. We do this, as you Americans say, one day at a time. Yes?"

Closing her eyes, unable to handle the intensity of his gaze, she tried to process their conversation, but her body was more interested in having him inside of her again. He shifted slightly, his thick erection pressing into her mound. One twitch of her hips and now his dick was sliding against her, separated only by his thin pants and her practically non-existent panties. All attempts to focus on anything but enjoying his touch fled when he groaned then rubbed his hips in a circle against her needy sex.

His voice was strained as he whispered, "Jessica, the things you do to me."

She ran her fingers through his hair, luxuriating in the lush feel of it against her skin, her heart rate slowing as she took in deep breaths. This brought a hint of his cologne to her, and she leaned forward to rub her nose against his. He didn't respond verbally, but he did give her a slow, sexy smile when she pulled back. Her whole body ached for him, but she had calmed down enough that she could kinda, sorta think.

Before she got carried away again, she took a deep breath, glad to see some of the tension gone from Alex's face. In her heart of hearts, she had a feeling that what Alex and Peter did wasn't exactly legal. It was such an absurd thought she kept rejecting it, but she was also pretty sure she was in some serious denial. She noticed little things, discrepancies that had caught her attention. Like the fact that no one treated Alex like a bodyguard. Oleg, Luka, and Maks, yes, but when Alex was with her, people were deferential to him. She was so googly-eyed over him she didn't notice it at first, but once she'd relaxed around him, she saw that Alex was given preferential treatment all the time. Of course, people kissed her ass because her Uncle Peter was in politics, but there was no reason for Alex to have the kind of...notoriety like he did.

People knew who he was and were afraid of him. Probably for a good reason.

But she wasn't.

Probably never would be.

Something deep inside her belly settled, and a sense of acceptance filled her. She smiled at him, a slow curve of her lips that seemed to coax his mouth into tipping up at the corners. She loved that about him, that he couldn't help responding to her smile. It gave her a heady sense of power to realize she made this broody, dangerous man happy. No man had ever responded to her like Alex did, and despite their differences, they blended together just right.

"I've come to a decision." She brushed his dark hair off his forehead, keeping her gaze on her fingers. "I would love to spend time in Rome, Alex. There is nowhere in the world I'd rather be than with you. Just...be patient with me, okay? You're a global playboy, but I'm still new to all of this. And promise me you won't keep me in the dark forever, that you'll tell me the truth."

"I swear to you, Jessica, I will tell you as soon as I can." He held her hand then brought it to his lips and kissed her knuckles, his facial hair tickling her skin. "You have nothing to worry about. I know you do not understand now—you are young—but you will."

That took away some of her happy glow. "Stop with that too young bullshit. I'm old enough for you to fuck, aren't I?"

His jaw twitched, but his amused smirk irritated her. "Yes. Perhaps I need to fuck you more. I think you are woman with vast sexual appetites. Tastes for things you do not even know you crave. Things that I will teach you."

Her mind skipped back to the overheard conversations about Alex's fondness for being dominant in the bedroom. "What kind of things?"

Her body was tired of his teasing talk, and she wanted him to slip that wonderful dick he kept teasing her with into her wet pussy. She felt tender down there, more sensitive, her arousal driven to the point that she was going to finger fuck herself soon if he didn't do something. Her hips tilted up of their own accord to grind against him, and his nostrils flared.

He captured her other hand and brought it to his lush lips, kissing the veins visible in her wrist through her pale skin. "Anything you want to do Jessica, any pleasure you want to explore, tell me. I want you to be honest about what turns you on. We will only do what you want, but I will ask for your trust to push you a little bit, to expand your horizons."

She bit her lower lip, knowing there was no way in hell she'd tell Alex about some of the kinkier fantasies she'd had. Yeah, an orgy was fun to imagine...but to actually do? Dirty, explicit mental images of fucking Alex while people fucked around them and watched set her body on fire, and moisture welled between her legs. Thank goodness Alex was kinky 'cause it looked like she was as well.

Looking up at Alex, she bit her lower lip then

whispered, "Okay. I'll tell you."

"Okay?" He smirked. "Did not sound very convincing."

She resisted the urge to squirm beneath his gaze. "What?"

His grin was downright wicked as he said, "We going to play interrogation."

Chapter Fifteen

J essica pushed her hair off her face, trying to see if he was serious. "What?"

He stood abruptly, hauled her up, and tossed her over his shoulder with her ass in the air and her face against his back. "Alex!"

"Hush, my captured spy. You need to know this now. In bedroom, I like complete control. That does not mean we will not play your games or I will not indulge your curiosity, but I own you, and that includes your pleasure. You are mine."

She was starting to find the whole you-are-mine thing arousing, but she wasn't going to tell him that. He couldn't just haul her around and demand things of her. And if she didn't want to tell him, that was none of his business. The thought didn't even make sense to her, and she sighed then watched the floor pass as he hauled her to their bedroom.

Before he set her down on the bed, he gave her butt a slap.

She yelped and glared at him when he gave her nipple a tweak. "Stop that!"

The lines around his mouth disappeared as his smile dropped from his face. "You need safe word."

"What?" She rubbed her sore nipple, trying not to acknowledge how strangely good it felt as her palms soothed the hard tips.

"You say word, we stop what we are doing and talk. Will allow me to push your boundaries. Is word you would not normally use in sex so, if I hear, I know you are troubled."

She considered her boundaries pretty wide, so she didn't put up a fight. If he wanted to give her a safe word, that was fine. The very fact that they would need something like that made her nervous, but she wasn't going to chicken out now

"Butter."

He frowned. "Butter?"

"Yes." Her breath hitched when he reached out and flicked her nipple—hard.

"On your back, Jessica. Feet on the edge of the bed with knees up, legs spread wide."

She balked, unused to anyone being so direct with her during sex. Looking up at him, she did as he asked, glad the nightgown had slid between her legs and covered her sex. Although by the look on Alex's face, that flimsy fabric wouldn't be there for long.

He shed his pants, leaving himself clad only in a pair of tight, dark gray, boxer briefs with his erection plain to see. Arousal lit her nerves, making her nipples pucker up into painful points. He was so built, including his cock. There was something deliciously obscene about the way he filled out his underwear, the fact that his hard shaft stretched the fabric, outlining him perfectly. A damp spot darkened the fabric at the head of his cock, and her belly clenched with need.

He was big, so big. Yeah, she'd been with endowed men before, but Alex was thick. He was long enough that he went deep, but it was his girth that made her breath catch. She fisted the soft blue comforter beneath her at the memory of the burn as he stretched her.

Sunlight shown around the edges of the closed curtains, slices of illumination that graced his spectacular body. She loved the way his muscles moved, smooth shifts beneath his skin that drew her eye and had her yearning to touch him.

Instead of moving between her legs like she'd anticipated and hoped, he stretched out next to her. The bed creaked slightly as it absorbed his weight.

There was an indulgent look in his eyes she'd glimpsed before, an incredible tenderness focused totally on her. He spread her hair over to the side, pausing for a moment to thread his fingers through the silky mass. Her nipples tightened until she was ready to lean up and rub her breasts on his chest. She was soaked and so ready for him.

"*Krasavitsa*," he murmured. "Am lucky to have found you before you realized how beautiful you are."

She sucked in her lower lip and tried to look away, but his hand on her chin made her face him. "Um...thanks."

He smiled and rubbed his thumb over her lip, making her release a soft sigh. "You do not believe me, but you will. One day, you realize I am right. I will help you see your beauty."

Licking at his thumb, she enjoyed the way his hips pushed against her, flexing the tight muscles of his belly. Pulling his thumb from her mouth, he ran it down her neck, over her chest, and almost to the peak of her breast. A shiver ran through her, and she marveled at how her body responded to everything he did. She was by no means a virgin, but she'd never felt the sexual intensity she experienced with Alex.

To her disappointment, he merely moved the top of her nightgown enough to expose her nipples, but didn't do anything more than stare at them.

She started to reach for him, but he shook his head. "Hands at sides."

Of course, her first instinct was to snark back. "You're so bossy."

He chuckled. "Someday I will spank you for that remark. Make you stand against wall wearing those incredibly sexy shoes that you had on and turn your delicate ass pink. I do not want to bruise you, so my touch will be highly controlled. And I guarantee you will come all over my cock while screaming my name.

However, I will also take you over my knee at some point, maybe in front of a group of people, and spank you like filthy girl you are. So dirty, so kind, so sweet. It pleases me to know you will try some of my darker desires, that I get to warm your ass with my hand, watch it bounce with each hit. And your pussy will be dripping wet when I fuck you."

"Oh."

Her breath came out in a soft sigh not only from the mental image of Alex taking her over his knee for being naughty, but also because his free hand had reached her hips and was slowly exploring the skin of her inner thigh. She wiggled, squeezing her thighs and sending bursts of warmth from her sex to her lower belly. A soft moan escaped her when he tweaked her nipple hard enough to sting.

"Be still."

It was impossible to keep her hands to herself with a nearly naked Alex stretched out next to her. When his calloused fingers slipped beneath her panties, they were so close to her clit that they barely grazed her, her hips twitched up, silently begging for his touch where she needed it most. Another brush, whisper soft over the hood of her swollen nub. His soft laughter made her grit her teeth.

"Alex, please."

"I told you, be still."

"But—"

Her words were cut off when he gave her a sharp slap right on her pussy, the pain stunning her before an equally strong wave of desire made her whimper with need.

"Be still."

"What the hell?"

Before she could go off, he pinched her clit then began to rub his thumb ever so gently on the fully exposed tip. "Shhh, let me take care of you, *prinsessa moya*. I need to give you the sweet before the bitter."

Her lips parted to question his odd word choice, but instead, a thick, heated moan rose from her. Alex had such skill in pleasuring a woman. A small part of her was irritated by how he'd gotten so good at it, but he was hers now—at least he said he was—and she wasn't going to let the past ruin the moment. She was beginning to understand the term 'living in the now'.

Alex rubbed his thumb on her almost too-sensitive nub with just the right amount of pressure and sent her body convulsing into an orgasm. The pleasure struck out of nowhere, and she arched violently, writhing as she begged him to fuck her. She didn't care if it was his fingers, tongue, or cock, she needed to be filled.

"Take me."

The words had scarcely left her lips before the tip of his shaft pressed into her, drawing out her climax. Her pussy gladly milked his cock, the orgasm extending while he slid gently in and out. His movements were languid, easing her down until she stopped twitching from overstimulation and relaxed around his dick. When her body finally unclenched, he hissed out a breath and pulled almost all the way out until only the bulbous tip stretched her entrance.

"You will make me embarrass myself with your strong pussy."

She reached up and cupped his cheek, enjoying the way he nuzzled against her hand as he began to move a little faster, his gaze growing darker. "So tight that I can barely move in you, and when you release..." He shuddered atop her and leaned down to lick at her nipple. "I want to pierce these. And your clit."

That thought cleared her mind enough for her to gasp out, "Pierce them?"

With a low growl, he pulled out only long enough

to flip her over onto her belly before surging back into her wet, welcoming warmth. "Beautiful, delicate gold hoops. Would look so stunning and would increase your capacity for pleasure."

Her body sure liked that idea because heat flashed through her, and her pussy contracted, earning her a groan. Turns out doing Kegel muscle exercises paid off. Guess that women's magazine was onto something after all. Jessica did Kegel exercises because it improved the strength of her orgasms. The more tension, the greater the climax.

Giving Jessica an experimental squeeze, Alex froze then slapped her ass. "Relax."

The heat of his smack only made her sex clasp him harder as an involuntary wave of tingling pleasure danced along her nerves. His hands felt huge as they rubbed her heated bottom. "You will bruise easily. I will take care how hard I hit you."

She let out a soft moan as his cock hit a new angle inside of her. "Please don't. Do to me whatever you want, I trust you to make it good for me."

His jaw clenched, and his hips pushed forward until he was filling her, deep enough that it stung, burned, felt amazing. "I do not have to hit you to make it hurt."

Rolling her hips, she moaned and moved her body so his cock rubbed her G-spot just right. That intense bolt of sensation made her toes curl, made her wanton. She didn't want Alex controlled above her. She wanted him to fuck her, now. She began to rock back against him, squeezing tight when he was all the way in and relaxing on the slide out. It actually heightened her own pleasure as well to grip him internally. Made his already substantial cock feel huge.

Alex went perfectly still behind her, his muscular body surrounding hers as he whispered against her

232

neck, "Do not move."

Her clit actually twitched as she froze, undone by the command in his voice. Even now, in bed with his dick buried in her, he radiated an authority she secretly loved. People were wary of him, deferential, and he acted like it was his due. Except with her he was protective, possessive, and seemed to delight in her happiness.

She was falling—or maybe had already fallen—in love with him.

Her whole body clenched, and she yelped when he thrust in hard enough to bring back that internal sting, his dick stretching her while her pussy resisted the intrusion. "I said, do not move."

She whimpered, drawn from her thoughts by the overwhelming sensation of his cock making her ache, the sweat on his skin scenting the air and mixing with the musk of sex. He was a total tactile experience, from the rough brush of the hair on his legs against hers to the magnificent body built for fighting. She blindly reached out and clasped his hand, holding it tight.

"I'll try," she whispered.

He went down on one elbow, still filling her, and moved her hair over to the side so he could kiss and nibble her neck. His voice was thick and raspy as he growled, "There are some things you should know about me, Jessica. Some kinks that I have that may be new to you. Understand that even if you do not want to do something, it does not mean I do not want you or I will be disappointed. Only means is off the table for us."

Confused by the arousal still coursing through her, thanks to his gently rocking hips, and the need to pay attention, she gently shoved against him so she could roll over onto her back. As soon as she did, he moved back between her legs. They both gasped as he filled her once again.

Giving her a challenging look, he said, "I like other men and women to watch me fuck you. To see the beauty that is mine. To covet you. Seeing you come is a sight to behold, skin flushed, lips swollen, and your nipples begging for my lips."

The mental image was so instant, so hot, that she couldn't help her body's reaction. When her pussy spasmed, he chuckled then nipped at her skin, earning another squeeze. "I would also like to watch a woman touch you, taste you. Watch you come in her mouth while I play with your perfect tits."

Her breath caught at how downright naughty that was, and her hips pressed up into him. The thought of being with a woman while he watched was a little intimidating, and a lot hot. Her imagination conjured images of some pretty blonde woman licking between her legs while Alex fucked her mouth.

"Mmm, *prinsessa moya*, you never fail to please me. I also want to watch a man touch you, taste you, make you climax." She shivered beneath him, being seduced by his dark talk as his movements began to speed up, drawing her mind back to her body. "Maybe I watch him fuck you."

Her heart skipped a beat at that one, unsure if she liked the idea or not. It felt too close to cheating and she would never do that. Ever.

"Not yet," Alex mused, "but the desire is there."

Before she could protest, he reached between them, his fingers stroking her mound just above her pulsing clit, their harsh breathing breaking the quiet of their bedroom, along with the occasional car horn from outside. While they lounged in bed, the world outside their room continued on, and she found the idea of spending the rest of the afternoon making love with Alex was exactly what she wanted. Her heart lurched as she stared up into his eyes, her fingertips grazing his face as he rocked slowly in and out of her. His body covered hers without crushing her. He easily held himself above her on strong arms, the muscles bulging enticingly while he made love to her. She gave him a small smile, and his breath came out in a low rush, an almost pained sound. Then she kissed him, the gentle strokes of her lips meant to soothe his pain.

"Perfect," he whispered. She laid back down, her hands still wrapped around his muscular neck. "I am lucky man."

Her reply was lost when he did a twisting thing with his hips that hit her deep inside, just right. A sharp burst of delicious sensation exploded from her belly out, and she cupped her breasts, rolling her thumbs over her nipples. He groaned, and she opened her eyes, watching him while she toyed with her breasts.

"I will tie you up, flog you, fuck you, and make you orgasm so many times you pass out. Then I will fuck you some more, in front of room full of people, your submission to me on display for them, the warmth of your passion warming their bodies even though they can only look, not touch without my permission. I will clamp your nipples then your clit, special made jewelry for your pretty cunt. I cannot decide if I want to put gold or platinum on you." He traced his fingertips lightly over her chest. "Maybe pearls."

Her body was too busy chasing her orgasm to filter her thoughts as she whispered, "Clamps? Won't that hurt?"

"Yes." His grin was anything but reassuring, more sinister promise than anything else. "But I will make it so good for you."

Their gazes met, and she forgot how to breathe,

235

too caught up in Alex's passion, his desperate need for her, and in the way he stared at her like he could never get enough of looking at her. It was all there in his eyes, plain as day, and she knew he loved her...maybe as much as she loved him. She wrapped her legs around his waist and cupped his face in her hands, trying to touch as much of him as she could.

The corner of his lips twitched in a smile before he leaned down and kissed the sweet spot behind her ear. "Perfect for me, Jessica," he whispered. "This feeling I have for you, it consumes me. You are everything to me. *Lyublyu tebya vsem sertsem, vsey dushyu.*"

He ground his pelvis against hers, hitting her clit just right and making her scream out his name. The taste of his salt filled her mouth as their lips met, his kiss devouring her as she shuddered against him. Her release was building in her, almost there, and it was going to be so very, very big.

"Come for me. Grip my cock, my filthy girl."

Just like that, electricity raced through her nervous system, tensing all her muscles, and she bit his shoulder, hard, when her orgasm crashed over her. Alex let out a startled bellow and ground himself into her body while he came inside of her. She could feel each pulse of his cock, and he twitched and groaned as she writhed beneath him, her overstimulated pussy tightening every time he surged into her. Once he was finally wrung out, he collapsed next to her and let out a weak chuckle, his hot breath warming the sweat on her face.

Damn, sex with Alex was awesome. Super awesome. Her hormone-saturated brain couldn't think of anything greater than that. Hell, she was struggling to breathe.

"I think your greedy pussy sucked me dry. Fuck."

Floating in bliss, she turned her head to look at

him and smiled. "Yep."

He blinked, then began to laugh, and pulled her to him, arranging her so her cheek rested on his chest, his lips against her hair. This seemed to be the spot he liked. She went to curl into him, but felt a bit of him seeping out and grimaced. There was no way she was sleeping in a wet spot.

When she tried to move he grumbled, "Stay."

"I have to clean up."

He opened one lazy eye. "Shower, bring back washcloth with you. I want you to clean me, then suck me, then ride me."

She hurried to the bathroom, eager to enjoy every moment she had with Alex.

Chapter Sixteen

Early the next morning, just as the sun was rising, she woke up and couldn't go back to sleep. Blah, traveling always sapped her energy. That and being Alex's fuck toy last night. He'd used her every way he saw fit and then some. She loved it all, wanted more, and sucked his cock back to hardness more than once just so she could feel the bliss of him entering her body.

She sighed, the scent of sex still heavy in the air. They should really open a window. If the cleaning ladies came in here, the pheromones might kill them. And if Alex was still asleep next to her when the unsuspecting staff opened the door, they'd get a glimpse of a world-class perfect ass that any woman in her right mind would want to grope. The temptation to touch him filled her, and she grinned at the sight of her teeth marks on one of his perfect ass cheeks. Alex had become rough and growly at one point, pinning her over and over again as she tried to fight him off. It was pretend, of course, but she loved the freedom he'd given her to really try and give it her all without fear of hurting him. The moment when she'd finally given in, exhausted and panting beneath him, he'd slide slowly and gently—if such a thing was possible for a man of his girth—into her.

Her sex began to tingle then ache in protest. She was ridden hard last night, for sure, and she rode him hard a couple times as well, which might have something to do with her Jello legs. Before she moved out of bed, she leaned over and whispered in Alex's ear.

"I have to use the bathroom, I'll be back."

He lazily opened one eye, and when his sleepy

gaze found her face, he smiled. "You will not run away again?"

Unable to resist, she leaned forward on her sore arms and placed a kiss on his forehead. "I can't run anywhere right now. My body has been...well-used."

The smug look he gave her irritated her, even if it was well-deserved. She'd finally found a man with a sexual appetite to match her own, but goodness, her body was not ready to fulfill her greed for him. Even her mouth was sore from endless kissing, and she wondered if her lips looked as swollen as they felt.

"Take bath. In my bag, there is clear glass jar with some bath salts. Use that. Is special mixture I have for sore body."

His words were thick with sleep. She smiled, then leaned back, and pulled the comforter over him. "Thanks."

Leaving him to get some more rest, she wobbled to the master bathroom, sighing with delight. It was the most beautiful bathroom she'd ever been in, and she was totally in love with it. Gleaming bronze marble, antique brass accents coupled with some of the most beautiful mosaic work done in turquoise and gold. Unusual and gorgeous. The marble bath was deep, and she grinned when she noticed there were two taps for filling the tub up. It was that big. After turning the water on, she stumbled over to the vanity and brushed her teeth, and her stomach growled.

She thought that maybe she should eat first, but she felt grungy. Their energetic bouts of sex had often resulted in both of them collapsing in a sweaty heap. A quiver of arousal tightened her nipples, and she winced and looked down. Alex had mauled her poor breasts, and she could see his bite mark on the side of her cleavage near her heart. Shit, it hurt to touch it. She should be a little more pissed off at him for bruising her like this, but she'd bitten him worse. His yelp then growl had been sexy enough that she tempted him into taking her again.

Groaning, she rinsed off quickly in the shower before eyeing the tub. It was more than half full, and she figured that was good enough for her. Steam rose into the air, swirling in the diffused light coming in through the smoked glass windows.

The bath salts smelled like Alex's cologne, and she sank into the water slowly, her body protesting every shift. Man, she needed to take up yoga and start doing cardio. Then again, she could keep having energetic sex with Alex and be in the best shape of her life. She could probably start a new exercise craze, the nympho workout.

That thought made her giggle as she relaxed her head back on the awesome padded headrest things on either end of the tub. The space was large enough that even stretched out her full length her feet didn't touch the other edge of the tub, and she floated. It was absolute heaven, and she let out a grateful moan as her muscles began to relax. The heat seeped into her, calming her as she lazily kept watch on the rising water level.

She must have closed her eyes at some point because the water shut off, the sudden absence of noise startling her out of her doze. Before she could freak out, Alex had her in his arms, pulling her to the side of the tub with him. He reclined back on the padded surface then pulled her to him so she was floating in his arms with her back to his front. Too comfortable to protest, she merely gave into his hold and sighed.

"This feel so good." His cock twitched beneath her at her breathy tone and she snorted. "If you think you're putting that thing in me anytime soon, you're crazy."

"I used you rough," he whispered against her neck. "I am sorry I lost control."

"Don't be. I loved it. No one has ever given me their passion like you do. It's addicting."

"Good, I want you addicted to me." He kissed her neck. "Room service will be here soon. There are a selection of clothes that have been brought in for you to choose from."

"What?"

He smiled as he ran his hand over her face, his touch light and perfect. "One of my friends is here, Nico with his girlfriend Catrin, who is a world-renowned stylist, though she's retired now from the fashion industry. She is familiar with the events we are going to so she will be able to help you find something for those occasions."

"Oh." Apprehension filled her at the thought of leaving Alex's side. "Are you coming with us?"

"*Nyet, prinsessa moya.* I have business."

"Oh. Is this business dangerous?"

"No more than usual."

She looked at him with narrowed eyes, "That's not very reassuring."

She expected him to be irritated. Instead, he gently kissed her bruised cheek. "I think the sex is good for you. Mark on cheek has faded."

She'd noticed that when she brushed her teeth, but she wouldn't let him distract her. "Can you at least tell me if the woman I'm going with is safe?"

"Catrin is the beloved of Nico Tezkin, an old friend of mine who was raised in a rough ghetto in northern Russia. First generation Russian, his parents had been brought there from Somalia as workers to fish the Barents Sea. His father died in storm out at sea, leaving behind Nico, his mother, and his three sisters. Was not good. Nico clawed his way out of ghetto, took care of his family, and now owns one of the best pharmaceutical businesses in the world. Is good man, does much charity work. Is how he met Catrin."

He got out, and she followed suit, wrapping her hair up in a towel while he dried her off, his touch lingering. She patted her hair and watched him admire her body as he dried it. "And how did they meet?"

"Catrin's father is boring politician who needed to kiss Nico's ass. They were at one of those dull dinners that seemed to never end, and according to Nico, his eyes met Catrin's across the table, and that was it. He was in love."

She couldn't stop the flush that burned the tips of her ears. "Love at first sight, huh?"

Avoiding his gaze, she went into the bedroom and smiled at the sight of three different, lovely outfits on the bed. She dismissed the bright green dress, feeling like she'd glow as she walked down the street, and focused on the remaining two. Alex moved around behind her while she studied the clothes. After her brunch yesterday among Italy's most beautiful people, she had a newfound appreciation for fashion. Of course, she'd watched those brain-candy fashion shows on TV, but it was a little different looking at it on the screen and seeing it spread out on a bed.

The dress on the left was a classic cream strapless sundress. It was fitted through the bodice with a sweetheart neckline lined in yellow ribbon and flared out a bit at the hips. There was an underskirt of yellow silk and a pair of awesome red leather wedge sandals. The dress on the right was a appealing purple confection with lots of embellishments, a little too fancy for her taste. The heels with that dress were stilettos, and she did not want to walk the streets of Rome in those torture devices. The wedges were tall, but they wouldn't kill her feet as much. And she was less likely to fall.

She hoped.

With her decision made, she began to get dressed, smiling at the sight of the lacy white panties and strapless bra that went with the dress. Thankfully, her hair would dry pin straight, but she tried to smooth it down as she brushed it back then twisted it up, digging through her makeup bag to find more hairpins while Alex talked on the phone. By the time he was finished, she was slipping in her small gold hoop earrings, a birthday gift from her best friend. Homesickness tightened her stomach for a moment at the thought of how much she needed to tell her best friend about how her world had changed, how it had become an exciting and frightening place that she sometimes didn't recognize.

"Jessica," Alex whispered, and she let out a soft sigh at their reflections in the mirror.

He stood behind her, and she came up to just under his chin without her heels on. His broad shoulders framed her body. The softness of his black suit jacket brushed against her, and she once again marveled at how debonair he looked. The black and yellow tie he wore complimented her dress, and she wondered if he'd done it on purpose.

He bent down and pressed his lips to the side of her throat, lightly licking her skin and causing pleasure to spark through her. "You have a beautiful neck, graceful and elegant. Like ballerina."

She giggled, the compliment making her both uncomfortable and happy. "Thanks. You have a beautiful everything, big and hard like a sex god."

That made him chuckle, and she beamed at him, enjoying the open happiness on his usually guarded face.

There was a knock on the door, and as soon as

244

she smelled the food, she was starving. They ate quickly, almost wolfing down their breakfast. By the time she'd drank the last of her coffee, she was full and sleepy. Alex smiled at her from across the table.

"I like that look on you."

"What look?"

"Pleased, content." He frowned momentarily. "Is hard to find word, so I explain. It is plain for any man to see when he looks at you that you are happy to be my woman, that I am taking care of you and providing for you. That I am doing my job of being your man. Is very important to me that you are satisfied, content. If man who wanted you were to see you upset, he might think he could lure you away."

"Alex, no one is going to try to lure me away."

He shrugged. "Besides, when I see you like this, it makes me feel good inside."

She reached behind her and touched the rough hair of his goatee. "You don't need to go to all these crazy lengths to make me happy, Alex. The only thing I want is you."

He kissed her wrist. "Come, you make me forget myself. I take you somewhere special."

The rapid thunder of her pulse filled Jessica's head as they stood before an elegant store not too far from their hotel, down the Spanish Steps and off on one of the side streets. The building she stared at was made of a beige stone, with three amazing brass-lined arches splitting up the façade. The window on her left held glittering diamond necklaces and bracelets, each exquisite and amazing. The window on her right displayed what looked like an emerald jewelry suite with stones bigger than her thumb nail in the necklace and earrings. The marble arch in the center led to the front doors of the famous Bvlgari jewelry store.

What the hell were they doing here?

Her apprehension must have registered with Alex, or he noticed that she was frozen in place.

"Jessica?"

Behind her, Maks took a step closer, his eyes, covered by sunglasses, constantly scanned the crowd that flowed around them. He was also in a perfectly tailored gray suit that set off his red hair nicely and clung to his lean frame. She had to admit, it was enjoyable being surrounded by so much male yumminess.

They were in some crazy high-end shopping district, and she was glad she had dressed up. Gorgeous women strutted their stuff left and right, their swaying walk meant to entice the male eye while their haughty expression told men to back off. Look, but don't touch—until they caught sight of Alex. Their gazes would warm as they took him in. He ignored them and kept his attention focused on her, more specifically, on anyone near her. Ahead of them, Krom played advance guard while one of Uncle Peter's men made sure they weren't being followed.

It was crazy. It was excessive, but if she was being honest, it also brought a welcome sense of safety.

"Jessica?" Alex asked again with a little more concern in his tone.

"What are we doing here?"

He took in her expression, and the corners of his lips curled up. She noticed that when they were out in public among strangers, he rarely, if ever, smiled. The most she got usually was a small twist of his lips. His don't-fuck-with-me vibe was out in full force, seemingly strong enough to dissuade anyone from getting near her. But as he slipped off his sunglasses and put them in his pocket, his gunmetal gray eyes softened to silver while his gaze roamed her face.

"If I told you, would not be surprise."

As they approached the front doors, they were held open by a tall, well-built Italian man who was almost as stone-faced as Alex.

Definitely hired muscle.

As soon as they were inside, an elegantly dressed brunette woman in her early forties escorted them back to what looked like a private room. She chatted with Alex in Italian while Maks trailed behind them. The lovely scent of lilacs flavored the air, and Jessica noticed a big silver vase on a small table stuffed full of purple and white lilacs artfully arranged with some greens. The woman took them through yet another door and down a short hallway where she opened a door to the left. Once they reached the well-appointed room, Jessica focused on the two comfortable cream leather chairs that had been set before a desk with a pristine black velvet mat. Beautiful classic art graced two of the walls, pastoral scenes that were a soothing blend of colors. A bottle of champagne had been opened and chilled in an ice bucket, along with two glasses and some beautiful strawberries.

Jessica was contemplating whether or not she should have a drink—after all, it would go to waste if she didn't—when she heard Alex say her name.

Calming the butterflies in her stomach, she turned and smiled, the tilt of her lips becoming genuine when she saw Alex gazing warmly at her, but faded a bit when she noticed they had unexpected company. Next to Alex stood an enormous man with the build of a bulldozer. His nose had been broken more than once, and he reeked of danger. It was only when she looked into his really pretty teal blue eyes that she noticed he was dressed in a suit as nice as Alex's, and that he was giving her an appreciative look that made heat prickle in her lower belly.

She couldn't help but lower her gaze and bit her lower lip, an action that made Alex chuckle.

"Ivan, she likes you."

"What is not to like?" Ivan remarked with a slow smile.

Goodness, he was handsome in a non-traditional way. No, not handsome...memorable. She tried to keep her heart from racing, but with Alex and this Ivan guy staring at her, she could almost feel their hot looks like a physical touch. The only consolation over her fluttering pulse was that the über-professional woman who worked here also looked a little glassy-eyed and stunned as she stared at the men. Not that Jessica could fault her. The chance of seeing two guys this striking together in a lifetime was rare, at least it was in Iowa. Then again, all of Alex's friends she'd met were hot.

Even his bodyguards.

Well, except for Oleg, because that was just ewww since he was kind of like an uncle to her now, but the rest were pretty fine in their own different ways.

"Lovely, isn't she?" Alex murmured in English.

"Stunning." Ivan gave her a little incline of his head. "It is a pleasure to meet you, Jessica. My name is Ivan, and I have known this bastard next to me for as long as I can remember. He does not deserve you."

To her surprise, Ivan's English was excellent. "I...that is...thank you-I think, but trust me when I say if anyone is unworthy, it's me. Alex is wonderful."

Alex frowned, but before he could say anything, Ivan chuckled and looked at his friend with a raised brow. "Lucky bastard. Sweet and charming, with beautiful legs I would like wrapped around me."

Instead of being pissed, Alex seemed proud, his shoulders straightened and his chest puffed out as the men chuckled and said something to each other in Russian. She was quickly realizing he liked showing her off like she was the treasured prize in some mighty conquest. There was a definite possessive gleam in his eyes, yet he seemed almost pleased that Ivan was openly devouring her with his gaze. The fact that this was taking place in the most elegant of establishments only made her body heat faster.

So forbidden.

So taboo.

So hot.

"Come here, *prinsessa moya*," Alex purred.

The carpet softened her footsteps as she went to him, taking his hand when he held it out to her. He pulled her to his side in a blatantly possessive move. As if to reinforce this, his hand slipped around her waist, his fingers resting on her hip. Ivan took all of this in with an amused look, and she could see Maks across the room trying to hide a smirk. It was good to see him smiling again. For a while there, she thought he was going to be stuck in a constant pissed off I-failed-you angst mode. That attitude would have driven her nuts.

Alex looked over at the saleswoman openly observing them with great interest. "Bring me the first two sets from her collection."

The woman blinked at his curt tone then scurried off.

Jessica frowned up at Alex. "What collection?"

"I had line of your own jewelry started. Unique pieces that you can pass down to your children. Things that will become treasures they will cherish as the years pass."

"Alex, that's outrageous!" She could feel her eyes grow wide, and Alex frowned when she squeaked out, "You can't do that!"

"I can do whatever I want, Jessica." She opened

her mouth to argue, but he silenced her with a kiss then whispered against her lips, "Let me do this for you. It brings me pleasure."

"But it's too much. I don't want you thinking I'm using you for your money."

He laughed against her mouth. "Jessica, I believe you. I know many, many women that are gold diggers. You are nothing like them. Let me spoil you, please."

Before she could respond, he proceeded to kiss her into a near-stupor, sucking on her lips, biting her tongue, mauling her in the most delicious way. By the time he eased off, she was swaying with her hand pressed to her lips. They were tender to touch, but she could still taste him.

"Will you let me do this for you?"

Completely dazzled by his kiss, she nodded slowly and murmured, "Okay."

Ivan laughed then patted Alex on the shoulder. "You will have your hands full with this one, but I think you will be all right."

She narrowed her eyes at Ivan, but before she could say anything, the saleswoman returned with two middle-aged men. Each of them carried a small stack of boxes. Some long, some square, and a couple small ones. A tremor ran through her, and she fought the urge to flee when they set the boxes down on the table to the left of the square of black velvet. She had a feeling Alex had done something extravagant, outrageous even, and she swallowed hard.

Ivan cleared his throat. "Jessica, it was my pleasure to meet you. I am glad to see reason behind my friend's happiness. Be good to him, yes?"

Still dazed by the sight of all those boxes, she nodded, her gaze darting between Ivan and Alex, who now sat in one of the chairs in front of the black velvet table. He didn't look uncomfortable in the least. No, he was the master of his world, in control of every situation. Once again, the clerks were kissing his ass as they waited on her. That only made her more nervous, and she almost jumped when something cold and smooth was put in her hand.

Ivan wrapped his big hand over hers to hold a full champagne glass in her hand. She noticed the scars on his knuckles.

Yep, definitely a fighter. Big time by the looks of it.

"Drink," Ivan prompted.

There was something about him that reminded her of Alex, an intangible force that compelled her to drain the glass of the crisp champagne. She handed the empty flute to Ivan who smiled, his blue eyes lighting up. Once she got past his scary appearance, he seemed like a nice guy.

"I must go, but I hope to see you again soon, Jessica."

"Nice meeting you, Ivan."

He tossed a strawberry at her before he left, which she caught with a grin. Taking a bite of the tart fruit, the champagne already warming her blood, she sauntered over to the table with a sway to her step thanks to the tall wedge heels, but she wasn't complaining. The way Alex watched her made up for any lingering self-doubt, and his open admiration made her brave.

As she sat in the chair next to his then arranged her dress around her legs, she looked up at Alex from beneath her lashes. "Open."

She popped the last bite of the strawberry in his mouth then smiled at him.

The woman across the desk cleared her throat. "Mr. Gorev, which set would you like to start with?"

Her nerves began to clamor again, but before she could freak out, Alex leaned over and whispered into her ear, "For the last few months, I've known you would be mine, so I began to design your line of jewelry."

"You...you had this made when we hadn't even..."—she cut a glance to the people watching them with feigned disinterest then back to Alex who was watching her intently—"kissed yet?"

"Yes." He leaned forward, his chair creaking slightly as his weight shifted. "You already belonged to me. I just had not claimed you yet."

"What?"

He laughed, then held her hand in his, and kissed her knuckles. "*Prinsessa moya*, I am trying to shower you with jewels. The least you could do is pretend to be excited."

When he put it that way, she felt like an ungrateful shit. "I-I'm sorry. Thank you. I'm just not used to this. People don't live like this where I'm from. Guys don't do things like this."

"Is not true. If your adoptive father had financial means, would he not have done same thing for his wife?"

"Well, yeah, he would." She sighed in defeat and tried to shake off her negative thoughts. He was right. Her dad would have given her mom the sun, moon, and stars if he could have. Her parents had the kind of loving relationship she wanted, but she hadn't realized what being with Alex would mean financially to her. If him giving her nice things was going to be a way of life with them, if he truly needed to do it in order to feel happy, she could at least be gracious about it. Hell, he was giving her a personal jewelry line.

And he said he'd had them made just for her.

If she wasn't already sitting down, she was sure she would have been swooning like some leading lady in an old black and white movie. "Alex, did you really design these pieces?"

"I gave them ideas on what I wanted. We have great deal of jewelry in my family. Is tradition to buy our women beautiful things, and I have seen many pieces that belonged to my ancestors. And you, *dorogoya*, are an excellent muse."

A frisson of excitement heated her blood, and she gave him a tentative smile. "Thank you."

Alex jerked his chin. "I want the Spring Collection first."

"Of course, Mr. Gorev," the woman murmured, giving Jessica a quick, envious look before nodding to the two men standing on either side of the table.

With perfect synchronization, the two men placed boxes on the velvet before Jessica. The boxes were what looked like black leather with the Bvlgari name in gold on the top. The chair Jessica sat in creaked a bit as she leaned forward, eager to see what she'd inspired Alex to make more than the actual jewelry itself. The woman slipped on a pair of what looked like white silk gloves and opened the first case.

Her English was decent as she said, "The first piece in the Spring Collection is a pair of pink diamond and pearl earrings. The main stones are one and a half carats while the pearls are an exceptional South Sea natural pearl."

Jessica blinked rapidly, dazzled by the elegant beauty of the jewelry. It was simple, the pink diamond studs with the pinky sized white pearls dangling beneath, but at the same time crazy extravagant because those were *pink* fucking diamonds. She tried to slow her breathing, and Alex squeezed her hand.

He leaned over, his citrus and sandalwood cologne somehow reassuring her and whispered, "Someday, you will get used to this and enjoy it."

253

She was spared from answering by the woman revealing a stunning white pearl necklace with a large pink diamond in the center. The woman rattled on about the details then showed Jessica a bracelet that went with it, as well as two cocktail rings. Her mind couldn't comprehend that these exquisite things now belonged to her, but that didn't mean she didn't want to clap and giggle just a little bit.

They were so *pretty*.

Alex said something in Italian, and the staff as well as Maks left the room, closing the door behind them and leaving her alone with him. It took some effort to tear her eyes away from the sparkly jewelry that seemed to call her name, but she managed to look at Alex with a big, genuine smile. "It is amazing, Alex. Really. It takes my breath away. I can't believe you made this for me. No one has ever done anything like this for me before."

She didn't even realize she was crying until he brushed his thumb beneath her eye. "Shhh, no tears. Will ruin makeup."

"Crap," she said with a shaky laugh while she got herself under control. "Right. Okay. I'm okay. It's just kind of overwhelming, but very much appreciated. Holy cow."

He stood and grabbed another box, this one a long rectangle. As soon as he sat down he tugged her out of her chair then pushed his chair back. "Kneel before me."

She swayed on her heels in shock. "What?"

"I have a gift for you, but it will only be given to you if you are on your knees."

"We are in a public place, Alex, a fancy one! We can't do that here."

"Jessica, I will not tell you again. On your knees. Now. No one will come in. Maks will make sure of it."

Swallowing hard, she nervously knelt before him,

ready to leap to her feet the moment anyone came in. "They won't leave us alone with all of this stuff. They'll come back for it, and I really don't want to be on my knees in front of them. It doesn't turn me on, Alex."

Instead of being mad, he leaned forward and tucked her hair behind her ear with that soft smile that melted her heart...and her panties. "Thank you for being honest with me about your needs. They will not come in here because you own this jewelry. It is in your name, and you cannot steal from yourself."

"But—"

He cut her off by placing his hand firmly over her mouth. "Only acceptable words are 'thank you, Alexandr'."

When he removed his hand, she gave him a surly, "Thank you, Alexandr."

For a few long moments, he merely looked down at her, studying her face as she looked back at him, getting turned on by the heat in his eyes. "Jessica, I have something for you that is very important to me."

For a second, she thought he was going to propose to her and was relieved then shocked when that wasn't what he had to say at all.

He tapped the rectangular box on his lap. "This is your collar, Jessica. A symbol that you belong to me."

"A-a what?"

He made a soothing sound. "I told you I want to own you. This is part of it."

"But, Alex, I can't go around wearing a dog collar."

The rich tone of his laughter filled the small room, and she relaxed marginally. "*Lyubov moya*, is not what you think. Go ahead, open."

Trying not to be too apprehensive, she slowly opened the lid and let out a soft gasp.

It was a choker made of gold bars encrusted with sapphires, interspacing a triple strand of creamy pearls. At the center of the choker hung a large heart shaped sapphire surrounded by gold and baguette diamonds. She reached for the beautiful jewelry, then hesitated, and looked up at Alex.

"May I?"

"It is yours, Jessica, but only by choice. You willingly wear my collar. I do not force you. Is gift you give me, gift of yourself."

She ran her hands over the necklace, the smooth pearls teasing her fingertips. "Gorgeous. But how do I put it on?"

He pressed two diamonds surrounding the sapphire heart, and it opened somehow, the sapphire heart sliding off and revealing a small locking mechanism. She gasped then looked up at him with a huge smile. "That is so cool!"

Her reaction seemed to startle him, then something deep in his eyes softened, and she felt suddenly shy at the intensity of his gaze. Oh yeah, he had feelings for her, big ones. Although she was experienced sexually, in relationships, she was still learning as she went, but even she recognized that Alex's feelings for her were...undeniable. He made her feel almost constantly adored, when he wasn't being an arrogant dick.

The light gleamed off the exposed gold, and she took the open pearl and sapphire choker from him. To her surprise, it fit just right, and as she took the sapphire heart, ready to put it on, Alex stopped her by grasping her hand in his, and she pondered how big his hands were. Yes, she'd felt them on her and adored his touch, but damn, her man made her feel delicate. So much power, yet he handled her like she was made of crystal.

"You understand when you do this you are

accepting another layer of my ownership over you, yes? You must think about this. Is not a decision to be made lightly. This collar means I own you in a way that cannot be denied. My stamp, warning off those who would try to take you from me."

Considering him, she took a deep breath and forced herself to clear her thoughts. After a few moments, her mind had focused enough to think. "Alex, I know you. Well, sort of. There is that whole 'secret world' shit I have to deal with. For God's sakes, only I would fall for a man who can't tell me who he really is. It's scary, and it's intimidating, and it's daunting for me to be your woman."

He looked her in the eyes, pinning her in place with his anger. "Who has tried to intimidate you, Jessica? Is important you tell me."

Blowing a strand of her hair out of her face, she tried to ignore how hot he looked when he was angry. It was like visual sexual candy. Especially when his hand still held hers tightly, not letting her pull away in the slightest. Claiming her...holding her in place. She couldn't get away from him. Especially if she wore his collar.

Without another word, she gently removed his hand from hers then slid the lock closed. When it clicked shut, she shuddered, puzzled by her strong reaction to wearing this beautiful piece of jewelry. Her pulse quickened, and she had some rather naughty thoughts about doing things to Alex in this room. Surrounded by millions of dollars in jewelry.

In Rome.

She could use another glass of champagne.

"Now," Alex said in a soft voice, "let me show you how to take it off."

Feeling strangely possessive of the choker, she placed her hand over the clasp. "Why would you do that?" she murmured.

257

He gave her a slow, easy smile. The light caught the silver in his eyes, making them shine at her. Goodness, her panties were about to fall off. The fact that she was the one to make him happy like this delighted her, even as she frowned over having to fasten and unfasten the lock several times.

"Do not get too attached to the choker. Is one of many. When you wear any piece of jewelry I've given you around your neck, it all means the same thing. You are mine, mine to spoil, mine to love."

Her nose burned, and tears prickled her eyes. "You need to stop, right now, before I cry. And if you make me walk down that street with raccoon eyes among all those fabulous people, I'll be really irritated with you."

He laughed again, and with a firm touch, helped her stand. Then he gently pushed her back so he could stand. With her free hand, she brushed back her hair from her face and realized she could smell him on her skin now. His cologne scented her fingers, adding another layer of his ownership to her. Christ, now she was thinking like him. That couldn't be good.

"Jessica, why are you sniffing your hand?"

She startled and gave him a slightly guilty look. "I could smell your cologne on my skin."

Oh, that pleased him.

With a noticeable growl in his voice, he cupped her cheek. "I like when you smell of me, Jessica. There is no mistaking you have been with a man when my scent clings to your skin."

She couldn't help but laugh, and her tension eased. "Jesus, why don't you just pee on me?"

Shaking his head, he strode over to her with a small box then handed it to her. "Earrings."

Inside the box was a pair of sapphire studs, not huge, but tastefully large. Part of her mind tried to figure out how much they cost, but she squashed

258

those thoughts. She was tired of freaking out. "Alex, these are gorgeous."

He helped her change out her plain gold hoops, handling them with the same care with which he'd handled a pair of earrings that cost more than ten thousand dollars. Her hands shook as she put them in, finally getting the tricky backings on with Alex's help. When they were in, he leaned back, quickly scanning her features, then smiled, big.

"As I thought, the sapphires bring out the lighter blues in your eyes. Such beauty, and all mine. Come, you need to see."

When they neared the mirror, she saw her reflection and immediately stopped chewing on her lower lip. Jeeze, she had no idea she looked that weird when she was doing it. Trying to smooth out her expression, she couldn't help but stare at her reflection. She looked beautiful, sophisticated, and elegant, things she never would have thought about herself before. Though she knew she was pretty, Alex truly brought out the beauty in her, and it wasn't just cosmetic. Her whole face glowed with happiness, probably a result of the plethora of orgasms Alex had given her.

Or maybe just because he was a super awesome boyfriend...or Master...or whatever.

He kissed between her eyebrows. "That little line means you are thinking too hard. Enjoy the moment, Jessica."

Meeting his gaze, she smiled and admired the necklace and earrings in the mirror. "These are so beautiful. Everything is gorgeous. Thank you, it really means a lot to me that you went to all this effort to make me happy."

"You are most welcome, *prinsessa moya*." His obvious satisfaction at having given them to her almost rolled off of him, and she had to hide a smile.

"Come, we need to return to the hotel. I have a meeting to attend to, and Catrin is taking you shopping."

Pulled away from watching the sapphire heart sparkle, she startled. Crap, she'd totally forgotten about that. Once again, the idea of being away from Alex didn't appeal to her, but she wasn't going to be one of those women who stuck to their man like glue. She needed her space, liked her space, and could use a little time away from him to get her shit together. Hopefully, this Catrin wasn't too scary. From what Alex said, she was some kind of socialite superstar and had been in more than a few scandals. He wouldn't say what they were, but she hoped it wasn't for being a raging bitch.

They left soon after, Alex holding her hand as she floated on a cloud of happiness next to him, proud to be on the arm of such a wonderful man. As they slowly strolled together, she could understand his pleasure at showing her off because, in a way, she did the same with him. Yeah, she wasn't a fan of women openly flirting with Alex right in front of her, but their admiration of him made her feel good because he was hers. This handsome, extraordinary, generous, amazing man was hers.

She tugged him to a stop, moving out of the way of foot traffic, and leaned against the dark stone of one of the exquisite shops. Not too far away, the Spanish Steps gleamed in the morning light, and the spray from the fountain in the plaza below threw little rainbows into the air. With the sun warm on her face, she looked up at him and wished he wasn't wearing his sunglasses.

"What is it, Jessica?"

Standing on her tiptoes, she placed a sweet, lingering kiss on his lips. "I'm just so happy to be here with you."

260

His small smile warmed her more than the sun as he rubbed his nose against hers. "So am I."

Before she realized it, they were back at the hotel. Instead of heading to their suite, they continued through the lobby, hooked a left, and Alex led her into the bar. Adrenaline cleared her head of her happy buzz when Alex called out, "Catrin, Nico."

She followed his line of sight through the busy room and saw a curvy, lush, little blonde smile at them and wave. Her lips were pink, her skin like porcelain, and she had big, blue eyes that looked like they belonged on a Disney princess. Based on looks alone, Catrin seemed like she should be teaching kindergarten, or riding on a unicorn while birds flew around her like princess out of a cartoon. For sure, sweet looking Catrin wasn't the kind of woman Jessica had pictured when Alex described her as a scandalous socialite. And Nico...wow. He was an intimidating, very suave black man with short hair and a sharp bone structure that looked good on him. He wore a black suit with a tie that complimented Catrin's red and black block print dress. When his gaze met hers, his smile was dazzling.

Boy howdy, Alex had some beautiful friends.

The black man spoke first, and she was a little shocked at his heavy Russian accent. "This must be Jessica. Is good to meet the woman that has stolen my friend's heart."

Catrin stood with a little squeal and hugged Alex tightly then hugged Jessica with equal enthusiasm. "Hello, darling. I've heard so much about you from Maks and Dimitri."

A little surprised by the woman's bubbly enthusiasm, Jessica smiled. "Uh...hi. Nice to meet you."

With a giggle, Catrin leaned back and studied Jessica from the top of her head, her gaze lingering on the collar, down to her feet before she clapped her hands and declared, "Gorgeous. I am so happy for you, Alex! She is stunning. And such lovely skin and hair with those unusual cat-like eyes. And she is sweet, I can tell. No, I have decided she is too good for you. I will have to keep her for myself...but if you are nice, I will share. Or maybe just let you watch."

Well, that answered why Catrin was the focus of so many scandals. The people in the bar area all looked mildly shocked, which for Europeans was like an American OMG face. Instead of hushing her, Nico and Alex merely laughed and ignored the disapproving looks thrown their way. It dawned on Jessica that they genuinely didn't give a shit. They merely shook their heads as Nico gently took her hand in his big, well-manicured one.

His grip was firm and his voice low. "Hmm, perhaps if I promise you as a wedding present, I can get Catrin to marry me."

Catrin said something in a rapid, and what sounded like pissed off, stream of Russian before stomping back to their table, grabbing her purse, and giving Nico a dirty look before she latched her arm through Jessica's.

"We are going shopping."

Alex sighed and held his hand out. "Jessica, come here."

She managed to untangle herself from Catrin, who was glaring at a smirking Nico, and went to Alex.

He leaned down and whispered in her ear, "As your Master, I give you permission to enjoy anything you want with Catrin."

"What?"

"You are in different world now, my world, and in my world, I make rules. You do not worry about right and wrong. If I say is okay, is okay. I want you to enjoy yourself, to take all pleasure life has to offer."

Conscious of curious eyes on them, she leaned in and whispered, "I don't understand. Do I get to make the rules, too? What are you talking about?"

He merely grinned at her—the jerk—and she found herself being dragged out of the bar by the hand before she could draw a breath.

"Darling," Catrin slowed their pace once they were out of the lobby, "I'm sorry about that unpleasantness. Nico and I are having...issues at the moment."

She thought about beating around the bush and decided against it. "Was he serious about wanting to marry you?"

The other woman gave an adorable pout then nodded. "Yes, the bastard."

"Umm, that's a bad thing?"

"Yes and no." Catrin led her into a waiting silver Rolls Royce where a burly guy held the car door open for them. "I love him to death. I just don't do marriage."

Eager to change the subject, Jessica said, "Where are we going?"

"A private designer I know. You can get anything in Rome, but we're not buying you clothes."

"We're not?"

"No, we're buying you lingerie."

Chapter Seventeen

During the limo ride, Jessica learned the bubbly woman spent a lot of time in the States—she was the daughter of the Russian Ambassador to the US—and had lived in Washington DC for nine years while growing up. As they talked about life back in America, Jessica realized how much she missed home. Before she could dwell too long on her homesickness, Catrin's cheerful gossip about the famous people she knew in Hollywood had them both giggling. A man wearing a black helmet on a motorcycle pulled up next to them, and Jessica was shocked when Catrin proceeded to flirt with him, lowering the top of her dress almost all the way so her breasts were fully exposed and leaning forward so he got a good look.

"Oh my God!" Jessica laughed as Catrin blew the man, who shook his head and fell back a pace behind the car, a kiss. "What are you doing?"

"It's just Maks," Catrin replied with a smile. "He's seen much, much more of me than this."

"Did you two...uh...date?"

"No, but we've fucked many times." She giggled when Jessica blushed bright red. "What has Alex told you about me?"

Still trying to find her footing around this somewhat intimidating woman, Jessica looked away. "Just that you are a socialite and one of his good friends."

"Hmm, that's it? He didn't mention that Nico and I are...what do you Americans call it...swingers?"

The casual way she said that made Jessica whip her gaze from studying the buildings they were passing in downtown Rome to Catrin. "What?"

"You should see your face." She giggled and reached over to lightly tap Jessica's nose. "Most of Alex's friends are into sharing."

A terrible thought twisted in Jessica's stomach, jealousy clenching her muscles mixed with pain. "I see."

"That upsets you. Why?"

She licked her lips then looked away again, fighting back tears at the thought that Alex might expect her to share him with another woman. "Nothing."

Catrin took her hand and squeezed it gently. "Please, Jessica, tell me what I said to make you so unhappy. Alex will skin me alive if I make you cry. He is very protective of you, and I did not mean to upset you. I am...honest to a...fault? I think that is the term."

"Do you think Alex will want to share me...or himself?"

"Oh, darling, is that what you're worried about? Nico and I have sex with other people, it is true, but only when we are together. I find watching him fuck other women to be highly arousing, but only women I choose. Let me think of how to explain this." She continued to hold Jessica's hand, but her gaze went distant. "The women we share, and the men that he gives the privilege of touching me, are all good friends who know the difference between sex and love. Nico is a handsome man, and very sexual, but his heart belongs to me. He could fuck a thousand women and that wouldn't change his devotion to me."

"Don't you get jealous? I'll be honest, the thought of Alex touching another woman makes me feel violent."

With a soft laugh, Catrin nodded. "Of course, but not with the women we play with. They're mostly submissives from the BDSM club we belong to back home, women who belong to his friends. It is almost like a bonding thing in our close circle, the ultimate act of trust. These men know my devotion to Nico and are aware that, not only would I not cheat on Nico, but that he'd kill them if they tried anything without his permission."

Turning more fully on the plush leather seat to face Catrin, she studied the other woman. "I guess that kind of makes sense. But I don't think I could watch Alex have sex with anyone else." She paused a moment. "No, I know I couldn't. Do you...do you think he'll be mad if I say no?"

"Of course not." Catrin smiled. "I don't think you understand how in love with you Alex is."

"He loves me?"

"Jessica, he is moving heaven and earth for you."

"What do you mean?"

The humor dropped from Catrin's gaze, and Jessica wondered how much of the other woman's bubbly personality was an act. There was a fierce intelligence hidden behind her soft beauty. "In all the time I've known Alex, he has liked easy women. Not like the American slang of easy meaning a woman is a slut, though he's had those as well, but women who do not complicate his already complicated life."

"Oh." She thought of all the effort Alex had gone to on her behalf, and doubt pierced her like an arrow to her chest.

Catrin made a tsking noise. "Do not look so sad. My point is that, for you, he has asked all of his friends to come meet you because you are *very* important to him. He has never done this with a woman before. Ever."

She couldn't keep the pleased smile off her face. "Really?"

"Absolutely." Catrin leaned closer, their knees

touching as the scent of her floral perfume tickled at Jessica's nose. "Be patient with him. This loving a woman is all new to him, and there will be a...I can't think of the word...there will be bumps in the road, yes? There will be people that will try to tear you apart, people that will try to use you against him, but you must hold onto your feelings for him. It will take a strong woman to love Alex, but I promise you, it will be worth it."

"People are going to try to tear us apart?"

Leaning back, Catrin shrugged. "Is the way of the world. People are jealous and greedy. They will tell you lies and try to manipulate you."

Jessica rubbed her temples. "Great."

"I am not making this any better, am I?"

"No, no, I appreciate your honesty. I just...I guess I didn't think about what being Alex's girlfriend would mean. You probably think I'm really dumb."

"I do not think you are dumb. I think you have been thrust into a world you are unfamiliar with, and that you are doing the best you can to understand it." She smoothed a strand of hair from Jessica's face. "I will be your friend and help you, not only because I love Alex, but because I think you will be very good for him. Our men lead hard lives, make hard decisions, and are under a great deal of stress. We, their women, are the one comfort they allow themselves. It makes us the most precious thing in their world."

"Really?"

"Darling," she chided gently, "you make him happy. It is a priceless gift to Alex. He will do everything in his considerable power to make you happy as well."

"He already has," she whispered and touched the necklace.

Catrin's eyes gleamed as she leaned forward.

"Please tell me if I am being too nosy, but is that necklace...special to you? Did Alex explain what it is?"

Sure that her ears were about to burn off, Jessica whispered, "He...uh...said it was my collar."

"Fantastic!" To her surprise, Catrin squealed and clapped. "Goodness, that is so exciting!"

"What?"

Still bouncing in her seat, Catrin smiled. "Alex has never collared a woman before. Oh, he is a much sought after Master, and he's had plenty of submissives, but never anything like this. Is very big deal."

That stupid jealousy twisted her gut again. She knew Alex had probably slept with half of the vagina-endowed population of Europe. Even so, that didn't mean she wanted to think about his past conquests. Then the wording of Catrin's statement hit her. "What do you mean 'he's a sought after Master'?"

Catrin's gaze swept over her face, and whatever she saw there seemed to drain away some of her excitement. "How much do you know about BDSM?"

"I've read about it and stuff, but I've never done it."

"Ohhh," Catrin gave a little mock shiver, and her blue-eyed gaze heated. "A virgin."

Unable to help herself, Jessica laughed at the almost greedy look on Catrin's face. "Hardly."

"I do not mean physically. I mean you have never experienced the pleasure of subspace?"

"I'm not even sure what subspace is."

Catrin gave her a huge smile. "It is the best feeling *ever*."

"Well, that's helpful."

With a giggle, Catrin took her hand again. "Technical explanation. Subspace is a chemical reaction that leaves you with very good, very intense,

269

yet relaxing, floating feelings. Or at least it does with me. Time becomes...like taffy? Is stretched and pulled, and pleasure is more intense, much more intense. Like so intense you will do anything your Master wants, happily, in order to fly in subspace."

"And how do you get there?"

"Is different with every woman. Some through pain. Some through domination. Some through mind games. Do not worry. Alex will figure out what works for you. Is part of the fun for him."

"And what does he get out of it?"

"Why, making you happy, of course. You need to understand that for the men of my culture making their woman pleased is their number one priority, though to those on the outside, it may not look that way. We give them ourselves, and in return, they give us everything. I need only to mention that I like something, and Nico will buy it for me. Not because I asked him to, but because it is something that will bring me pleasure. It makes him feel good to know he can provide for me." Catrin sighed then gave Jessica's hand a squeeze, old sorrow dimming her gaze. "Nico did not have an easy life. He was born into a poor family, and because of the color of his skin, he has had to fight for every penny, and ounce of respect, that he has. A lesser man would never have survived my beloved's childhood."

It had never occurred to Jessica that there would be racism in Russia. "You mean people are prejudiced because he is black?"

"Extremely prejudice. If not for Alex, Nico would probably still be living in the godforsaken slums of his hometown."

"What do you mean?"

"Many years ago, Alex and his father were spending time with their...business associates in the city where Nico lived." She pressed her lips together then looked away, and her voice became thick. "Nico's mother was a prostitute, his father a drunk who would disappear in and out of their lives. In order to make extra money, Nico would work at the brothel where his mother sold herself as an errand boy and a form of protection. Even though he was only fifteen, Nico was big for his age and a fierce fighter. He had to be in order to survive. Because of the color of his skin, he was often targeted, and with no father to defend him, he had to learn how to defend himself."

"That's terrible," Jessica murmured. Compassion for the man made her chest ache.

"Gets worse. The pimp that ran the brothel accused Nico's mother of stealing from him, and in order to make an example, he took Nico's mother outside into the courtyard and in front of the rest of the whores he…" Catrin sucked in a harsh breath then said in a rush, "he had her pinkie finger cut off."

Nausea roiled through Jessica's stomach. "Oh, my God!"

"Yes. One of the other prostitutes told Nico what was happening, but by the time he arrived, the deed had already been done, and the pimp was watching his mother scream in pain while she bled into the snow. Nico went insane with rage and almost beat the pimp to death before he was hauled off of him. Certain that he was going to die, Nico fought with everything he had, not realizing that the men holding him back were not the pimp's men, but instead, part of the Novi— I mean, worked for Alex's father. They'd been in the area and had heard the woman's screams." Her face was momentarily shadowed as their car passed by some tall buildings.

"What did they do to him?"

"Alex had recently lost his mother and half-sister, so he understood Nico's rage. He intervened on Nico's behalf and managed to convince Jorg, that's

Alex's father, to take Nico on as a sort of apprentice. It did not take them long to realize that Nico is brilliant, and I am not bragging like a woman in love. Nico's IQ is 139."

"Holy shit," Jessica breathed. "He's a genius."

"He is, and not only that, he is ambitious. He recognized the priceless gift Alex had given him that day and worked hard to repay his kindness. Jorg may be many things, and most of them not good, but he did not care that Nico was black, only that he was smart and fiercely loyal. The Nov—Gorevs sent Nico to school in Zurich where he studied chemistry, and now, after many years of hard work, Nico owns one of the most profitable pharmaceutical manufacturing firms in Russia." The pride in her voice was evident, reinforced by Catrin sitting straighter and lifted her chin. "But he never forgot where he came from. He donates a great deal of money to various charities for the poor, and while there are still whispers behind his back because of the color of his skin, they no longer say it to his face. They don't dare."

"Wow," Jessica breathed. "Just...wow. He's amazing."

"He is," Catrin agreed with a small smile curving her full lips, "And so is Alex."

For the rest of the ride, they were silent, each wrapped up in her own thoughts. Jessica tried to imagine the world Alex had grown up in, one where women's fingers got cut off and fifteen-year-old boys made very adult decisions that quite literally saved the life of a remarkable man. The more she learned about Alex, the more she realized just how complex he was, and she couldn't help but feel a sense of pride that he loved her. Or at least Catrin was sure he loved her. She sure hoped so because it felt like her love for him was growing by the minute.

Chapter Eighteen

Maks sped past them and up a winding drive as they came to what could only be described as a dream villa on a hillside peering out over Rome. White marble columns supported a slate roof while lush plants and flowers grew in carefully arranged mounds. They were far enough away from the city to hear only the faint sound of traffic, and the air smelled cleaner out here. A steady breeze hissed through the leaves of the old-growth trees surrounding them and she took a moment to enjoy the feeling of the sun on her face. Opening her eyes, Jessica took a deep breath while she followed Catrin up the steps to the dark, heavy-looking wood front door. Before they could knock, the door opened, revealing a lovely, older woman with long gray hair held back in a braid. With a smile she ushered them into the house while speaking Italian.

From their left, a woman spoke in a heavily Italian accented voice, "*Bella*, it is so good to see you again."

They turned, and Jessica hung back as Catrin and a middle-aged woman with a hawk nose and long, dark hair exchanged cheek kisses. The other woman wore all black with only the chunky jade necklace around her throat giving a hint of color. She was very elegant, and when she exchanged cheek kisses with Jessica, she smelled good, almost like baby powder.

Stepping back, she smiled and clasped her hands together. "Ms. Venture, welcome. My name is Oriana."

"Thank you, but please call me Jessica."

273

The woman gave her a head-to-toe perusal before briskly clapping her hands together once and looking at Catrin. "You were right, jewel tones. And ice."

Moving behind Jessica, Catrin ran her fingers through Jessica's hair. "Gorgeous, isn't she?"

"Stunning. Have you done any modeling, Jessica?"

That startled a laugh out of her even as she wondered why Catrin was playing with her hair. "Me? Uh, no."

Oriana arched one perfectly shaped brow. "Really? I'm surprised you haven't been scouted yet."

Thankfully, Jessica was saved from answering when Maks came in through the front door. At the sight of the handsome man, Oriana beamed. "Maks! It's so good to see you again."

The smile he gave Oriana was downright wicked when he replied back in Italian. Whatever he said made the other woman blush bright red while Catrin and Jessica shared an amused glance. Evidently, these two had some history between them because Oriana looked like she was ready to jump Maks any second.

"Oriana?" Catrin said with laughter in her voice.

Giving them an almost guilty look, Oriana cleared her throat. "Please, follow me."

She led them down a level to a gorgeous, huge room lined with racks and racks of clothes, shoes, jewelry, more clothes, more shoes, and a spectacular set of floor-to-ceiling windows that looked out over a senic orchard. Farther down the slope sprawled Rome. It was late afternoon, and a golden haze hung over the city, a beautiful ambient light that made her wish she could take a picture of it with her phone without seeming tacky. Catrin moved up next to her and looked out at the view as well while Oriana bustled around behind them.

"Magnificent, isn't it?" Catrin remarked in a soft voice. "When bad things happen in my world, I try to remember that there is beauty like this that is worth living to see. Places that God gave us to enjoy, to lift our hearts. The world is filled with them, but most people don't get to experience it. Because I am lucky and I was born into wealth, I've been able to go to these places, but I feel like everyone should experience this. God made His gifts to be shared, to be enjoyed."

Moved by the honest passion in the other woman's voice and trying to regain control of her runaway emotions—she was such a softie sometimes—she whispered, "Would it be tacky of me to take a picture with my cell phone to send it to Alex?"

Catrin turned, studying Jessica's face with unexpectedly soft eyes. "I think he would love to hear from you. Nico sent me a text that said Alex has been pining for you, and that he's been a bastard to deal with. Maybe we send Alex a picture to cheer him up, yes?"

Smiling, she dug through her purse. "I'm totally going to do it."

When she held her camera phone up to take a selfie, Catrin made a tsking sound. "No, no, no. That will not do."

"What?"

Snapping her fingers, Catrin barked, "Oriana, I need a camera."

Instead of telling her to fuck off, the elegant, dark haired woman calmly removed a nice looking digital camera from a cupboard and brought it to Catrin while giving Jessica a critical eye.

"Maks, what do you think? I need to capture..." then Catrin launched into Russian, gesturing to

Jessica while they both examined her from head to toe.

Fidgeting, she shifted uncomfortably in her heels. "Um...guys? I just want to take a picture of the city. No big deal."

Catrin finally looked at Jessica, really looked at her, then sighed. "I forget you are not used to this, but trust me, some of my photos are in major fashion magazines. I know what I am doing, and Maks is an artist, oil painting, who does beautiful things with lighting. We are speaking in Russian because it is easier for both of us to put complex thoughts into words. Make sense?"

Before Jessica could answer, Maks stalked over to her. He said something in Italian, and Oriana brought them a set of gorgeous silver combs from one of the deep drawers along the wall. The warm lighting brought out the pine green in his eyes, and she sighed inwardly. He was such a good-looking man. Too bad he broke hearts like it was his job. She'd seen him win women over surprisingly fast, but once he'd had sex with them a couple times, they were done whether they wanted it to end or not.

He was kind of a dick like that.

Handing the combs over to her, he ignored Oriana and Catrin talking behind them, focused totally on her. "Put your hair up. Have beautiful neck, flowing lines. You display Alex's collar, and he be proud."

After taking the combs from him, she pulled her hair up into a messy bun, long tendrils hanging down here and there.

When she turned back to Catrin, she found the other woman was smiling at her. "Darling, the camera loves you. I took a couple test shots. Come see."

Flushing at the thought of pictures taken in the

past where she looked weird flashed through her mind, but when she looked at the screen on Catrin's camera, she sucked in a quick breath. No one had ever captured her image like this. In the first one, half her hair was up, the comb in her hand, and a dreamy smile hovered on her lips. She was looking out over the city, and the illumination gave her pale skin a golden tone, like she was reflecting the light. Her collar sparkled and while she definitely looked like herself, but at the same time she didn't.

"Holy moly. You're amazing"

Maks laughed while Oriana rolled her eyes. "See, you could easily be a model."

"Forget it," Catrin said while studying Jessica's dress. "Alex will never allow it. I want her in something different. With her hair, fire and ice. Something to set that sapphire off. Goodness, Alex is wasting no time proving to you he can be a good provider."

Unconsciously reaching up to touch the heart, she frowned. "What do you mean?"

"He is showing you how much you mean to him." Her camera beeped, and she looked down then smiled. "Alex says your beauty stuns him."

"Pardon?"

"I sent him one of the pictures of you to see how he would react. He is extremely pleased. I bet he is showing you off to Nico right now."

"Oh," Jessica whispered, happiness tickling her belly. "Really?"

"Mmm-hmm. He is asking for more." She looked up, a hint of heat in her big, not-so-innocent blue eyes. "Shall we give him something to look at?"

Her heart rate increased as the mood in the room changed. Without consulting anyone, Maks growled out, "Oriana, outside. This is now private sitting."

The other woman raised a brow, but nodded and

gently set aside a shirt she'd been looking at. "Of course. I will see that no one disturbs you."

"Krom is on exterior guard. Do not be alarmed if you see him."

Oriana walked through the room, her laughter filling the air. "If I can see Krom, he isn't doing his job."

When the door snicked closed behind her, Jessica bit her lip and took a step back, the blatant hunger in their combined gazes stroking her body like a touch. Her throat thickened as she tried to think of something to say to break the tension. When the cool glass of the window met her back, she jumped.

Shaking his head, Maks smirked at her. "You look like you fear for life."

After giving Maks an elbow then handing him the camera, Catrin sauntered over to Jessica. "We had to send her out. Alex would not want that woman to see your body."

"Uh...why?"

"Because he does not consider her worthy."

"That's kind of an asshole thing to do, but also kind of sweet."

Laughing, Catrin gave her a gentle hug and whispered in her ear, "That is the way it is with our men. They can be sweet. They can also be bastards, but everything they do is for us. Now, shall we do something for Alex's pleasure?"

Maks interrupted with amusement in his voice, "Alex is growing impatient."

Catrin's golden brows rose in an unspoken question, and Jessica blurted, "Okay."

The other woman didn't waste any time, taking Jessica behind a white silk and bamboo screen where there was a clothing rack stuffed with gorgeous pieces of lingerie and some dresses that were scandalous, yet obviously of haute couture quality.

"Let's get you undressed," Catrin said in a low voice and took a step closer.

With her heart pounding, Jessica started to fumble with the zipper on her dress, but Catrin slapped her hands away. "Let me."

Looking Jessica straight in the eye, she wrapped her arms around Jessica and tilted her head up so their lips were close enough for Jessica to notice that Catrin smelled like expensive bubble gum, if there was such a thing. Sugary, yet refreshing, but also delicious. Ever so slowly, Catrin lowered the zipper on the back of Jessica's dress, her fingers caressing the skin revealed as the dress parted. After what seemed like an eternity, the material pooled around her feet. Slowly, her hands lightly trailed Jessica's suddenly sensitive skin the whole way. Catrin gave Jessica a languid smile.

"I see now why Alex is so enamored with you. So beautiful and responsive." She took a half step back, her gaze taking in the strapless, white lace bra that Jessica wore. "You are going to drive Alex mad when he sees the pictures we will take for him. Do not worry about privacy, Alex's phone is secure, and I will be taking this camera with us. No one will see but him...and maybe Nico. I wouldn't put it past Alex to show my husband the pictures just for bragging rights."

Jessica was a nervous wreck of hot desire and guilt at this moment. Her pussy was wet, slick with her arousal at Catrin's open flirting. When Catrin reached around Jessica to unclasp her bra, she barely placed her lips on Jessica's throat, giving her a soft kiss on her pounding pulse. Rational thought was quickly being replaced by hunger, her kinks tripped by the fact that Maks was in the room with them. Could hear them. Wanted to watch them.

"Did Alex say you could play with me?" Catrin whispered against Jessica's skin, making her nipples bunch painfully.

"Yes."

Her voice came out in barely more than a whisper, and she closed her eyes, overcome by the intensity of Catrin's light touch as she removed Jessica's bra. Once again, she trailed her fingers over the sides of Jessica's back, but this time, her fingertips glided up the side of Jessica's breast then grazed over her nipples, making her moan in delicious torment as her tight buds crinkled further. Unable to think beyond the pounding in her groin, she moaned and arched forward, silently offering herself to Catrin. Maks' voice came from deeper in the room, speaking Russian, but Jessica was unable to focus on anything but the warmth of the woman standing before her.

She'd hadn't been this attracted to another female before. Yes, she'd fooled around with girls, but at the end of the night, she always wanted dick. The girls were just like a snack, while men were the main course. But with Catrin, she found herself fiercely attracted to the sexually confident woman and curious about what it would be like to be with someone so obviously experienced in the art of pleasuring women. Catrin ran her fingers down Jessica's ribs, making a pleased sound as that teasing touch tickled along Jessica's body, little shivers raising the fine hairs on her arms as she got goosebumps.

Instead of touching her breasts, the blond woman slid her hands into the edges of Jessica's underwear on her hips. She gently lowered them until she was bending with her face right in front of Jessica's pussy. Her clit was hard, and her thighs were trembling as she tried to stay still. Catrin could probably see the thick arousal coating her shaved pussy lips, and that knowledge made her belly quiver.

"Step out of your panties," Catrin murmured. "We must put you in something to show off your pretty pussy. Alex is lucky man. You smell so good. Wonder if taste is same."

An incoherent groan was Jessica's only response, the sound turning to a strangled gasp when Catrin leaned forward and licked her slit three times, each stroke ending with the flat of her tongue rubbing slowly against Jessica's clit. Her arousal shot through the roof, her pussy hurting for Alex's hard cock, for Catrin's fingers, for something to fill it. Then Catrin circled Jessica's clit with a delicate touch, making her stumble back a few steps. Laughing, Catrin stood, her warm blue eyes devouring Jessica and licking her lips.

"Sweet and tangy pussy, my favorite."

Unsure what to do and feeling out of her element, Jessica simply stood there while Catrin stalked closer to her. On the way, she snatched up something that was a lovely ice blue color. There was an authoritative snap in Catrin's voice. "Take your shoes off."

Another tingle went through Jessica, harder this time, and she quickly removed her shoes. With Catrin still wearing her heels, they were almost the same height. She gave Jessica a slow, somewhat intimidating smile. "Oh, Alex is a lucky bastard. You are delightfully submissive. Look how wet it makes you."

Flushing, Jessica tried to cover herself, but Catrin slapped her hands away. "Do not touch. Is my job to dress you. Alex gave me permission to play with you. I am...how would I say this? You are new to lifestyle, yes?"

"Lifestyle?"

"BDSM?"

Blinking, she nodded. "Yes."

"Then let me explain. I am switch, meaning I like to both dominate and submit...though I never dominate Nico. He is too much of an Alpha male. Always my Master." A little purr entered her seductive voice, and she stepped close enough that Jessica's aching breasts rubbed against the other woman's abundant chest. "But I do have a dominant streak for women. Not all, but the true submissives make me want to play with them. You have allure you do not know, an energy that Dominants find irresistible."

Jessica was equal parts freaked out, turned on, and curious. "What makes you think I'm a submissive?"

Leaning in, Catrin whispered, "Everything, but especially this."

With no preamble, she rubbed Jessica's pussy, her fingers sliding through the wetness, the heel of her palm teasing Jessica's clit. Her breath caught in her throat, and she moaned when Catrin slipped a finger inside of her. Right away, her pussy clenched down, and Catrin made a soft, purring noise. "That's it, beautiful girl, get nice and turned on. I want that pussy red with desire. Alex says he can turn your pink sex the color of red roses. Let's see if we can do the same."

Unable to help herself, she rocked against Catrin's fingers, her arms rising to wrap around the other woman's neck, more than ready to let the beautiful Russian switch do anything she wanted.

"Do you want my kiss, pretty girl?" Catrin whispered while she worked a second finger into Jessica's sex.

Oh, that was so much better.

"Mmm, you have a hungry pussy. It wants to be

filled. My fingers will have to do, because Alex will not let Maks fuck you," she whispered against Jessica's mouth, her fingers moving faster. "But you know Maks wants to fuck you. He has a very thick cock, with a few piercings for women's pleasure. And he is a Dominant, helpless to resist your need for a Master. You tempt him by just being you...the same way you tempt me. But luckily for me, I can touch you, fuck you, spank, and dominate you all I want."

"Please," she whispered against Catrin's lips, "kiss me."

"Say 'Mistress, please kiss me.'"

A forbidden tingle raced down her spine to her pussy. This was so kinky and surreal, but since she had Alex's blessing, she embraced the experience. Knowing that he was okay with this, even encouraged her to play with Catrin, allowed her to let go of most of her guilt, yet hold onto just enough of it to add an illicit thrill that made her all the wetter. "Mis-Mistress, please kiss me."

Instead of devouring her, Catrin's first brush of Jessica's lips was gentle, smooth skin sliding over smooth skin, the nerves of her mouth positively buzzing from the touch. She was right. Catrin tasted like bubble gum. It must be the lip gloss the other woman was wearing. Yummy. Softly caressing just Jessica's arms, Catrin stepped back and gave Jessica a naughty wink.

"Now, you are ready to wear what I have picked out for you. I promise, Alex will lose his mind."

Twenty minutes later, a very sexually frustrated Jessica stood before the windows in a piece of lingerie that was at the same time the most beautiful thing she'd ever seen and the most scandalous.

A constant heat flushed her body, embarrassment and arousal in equal measures, lending her skin a pink tint that made Catrin and

283

Maks grin.

Jessica tried not to think about the outfit she was in, but her mind kept flashing to her reflection in the mirror, her breasts encased in some shimmering blue fabric, with circles cut out in the center so her nipples protruded in an obscene manner. If that wasn't bad enough, Catrin had attached a pair of—no kidding—diamond and platinum nipple clamps that Oriana just happened to have in stock. They reminded her of a bobby pin with a little slide that Catrin adjusted. She was delighted to find that Jessica was sensitive and made sure she used the perfect amount of pressure.

Right now, her nipples felt like someone was gently squeezing them, driving her crazy with the desire to have someone suck the sting away. Catrin, the evil bitch, wouldn't allow Jessica to orgasm. It was making her ravenous. She wanted to come so badly and attempted to touch herself, but Catrin had forbidden her, which caused Jessica to growl like an irritated lioness. That made Maks laugh, the sexy bastard, and she glanced over at him, finding his gaze once again locked on her exposed sex. She wore this crazy platinum belt with trailing ice and sapphire blue crystals that barely shielded her pussy and made the auburn hair between her legs stand out. His open desire wasn't helping things nor was the knowledge that he possessed a big, thick, pierced antidote to her ache.

And if he licked his lips one more time while looking at her, probably thinking about eating her, she was not going to be responsible for her actions.

Catrin laughed and showed a text message in Cyrillic to Jessica, translating it for her. "Alex says he's going to kill the people he's with so he can come to you, Jessica."

Her laugh came out a little strangled, and for a

moment, she shifted out of the pose Maks had put her in, earning her a displeased glare from him while he cleared his throat. With a sigh, she reclined back on the modern divan covered in deep burgundy velvet, placing her hand so it lay curled on her lower belly, her back slightly arched, nipples hard, and going out of her mind with the need to be fucked. Her pussy *throbbed,* and when she replied, her voice easily reflected her frustration.

"Yes, please."

They burst out laughing, and she turned to glare at them, clenching her jaw as Catrin took another picture.

A few seconds later, Catrin let out a giggle. "Alex said that whatever we're doing to piss you off, keep doing it. You are sexy when you are angry."

By this point, Jessica should have been used to Catrin's unapologetic sensuality, but she and Jessica had some kind of deep connection between them, an instant attraction. Jessica was at once nervous and having one of the most erotic moments of her life. The fact that Alex, and probably Nico, were looking at these pictures while in some kind of meeting only added to the sexual fire burning in her.

When she saw Alex, she was going to jump him, then ride his face, then fuck him.

Repeatedly.

Catrin let out a soft, almost crooning sound. "What are you thinking about, sweet girl. Your eyes went dreamy."

"Alex."

Maks sucked in a quick breath, almost as if he'd been hurt, then shook his head. "Lucky bastard."

Giggling, Catrin handed the camera to Maks, a wicked smile on her lips. "Alex wants me to lick your pussy."

"Lucky bitch." Maks was scowling again, but his

285

gaze had heated immensely. Oh yeah, he liked watching her, and the thick erection pressing against his fly twitched as she watched. Movement from her left caught her eye, and Catrin was approaching her with a new outfit.

"Now, darling, something a little more you. That was for his visual fantasy."

This time, they didn't bother to go behind the screen. She stretched out with the knowledge that Alex was watching via the pictures. As Catrin removed the first outfit, she placed gentle kisses on Jessica's throat. Maks moved around behind them, his gaze ravenous as he snapped picture after picture.

He said from somewhere right behind Jessica, "Alex is on his way. He wants to taste pussy on your lips, Jessica. He wants you to lick Catrin's *pizda*. She will teach you how she likes it."

"Mmm, excellent," Catrin purred and winked at Jessica.

Her jaw dropped while Catrin let out a peal of laughter that made her smile despite her shock. Catrin kissed Jessica quickly on her mouth. She leaned back and grinned while she shook out a silky navy gown with hip-high slits on either side with what Jessica could only think of as a mandarin collar. It was tight, and it was sheer, but it was also amazing. Without thinking, she reached out and stroked the gown, sighing at how satiny it was.

"This is beautiful."

"It feels good on a sensitive body. Skin like yours can gain sensations from touching things that most people can't. My first girlfriend was like this, worse even than you. The barest of sucks on her clit, and she'd be coming all over my face. Just like I'm going to come on yours. Follow me."

Blinded by the rough desire overwhelming her, she followed Catrin across the room on shaky legs.

286

The other woman pulled down a thick, large, sheepskin rug that was folded up on a shelf. With a few brisk movements, she spread it out on one of the Persian carpets. Catrin helped her to lie down on the rug, which felt decadent beneath her. She let herself relax further, even as she rubbed her thighs together, trying to find relief.

Catrin gave her leg a slap that stung. "Stay still. I want you on hands and knees. You are a naughty girl trying to pleasure yourself, so we will put a nice shade of pink on your ass as punishment for Alex."

A shiver went through Jessica, and she stared up at Catrin, who was slowly removing her dress, revealing a very sexy black lace panty and bra set. She licked her lips at the sight of Catrin's large, natural breasts and wondered how they felt. They looked really soft. Catrin cleared her throat, and when Jessica's gaze hers, she was captured by the anger on Catrin's face.

"I said, on hands and knees. Move quick or I make spanking punishment instead of pleasure."

Melting inside at the command in the other woman's voice, Jessica did as ordered, her legs unsteady as she moved into position, one that Alex put her in regularly.

Once she presented her bottom to Catrin, she gently rubbed it. "So wonderfully built. Usually women as slender as you are like sticks, but you have some curves. Makes you even more beautiful to me."

With no more preamble, Catrin gave Jessica's ass a sharp tap that made her gasp.

Shit, that hurt.

She whined low in her throat at the next hit, which only made Catrin and Maks chuckle. The other woman gave a harder swat, and Jessica's spine bowed.

"Alex said she is his beautiful, filthy girl," Maks

murmured, "and he is going to fuck Jessica raw tonight."

"I bet," Catrin murmured, skating her fingertips over Jessica's heated, stinging bottom.

Sheesh, less than a dozen spanks and Jessica was ready for Catrin to do anything she wanted. Her mind buzzed, and she felt almost drunk as Catrin flipped her over to her back. Jessica could only moan in approval when Catrin removed her bra, revealing tight, pink nipples perched atop her large breasts like gumdrops. There was something about Catrin that was like the sweet version of Alex's spice, and when she knelt down, she took Jessica's hand and placed it on her breast.

"Go ahead," Catrin said with a gentle smile, "you can touch me. I like it."

Eager to explore, Jessica sat up a bit and cupped the abundant curves of the other woman's right breast, exploring the warmth and hefting the weight of it in her hand. No wonder guys loved breasts so much. They were so soft and cuddly. Yes, it was odd to want to cuddle with a breast, at least in her mind, but she really just wanted to sit here and stroke Catrin and enjoy the silk of her skin. Ever so slowly, Jessica leaned forward and stuck her tongue out to lick Catrin's breast. Maks gasped next to them as he moved to a different position, growling deep in his throat as he took a photo. Her pussy clenched at the thought of how this would look to Alex and how it must be driving him mad that he couldn't touch her right now.

"He is almost here," Maks muttered. "Wonder if he did kill people he was meeting with to end discussions."

Catrin ignored him as she guided Jessica back so her head rested on a small pillow the blond woman had pulled over from a nearby chair. As Jessica arranged her head into a comfortable position, Catrin gathered Jessica's hair and spread it out it above her head. "I want to run my fingers through this Irish fire while I ride your face. Is easiest way to show you what I want, how to make love to my pussy."

Jessica sucked in a quick breath, aroused beyond belief, then groaned softly when Catrin pulled her panties aside to reveal her pretty sex covered with well-groomed, golden blonde hair. Evidently, Nico liked his woman's pubic hair, and Jessica could see why. It looked downy soft, and the little bit of liquid arousal wetting the curls made Jessica's empty sex clench down in need. It was a heady feeling, to know she'd aroused Catrin like this. This stunning, exotic, achingly sexy woman was aroused because of what Jessica was doing with her.

She wanted to make Catrin burn even hotter.

Without any hesitation, she helped Catrin kneel over her face, then plunged her tongue between Catrin's pussy lips, and proceeded to devour her.

With a shuddering gasp, Catrin said something in Russian, and Maks was at her side, holding her while Jessica let out all her pent up sexual frustration on the woman. Jessica had watched plenty of girl-on-girl porn during the sexual dry spells in her life. And she'd watched a bunch of really good instructional ones by Nina Heartly that had given her the inside scoop on eating pussy. Her boyfriend at the time didn't know what he was doing down there, and she wanted to be able to give him hints.

Now she employed those unpracticed skills on Catrin, smiling against the other woman's wet sex then attempting to lick up the sweetness between her thighs. She sucked gently on the other woman's clit then a little bit harder, which made Catrin moan, a sound Maks echoed—except he sounded tortured.

She was right about Catrin's pubic hair. It tickled

her lips as she began to rub her tongue against her clit. That hard little nub stiffened further when she sucked it, and Catrin let out a soft cry then shivered. In an unconscious begging gesture, Jessica spread her thighs and lifted her hips, sucking harder on Catrin, wanting her to come. She remembered that Catrin was a submissive and might like a little spice with her pleasure, so she gently raked her nails down Catrin's back then did it again, this time harder.

Catrin arched with an agonized wail, grinding her pussy against Jessica's face, her soft flesh quivering beneath Jessica's tongue. Every inch of Jessica's body ached to come, and she groaned in anguish, wishing someone would just touch her. If someone brushed her clit, she'd explode. As soon as the thought left her mind, Catrin was plucked from kneeling above Jessica's face, and a hard, almost too thick cock slammed into Jessica, making her writhe and scream.

Alex growled, "My filthy girl."

She saw the surprise in his eyes when she grabbed his unbuttoned shirt and jerked him down to her, rubbing her hips against his while she clung to his body, needing him, riding him as much as she could in this position. Within three thrusts, she was coming so hard tears slipped down her cheeks as she wailed. He made an approving noise, his lips gentle as he kissed her tears away.

"Good girl, give me your pain. I will take it away and replace it with love."

A few more tears slipped free, but when she opened her eyes, she saw his devastatingly handsome face above her, his burning gaze filled with a need almost as fierce as her own. She arched against him again, nowhere near fulfilled. That orgasm had been like a tease. She needed more. With a low growl, she clasped her legs around his waist and rocked on his steely hard cock, marveling at how deep he felt inside of her and how well he filled the hollowness in her heart. Tingles raced down her spine, and she let out a choked cry.

Unable to stop herself, she buried her face against his neck and whispered, "I love you."

He froze, his body turning to rock beneath her fingertips, but his voice came out tinged with humor as he said, "I know."

She was about to call him an arrogant jackass, but he flipped them around so she suddenly found herself straddling him. The position pushed him deep, and she gasped, so full of dick it stung. He slowly ran his hands up her torso, cupping her breasts while she took him all the way, her gaze going distant as pleasure unfurled within her. The sheepskin was soft beneath her knees, and it framed his dark, masculine looks perfectly. She wasn't sure which she liked better: Alex naked or Alex looking debauched as he fucked her in the suit and ruined shirt he hadn't even bothered to take off.

"Do you know"—he punctuated his words with a hard thrust—"how insane I was to be inside this hot *pizda*?"

"Yes," she cried out. She didn't give a shit about anything but how good he felt inside her.

He stilled then shuddered against her, grasping her hips hard enough that she vaguely wondered if she would bruise. "You are everything to me, Jessica. I promise to take care of you for the rest of your life. To provide only best for you. To put you and your safety first."

She frowned and fought to think past the sudden flash of desire when he tilted her hips, forcing her to fall closer to him and brace herself on her arms as he began to move. This put her clit against his pelvis, and she gave a throaty moan when he fucked her with

291

this amazingly dirty roll of his hips. She had to dance with him because, if he danced like he fucked, she was going to marry him.

The thought startled her, but Alex chose that moment to start speaking to her in Russian. The words meant nothing, but by the reverent tone of his voice, she knew he loved her, truly and deeply. Her whole body tightened, and she groaned as she almost reached the point of coming. Eager for her release, she began to ride him harder and gave a small smile when his words trailed off.

"Hungry for my cock, aren't you, my filthy girl," he murmured and smacked her flank hard. "Show me how much you want my cum."

Instead of answering him, she met and held his gaze then began to milk his erection inside of her by clenching her internal muscles. His eyes narrowed and he growled, darkness spreading in his gaze as he flipped her to her back then began to fuck her in perfect time with her contractions. It felt so good that she melted against him, rocking into his thrusts when he set a bone meltingly unhurried pace.

Despite the slowness of their movements, there was an intensity between them that was so good it was addicting. This had to be love, because she would do anything to keep this euphoric feeling and indulge in it as often as she wanted with Alex. Maybe she was moving a little fast from lust to love, but they'd been friends for a while. When he touched her like this, she just about came out of her skin with happiness. Every caress of his calloused hands against her body was reverent, even when he was fucking her brains out and building her quickly to another intense orgasm.

When she climaxed this time, it was with a smile, contentment mixing with relief and a rush of love so strong it staggered her. Alex covered her body and held her tight while he surged into her, kissing her neck just above her collar. The hair on his body tickled her when he collapsed atop her, both of them panting as they lay sprawled on the sheepskin rug. She was wracked with shivers, and when a particularly strong one happened, he made an almost pained sound.

"Vibrating *pizda*," he muttered as his hips jerked.

She squeaked, "Oh, God, please, I need a minute before you fuck me blind."

"Fuck you blind?" He leaned up, and his smile was so gentle she simply soaked up his affection.

"I love you."

Again, he smiled. "I know."

"How do you know?"

"Jessica," he chided. "You left behind your family to come with me. Women do not do that unless they love a man, unless he is where their heart wishes to be."

"Have many women loved you?" She had no idea where that jealous thought came from.

Instead of being offended, he shrugged. "Maybe. I do not know because I never cared. I never wanted anything with them. But you, you *prinsessa moya*, I want you more than anything. You are my ultimate treasure, my prize. My heart beats for you now."

The best she could manage was a nod, blown away by the fact that he meant every word. When his gaze dropped to her collar, he smiled. "In pictures, I could see how much my collar meant to you."

Remembering her conversation with Catrin, she stroked it. "Alex, honestly, this is the most beautiful thing anyone has given me other than my princess crown."

"Princess crown?"

She nodded. "I got it when I was seven. My mom made it for me. She was crafty like that. She enjoyed being a stay-at-home mom, loved being a housewife. I was lucky to have ended up with two amazing people. When I put it on for the first time I felt like a real princess. But with you, I *am* a princess."

He smiled and placed a gentle kiss on her lips. "You are most beautiful woman I have ever seen. Those pictures of you...they distracted me in a very bad situation. Helped me to keep my temper."

The sun had almost set by this point, giving the room a red hue that tinted Alex's skin, making her think of the war god, Ares. "What happened?"

"I had a...disagreement with some of my father's corporate policies. I may have to return to Ru-Belarus sooner than I anticipated."

Suddenly deflated, she closed her eyes. "Oh."

He kissed her lips. "Is not as likely now. I was able to maintain my temper, and he agreed to my terms. Thankfully, Oleg is there, and he is a calming presence with my father."

Uncertainty began to fill her, but she pushed it back. She knew going into this that Alex traveled. It was how his life was. Instead of forcing him to stay with her, she needed to let him go do what he needed to do. She'd seen her mother do it with her father during the busy seasons on the farm, only seeing him when he came home to eat and sleep. Still, Alex wasn't a farmer, and she knew when he was away from her, he was in danger.

"I hope you can stay."

His eyes half-closed, and he brushed her hair back, studying her eyes. "So do I."

Someone knocked on the door. "Time to go."

With a smile, he gently pulled out of her and cleaned her with a handkerchief. "Come. I will give Catrin my credit card and tell her to buy whatever she fancies for you."

At the mention of Catrin, Jessica flushed bright

red. Now that she was deeply satisfied, she couldn't bring herself to get too upset. Wanting to know how Alex felt about it, she looked at his chest while he cleaned up. "Did you like your pictures?"

"I almost came in my pants, and Nico was ready to fake a heart attack so we could leave and claim our women."

Her gaze fell to his feet. "Nico really saw them?"

"Catrin loves to tease. She knows sending him pictures will drive him crazy, make him fuck her hard. What she also now knows is that being teased makes you very sexually aggressive, eager to please. She looked like she was going to pass out as you licked her." As if sensing her discomfort at his frank talk, he wrapped his arms around her. "*Devushka milaya,* do not worry. I find it very attractive to taste pussy on your lips. And I know Catrin will be not only good lover, but good friend."

"I wouldn't know about the good lover part," she muttered. "She wouldn't let me climax."

He made a pained noise. "Your submission to her was beautiful. You enchanted her. Do not be surprised if she...what is American term...she has crush on you. Would be good thing. Catrin is smart. She would be good to help you learn my...culture. Make loyal friend"

Suddenly chilly, Jessica rubbed her arms. "Have you seen my dress?"

He helped her into it then walked over to a rack of what looked like shawls and selected a buttery yellow one with a soft sheen to it. When he slid it around her shoulders, she sighed, nuzzling her cheek against the fabric. Once again trying to let him know how much this meant to her, she kissed him on the cheek and whispered, "You always take such good care of me."

His arms wrapped around her in a strong hug,

pulling her to his chest. "That is because you are the most precious thing in my universe."

Chapter Nineteen

Nine days later Jessica found herself in a stables on Laz and Melanie's estate, waiting to learn what this 'hunt' that she was invited to attend with Alex was really about. She wore a pretty, very short, and totally sheer, sparkling black dress that barely skimmed her pussy, so she was sure this wouldn't be a hunt in any traditional sense of the word. If there was a breeze, her goods and the professional coochie spa treatments she'd had with Catrin and Melanie were going to be on full display. Made her glad she'd endured the embarrassment of having the esthetician all up in her lady business in order to have her pussy almost entirely hair-free except for a thick strip. The ladies from the spa insisted her red pubic hair was too pretty to remove entirely, so after discussing her vagina with Melanie and Catrin like it was the cool thing to do, they ended up leaving her with a patch big enough for Alex to 'rub against his lips'.

Alex had indeed appreciated her efforts and expressed his appreciation by eating her until her pink pussy was a deep rose red. Just the memory of his amazing mouth resulted in a nice tingle warming her blood. She smoothed down the sorry excuse for a piece of clothing that clung to her body, transparent to the point that she could see where her freckles ended on the creamy skin of her chest right above her nipples. It was scandalous, but all the women were wearing something similar so she couldn't complain. Long, ice blue ribbons trailed from the bottom of the barely-there dress and fluttered around her legs. The ribbons were snapped on to the sheer fabric, making them easy to snatch off. A breeze blew through the stables, and sure enough, her dress lifted and her pussy was on full display, but she was too busy freaking out to really care.

Dressed in his own version of hunting gear, Alex looked so damn good that she was having a hard time keeping her hands off of him. Cream pants hugged his muscular thighs, outlining his cock well enough that she could easily make out the plump head of his shaft. Those pants made her want to touch him in the worst way, but it was the jacket that got to her. It was a beautiful, velvet-soft, black leather trench coat that had some kind of lacing for the closures, which hugged Alex's trim waist and highlighted how fit, how virile he was. And his hands... The sight of perfectly fitted, black leather gloves on his big hands made her quiver inside.

The gust also picked up her fine, straight hair that had been left loose, mingling it with Melanie's dark blonde curls. Melanie gave her a teasing wink, and Jessica found herself relaxing a bit. Despite her elevated status in the world, Melanie was different with Jessica than she was with most people. When they were alone, Melanie was unguarded, bubbly even, but in public, she had a haughty look that could slay a person at twenty paces. It made people treat Jessica differently now, like she was someone important.

Jessica was having her ass kissed left and right because the Queen Bee of the social scene in Rome, the Mayor's wife, adored her and wasn't shy about letting other people know. Thankfully, Melanie preferred to hang out with her true friends out of the public eye, and last night, Melanie had hosted Jessica, along with a bunch of other women, for a private screening of a romantic comedy that wasn't even out in theaters yet. After the movie was over and everyone was leaving, Jessica was astonished to learn that one of the nice women she'd met that night, an older brunette named Mimi Stefano who was Laz's cousin from the US, had actually been a feared assassin before she got married and retired. The stunning older woman had been so sweet and charming that she couldn't imagine her hurting anyone. Jessica wasn't sure if Melanie was joking or not, but she did know that the women at the Stefano's palatial home that night were all either important in their own right or, like her, were loved by powerful men.

So far, everyone Alex introduced her to was either formidable, dangerous, or both. It said a lot about the man she'd tied herself to, some of it scary, some of it good. One thing was for sure, at times, he seemed to know her better than she knew herself. When they'd arrived tonight, Alex had given each woman a long look and made an appreciative comment to the woman's Master about his submissive, but that was it. His attention was, from that point on, entirely on her as he watched her experience the apprehension of the hunt, urged her to embrace her emotions and think with her body, not her mind. Then he'd whispered seductive things in her ears while Catrin kept giving her a knowing smile. Nico stood right behind Catrin, plumping her full breasts in his dark hands while she arched and moaned. They made such an erotic picture, and Jessica thought she could watch them love each other all night, because it was beautiful. While observing Catrin and Nico play was sexually arousing, it was their shared adoration for each other that made her heart race.

New men's voices rose from the back of the group, but she forced herself not to look. As she tried to figure out how many men were here now, she became increasingly anxious. With a slightly shaking hand, she rubbed the sapphire heart on her collar with her thumb. The physical reassurance his collar represented was like a lifeline of comfort to her now. Her whole outfit showcased her collar, and she had a feeling Alex preferred it that way. Despite his willingness—no, his eagerness—to watch her orgasm with other men...and women, he was very possessive of her and wouldn't allow anyone near her he didn't approve of. The metal of the collar was warm beneath her fingertips as she stroked over it and remembered what it represented.

The promise of protection, love, and freedom.

That was the reason she stood here with three other women, one of them being Catrin, practically jumping out of her skin. The Master of the Hunt explained how the game would be played in his deep, accented voice. In this case, the Master of the Hunt was Alex's friend, Ivan, who smiled at them and switched back and forth between English and Russian. Jessica probably would have been more impressed by his bilingual abilities if she wasn't now fighting an unnatural, powerful arousal slowly sensitizing her body.

As scared as she was, there should be no way her body was heating like this, but Alex, damn his black heart, had put some kind of special, golden oil on her clit and nipples. Catrin called it "Aphrodite's Honey", and the other Masters applied it to the their women as well. When she asked Alex about it, he would only give her a rather wicked grin.

He watched her as Ivan spoke, and when Alex frowned and nodded in Ivan's direction, she realized she'd been staring at him and daydreaming. It would really be to her advantage to pay attention to what she needed to do in order to survive this hunt. The heat from the damned oil increased on her pussy and nipples, almost like the feeling of someone breathing fiery, moist air on her body. Her skin had sensitized, and she fought her growing arousal. She needed to focus on the rules of the hunt, not the memory of Alex's cock splitting her open as he eased his painful girth into her.

Melanie, in all her barely covered, elegant glory, now stood next to Jessica in the stables, holding hands with a curvy, lovely Mongolian woman named Sarnai who belonged to Ivan. She was sweet and had immediately made Jessica feel welcome. Sarnai and Ivan made an interesting pair. She was soft and cuddly, while Master Ivan was a beast of a man. Something about that image aroused her and she wondered if she would get to see them have sex tonight.

Ivan—no, she needed to call him Master Ivan right now—examined her closely, his gaze smoothing over her body like a slow physical touch. "The ribbons on you are tokens. If one of the riders collects a ribbon, he can request a favor from your Dominant, including sexual ones. Nothing will be done that your Master does not agree to, but if you do not agree to the favor, simply use your safe word, and something else will be selected. Do not try to shirk your duty. If your Master feels you are merely being a brat, you will be punished for using your safe word in such a manner. A punishment, I assure you, I will enjoy giving. Turning pretty skin red with my spanks is particular...taste of mine. I share this taste with many of the hunters tonight, so be good little submissives, yes?"

The men all laughed, the deep, almost menacing sound filling the room, while she squeezed Melanie's hand even harder.

And now she was close to shaking with fear.

As if it wasn't bad enough to have Nico, Alex,

Master Ivan, and Laz hunting the women, some other men would be joining in as well, including her bodyguards, the serial killer scary Krom, and Maks, who regularly fucked her with his gaze when he thought she wasn't looking. From the way the Mayor was treating Alex's bodyguards, they were more friends than hired help tonight. Not that anyone would tell her anything about Alex and his business. It was frustrating as hell, and the only one that she might be able to get info out of, Maks, would have to be seduced to give it up.

She'd never be the kind of woman to lead a man on, and Maks didn't seem to understand that even if she had sex with half the free world, no one and nothing could ever tempt her to leave Alex. Playing with other people was just that, playing. It was fun and friendly, even when it was hot and steamy. With Maks, it would not be fun or friendly, only intense and emotional, so she planned on keeping her distance from the handsome man with the reddish-blond hair and pine green eyes. To make matters worse, the hunger in his gaze, when he allowed it to surface, made her pussy clench. She couldn't help it, her body recognized a man who was attractive and wanted to fuck her blind.

No, that was a temptation better left alone.

She needed things to return to how they were before the attempted kidnapping, to the Maks who was her friend, a man who was surprisingly gentle and funny once a person got past the rather formidable walls he kept around himself.

Alex found her worry over Maks amusing, assuring her that Maks was harmless, and he had allowed Maks into the hunt along with Krom. The men outnumbered the women, and she couldn't help but fear....or maybe yearn for the experience of having more than one man at a time. Her gaze roamed over the men, and she wondered if she'd kiss any of them tonight, if she'd know what they tasted like.

Catrin grabbed her hand and gave it a squeeze before whispering, "Breathe. I swear you will love this once you get over your fear."

"There are so many men," Jessica wheezed.

Laughing softly, Melanie leaned closer while keeping an eye on Ivan. "Darling, you throw any men you can't handle my way. I love to be buried in cocks."

The women giggled, Jessica with a bit of shock. Then they quieted when Ivan gave them a stern look. Shuffling her feet, she watched Master Ivan from beneath her lashes as he fought a smile while shaking his head.

She sucked in a breath that brought the scent of horses and hay to her, soothing smells that reminded her of home. The aromas of horses, sawdust, and clean hay sunk deep into her, triggering memories of the life she'd left behind, of her home where her strong, brave father had provided a good life for his girls. They'd had a massive barn, and after a hard day of working, she'd climb up in the hayloft and watch the sun go down. Her mother had given her an old blanket that protected her from the straw, and she'd spend an hour or so reading in silence while the light faded over the fields that seemed to go on forever.

Homesickness filled her, and she didn't protest when Catrin drew her closer and gave her a one-armed hug.

Master Ivan cleared his throat. "Nothing will happen that you object to. Your Masters will be overprotective of you, so you must be honest with them if something is too much. No one will have their feelings hurt or be disappointed if you do not wish for a sexual favor."

"But," Catrin murmured, "you'll be kicking yourself in the ass for the rest of your life if you miss out on the men who will be hunting us. Each and every one of them is...talented in pleasuring a woman."

"Is like being hunted by wolf pack," Sarnai said with a soft smile.

Realizing that everyone was staring at her, Jessica ducked her head down against Catrin's, hiding from their intense gaze. Before she had time to take a deep breath, Alex was there, pulling her into his arms and surrounding her in warm leather. There was no judgment or disappointment in his gaze, only worry.

"Jessica? Do you not wish to do this?"

Part of her, the scared part that somehow felt like she should be ashamed of even considering this, urged her to say yes and run away. But the wildness that Alex had given her permission to let loose was hungry for this experience, starving to drink down everything life had to offer with him by her side. His thumb brushed her nipple, and she startled, not realizing how sensitive they'd become.

The corner of his full lips twitched. "I only used small amount of the oil, but already it is making your body ripe for me. Nipples are hard, sensitive. Pussy wet. Trust me, Jessica, I will make this pleasure for you. Trust me to understand what my woman needs. I know you do not want to see me with other female, so do not fear that. We discussed already, and I promised. You are everything I need, your pleasure the only I am interested in. Because I know no matter how many orgasms you have, you are still hungry until you have me. Your body craves mine, craves my shaft deep inside of you no matter how many orgasms your little Mistress Catrin gives you. I will give you what you need...eventually."

He had that right. When she'd played with Catrin, the need to fuck Alex had burned inside of her, making her unusually aggressive with him afterward. And the sex was always raw, hungry, and out of this world. Evidently, Alex had noticed her increased libido and had enjoyed it.

"I will always need you," she whispered as her clit began to throb.

"*Ya palyubIl tebyas pervava vzglyada*", he murmured.

"What does that mean?"

"That I have loved you since first moment I saw you."

"Alex," she leaned up and gave him a gentle kiss, trying to put the emotions racing through her into her touch.

All she could do was groan deep in her throat when he rolled her nipple between his gloved fingers, sending bolts of hard desire to her swollen clit, making it throb while they kissed. Alex pulled back and made a soft noise of approval, forcing her to focus on him. His gaze was dark with desire, and she pressed her body against his, feeling his arousal thick against her. The skin between her legs was sensitive even to the press of her thighs, and she groaned again when she brushed her pussy against his pelvis, wishing he was inside of her, easing this intense sensitivity that was driving her crazy.

"Do you trust me, *prinsessa moya*?"

Her voice came out unsteady, but she managed to hold his gaze, knowing this was important to him. "I trust you."

He removed his hand from her breast then said something in Russian. A moment later warm, gentle hands caressed her body from three sides, and she sucked in a harsh breath, panic warring with desire. That fear eased when she realized she was being touched by women, not men. Catrin drew down the flimsy top of Jessica's dress and blew a puff of cool air on Jessica's nipple, the flesh hardening until it was painful. She whimpered while Melanie ran her fingers through Jessica's hair, her nails lightly scraping her scalp. The gentle feeling was divine. Sarnai was softly stroking low on her belly, just above Jessica's mound. Their silken hair brushed against her body as their perfume swirled around her. She was surrounded in rounded limbs and warmth. She couldn't do anything but relax back in their arms, her hips chasing the slender fingers teasing her slit now, making her belly quiver.

Melanie drew her hair to the side then gently bit and licked Jessica's neck. A keening whine escaped her, and her eyes flew open when she heard the rough murmur of men's voices and more menacing laughter. All the men were here now, dressed in their crazy, sexy BDSM hunting gear, and their gazes fastened on the women touching her, and many of them studied Jessica's face with as much interest as her body. Her back bowed with the illicit pleasure that came with the knowledge that all these handsome men were aroused and wanting her. There was power in that idea, a heady feeling that these commanding males would only hold back for so long before their formidable control broke and they took their pleasure.

Catrin captured Jessica's nipple in her mouth and sucked hard while sharp fingernails dug lightly into Jessica's buttocks. It felt so damn good, and she wondered what the hell was in that oil Alex had put on her. She was desperate to get fucked, to orgasm, and she felt like she could devour the men who watched them with such raw hunger.

Before she could climax, Alex snapped something, and the women reluctantly left Jessica standing on shaking legs, exposed and feeling vulnerable while she sucked in harsh breaths.

Ivan clapped his big hands, looking more intimidating than ever in a pair of skintight black riding pants. She swore she could see every detail of his cock through them. Normally, that would have been enough to distract her, but not even the sight of all that magnificent male flesh on display could completely ease the nervous twisting in her gut.

Seemingly unaware of Jessica freaking out, Ivan scanned the small group of women, his expression cold and intimidating. As his gaze came to hers, she found herself trapped by his radiant blue eyes, so out of place in his harsh face. His eyes reminded her of warm Caribbean waters, the kind she swam in when she was on spring break her freshman year of college. Inviting eyes in a decidedly unfriendly face. Then again, some of the coldness bled out as he held her gaze, his expression softening the slightest bit, allowing her to suck in a quick breath then slowly let it out. Ivan was the kind of man who didn't ask for control, he took it, and she was more than happy to give him the proverbial reins. To her surprise, he winked, and she clamped down the urge to giggle. Then she finally began to pay attention to the fact that he was talking, instead of freaking out.

"You will have ten minutes to hide as best you can. The estate is vast, and you can run as far as you want and hide anywhere on it. There is the maze where horses can't enter, the fields where a clever girl might hide among the grasses, and the orchards as well as the pool and gardens. You should have no trouble evading us. The main house is locked, but that is merely because Melanie frowns on people riding their horses through her kitchen." His grin was less than reassuring. No, it was downright predatory as was the way he paced before them, clearly eager to hunt them down. Shit, why did that turn her on so much? "The Masters will then begin the hunt, and they will only have thirty minutes to find each of you and collect their ribbons. Any questions?"

Adrenaline began to pump through her, and she glanced at Catrin. The image of her sucking Alex's cock flashed through her mind. While she didn't think she could share Alex with Melanie or Sarnai, she thought she could with Catrin because she knew Catrin loved Nico to distraction. Then she imagined kneeling next to her, sucking Nico's dick while Alex watched, and a low groan almost escaped her. Thanks to the blonde's openness, Jessica knew that Nico was not only well-endowed, but also extremely gifted in the art of pleasing a woman. Plus, Catrin had invited Jessica to have Nico eat her pussy so she could experience his thick lips. "Like clouds kissing your clit," she had said.

The memory made Jessica smile at her sexually adventurous friend. Catrin smiled back, and the worried look left her gaze, replaced by excitement. She winked at Jessica before turning her attention back to a now silent Ivan.

"Go!" Ivan shouted, and Jessica ran, losing ground behind the other women as they took off.

"Split up," the Sarnai said in a low voice. "Do not make easy."

With that, the women began to peel off one by one as they raced away from the stables, and Jessica's breathing deepened while the wind brushed over her body like a caress, her hair streaming out behind her as she got into her rhythm. Her competitive instincts kicked in, and she took off after the other women, her long legs eating up the ground. She'd run track in high school, and the old patterns came back of how to breathe and move her body. The sun set over the forest and grape vineyard on the isolated country manor that was a three-hour drive from Rome. They were all alone, the staff long ago dismissed, except for their bodyguards.

Bodyguards.

Shit.

Christ, Krom was going to be hunting her.

And Maks.

A naughty tingle warmed her sex while she darted off in the opposite of the direction from the one most of the other women had taken. When she saw the other side of the house, she knew why they hadn't come this way. There was nothing but a large grassy yard, an elaborate pool complete with a two-story pool house, and a steep drop-off on the edge of the rocky hill that the house perched on. It was far too dangerous for her to even consider descending so she could either backtrack and hope she made it in time, or keep going.

Shit, she'd messed up.

No way she could find another hiding place now. She'd been running around for at least five minutes, so she had to work with this. Sprinting across the lawn, she made it into the pool house just as the horn sounded signaling the beginning of the hunt. Okay, she had to remain hidden for thirty minutes. Piece of cake. She darted for the stairs, daring a glance out the window that revealed no one was in this area yet.

The upper portion of the pool house was a loft with full bookshelves and a massive futon drowning in pillows. She saw nowhere else to go except a closet that was almost empty and a bathroom with a glass shower, so she darted into the mound of pillows, concealing herself in them as best she could. The moment she settled she became aware of how tingly her body was, of how her sex was swollen and wet. The urge to touch herself grew stronger by the second, but she managed to lace her hands together and not wiggle too much.

Silence reigned, and she was sure almost eight minutes had passed when someone entered the loft. Her pulse pounded between her legs, her nipples ached, and she found herself almost wishing that whoever was down there would find her.

She needed relief, and if she was lucky, it would be Alex.

She was not lucky.

A sharp scream escaped her when big, rough, tattooed hands pulled her back from the pillows then threw her down on them with her butt in the air.

Before she could say anything, a large palm pressed on her lower back. "Stay."

She recognized that voice. Turning her head, she found Krom studying her sex, his wide nostrils flaring. His gaze was almost detached, but a muscle in his jaw twitched, and his broad chest lifted as he took a deep breath. He raised his hand just above her pussy. She could feel his heat and the promise of his skin, but he gave her nothing. Unable to help herself, she pushed back, seeking relief.

"Bad baby," Krom growled out, his hand gripping her thigh. "If I took what you offer, Alex would have my head. Almost worth for taste of *pizda*. Wet, swollen. Would be hot on my dick."

Before she could react, he jerked off one of her ribbons. "We will see what he will do to punish his little girl for being so tempting."

She sat up, wondering if she should run again, but before she could move, someone else entered the house. He laughed when Krom said something, and she knew there was no use in running. With a sigh, she rolled over and sat up, leaning back on her elbows as Nico entered the room. He wore leather garb similar to the other men, but he had a riding crop as well. There was something about the way he held himself that was masterful and intimidating. This was a man secure in who he was, confident in his own power. Her body tightened, and she almost moaned aloud when he stopped before her, his dominant personality rolling over her, draining her will, leaving her weak before him. He ran the tip of his ridding crop over her breast and she melted for him, her muscles relaxing even as her lower belly tightened, especially when he gave the tip of her breast a little flick with the crop, the burn making her gasp then whimper.

His cold look softened. Then he leaned over then rubbed his thumb over the apple of her cheek. "My Catrin is right, you do submit beautifully. Will you send me to find her with the taste of you on my lips?"

Her thighs squeezed, and she swore her breasts were shaking with her heartbeat. "Pardon?"

His full lips twitched, humor further softening his expression. The edges of his eyes were tilted, giving him an almost Asian look, but his lips were large and, from what Catrin said, incredibly soft. Need tormented her as she thought about those lips on her pussy. Then Jessica thought about Nico and Catrin sharing a kiss with the taste of her arousal on their lips, and her desire to have him lick her increased tenfold.

Squatting before her, Nico eased her thighs open. "Safe word?"

"Butter."

With that, he jerked her thighs wide and stared at her sex. His pleased murmur made her twist beneath him. He smacked her pussy with his hand as he scolded her, "Behave. Spoiled *malysh*. Alex is too easy with you. But you are sweet, so I understand why he is this way."

Kneeling between her thighs, he placed his large hands on her hips, pulling her forward. The sight of the contrast of his dark skin and black leather against her pale thighs made her clit swell. At the first touch of his mouth, she gasped and clutched at his head. Catrin was right. Nico's lips were as soft as pillows, and promptly, he used them to drive Jessica out of her mind. Not only could he eat pussy, he knew how to work her, and Jessica wondered if Catrin had told him what she liked. He looked up and held her gaze while he lapped her softly. His tongue drove her straight into a brief, intense orgasm that blind-sided her. With her raw moans still echoing through the loft, Nico continued to suckle at her flesh, rubbing his tongue against her sensitive clit and holding her in place with his strong hands. He made pleased noises, and when she was shivering with an overload of pleasure, he leaned back then stood, his mouth glossy with her release.

"Thank you."

"Huh?" was the only thing her dazed mind could spit out.

Laughing, he gave her pussy a sharp slap with the crop. Her neck arched, and she gasped. "Krom was right. You are naughty girl. In best way."

His erection strained against his pants when he stood. Then he grabbed a ribbon and headed out the door, passing...

Oh, shit.

Maks.

His energy seemed to fill the room, obvious enough that Nico gave Maks a curious look before leaving. With Nico gone, the tension only got worse, and she was all too aware of her debauched state. Maks stared at her, spread out before him, with such open hunger and emotion that she felt like she should cover herself. The way he wanted her made her uneasy, but she was helpless as he prowled to her, his green eyes dark, almost violent.

"Rose-red pussy, wet and hot. You torment me."

Instead of grabbing her body, he lay down next to her on the bed then pulled her into his arms. This surprised her so much she didn't even fight it when he pressed his lips against hers and proceeded to kiss the hell out of her. Slow and sensual, his tongue stroked against hers as she enjoyed the moment almost against her will. His arm clamped around her, pulling her so tight against him they were flush from torso to pelvis, his erection digging into her. With a low groan, he sucked on her tongue, and she rewarded him by throwing her leg over his hip, whimpering when his fingers moved lower, the tips almost touching her pussy.

He pulled back and began to whisper in Russian against her mouth, his tone so gentle...seductive in a way that could be dangerous. His fingers pressed in, grazing her wet labia, and he placed a stinging bite on her neck. A moan escaped her, and he pressed another soft kiss on her sensitive mouth. Her body wiggled against him in an instinctive plea for release. He smelled good, like a winter forest at night with hints of pine. Fresh and wild. She cautiously licked over his pulse, enjoying his groan of pleasure and the way he whispered her name.

Shit, she was playing with fire.

"Let me fuck you," he whispered against her mouth. "When I give Alex my ribbon, let me fuck you. You almost died, Jessica. I have to feel you alive."

Her breath came out in a rush, and she leaned up on her arm and stared down at Maks. The desperation in his words mixed with desire helped clear her head enough to understand something wasn't right. She knew the attempt on her life had bothered him, but evidently, she'd underestimated his feelings. "Honey, I'm all right."

His grip on her tightened. "You almost died."

"I didn't." She internally sighed. She never wanted to be in a situation like that again. Not only because she had no interest in being tortured to death, but that she'd have to put up with the men in her life getting all moody. "What do I have to do to make you smile?"

"What?"

She sighed then smoothed his hair off his forehead. "I don't like seeing you unhappy like this."

He closed his eyes, then reached up, and stroked her face with reverent fingers. "So sweet."

She kissed his fingertips, and his eyes opened again, calmer now, filled with more warmth than tormented worry. His gaze dropped to her breasts, and he licked his lips. "Let me taste them."

"Maks...I'm not sure—"

Lowering his head, he blew on one tip, but before he could take it into his mouth, someone came in downstairs. With a sigh, Maks backed up and snatched a ribbon. "Think about it, Jessica. I have watched you with Alex, have watched you with Catrin and Nico. I know what you like. I would make it very good for you."

Once again, as soon as one man left, another appeared. This time it was Master Ivan. All the breath left her body as his predatory gaze scanned over her. He stalked closer, his trench flaring slightly behind him, showcasing his thick, muscular thighs. The man was huge, and authority seemed to roll from him in pussy-tingling waves. He leaned over, grabbed both of her hands, and held them over her head, his teal eyes blazing as he restrained her.

Dipping his head down to hers, he whispered, "Kiss me, Jessica, and taste Catrin's pussy on my lips."

She didn't even bother to fight it. She couldn't. Ivan wasn't allowing her a choice. Eager for a taste of him, she licked at Ivan's mouth. He groaned and pressed his hips against her, teasing her wet pussy with his thick cock. The leather of his jacket creaked as he shifted, allowing her to wrap her legs around his waist and rock her swollen slit over his erection. She swore stars exploded behind her eyes at the first movement, and her legs clutched him tighter, her hips working against him while she panted into his mouth.

A deep chuckle rumbled through his wide chest like thunder. "The oil has made you hungry."

He bit her lower lip hard enough to sting, and she whimpered, earning a bite on her neck this time. That sting translated to pleasure, and she growled into his mouth, swallowing his answering snarl as her body tensed harder, raw need sweeping her away. She circled her hips and let out a startled squeak when Master Ivan clasped her neck, choking her while he ground his pelvis into hers. It wasn't choking in a scary way, but in a very controlled, dominant fashion, and it drove her crazy, the physical threat of him while he tortured her with pleasure.

A hard buzzing filled her body, exploding from her pelvis and blanketing her in ecstasy when she began to climax.

Master Ivan growled his encouragement. "You soak my pants. Can feel wet, hot pussy. Smell it."

She could only moan and rub her nipples, the fires inside of her momentarily banked, leaving behind a drugging warmth. Leaning over her, Master Ivan began to place gentle kisses on her jaw and neck, his heavy warmth increasing the sensation of being protected, cared for. She stretched out, enjoying his touch and just living in the moment. In the distance, the horn sounded again, and Ivan pulled back and grinned. "By the way, Krom told us all where you were."

If she could have opened her eyes, she would have glared at him. "Cheating asshole."

Chuckling, Ivan stood then scooped her up into his arms.

"Wait, what are you doing?"

"Returning you to Alex."

"I can walk."

"And I can carry."

"I don't want you to hurt yourself."

Ivan burst out laughing. "Do you know how I train? I lift things that weigh four times the size of you. Could carry you for miles with no hurt."

As if to reinforce his words, he took her down the steps and out of the pool house with almost no effort. Ivan had left his mount out front, and the beautiful roan gelding gave a soft nicker. He let her slide out of his arms to go to the horse. Happiness filled her as the beautiful creature snuffled at her before butting her hand for attention. Resting her forehead against the horse's neck, she gave him lots of love.

"You're just a big baby, aren't you?" she whispered as the horse shivered when she got to an itchy spot by his ear.

Ivan swung up into the saddle, then reached down, and hauled her up with him. Instead of having her face forward, she was facing him with her thighs over his, her cheek against his wide chest. This placed his erection against her sensitive core, something she became all too aware of as the horse carried them back to the stables. Each step produced a rocking motion of her pussy against him, turning her on all over again until she wondered when the hell the effect of the damned oil was going to fade.

Just before she gave in and allowed herself to orgasm, they arrived back at the villa. Ivan lifted her from the horse and held her hand as he led her inside on shaky legs, his smile warm. When she got over how physically scary he was, Ivan was really a softy beneath it all. Gentle even when he was violent, if that made any sense. They arrived in the large living room, and each of the Doms held their submissives in their arms. She practically ran to Alex and threw herself into his arms when she saw him. She placed her mouth against his and wound her arms around his neck, drowning in the taste of him while she sank her fingers into his hair. Just the sensation of his lips was better than anything she'd experienced tonight, and she felt as if she was flooded with happiness.

He broke their kiss then growled softly, tightening his grip on her. "You taste like *pizda*. I fucking *love* it."

Melting into his arms, she wrapped her arms around his neck. "I missed you."

"Did you find pleasure?"

"I...yeah." She whispered the last word as she tried to deal with the instant, almost reflexive guilt.

He tsked then tipped her head up. "Do not be ashamed. I gave you permission, and I am your Master, so that is all you need."

Her eyebrows drew up. "Arrogant, much?"

"*Prinsessa moya*, I own you." He touched her collar, and she instantly smiled.

"Yes, you do."

She became aware of everyone watching them and flushed, pressing into Alex and trying to ignore what she was pretty sure was jealousy in Maks' eyes. Yeah, she'd need to talk to Alex about Maks' more-than-friends feelings. Playing with other people who knew the rules was one thing, starting something emotional with someone that could never go anywhere was entirely different. Maks had feelings for her, all wrapped up in his guilt over her getting hurt.

They were good friends, and she had shared

317

things about her life with him that she didn't tell most people. He loved hearing about her family and had even enjoyed it when she showed him her family's photo albums. He'd studied the pictures like an anthropologist looking at an ancient culture, his attention totally on her when she'd go off on tangents about the people in the pictures, sometimes getting one of his rare laughs.

Damn, she liked to make him smile.

Was she leading him on?

Her worried gaze met Alex's, and he frowned when she declared, "I need to talk to you."

"Of course."

He led her farther into the house until they came to a solarium with a huge lounge sofa long enough to fit ten people lying side by side. There was also a couch and a small bar set up among the plants, but the majority of the space was taken up by the carefully cultivated vegetation and the profusion of orchids scenting the air. Alex stopped in the middle of the room then turned to face her, looking like some kind of kinky, dashing eighteenth century lord in his Victorian conservatory. He held his hand out and she slipped hers into it, a sense of peace settling over her.

Holding her gaze, he pulled her down onto the lounger. "Relax."

With swift movements, he began to remove his gloves, but she stopped him. "Leave those on."

Wickedness filled his expression. "You like?"

"I love. You have such big hands, and your gloves make them seem even bigger. It's totally pornographic. Those pants make you look bigger as well. You look so good in those it should be illegal."

He laughed and shook his head then quickly removed his jacket and shirt, leaving him in only his knee high boots, tight pants, and black leather gloves. She shivered with delight. This was the body built to please her beyond all others. Perfect from his broad shoulders to his muscled calves, the dark fur on his chest accenting how masculine he was. She held her arms out to him, and he gathered her against him, allowing her to press herself as close to him as physically possible.

"Now, what is wrong? Did you not enjoy yourself?"

"No, I did. I..." She debated how to put this in the most non-confrontational way possible. The last thing she wanted was for Maks to lose his job. He took great care of her, and before her almost kidnapping, they'd had a good friendship. "I think Maks has feelings for me way beyond friendship."

"I know." Alex sounded unperturbed.

"Uh-Alex, I think he might think he really, really cares for me."

"Is good."

Totally thrown off by his reaction, her brow scrunched. "What?"

He sighed, smoothing her hair back with his gloved hand. "Devotion will keep you alive. I will let you in on secret. If man cares for you, he will do anything to keep you safe. Is way of the world. I am selfish man and want Maks to care deeply for you because he is your main bodyguard. Just like Nico cares deeply about you because Catrin loves you. An army that loves their ruler will keep them alive."

"Army?" Her eyes widened. "Wait, Catrin loves me?"

"Not the same as she loves Nico, but yes. There are many kinds of love, *dorogoya*. You do not understand the...impact you have on the lives of those you know."

"Like Maks," she muttered. "Alex, I don't want to hurt his feelings, but I will never feel for him the way I feel about you."

"I know. Believe me when I say he understands that I will never allow another man to try and take what is mine. With Maks, circumstances are different, special. Hard to explain in English. He has this...what is word...habit...no is not right. His lost first love died of cancer at seventeen, and he has need to reconnect with a woman he cares about if she is hurt."

"You mean he fucks every woman he likes if they get a paper cut?"

"What? No, no." His lips thinned in obvious frustration. "Once he feels like he has reconnect with you, he will calm, go back to friend you know. He will still want to fuck you, because you are magnificent, but he will not want to take you from me."

"That...Alex, that's crazy."

Shrugging, Alex gave her a hard look. "It is way of my world. Try not to judge him so harshly. Maks has been through much, has not had easy life and must deal with it however he can. He likes you, Jessica, and it would hurt to have you withdraw your friendship because of his way of dealing with his grief. I hope you never understand what it is like to suffer loss like that."

To her surprise, she was now drowning in guilt, guilt that she was uncomfortable with the fact that Maks liked her, guilt that she was so self-centered that she never considered he might have reasons of his own for the way he reacted. Why was nothing in her life simple anymore? She always felt like she was on a rollercoaster with Alex, never sure what would happen next or how his words would change her view of a situation. Either he was a master manipulator or she had a lot to learn. Probably a mixture of both.

"I'm not trying to be mean to him. I just don't want it to upset what we have, Alex. I mean...if I knew a girl liked you the way he likes me, I would never want her near you." She chewed on her lip, the thought having awakened her jealousy. "I wouldn't like that at all, and I can't help but worry that you'll resent me for not being as free as you are with my playing with other people. I mean, you asked about my pleasure, but I don't want to know if you touched any of those women when I wasn't around."

"I kiss—"

"No, seriously, I don't want to know. It makes me jealous and uncomfortable."

The tension grew between them as he blew out a frustrated breath, and she braced herself for the coming blow. This was it. He was going to realize they wouldn't work out in the long-term. This was when he would break her heart. Looking away from him, she tried to keep her composure.

"Jessica." He gently placed his fingers beneath her chin, turning her to look at him. "If I only have you for the rest of my life, I will be blessed."

She wanted to believe him, she really did, but her insecurity had manifested, and she hated how crazy it made her. It didn't used to be this bad, this fear of someone breaking up with her or going away, but since her parents' deaths, anyone she loved leaving her life made her profoundly sad. Yeah, at some point she was going to have to talk to a therapist, but right now, she battled with the desperate need to cling to Alex, even though she realized that was not a good idea. They needed to have this conversation, and this might not be the ideal time for it, but she had to let him know her concerns.

She looked him in the eye. "You say that now, but Alex, you've basically lived the swinger lifestyle for years. It's what you like. I understand that. I like it, too, but I'm selfish, and while I think the idea of sharing you in certain ways, with only the women I approve of, is arousing, the idea of you touching another woman while I'm not there makes me furious."

He shook his head, his expression bemused. "What I love is to watch you explore your world, to grow, to experience new pleasures that you would deny yourself if I was not in your life. It is gratification better than anything I have ever experienced. It feeds my body and soul. What arouses me is not having sex with different people—it is you. This emotion you call forth so easily from me is something I have longed for but never found—until you became mine. I love *you* and only you."

Her ire faded beneath the strength and conviction in his voice.

"I love you, too."

"I know." He winked, lightening the mood enough for her to draw a deep, calming breath. "For you, I am ultimate voyeur, eager to watch you give yourself to others so I may see your passion, because when you are done with them, you will always return to me. I know this—is not question in my mind or heart— and allows me to share you without anger with those that I choose."

She tensed against him, and as usual, he read her emotions easily and sighed, his dark gaze scanning her face.

"Alex..."

"You doubt me, and nothing I say will change that, only time. Is okay, I am patient man. You will see that I am telling the truth, that you are...what is American saying...you are it for me and I am it for you. I am both your Master and your most humble servant."

That made her giggle, and she liked the way his lips immediately curved up in response. "Servant? You? Whatever. You're so bossy you'd tell me when to brush my teeth and go to bed if you thought you could get away with it."

His tight expression faded, and he softened against her, his gaze warming as he studied her face. "Do I not already do that? I bring you to bed, fuck you, send you to clean up. Then when you come back, I usually give you another orgasm with my mouth, and maybe fuck you again in the middle of the night."

"You always fuck me again in the middle of the night."

His arrogant, satisfied grin made her heart skip a beat. "This is true."

Eased by his love and efforts to reassure her, she sighed. "I'm sorry I'm such a pain in the ass. Really, I'm not sexually repressed in the least. I'm just...well, I feel guilty that I don't feel ashamed about what I did tonight, only excited. It's like I'm punishing myself for not feeling bad. If I was a good girl, I'd be appalled at some of the things I have done, that I've fantasized about."

"Jessica, listen to me. You have no reason to feel shame, at all. You are magnificent in your pleasure. I will tell you when I do not like something. Rest assured, and you are silly for giving yourself guilt when none is needed."

"I can't help it!" She blew out a frustrated breath. "It's like I've been brainwashed to feel ashamed for enjoying sex that's taboo for most people. Like I'm a bad person and you'll leave me."

"Jessica, I will never leave you. Feel inside your heart, and you will know truth." He placed gentle kisses on her face. "I believe I understand your problem, is not uncommon with women, especially submissives. Maybe you need to feel punished, need sting of redemption, to give self permission to enjoy."

Her brows flew up. "Uh...what?"

"I am going to have Maks punish you tonight. If you feel sorry for him after he is done spanking you, I give you permission to make him feel better, however you choose."

Her lower belly tensed in a not unpleasant way. "Wait, why am I being punished?"

His gaze darkened, and her nipples tingled against his chest. "Because I wish it to happen."

Chapter Twenty

A lex watched Krom sigh, his big body putty in Jessica's hands. And feet. She was currently walking on the other man's bare back, giggling as she rocked her feet back and forth. One of her good friends had studied how to walk on someone's back in Japan and taught her how to do it. Now she was cracking Krom's spine, and the man groaned each time like he was having a really good orgasm, which only made Jessica giggle harder and almost lose her balance.

"Did you just purr?" she asked him with amusement bright in her voice.

Krom merely grunted, his eyes closed and his face harsh even in relaxation.

Alex held out his hand, and she grasped it with a happy smile. As soon as she found out she wouldn't have to do anything sexual with Krom, she volunteered to walk on his back. Now Alex was wondering why she hadn't offered to do this for him yet. It looked good, because he got to watch her petite breasts shake as she moved, and he got a flash of her pussy when she widened her stance. She still wore her dress, but all the ribbons were gone now, and her stiff nipples pressed against the thin cloth.

Krom had been after her from the start, and he tracked her down just on principal. Then, with Alex's blessings, he'd told the other men where to find her. While Alex snatched ribbons from Melanie and Catrin, he'd left Ivan's girl alone because his woman did not know her. There was no need to push Jessica. He was letting her set the pace, permitting his sweet girl to stretch her wings within the safety of his protection and with his friends. Watching her begin to embrace her sexuality was rewarding on levels he'd never even imagined, making him wonder how he ever thought he could live without her. He was connected with her in a way he'd never imagined, their bond going beyond flesh and blood to a soul-deep level.

She was his heart, his reason for living, and his love for her seemed to grow by the day. Every night he went to bed thinking he couldn't possibly feel any stronger about her. Then he'd wake the next morning, and the moment he saw her his love would deepen, as would his determination to own every moment of her pleasure. His friends were his allies in seducing her, in working Jessica up to the point she stopped fighting the gratification and gave in. Once she embraced her need, she became glorious in her raw, honest lust.

Like she was right now after his friends had worked her up for him.

He was rewarded for his sharing by now having a very aroused Jessica practically squirming with need. Her pupils were huge, and she trembled beneath his touch. One of his favorite kinks was delayed gratification...then multiple orgasms. So far, Jessica had not complained about the play they'd done in private. In fact, she begged him for it. She'd embraced his lifestyle with open arms, and he gloried in this beautiful woman who gave herself so freely to him, trusted him to make the right decisions for her. At least that's what he hoped.

Krom grunted and looked at the door of the conservatory. Alex followed his friend's gaze to see Nico coming in with Catrin stalking forward from his side. The soft pink scrap of silk she was wearing had been torn open to reveal her breasts, which jiggled with her every step. An unusual dominance had entered Catrin's normally sweet expression, and it was all aimed at his blushing little Jessica, who was staring at Catrin with complete submission turning her expression dreamy with lust.

He'd underestimated how much Jessica enjoyed Catrin. The two had hit it off, and he was sure his sweet girl had a crush on Catrin. It was cute to watch and arousing to witness real attraction between two different, but stunning women.

His cock thrust against his pants when Jessica looked at him as she stepped off Krom. "Alex...you wanted me to be honest with you and tell you when I like someone, right?"

"Yes."

His lips twitched with a suppressed smile as he watched her gather up her courage then whisper, "I like them."

"I know."

She chewed on her lip. "Oh. Okay."

Bemused by her sudden bout of shyness, he looked forward to the day when she asked for what she wanted without fear. He would not only provide it for her, but enjoy it. "What do you want? What have you fantasized about?"

"What?"

He held up one of Catrin's ribbons. "What do you want her to do to you? Her ribbon is my gift to you, *prinsessa moya.*"

Heat made her blue eyes burn, and he smiled down at her, delighting in how hungry she was. Truly, he was blessed. So beautiful, but also loyal and smart. In a few years, she would be a woman to reckon with, and he was thankful he would be the man lucky enough to watch over her. He would nurture her and help her find her inner strength.

God, he loved her.

Something must have reflected in his gaze because she began to press sweet kisses on his face.

"You have been so good to me, but now it is my turn to be good to you."

"What do you mean?"

"You like to watch me with someone else, right?"

"It makes my dick hard."

She let out a shuddery breath, and he smiled against her lips. "Okay, right. So I would like to trade in her ribbon for Catrin to suck your cock with me."

His balls pulled up tight, and he clenched his teeth to keep from throwing her to the floor and fucking her.

"Are you sure?"

A full body quiver vibrated through her, and her pale chest flushed pink. "Yes."

"As long as I come inside you, is fine."

"How generous of you," she replied with a grin.

Krom was sitting on the edge of the lounger, his long legs crossed in front of him and his gaze on Catrin. He was a regular third with Catrin and Nico, and Alex wondered how Jessica would react to that. Right away, Jessica seemed to notice Krom's heated looks as he gazed at Catrin. His little girl sucked in her lower lip, and her gaze darted between Krom, Catrin, Nico, and back to Krom again. The flush on her chest spread, and Alex smiled at how easy she was to read as her eyes widened and she blinked rapidly. Her expression of shock was quickly turning to curiosity and desire. As was the case with most exhibitionists, Jessica had a healthy dose of voyeurism as well.

"Nico," Alex greeted his friend, not at all surprised to see Maks following them. "I have a ribbon for you."

"I have one for you as well," Nico said with a grin and held up Jessica's blue silk ribbon.

His girl shifted next to him, and he decided now was the time to test her and help her get over her fears. It was time for a lesson in what it meant to belong to him.

"I need your assistance with something."

The two women eyed each other, the sexual tension between them thick enough that he could almost see it arc between them. Without hesitating, he slid his finger between the swollen lips of Jessica's sex, cupping her tight when she startled. For a moment, he wondered if she was going to safeword out. Then she moaned as he slid two fingers into her grasping sex.

"I'll trade you. Catrin will suck my dick, while Jessica sucks yours." As soon as those words left his mouth, Jessica's pussy clamped down on his fingers, and he swore he could feel the rush of wetness spilling from her tight cunt over his knuckles.

Nico licked his full lips, as unapologetic about his desire as his woman. They were a perfect match for each other. Alex just hoped Catrin would realize that. Nico was proposing daily now, and no one was sure if Catrin would say yes or not. Even Jessica didn't know, and she had spent a great deal of time with the little blonde minx lately.

Jessica looked up at him, and he glanced down, giving her time to protest. She studied his face for a moment, the apprehension clearly visible in her enchanting blue eyes, but she reached out and laced her fingers with his then nodded. He took a moment to give her a gentle, reassuring kiss and nose rub, then turned his attention to Nico, who was watching them with a small grin, and Catrin, who was outright beaming at him. They both adored Jessica and thought she was perfect for him. Something he happened to agree with.

He gave her pussy a light spank then released her. "On your knees. Catrin, I want you next to her."

Nico sat next to Alex on the lounger and slowly

unfastened his tight pants, freeing his erection, which bobbed dark and thick against his jacket. Letting out a little hiss, Jessica blinked as she studied Nico. Catrin was a size queen. She loved big cocks, and Nico was a large man. Jessica blinked hard, then started to raise her hand. Pausing, she looked over at Alex.

Answering her unasked question, he nodded. "You may touch him, my filthy girl, but only with Catrin's permission."

Catrin groaned. "Please, touch him."

Reaching out, Jessica softly stroked the delicate foreskin of Nico's cock, her fingers an erotic white against his dark tone. Alex groaned and looked down at his own lap as Catrin began to free his dick with a familiar, naughty smile. He'd been having sex with her for years, and she knew how to pleasure him. The added stimulus of watching Jessica take her first, hesitant lick of Nico's shaft made his balls tingle before Catrin even took him into her mouth. Jessica's tongue was so pink against the darkness of his friend's cock. Her mouth looked small and tender as she stretched wide to envelop the head. With a low moan, she began to work Nico's shaft with both hands while Catrin moaned and sucked Alex off, wiggling with arousal as she stole hungry glances at Nico and Jessica.

Nico sank his fingers into Jessica's hair and spoke to Alex in Russian. "She is going to make me come quick."

Alex grunted as Catrin took him into her throat. "Same."

Aware of Krom watching them, Alex pried Catrin off his cock, his balls drawn up tight. "Go get your face fucked by Krom."

Eagerly, Catrin complied as Nico slowly eased Jessica off of his visibly throbbing dick. "Such a good girl. You pleased me very much."

Gesturing to Maks watching them with such hungry eyes, Alex smiled down at Jessica. "Did you enjoy that?"

As predicted, a flash of remorse dimmed her passion, and she looked away, a flush turning her ears red.

"Maks, my little girl likes to feel guilty about doing what her Master ordered. I need you to punish her for doubting me."

Jessica trembled while Maks stalked toward them, his attention totally focused on the fidgeting submissive kneeling between them. His poor girl was about to pass out if she didn't get her fear under control. Perhaps he needed to take more power from her, to make her feel helpless. With this in mind, he looked over at Nico, who was watching Ivan throat-fuck his girl across the room.

"Nico," Alex said in a rough voice, "I need restraints."

Catrin removed her mouth from Krom's rock hard erection and winked at her husband. "Put her in something comfortable, nothing too harsh. I have plans for her. She responds well to teasing, especially if it is in front of her Master."

With a low growl, Krom forced her mouth back onto his cock. "You may get to order around sweet little Jessica, but I will not put up with you misbehaving in my presence. Now suck."

Nico chuckled and shook his head when Catrin let out a little whine, her pussy wet and pink while she serviced Krom. A moment later, he took a pair of dark green leather cuffs lined with black rabbit fur from a space beneath the lounge. Alex caught them neatly, and when he looked back down at Jessica, he found her gaze had gone hooded, her attention totally focused on the cuffs. Much to their mutual delight, they'd discovered she loved being restrained, and he'd given her some powerful orgasms in return for her trust.

When she eagerly held her hands up, he smiled and buckled them around her slender wrists, the black fur a stark contrast to the speckled cream of her skin. Because she was so fair, he could easily see the delicate veins at her wrists, hints of blue that called to his lips. Before he buckled the second cuff, he kissed her there, the smoothness of her skin always a pleasurable sensation. The previous week, he'd spent an entire day with her in bed, naked, reveling in just touching her. By the end of the night, she was so sensitized to him that the softest caress made her shiver.

Hooking the cuffs together, he licked his lips at the thought of the visual feast to come. Hopefully, this act of trust on both their parts would help soothe Maks. His friend did not lose his grip often, but Jessica was a member of their close-knit circle of friends now, and Maks fretted over her like he did all the women he allowed himself to care about. Alex could only hope his girl would give Maks the gift of peace of mind...and body in a way only she could. Once Maks got past her initial resistance, Jessica would be melting all over him. It was just a matter of pushing past what society said was right and wrong to what was the actual truth for her.

With this thought in mind, Alex stepped back and fisted himself, groaning at the sensation of the leather of his glove working his shaft. Jessica responded immediately, her gaze focused on his movements, her entire being hungry for him. Her pretty pink nipples, all swollen from the oil, begged for his touch, but he kept his hand working his dick then nodded to Maks. "Spank her. Make her come if she pleases you. Make her come twice if she misbehaves."

Everyone in the room chuckled as Jessica blushed so hard she turned cardinal red then hissed, "Alex!"

To his bemusement, Jessica found herself spun around with Nico holding her arms, keeping her draped over Maks' lap while Krom lay back next to Alex with Catrin atop him. Jessica's startled gasp made Alex fight a smile as she watched where she could no doubt see Krom's pierced cock stretching Catrin wide. The little blonde Russian woman looked like her snug pussy was about to tear around Krom's girth, but Nico was even bigger. He'd seen his friend fuck Catrin many times and knew the sight was sweet.

Watching Catrin distracted Jessica enough that she didn't realize her cuffs had been chained to a bolt in the floor until Nico stood then gave those chains a jerk. "She's ready, Maks."

His little enchantress wiggled on Maks' lap, unaware of the pained expression on Maks' face as her struggles rubbed her body against his and exposed her firm ass and wet, puffy *pizda*. Fuck, she had such a delicious cunt and thanks to whatever spa treatments she'd had done, her lips were totally bare, allowing him to eat her smooth flesh until he would come close to losing his mind with the need to fuck. And the feeling of that hot, slick cunt parting for him, drawing him in with her tight *pizda* muscles...his cock throbbed in his fist, and he pinched the base hard enough to chase back his orgasm.

A sharp crack rang through the air, followed by Jessica's scream. "What the hell!"

"Hush," Maks murmured, his attention totally on the pink flushing the skin of her butt cheek. "You are tender. I will be gentle."

This time she couldn't even get her protest out

333

before he slapped her again and again, slowly warming her skin, taking his time to work her up and treat her as she deserved. Yes, Maks was a man worthy of touching Jessica. He knew what a privilege it was, how Alex and Jessica were honoring him by allowing this. Alex had to remove his hand completely from his cock when Jessica began to cry, tears dripping down her face even as she raised her hips to meet each slap.

Alex would bet his home in Siberia that Jessica's tears were because of misplaced guilt rather than true pain. As sensitive as her skin was, if Maks had been using an ounce of his strength, she'd be bruising already. Instead, she hung limp over his lap, her hair falling to the floor around her face. Alex took a step to the side, and he could see the sheen of her arousal wetting her thighs and her beautiful cunt. Truly, Alex had never seen any woman as beautiful as his Jessica.

Maks noticed his movement, and when their gazes met, Alex was pleased to see the relaxation of his friend's facial features, that some of the terrible fear had drained away from the other man's green eyes. As that dread finally left Maks entirely, Alex was glad to see his friend once again in control of himself. Now there was mischief instead of grief tightening his lips, and he deliberately traced his finger down the swollen slit of Jessica's sex then gave her a little spank on her inner thigh, drawing an arousing, pleading noise from his girl.

Fuck, she was going to go wild when Alex finally got his cock in her.

Maks raised his eyebrows and stroked his fingers closer to Jessica's pussy, the back of one finger barely grazing the side of her puffy labia. She froze, her thighs tensing, and Alex had to bite back a laugh as Maks grinned at him. With a light, tender touch, Maks began to stroke the back of her thighs, now pink from his blows. He traced circles inward while Jessica jittered and twitched. He was almost at her center when she abruptly widened her stance and tilted her ass up, silently pleading with him while she clutched the cuffs of his pants, her face turned into his calf.

With a low groan, Maks sank two fingers into her pussy, and she keened, the lovely muscles of her slender back twisting as she rubbed herself into his touch. Alex loved it when she got wild like this, when her hunger overwhelmed her and she became almost animalistic in her pursuit of gratification. Maks gave her ass another slap, and she whimpered then stilled as he began to stroke his fingers in and out of her rose-red pussy.

Alex momentarily knelt next to her so he could pull her hair back and watch her face. When she looked at him, guilt and pleasure combined on her expressive face, and he sighed. Ahhh, his poor little one. She was so scared, but that made her eventual discovery of the pleasure they offered her all the sweeter. A hint of the forbidden to drive her desire even higher.

Catrin was crying out as Krom began to pump hard into her, his grunts a masculine counterpart to her pleading noises. Jessica stilled beneath Maks' touch then lifted her head, her attention totally on Catrin getting fucked into submission. Nico noticed Alex watching and shouted out, "Bring your girl over here. Catrin is being too noisy. I need something to keep her mouth busy."

Catrin moaned long and loud, making Krom curse as she twisted up against him, her orgasm making her hips work him in harsh jerks. Krom held on, his lips drawn back in a snarl while he slammed into Catrin. Ivan hefted his girl into his arms, the shine of her arousal coating his erection as he carried her over to the lounge and placed her next to Jessica. Sarnai gave a happy sigh, her breasts red from being struck, her pussy swollen from Ivan's hard fucking. Alex gritted his teeth, the need to be inside Jessica almost overwhelming him. Catching Maks' gaze, he unhooked the chains from Jessica's cuffs.

"Jessica, stand up and tell Maks thank you."

She stumbled to her feet, and he was there in an instant, holding her weaving body against his. Her voice was thick as she whispered, "Thank you, Master Maks."

Maks' gaze softened to the point that Alex wondered if he needed to reconsider allowing Maks any access to Jessica. There was devotion, yes, but also a tenderness Alex did not like. Before he could move his girl away, Maks had her chin cupped in his hand and drew her down to him, kissing her until she sank into his embrace, her ass pressed into Alex's erection as she returned Maks' kiss, her body undulating with need. That odd jealousy sparked again, and he gently guided her away from Maks and broke their kiss. When she focused on him, he saw that her eyes were fever-bright with need.

Without looking at anyone, he said in Russian, "Ivan, have your girl take care of Maks. I'm going to take my woman and fuck her until she can't walk."

Chapter Twenty-One

J essica could barely walk already as Alex led her over to a smaller, three-person size daybed covered in pale sage green silk and mounded with floral embroidered pillows. Tall, potted palm trees arched overhead, and a little fountain bubbled nearby. The atmosphere was at once comforting and sensual, exactly what she needed after that overwhelming scene on Maks' lap. As usual, Alex seemed to read her mind, sensing she needed reassurance, and placed a gentle kiss on her forehead. No matter how much she searched his gaze, she could only find acceptance and desire, no anger or anything like that. When she kissed Maks that last time, she was sure she saw jealousy in Alex's expression, but if she had, it was gone now.

Or she could be totally seeing things that weren't there because of her own internal conflict that was easing by the minute.

"Lift," Alex said as he removed her dress, leaving her standing naked before him.

Melanie and Laz came in, looking flushed and happy, their arms wrapped around each other as they scanned the room. Melanie was now nude except for a thick, gold waist chain, and she gave Jessica a big smile and a wink when their gazes met. Laz grinned at her before turning his attention to where Ivan, Maks, and Sarnai were playing. Her interest piqued as she watched all five of them descend into a laughing, touching, kissing tangle of limbs and groping hands.

To her shock, Alex gave her breast a hard slap. "Eyes on me."

Looking back to him, she swallowed down a

moan at his ravenous gaze going over her body, the sting from her smacked breast only adding to her arousal. "Someday we will play with them. Someday I will watch you take pleasure from as many people as you can handle, and I will love it. But right now, I am greedy for you, *prinsessa moya.*"

He tossed her dress to the side, his gaze devouring her. She started to shift, to hide herself, but his displeased sound made her freeze in place. A warm, disarming arousal moved through her, the satisfaction that came from realizing she was with a man who was in total control of himself, and her. Part of her was aware that more than one pair of eyes were watching them, but it didn't matter. The only person in the room who felt real was her Master.

Without thought, she reached out and cupped his cheek, rubbing her thumb over his goatee. "I missed you."

His stern expression fractured as he grinned then shook his head. "*Devushka milaya*, what am I going to do with you?"

"Love me?"

"Always," he whispered before claiming her lips in a slow, sensual kiss that left her gasping in his arms.

She'd experienced many different kinds of pleasure with Alex in their brief time together as lovers, but something about this night changed things between them. While she was not as experienced as Alex, she knew that accepting his lifestyle reassured him in a way she didn't understand yet. Thank God she not only enjoyed what he taught her, but yearned for it. The more control she gave to him, the more he helped her feel like it was okay to be as hedonistic as she desired, because she always ended her night in his arms.

His love for her shone like a beacon. Despite the

338

rather loud and aggressive activities happening on the other side of the room, they were in their own little sensual bubble. They took their time exploring each other with gentle touches, tasting and savoring the feeling of being together. This was one of the first things Alex had taught her, patience to build the fire inside until it was a roaring inferno, burning her with the need for his body. The salt on his skin sat heavy on her tongue as she licked his thick, corded neck, her hands working his large cock while he groaned against her lips.

"Put me in your tight *pizda*," he whispered against her mouth, the silk caressing her bare skin while he maneuvered her onto her side.

Facing each other, he flexed his hips as she fit his shaft to her entrance, pushing into her aching flesh. Unable to help herself, she gasped and moaned softly. "So good."

"Your body loves my cock," he ground out as he pushed into her all the way to the root, his balls pressing against her buttocks as he lifted her leg higher on his hip. "Grips me, tight."

At his rough talk, her pussy did indeed grip him tight, and he groaned. "You have velvet fist."

That odd phrase dragged her out of her arousal a bit. "Huh?"

Sweat popped up on his brow as he continued to move in and out of her at a pace that made her feel every inch of him. "Old courtesan trick. To squeeze the pussy like that, strong enough to feel like fist clenching cock, but better. Highly prized."

She almost gave him a lecture on Kegel exercises being beneficial to a woman's health, not just for sex, but her response was lost in a shriek as he slammed hard into her, hard enough that it stung deep inside.

"Do not argue with me when I am fucking you, unless you want me to fuck the fight right out of you."

She made a mental note to fight with him sometime in the future while they were having sex.

Leaning over, he kissed along her jaw, his chest hair scraping her nipples while he rocked slowly into her. "Your little clit is so hard. Ride me."

Her breath came out in a whoosh as he easily maneuvered them so she was on top, her body almost immediately moving as she fucked him. Yeah, he might have been making love with her, but she wanted to come, and she wanted it now. He grasped her breasts in a punishing grip, and she bucked against him, sinking his dick all the way inside. Bracing her hands on his chest, she rode him hard, her thighs aching as she bounced on his cock, her orgasm close enough that her thoughts had gone fuzzy, all of her focus now turned to the sensation of her muscles tightening and the wonderful euphoria that would soon flood her.

"Come for me, *prinsessa moya*. Soak me with your juice."

She shuddered and cried out as her orgasm overwhelmed her. Alex took over moving her body, his hands on her hips as he held her still so he could fuck her, pounding her pussy until another orgasm came close on the heels of the second, her poor clit so sensitive the rasp of his pubic hair against her exposed bud was too much. She began to fight him, and he snarled. She opened her eyes enough to look down at him. His face was a fierce mask of need, and she made a mewling sound low in her throat while he continued to fuck her hard enough that her teeth clicked.

With a final grinding thrust, he stilled beneath her, his back arched and lifted her from the daybed. He filled her up with throbs strong enough for her to feel, his head rubbing against the mattress as he thrust up into her, his body slick with sweat. He was magnificent—a study in power and strength, and he was all hers.

She wilted forward like a puppet whose strings had been snapped, her eyes closing as her body tried to slip into sleep. Alex stroked her back, his touch soothing as they panted. Making a low noise deep in his throat, his cock twitched inside of her. "I love you."

Snuggling against him, becoming more aware by the moment of how sticky they were, she ran her fingertips over the dark hair on his arms. "I love you so much, Alex. More than I've ever loved anyone or anything."

"When we get back to Ireland, I want to buy house with you, want you to live with me."

"Okay."

His breath ghosted over her head as he sighed. "Okay? No fight?"

"Mmm, no. I'm feeling really mellow at the moment. Enjoy it while you can."

"Someday, when you are ready, I will marry you, Jessica Venture." She tensed, but he merely patted her bottom. "Not yet, but ceremony is merely formality. You belong to me, my light, my love. We have much to discuss, but never doubt my devotion to you. Men of my family, when we fall in love, it is forever."

Her mind spun as she tried to absorb his words, and the first thing that her mouth spat out was, "You'll need to meet my family."

"I will," he said in an amused tone.

"I'll have to meet yours."

His body turned to rock beneath hers. "When you are ready."

"Alex..."

"No. We have discussed. Father is not good man."

"I know." Not wanting to ruin the mood between them any further, she decided to table that discussion for when she wasn't naked in a room full of people fucking. "Do you think we could find something in our budget for a place out in the country? Something with some acreage? Being out here today reminded me how much I miss my old house. My uncle lives there with his family running the farm, but I'll always think of it as my home."

Alex laughed and smoothed her hair back from her sweaty cheek. "Jessica, you have no budget. Anything you want, you can have."

She sighed. "So I guess my offering to pay half the rent on a place isn't going to happen?"

"No. I am the man I—"

Leaning up on her elbows, she smiled down at him and placed her hand on his lips. "I know, you provide."

He kissed her fingertips before she removed them. "I have some business to attend to when we get back. After that, I will go to America with you to meet your family."

"Thank you."

Rolling them so she was under him, he carefully slid his semi-hard cock out her. "Remember this."

"What?"

"Promise me you will remember us, like this, right now. Things will get bad, is way of world. You will need this to get through."

"Alex...you're freaking me out."

His eyes closed, and a tormented look came over his face. "Promise me you will remember how much you love me."

Reaching up, she cupped his face, her love for this complicated man overwhelming her. "I promise."

"Swear."

"I swear it."

He whispered a bunch of stuff in Russian against her head as she continued to pet him, her eyes closing for good as sleep claimed her even as she wondered what her normally unflappable man was so worried about.

Chapter Twenty-Two

Eight months later

J essica's new best friend, Catrin, leapt up onto
Jessica's massive four-poster oak bed, her
vibrant purple pajamas complimenting her light
tan. The small, curvy Russian woman had stopped by
with her new husband for a few days to visit Jessica
and see their new home now that the updating and
remodeling was finally done. Alex had to go away on
business—again—and he'd brought Catrin and Nico
over as a surprise for Jessica. Catrin had become
absolutely enchanted with Ireland and dragged
Jessica everywhere with her, doing tourist stuff with
such enthusiasm that it always made Jessica laugh.
Her friend was such a free spirit, but very smart, and
she made the world around her an interesting place.

Plus, Catrin was honest. Sometimes brutally
honest. Like right now.

Catrin squealed as she bounced among the navy
and burgundy silk pillows mounded against the head
of the bed. "Holy shit, bitch, you live in a castle! I
know Alex calls you his princess, but this place is
outrageous. You must let me help you decorate it.
The colors I could do here…"

The home Alex had bought for them four months
ago was actually an old manor on the outskirts of
Dublin that had been lovingly restored and updated
from its original neglected state, but sat mostly empty
of furniture. Alex wanted her to decorate the home
with things she liked, but she had no idea what to do
with all the space. In the past three weeks since they
moved in, she managed to get the essential rooms
done, but that was about it. There were nine

bedrooms, fourteen bathrooms, and close to a dozen sitting areas. That was a lot of space to fill for someone who'd only lived on her own in one-bedroom apartments. Like anything else in her life, she studied online about interior design and had struck up friendships on a couple decorating boards where she talked with interior designers about her ideas.

Their feedback had enabled her to start to slowly make the home that Alex deserved. He worked so hard, often coming back to her completely drained and exhausted. The first thing he did whenever he saw her was draw her into his arms and hold her tight, his body sometimes trembling with tension. She hated that whatever he did put him in such a state and would wonder when Alex was going to share that part of his life with her. As the months passed, she was getting impatient, but Alex always managed to soothe her—okay, he usually distracted her with sex—but when he wasn't home, her unanswered questions constantly rattled around in her head.

With a happy sigh, Catrin switched positions on the bed so she could peek through the open door of the master suite's spa/bathroom. It felt wrong to call that opulent space something as mundane as a bathroom considering it also had a steam room, a massage table, a massive shower with water spouts all over the place, and a bathtub big enough to hold eight people. There was also an area set up just for her to use whenever she had hair stylists and makeup artists come to doll her up before a big event.

All of it was done in winter white marble with pale green and copper veins, clean and modern but also welcoming, especially in candlelight. The memory of making love with Alex in that huge tub tingled through her, and she missed him immensely.

His larger-than-life presence was a part of her now, and she mourned when he wasn't home, which was becoming more and more of a frequent thing thanks to situations that he refused to discuss with her. But Alex was coming home tomorrow, and she couldn't wait to see him, taste him, feel his strength surrounding her again.

"Really, this place is marvelous," Catrin said while she clapped her hands together. "Oh, we are going to bring this magnificent home to life, and once we're done we'll throw the biggest party Dublin has ever seen."

Jessica had adored the sprawling two-story manor with its three separate guest houses on the grounds. While the home was amazing and the twenty-two acres it sat on were beautiful, it was the stables that had captured Jessica's imagination. She could easily see teaching her children to ride out there someday and imagined greeting Alex out at the barn then having a romp with him in the hayloft.

"It's not really a castle."

Laughing, Catrin smacked her arm. "What-the-fuck-ever. You have a seven-foot fence encircling the property, guards on all the entrances, and there is a lovely tower like something out of a Disney movie with your own private underground hot springs. Bitch, you live in a castle."

Jessica shook her head then grabbed a pillow and hugged it tight, the scent of Alex's cologne briefly filling the air. "Okay, I live in a castle."

"Alex has crowned you the new Novikov queen. Oh, there will be some broken hearts in Russia when they realize Alexandr Novikov has taken a bride," Catrin said with a laugh in her voice that abruptly cut off as she grew alarmingly pale. "I mean Gorev."

"Wait, you said Alexandr Novikov. Who is that?"

"Goodness, I'm tired. My mind is getting all

347

mixed up."

Catrin's unusual behavior, the almost glassy look in her eyes that was definitely more fear than humor, put Jessica on full alert. Going over what Catrin had just said, she sucked in a hard breath through her nose. A memory tickled at the back of Jessica's mind, something about that name, Novikov. She'd heard it often, usually when the bodyguards were speaking to each other in Russian. While she'd begun to learn some of the language, it was hard for her to get a grasp on it, and everyone spoke so fast. All she knew was that she heard that name a great deal, but had dismissed it as being some business partner she hadn't met yet. And she'd seen the name Alexandr Novikov on some mail, but hadn't really paid any attention to it, dismissing it as junk mail.

Her mouth went dry as she realized she'd heard Dimitri called Dimitri Novikov once. It had been to a man she was unfamiliar with, who was speaking in Russian, but she remembered thinking it was odd that the man called him that. Then again, she knew both Dimitri and Alex used aliases and had dismissed it as being one of them. Alex was revealing his world to her bit by bit, and among the things he'd shown her was where they each had two sets of fake IDs and a ton of cash along with keys to different safe houses and directions to them stashed away.

At the time, she'd been frightened that he had such illegal things. Now an even bigger fear gripped her, one so large she feared she might throw up all over her lovely bed, in her gorgeous bedroom, in her home fit for a princess...all built on lies.

"Alexandr Novikov," Jessica breathed, watching Catrin's pupils dilate in fear. "That's his real name, isn't it?"

"No, no, that is not true. I simply misspoke. Was error in translation."

"Oh, God." Her lower lip quivered, and she tried to ignore the burn in her nostrils, the taste of tears not yet shed filling her mouth. "I'm in love with a man who doesn't exist."

"No, Jessica, please don't." The fear was plain in Catrin's voice, and Jessica wondered what kind of monster she'd tied herself to. Catrin wasn't afraid of anyone, but right now, she was clearly terrified. "He loves you. He really does. It was for your protection."

"Are you telling me that Alex is so dangerous I can't even know his real name without being at risk?"

Catrin opened her mouth, but no words came out. Instead tears dripped down her cheeks. "I-that is...Yes. Jessica, their world is terrible, horrible place. They keep us, the women they love, as isolated from it as possible. They do not want any of that ever touching us. Is their way. I resisted Nico's proposal for the longest time because I do *not* approve of the world of the *Bratvas*, but they are a necessary evil. Is paradox, they do bad things but are such good men. Nico gives away almost all of his fortune to his charities, supplying entire villages in Siberia with traveling doctors and midwives as well as scholarships for the children of poor families."

Her heart pounded so hard she could hear her blood rushing in her ears. "That's great, I'm happy for you and Nico, but Alex has crossed the line with me. We're fucking done and I'm out of here. You can stay or go, but I'm telling you right now that I'll be gone before Alex gets here."

"Please, Jessica, you mustn't run away. Let him explain to you."

She pushed away from Catrin, rolling off the bed and pacing over to her closet. "Just to make sure we're clear, I'm in love with a man who has lied to me about his fucking real name since the moment we met, and he's somehow going to explain that away?

349

Are you for fucking real?"

Catrin followed Jessica into the closet, her cheeks wet with tears and her hands out in a pleading gesture. "Jessica, calm down. You are overreacting."

"Are you kidding me? Catrin, you lied to me as well, so forgive me if I tell you to go fuck yourself."

Red flared in the other woman's cheeks. "I couldn't tell you. Alex forbid it."

"Oh, right. Alex says you can't do something because, of course, you don't want to piss off Alexandr Novikov, whoever the fuck he is."

"He has reasons for what he does!" Catrin began rub her arms, her agitation rising by the second. "There is a long history you must know to understand why he is way he is. As soon as you hear his explanation you can judge him, but do not shut him out before he has chance to explain himself."

"No offense, but the only one I needed to hear explanations from was Alex, and he chose not to. He has had a thousand chances. So now, I'm choosing not to explain to him why I'm leaving."

Jerking off her pajamas, she avoided Catrin's gaze while getting dressed in a pair of jeans that fit her perfectly and a deep green sweater. Even though it was warm at night, she still got chilled, and she hated how her fingers would turn a weird purple red color when cold. That was part of the problem with having skin that was almost transparent. Maybe she should start using some kind of bronzing lotion so she didn't glow in the dark.

Her gaze locked on her image in one of the mirrors in the closet. She looked like shit. Her eyes were wide, almost as if she was in shock, but her hands trembled with anger, and her face was puffy and red. God, why did she have to turn instantly hideous when she cried? A tear slipped free, and she swallowed hard, the pain that had momentarily entered her gaze nothing compared to the way her chest hurt. With a start, she realized her thoughts were rambling through mundane things with a desperation that scared her. It was like she didn't want to think about what she'd just learned, was desperate not to consider the ramifications of what had just happened.

She needed to get to a computer right away.

Information was power, and now that she finally had a name she could get some answers.

Without sparing Catrin a glance, she pushed past the woman and grabbed up her tablet, typing the name 'Alexandr Novikov' into the search engine. Unlike when she typed in Alexandr Gorev and got practically nothing, a wealth of information came up, words like *Bratva*, mafia, murder, drugs, prostitution, extortion, blackmail, and just about every sin known to man was there on her screen. Her chest felt as though it had split open in a mortal wound as she looked at picture after picture of Alex with some of the most evil men in the world.

The man she loved to distraction was a monster.

Absently, she noted that Catrin was on the phone with someone, her voice close to frantic, but she was too busy feeling like she'd been kicked in the gut to pay any attention. Her pain became a physical thing as she read the story of the Novikov Curse, the real reason Alex was so paranoid about her safety. And the deaths...so many women had died in this stupid war between two criminal empires including his mother, half-sister, and stepmother.

Her breath came out in a harsh sob as she stared in disbelief when she scrolled down and saw a picture of herself on some crazy, mafia-worshiping website that was devoted to chronicling the lives of the underworld. They didn't use her name, just identified her as Alexandr Novikov's woman, but it was a picture of her walking down the street in Dublin with Oleg, who was also identified in the picture as one of Alex's best bodyguards and a high ranking member of the Novikov *Bratva*. Next to that was an image of Alex looking down on Jessica like the sun rose and set in her eyes, his whole body curved around hers as she touched his face with her fingertips. He never hid his affection for her, always letting her know that she was cherished and adored. The setting for this picture was the Spanish Steps in Rome, and she knew this was one of the paparazzi pictures from when they'd arrived.

The bed depressed as Catrin sat next to her. On impulse, Jessica did a search for Catrin and came up with nothing beyond gossip and fashion pages mentioning her. Then did one for Nico. It was bad, not as bad as Alex, but still not good. Nico was known as the drug manufacturer for the elite of the criminal world everywhere, supplying them with drugs, but not the recreational kind.

No, Nico made top of the line prescription drugs for a variety of ailments, including chemotherapy and experimental treatments. In the opinion of the person who had written the article on Nico, this made the black Russian rich enough, and powerful enough, that he'd done the impossible and rose to power in a society that was *extremely* racist. He'd conquered the world with the help of the Novikov *Bratva,* and he was now one of the world's richest men, untouchable because of his value as a healer.

At the bottom of Nico's article, there was a picture of Nico and Catrin dancing together at some ball. They were backlit by the mellow glow of a chandelier, and the smile Catrin was giving Nico was totally radiant. Their happiness with each other practically leaped off the page, and she knew that any enemy who saw this website would see how much

Catrin meant to Nico. A shudder worked through Jessica as she suddenly realized how big a target she had become by being with Alex. She let out a low moan, and Catrin slid the tablet off of Jessica's lap, her nose wrinkling in distaste when she saw the screen.

"They would have to use that picture. That dress is hideous."

"What?"

Catrin sniffed and turned the tablet off. "At least you look good in your pictures."

"Are you insane?"

"No, just practical. If I have to be on such a disgusting website, I at least want to look good. That color is horrible on me."

Unable to stop it, a startled giggle escaped her, the shrill sound making Catrin wince. "Am I dreaming?"

"No, *devushka milaya*, you are not." Catrin laid her hands on Jessica's thighs and looked her in the eyes, the light blue of her friend's irises burning into hers. "You have fallen in love with a good man who does evil things."

That seemed to sum up the situation nicely, and she pulled her hair back from her face, tension replacing the fear. "Evil things, Catrin. He does *evil* things!"

"But he is not an evil man. Jessica, you know this. He is good man, born into a world that he cannot escape. It is rule or die for him. Lead them all or become prey. If he does not rule with iron fist, they will think him weak. Trust me, there are much worse men out there that you do not want to be in charge of one of Russia's strongest *Bratvas*, men who would not hesitate to kill Alex if they thought they could get away with it."

"Kill him?" Her self-absorbed fear retreated a bit,

replaced by a worry that was somehow worse. "People are going to kill him?"

"No, well, yes, but they try to kill him all the time and do not succeed."

"Oh no," Jessica moaned as she began to cry harder.

Making an exasperated noise, Catrin hugged her close. "Is not so bad. I promise. You will never know that part of his world. You will be his joy, his life, his reason for living. Russian men are not like Americans. They can be hard to understand for woman used to the Western culture, but that does not mean they do not love. Alex loves you. You are only woman he has ever loved. You may not know his name, but you know his soul. He has spent the past months introducing you to everyone he knows and respects because he is so proud of you. Not because you are beautiful and charming, but because you are sweet, and kind, and generous. You represent a life that many men crave, but have never had. To Alex, you are the ultimate prize."

She hiccupped, then grabbed the edge of the sheet, and wiped her face. "This is crazy, I can't deal with this. I need to go home."

"You are home." Jessica started to protest, but Catrin cut her off. "You told me you sold your parents' farm to your uncle Adam, that your family is scattered all over the United States, and almost none of your friends are still living in your hometown. It would be a lonely, miserable life compared to what Alex offers you."

She fisted her hands on her thighs. "I can't stay here!"

"Jessica," Catrin said in a sharp voice, "you cannot run from him. You must be brave and face him. Give him chance to explain. You have no idea how much you will hurt him if you run."

She wanted to stomp her foot and scream, to just leave and never come back, but that wasn't exactly the right way to handle a relationship, even if it was one based on a confusing mix of love and lies. If she was going to end it with Alex, he deserved to have her do it to his face. The sooner she could get this over with the better.

"Fine, I'll let him explain, but I'm telling you right now, Catrin, there is nothing he can say that will make this okay. I saw pictures of him with other women. Beautiful women at charity and celebrity events in Russia. Recently. A few of them were referred to as old girlfriends, and there was talk of 'flames' being rekindled. Please tell me how I'm supposed to be okay with that level of disrespect? What, I should just trust that he's not fucking them? Because he's always honest with me, right? Or, maybe, because I thought we were becoming good friends you might have clued me in that he was cheating on me."

"He is not cheating on you."

"Right." She sneered, then stood up, and marched to the door. When she tried the handle, it was locked. Whirling around, she glared at Catrin. "They locked me in!"

"Yes," she whispered, "they did."

Furious that she was being held prisoner, she went to kick the door but decided against it when she noticed her feet were still bare. Stalking back into her closet, she put on the sturdiest pair of boots she had. If she had to fucking kick out a window and climb down the side of the house to leave, she would.

"Jessica, you have to calm down. It's not as bad as you think."

She balled her hands into fists so hard her nails bit into her palms. She contemplated using the sturdy oak chair that she'd gotten at an antique flea market

355

and loved to try and get through the windows. Then again, if that glass was bulletproof like Alex said it was, then it was also probably old-chair proof.

"I don't think you're quite getting this. He lied to me about everything, Catrin. Everything." With a low sigh, Catrin stood and started to approach Jessica. She stopped with a hurt look when Jessica backed away. "Don't touch me."

"Please don't be mad at me, Jessica. I couldn't tell you." Catrin's lower lip quivered, and Jessica felt like a bitch even though she was plenty pissed at Catrin. "I-I'll leave you alone so you have some time to think."

When the door opened for Catrin, Jessica considered bolting for it, but Krom and another man she didn't recognize stood there. Their faces were unreadable, but she was pretty sure Krom winced when he momentarily caught her gaze. Catrin looked back over her shoulder at Jessica then let out a muffled sob and fled. This time when Krom looked at Jessica, his expression was hard and accusing, like she'd been mean to Catrin, like she was the one at fault.

"Do you need anything?" Krom asked in a stiff voice.

"I need to leave."

"Anything else?"

The temptation to be snarky filled her, but she wouldn't put it past Krom to flip her over his knee for a spanking if she lipped off. "No."

He didn't bother with any further conversation, just shut the door with a resounding click as the bolt slid into place. The silence in the room weighed down on her, and she collapsed on her side and grabbed her pillow, crushing it to her chest as she cried. After what seemed like forever, exhaustion stole her away, and she fell into a dreamless sleep.

Loud, but muffled male voices came from the other side of her bedroom door, waking her from a restless doze. Sunlight shone from behind the curtains, and she still felt groggy. The door burst open, and Alex strode in, his handsome expression one of barely contained fury even as she noted the signs of exhaustion clear on his face. The last of the muzziness from sleep fled from her as fear made her scoot away from Alex on the bed, and she almost fell off in her haste to avoid him. He snarled at her, and she froze, but she was becoming more and more pissed off by the second, and she snarled back at him.

"Oh, hi, Alex. You know, I was looking at getting your initials monogramed on some towels for Christmas. Sure am glad I didn't, considering they would have been wrong. Wouldn't I have felt dumb when your friends, who know your real name, came over and saw the AG instead of AN."

"You must listen to me."

"No!" She surged off the bed, strode across the room, and pushed his chest hard enough that he took a step back. "You lied to me! Over and over and over again! Everything was a lie! You broke my heart, you fucking asshole! You cheating motherfucker."

He allowed her to pummel him, her blows not hurting him in the least. "It was for your protection, and I never betrayed you."

She choked on a hysterical sob and struggled to breathe past it, past the poison that was invading her system from her wounded heart. She wanted to believe him, she really did, but he was a pathological liar. "You lied to me about who you were for my protection. Are you fucking kidding me? That's your excuse?"

"I told you there were things I could not tell you, things you would not understand. I wanted to give

357

you more time."

"Alex, all the time in the universe is never going to make me understand how you can possibly justify being a criminal. You've killed people."

"I have," he replied without remorse, a cold look she'd never seen before that made her flinch. "There are the deaths of many, many people on my hands. Does it disturb you that the same hands that touch you with such love are capable of murder?"

Upset by his matter of fact attitude, at the control he was exhibiting, and how her own self-control seemed to have totally left the proverbial building, she slapped him. "Fuck you!"

He touched his jaw absently. "I would like to remind you that I have never ever struck you in anger. Me, the monster."

"You've been with other women," she screeched, then tried to walk away from him only to have him hook his arm around her middle.

"I have not. I have attended events with friends of mine, past companions, but none of those women got anything more than dance out of me. They know their place, and it is not as my woman. My heart is taken, and any female who tries to break my bond with you has been made an example of in a public way."

Her vision blurred as tears spilled down her cheeks, confusion and heartache overwhelming her. "Why, why would you do this to me? Do you hate me that much? What did I ever do to you to deserve being mentally fucked with like this?"

He grasped her by the back of the neck, and before she knew it, his hand held her firmly in place. "You will shut up and listen, or I will gag you, tie you up, and make you listen."

"I don't even know you," she wailed, her knees giving out and causing her to sag against him. Even though she hated him, he was her only source of comfort. Then he put his arms around her and she hated him even more because his touch gave her strength. "I loved you so much."

"Shhh, *prinsessa moya*. I have story to tell you."

He pissed her off using his pet name for her, so she tried to push away, but he held her strong...until she slammed her hand against his chest. Then he hissed and flinched like she'd really hurt him. Right away, her ears rang as she felt some type of bandage beneath her fingertips.

He'd been hurt.

Oh, God, he'd been hurt!

With a low moan pushing through her suddenly tight throat, she ripped apart his shirt, revealing a cloth bandage that spanned his chest between the two eight-pointed stars on his shoulders. Her mind trailed to the tattoos on his back, and she flinched. Fuck. Images from the website where she'd read about Alex flashed through her mind, and she recognized those tattoos now as marks of a very, very high ranking member of the *Vory*, known in some circles as the Thieves Guild and in others as simply *Bratva*. That symbol was universal in the world of the Russian mafia for what amounted to royalty. Her gaze skittered over his body, remembering where there were other, odd marks that now told a horrifying story of death and betrayal. Violence was written into his skin, testaments to the criminal things he'd done and the fact that he'd survived terrible situations. Like being in prison three times if she read the barbed wire tattoo on his bicep correctly.

After she'd scanned him and ascertained that there weren't any more injuries, she placed her fingertips as gently as she could on the bandages. "What happened?"

He looked conflicted for a moment then blew out

a harsh breath. "Is healing. I got it three days ago, but needed to protect it during traveling. I had to leave abruptly and have not had a chance to tend to it yet."

She had to remove her hands because they were shaking so hard she could have hurt him. "Alex, what happened?"

His hard gaze met hers. Then he carefully peeled the bandage off, and she frowned as she realized it wasn't covering some terrible injury, but a new tattoo. It took her a moment to realize it was letters in Cyrillic, and for some reason, it looked familiar. She'd seen it before...Holy crap! He had her name tattooed on his chest. There, for all the world to see, her name over his heart. Her lower lip quivered, and she was being torn in two by her internal battle. Part of her was relieved that he was okay, that he'd done something as lovely as having her name on him, while another part hoped he'd get it lazered off because she never wanted to see him again now that she knew he was all right.

"I don't understand you." She thumped him in his ribs, her overwrought emotions making her want to bite him. "You do such terrible things. You lie to me, but you tattoo my name on your chest? Why?"

"I have lied to you. I admit I do terrible things, and your name is on my chest because you own me, Jessica. You are my world. Everything I do, I do to keep you safe, including hiding my true name." His gaze was fierce, uncompromising. "I had a disagreement with my father about you. He believes that I put you in great danger by publicly declaring you are my woman. I responded by getting your name tattooed on me. He responded by...it was not pleasant."

Horror filled her as she ran her hands over his body, haunted by the pain in his voice when he said that last sentence. "What did he do to you?"

"Shhh, *lyubov moya*, is nothing I have not endured before. My father is...harsh man. He does not like to be defied."

"Alex." Her nails dug into his skin, a terrifying realization filling her. "Is he going to hurt you if you continue to see me?"

"See you?" He leaned up on his elbows and shook his head. "I do not want to see you. I want to marry you."

So thrown off her game by Alex's response, she just stared at him for a few moments. "What?"

"In my pocket."

Eyes wide, her hand hesitantly reached for him then pulled back. "Have you lost your mind?"

"Obviously I have. Now reach into my pocket."

"Don't get snippy with me, Alexandr *Novikov*. I don't deserve it."

"I just flew from Moscow to Dublin in record time so I could hopefully talk to you before you managed to run off and maybe get killed. The whole way, my mind was filled with images of burying you or you dying because I kept my true self from you. Is most horrible feeling I have ever experienced. I felt my soul rotting inside of me." He reached up and gripped her by the back of her head, tilting her slightly so he could brush his lush lips over hers. "So I do not care that you hate me. I am overjoyed that you are alive to hate me. I also know that no matter how much you despise me, you are alive so I can do what I should have done since the beginning."

Her irrational emotions took a blow from the sincerity burning in each of his words, but the wounds to her heart were too raw to ignore. "This relationship...no, this whatever we have is no longer working for me."

"That is unfortunate, because I am in love with you beyond all reason and will do everything I can to

361

earn my way back into your heart. Give me a kiss, but mind the tattoo."

"You are such an asshole!"

Moving quick for someone who had just arrived off a long flight, he snatched her into his arms, and she was annoyed with herself when she realized she was being careful not to touch his tattoo of her name because she didn't want to get it infected and screw it up.

Jessica, in beautiful Cyrillic letters, over his heart. Because his father had tried to keep them apart, he defied the head of the Novikov *Bratva* for her and had paid some kind of price for loving her. Maybe hiding his name from her wasn't the end of the world. As always, her body was starved for him when he first came home, and it was demanding the release it knew was on the way. Her pussy was soft and achy beneath her jeans and growing wetter by the second as her anger faded, replaced by grudging relief that he was home.

While she still had an ounce of sense in her head, she drew back, only to find Alex holding out a little, black box to her.

"Jessica, please do me the honor of being my wife." She started to protest, but he thrust the box into her hands. "Look at it before you say no."

"Alex, getting married is not the answer to...." Her breath left her in a rush, and not just because of the beautiful two-plus carat diamond ring surrounded by sapphires. It was the pattern of the tiny sapphires on either side of the ring, with their own twin slivers of green emerald leaves that had her eyes tearing up. It couldn't be.

"Is this...are these from my mother's ring?"

"Your adoptive mother, yes. Your aunt gave it to me after I asked for your hand in marriage from them. She said your father had this ring made for your mother when they adopted you because the first day they had you, your mother took you into the garden to pick blueberries for you, and it was one of the happiest moments of her life. It was then that she realized she was finally what she'd always wanted to be, someone's mother."

"You...you what? When did you talk to my aunt?"

"When you took me to meet them."

"But that was months ago!"

"Yes. And the reason I went to my father to talk about you was because I asked for a piece of my mother's jewelry that was kept in family vault. He objected, we had big argument, but he could not dispute fact that my mother had left those jewels to me to give to my wife. It was in her will. My father is...hard man...but he loved my mother enough not to block access. This diamond has been in my mother's family for generations. Was said to have belonged to the favored concubine of a Russian czar. How it ended up in the hands of my mother's family, I do not know. I can only remember my mother's fantastical story about this gem." He let out a soft sigh, his face gentling as she looked between him and the ring. "She did that for all her jewels, made up stories about them. She would let me play with her sparkling necklaces while she told me tales of princes and dragons, and other nonsense."

Alex had never shared this much about his upbringing, and she had to make herself focus on him and not the ring, which was a beautiful blending of her family and his. "She sounds like she was a wonderful mother."

"She was. And when she died, I wished that I had died with her. My father was not much better, his mind cracking beneath the weight of her loss. When he remarried a few years later, I was overjoyed. My stepmother was a wonderful woman, sweet and kind.

363

Then came my little sister and, close to a year after that, Dimitri. After years of being alone, I had a family that I adored...Then they were taken from me as well, worse this time because my father's mind broke even more than before, and he went on a bloody rampage, destroying entire families—every single one—in his unquenchable thirst for vengeance."

She sucked in a quick breath, all too aware of the rage that still filled him over their deaths. "You lost so much."

"I did, and I embraced the feeling of emptiness they left behind. For years, I felt nothing beyond friendship for anyone other than my brother and father. Then I met you. From moment I saw you, that hole inside of me began to fill. I felt alive, happy in a way I had never experienced. I tried to fight you, tried to ignore your pull. I was determined to give you the kind of life you deserved." Sorrow darkened his gaze. "I have seen where you grew up, the good people you are blessed to have in your life. It was perfect. I will never be able to give you that."

Almost against her will, she leaned forward and kissed the bristle along his jaw where he normally shaved to shape his goatee. It surprised her to see him with scruff. He was almost fanatical about his appearance, but it also made her aware that he'd been in a bad state before he came back to her. His need for her was staggering, and she could no more resist kissing him on the lips than she could stop breathing.

"You hurt me," she whispered. "Bad."

"I regret every moment of anguish I may have caused you." He took the box from her hands. The diamonds sparkled in the light while the sapphires practically glowed. "Marry me, *prinsessa moya*. I vow you will never regret it."

"Can we have a long engagement?"

"How long?"

"I don't know...uh, two years?"

"Two months."

"What?"

"Fine, three months."

"Three years!"

His lips twitched, and she wanted to knock him on his cocky ass. "Five months."

"Twenty years!"

"Seven months, final offer. If you test me, I will marry you tonight. Think about what you wish before you speak, because I am man of my word. You know this."

Fucker. She did indeed 'know that', which made her, for once in her life, think before she spoke. He wasn't going to budge. This was his final offer, and she knew he wouldn't give in on this. Secretly, a messed up part of her psyche really liked that he was so eager to marry her, to the point where he'd force her to give in to his wishes.

"Fine. Seven months."

His whole body relaxed, and he collapsed, pulling her with him so she lay curled into his side with her head on his shoulder. "Thank fuck."

Unable to help it, she giggled. "Thank fuck? Really? I agree to marry you, and all you can say is 'thank fuck'?"

Turning his head to her, their gazes met, and a full body tingle raced over her, lifting every minute hair on her skin, as his emotions were laid bare for her to see. Love, pure and shining with joy, filled his beautiful, storm-gray eyes with their ring of black, and her love surged in return. They began to kiss, long and deep, before Alex made love to her so many times that she wasn't sure she'd be able to walk the next day. It was only when Alex had come for the fourth time that he finally collapsed next to her, the sheets wet with their sweat.

"Jessica Novikov," he whispered, his hand spasming on her thigh. "My wife."

"Not yet," she whispered with a grin, turning her head so she could kiss his bicep.

Abruptly, he rolled into her and pulled her tight to his body. "I will never let anyone harm you, not even my father."

She tensed. "Okay."

He rolled out of bed and grabbed her ankle, hauling her after him. "Come, we sleep in different room tonight. Bed is wet."

When he said that he leered at her, making her laugh. "Don't look at me like that. It wasn't all me, buddy."

"Right. Shower then bed. I have next three days off to make love to you. Though I might let you out so you can show Catrin your ring."

"Catrin..." She winced at the memory of how she'd been to her tonight. "I was mean to her."

"Then tomorrow you will be nice. She adores you, Jessica, and will forgive you. Remember, at one time she had no idea what Nico did for a living. Learning the truth was hard for her, but her father was involved in a different *Bratva* so she was not totally ignorant of it."

"Not like I was...am. Shit. Alexandr Novikov, you're lucky you're so damn good in bed, or I would not put up with the amount of bullshit you've brought into my life."

Chapter Twenty-Three

Six and a half months later

Alex gritted his teeth as he strode through the front door of his stunning manor outside of Dublin. This peaceful place in the middle of the woods was home now. Not the pit of inhumanity he'd left back in Moscow. Things were going badly, really badly, for the Novikov *Bratva*, and he knew it was his father's fault. Men were dying because Jorg Novikov was determined to expand his territory while Alex had to work desperately behind the scenes to try and broker a peace not only for the good of his mafia family, but also for his fiancée's continued wellbeing. To say he was stressed was an understatement, but damn, the feeling of finally being home was like a balm to his battered body and soul.

Poor Dimitri, was having a tough time dealing with their father. While Alex loved the old man, he knew his father had major flaws. Dimitri, on the other hand, was young enough that he'd been sheltered from the worse of Jorg's wrath over the years thanks to Alex and the men loyal to him doing their best to protect Dimitri. Now, because Alex was spending so much time with Jessica, Dimitri was having to face some hard truths, one being that their father could be a demon in human form.

Unlike his younger brother, Alex had a home to escape to and a woman who adored him.

Alex spoiled Jessica, but she never asked him outright for anything. In fact, she got irritated when he'd buy anything she'd shown the slightest interest in. After much debate, she made him understand she didn't need things to feel loved, only him. He'd discovered that apples, more specifically a scent similar to apple pie, was the scent his Jessica wore. He ordered a case of her favorite products for her, her best friend from the United States helping him to assemble it for Jessica, and she'd rewarded him well for his inexpensive gift.

His Jessica made him the richest man in the world, but he knew others would try to take his happiness from him out of greed and avarice, so he'd taught Jessica to defend herself. As his father had continued to become more bloodthirsty by the day, Alex had instructed Krom and Maks to begin training her at least two hours a day, five days a week. Oleg, along with is adorable wife and girls, often attended, as well as Jessica's Aunt Mary and any friends who might happen to be staying the night, but it was Jessica who received the bulk of the instruction, and she'd taken to it with an ease that surprised him.

In what had to be some sort of divine and karmic revenge, it was beginning to appear his sweet little woman could possibly become quite the proficient killer if she tried.

That point was reinforced when Alex felt a gun pressed to the side of his head as soon as he entered the house, followed by the scent of apple pie. At that moment, Jessica held a 9 mm pressed to his head with the ease of an accomplished assassin. A gun she'd grown quite proficient with. Oleg had taken over her hand to hand-to-hand combat training, while Maks was giving her shooting lessons. Luka, though, taught her things she called her 'ninja' skills—Basically the art of stealth— and she'd gotten pretty good at it. Good enough to be arrogant as she stood there with cold steel, with the safety still on, against his temple.

There had been two attempts on Jessica's life since they'd returned, of which she knew nothing about. After the second one, they managed to keep one of the would-be assassins from using his cyanide capsule. They learned that one of Peter's enemies was behind this, not Alex's. Alex, along with his men, helped Peter annihilate the rival faction, sending a crystal clear message that anyone who threatened Jessica, Alex, or the families and friends they loved would face a horrible death. Alex had been honestly surprised it wasn't one of his enemies and relieved that the protection he'd managed to surround her with had kept her safe from rival *Bratvas*, at least for now.

That is, if he could keep his father from attempting to start a war with everyone.

He tried to keep from smiling as Jessica quickly frisked him while keeping the gun to his head. It was easy to recognize Oleg's training, and he approved of her following all the steps of disarming an opponent, even with him. She was skilled, her touch light and swift as she detected his various weapons, not bothering to remove them, just letting him know that she knew they were there. The fact that she found his carefully concealed knives swelled his chest with pride. She was good, really good.

But he was better.

His wrenched shoulder ached as he disarmed her, and he gritted his teeth when she hit him in his already bruised side, along ribs that flared with hurt.

As soon as he made a pained grunt, she backed off then set her gun on the foyer table within reach. Her hands shook as she clasped them together and stared at him. She wore a light gold kimono over a white cami and tiny pink shorts. Her hair was a wild mess pulled back in a ponytail, and her gaze was angry when he met it. Inwardly, he flinched, knowing he was about to get his ass verbally beat by her.

"Two weeks...two weeks, Alex, and you couldn't

369

call me once?"

He leaned against the wall and turned on the small lamp next to the light brown sofa that faced the riverstone fireplace. A vase filled with fresh, multi-colored tulips sat atop the coffee table, as did an empty coffee mug and a book. Some of the pillows were slouched on the back of the sofa, an obvious sign Jessica had spent a lot of time in here lately. Obviously, Jessica hadn't expected him to be coming home, and he sighed inwardly. Things were about to go from bad to worse, and he suppressed a groan of frustration. It had not been an easy journey, and all he wanted to do was collapse on the sofa, have her ride him to orgasm, then pass out right there with her draped over his body.

And sleep for ten years.

"No, *prinsessa moya*, I could not contact you. Was not safe."

"And you can't tell me about that 'not safe' stuff, right?"

Regret filled him. "I cannot."

She crossed her arms and frowned at him, adorable even in her anger. He'd grab her and kiss those pouty pink lips of hers until she was smiling at him again. From deeper inside the house, an old grandfather clock chimed, and he raised an eyebrow.

"Is clock new?"

So he was a bit of a bastard for trying to distract her, but he knew she'd purchased an expensive grandfather clock, and that she'd fretted the whole time about the price. Oleg had been amused by her...what did she call it...freaking out, but he had been patient with her. Alex had ordered her to pick out something for the home while he was gone, something that would make the place hers. He'd let Jessica know he had more money than she could spend, but she somehow didn't believe him despite the lavish lifestyle he gave her.

Her whole body softened, and she sighed. "Yes."

"I like it. The sound is very soothing."

"Well…good." She closed her eyes and whispered, "Are you going to tell me what happened that left you looking like you got gored by a bull?"

He wanted to, ached to, but the game he was playing right now was so dangerous he didn't need or want her to know anything about it. She would worry herself to death if she found out how much danger he was in. Not only did he have to worry about rival organizations, he was greatly concerned about his father's increasingly volatile reaction to Jessica. It was the oddest thing. He felt like Jorg actually cared for and liked Jessica, but he was adamant that Alex should leave her. It had gotten to the point where Alex didn't mention Jessica in his brief dealings with his father, but the previous week he couldn't put it off anymore. Not when his father had sent a whore to his rooms in an effort to tempt Alex to stray.

That effort to get him to betray the woman he loved had sent Alex into a rage. He'd gone to his father, and they argued until Alex had finally told him he was going to marry Jessica. He wasn't sure what to expect, but scathing anger had not been it. Jorg had railed at him about the Novikov curse and warned Alex to let her go. It was too late for that, and even his father's wrath hadn't swayed him from his decision. In fact, plans were now being put into place that would seal her to him forever. He was not his father. His efforts to keep Jessica safe would pay off, and he could only pray the old man would die soon. Everything would work out, and he could have his family without abandoning his duty to the men and women who loyally served his *Bratva.*

That is, if Jessica didn't kill him first.

"I am okay, *dorogoya.* Little bruised, but okay."

She went ashen and rushed to his side, ripping open his dress shirt with a mighty yank, and stumbled back with a pained cry. "Oh, my god, Alex! What happened to you? Who did this!?"

He eased his jacket off, knowing his bruised ribs probably looked as terrible as they felt. Not to mention the healing wound across his abdomen. If the shard of metal from the car's engine had been just an inch or two closer, it would have cut him open like a gutted fish. "I was in car accident."

With a trembling lower lip, she turned her tear-filled gaze on him. "A car accident?"

"Yes, a car accident."

The tears escaped and spilled down her cheeks, and he rubbed his hand along her delicate arm, reveling in the warmth, the life of her body against his skin. Outside, thunder rumbled in the distance and rain began to beat against the skylights stretching across the room. Somewhere in the house, a door opened and closed.

A soggy Oleg appeared a moment later, his expression apologetic as he wiped the rain from his face.

"Alex, is good to have you home. Everything is secure." His eyebrows drew down as he examined Alex's torso then said in Russian, "You got lucky."

"I always do."

Shaking his head, Oleg gave Jessica a small smile. "Goodnight."

His girl responded with a brave, but shaky, smile, but Alex hated the sorrow in her face. After his old friend left them, he tugged Jessica close again, rubbing his lips against her hair, breathing in her fresh apple scent.

She'd put on a few pounds since they'd met, and he loved how it had softened her frame, giving her subtle curves he adored. Her breasts were fuller and, if he wasn't crazy, even more sensitive than usual. The thought of making her orgasm by suckling her nipples like he had before he left heated his body, but he tried to banish that thought. Jessica needed him to talk right now. It was her way, and even if he inwardly hated it, he would give her whatever she needed.

Her whole body trembled as she whispered, "Oh Alex, I would die if anything happened to you."

He ran his fingertips over her creamy cheek then gently wiped away her tears. "*Dorogoya*, please do not cry. Kills me. Nothing will happen. I will not let it."

"I hate this," she whispered, her voice incredibly sad. "I really do."

Instead of doing the right thing and offering her an out, he sought to bind her closer to him. "My time away was worth it. For two weeks, I am all yours. No working, only you and me."

Light shone from her gaze, happiness easily replacing the sorrow. Not totally. There was still a tension to her frame he didn't like, but soon enough, he'd have her relaxed and blissful. While he was away, he'd been constantly worried about her, but hadn't dared call. Just because he was out in the open about his relationship with her didn't mean he'd make it easy for his enemies to track her. Plus, he didn't trust some of his father's men right now. The whole *Bratva* was off, as if they were an enormous house resting on a foundation of one shaky brick. The feeling of foreboding still clung to him, but not as much as it did while he was in Moscow.

She took a step closer, unable to resist the pull between them while he studied her in the low lamplight. "Will you let me take care of you for the next few days? Rest and heal?"

His sweet girl, he knew she needed to do this for

him, understood the urge to take away his pain in any ways she could. "Yes, but in two days we leave for surprise. You will have to satisfy yourself with caring for me for one day."

Looking at him from beneath her eyelashes, she gave him a wicked smile. "Are we going back to that club in Paris?"

At the mention of the BDSM club they'd visited on his last break from work, his cock twitched. "Mmm, did you like that?"

"I did," she whispered, a cute flush making her cheeks pink. "A lot."

He'd fucked her as part of a demonstration on orgasm denial for the club. Her screams of gratification when he finally let her come had been seared into his memory as had the way she'd smiled up at him afterward with pure love. "So did I, but no, we aren't going back there."

"Oh." She tried to hide her disappointment.

Easing her closer, he buried his face against her hair. "Nico and Catrin are having a private party up near the North Pole. A northern lights party."

The women had formed a close friendship in addition to their sexual relationship, and Alex knew Catrin adored Jessica. And as Alex had happily discovered, Jessica loved to watch big, muscular, dark skinned Nico fuck the curvy little blonde. Jessica also had a taste for voyeurism and had greatly enjoyed watching Catrin suck Alex's cock while Jessica sucked Nico's. They hadn't switched around for actual sex, but they'd played together in plenty of other ways that never failed to leave Alex's sweet submissive ravenous for him when they finally came together.

The sexual energy between them was intense, and he couldn't help but smile as Jessica gave that little wiggle of her hips again. She was definitely

374

thinking naughty thoughts. She always did that small hip wiggle when she was aroused, and he pressed back, rubbing against her pitiful excuse for shorts. He could easily slide them over and shove his way inside her. Hell, he'd done it plenty of times before. Once right in front of Luka and Maks. She'd been very naughty that day, being a brat and, in general, a pain in the ass. Their sexual relationship had progressed by this point into more than dabbling in BDSM, and Jessica got off on being punished.

The more she'd baited him the more he realized what she was trying to do, even if she was ignorant of the fact that she was trying to top from the bottom. He'd warned her twice before he had her bent over the kitchen table, spanking her ass while Luka kept her arms pinned and Maks had kept her torso pressed to the table with his hands on her lower back. Together, they'd restrained her while Alex punished her, noting how quickly her pussy grew swollen and wet.

She'd been shuddering when he'd rubbed her slit and had come almost the instant he'd slid his cock into her.

His little girl was filthy, kinky, and hungry to explore.

He loved it.

He loved her.

She gentled in his arms then placed a kiss at the skin exposed by the open collar of his ruined shirt. "I missed you."

"I missed you so much." He couldn't get enough of touching her, smelling her, craving her taste. "Every night I slept like shit. Every day I had to force myself to not think of you, to save all of my obsessing for the quiet moments when I could finally rest."

"Me, too." She took a step back then laced her hands with his. "Come on. I have some dinner I can warm up for you. Then you'll take some pain meds, wash up, and I'll put you to bed."

He chuckled. "No, little girl, we won't. You will feed me, wash me, then you will suck me dry, and I will return favor. Then I will fuck you, gently but make you come, hard."

She stumbled a bit then looked back at him with a hungry gleam in her eyes and replied with a sassy, "Yes, Sir."

His phone rang with the tone he'd assigned to Dimitri. Jessica knew that and called out from the kitchen, "Tell Dimitri I said hi."

Closing his eyes, he took out his phone and answered the call in Russian. "Hello."

"We found them," Dimitri said in a tired voice. "They'd been shot execution style."

Regret left a bitter taste in Alex's mouth. "What the fuck were they doing that deep in Tepov territory?"

"Father," Dimitri growled out, "had some intelligence that the Tepovs were behind the stolen shipment from South Korea."

"But that makes no sense!" Alex walked deeper into his home, not wanting Jessica to worry. "The Tepovs wouldn't have the first idea of what to do with that nanotechnology. Besides, they're our allies and have proven it over and over again."

"Maybe not anymore. I spoke with Yuri Tepov, and he gave me a warning that if we insult him like this by sending spies again he will have to rethink the relationship between the *Bratvas*. He knows it is our father, and he knows we are doing everything we can to do damage control, but he cannot allow such an insult to stand."

"Shit. What about the Boldins?"

"They don't appreciate our father's efforts to test their hold on the western zone."

"And the meeting?"

"Gedeon Boldin is keeping the peace with his family—for now."

Alex let out a sigh of relief. The Boldins were the last big hurdle, besides Alex's father, to bringing Jessica safely into his world. Gedeon had been eager to put an end to the stupid, fucking curse that had tormented their parents' generation, and both Alex and Gedeon had vowed to never target the women and children of the other *Bratva*. They weren't outright allies, and their dealings had been done in secret, but Alex respected Gedeon and knew the other man loved his wife and twin daughters more than anything in the world. He was as eager to make a deal as Alex was, if not more.

Focusing back on the present, Alex wandered through the old library of the manor, taking in the new odds and ends decorating the room that Jessica had placed in his absence. "Excellent. How are you holding up?"

Dimitri gave a dry laugh. "I am realizing many things in my life are not as I thought. We are still looking for who tried to take you out. Our bomb experts are analyzing the car so we should have an answer soon. You are one lucky bastard. That blast should have incinerated you."

"I am." The need to see Jessica, to breathe in her scent, to bask in the light of her smile filled him. "Is there anything else?"

"Petty things, but I will take care of them along with our lieutenants. Go. Enjoy your woman. I will see you in two days in that godforsaken, frozen hellhole."

Alex couldn't help but laugh. "You will love it. Thank you, brother, I owe you."

"You'll do the same for me when I find a woman like Jessica." It saddened Alex to hear his normally jovial younger brother sounding so...adult. "May it happen to me sooner than later. I envy what you have."

"Someday, my brother, you will fall in love with a good woman, and I will rejoice when it happens."

After talking for a few more minutes, he hung up the phone and made his way through the quiet manor to the kitchen. His accident had happened six days ago, and the worst of the pain from his bruised ribs had eased, but he was still not feeling his best when he entered the warm space, his gaze adjusting to the brighter lighting reflecting off the white marble counters and dark wood cabinets. All his aches and pains were swept away by the sight of Jessica moving swiftly through their specially installed, American style kitchen, grabbing the leaf green plates she'd chosen and heaping what looked like one of her casseroles onto the two plates. The smell of that food was something he'd come to associate with Jessica cooking in the kitchen, and he understood now what the American term 'comfort food' meant.

She smiled when she noticed him standing there, and he noticed her eyes were red from crying, and her cheeks were blotchy. Instead of saying something about it, he decided to give them both a break and keep things light. He was happy to be home, and he was going to leave his troubles at the front door for as long as he could. His time with Jessica had become his reason for living, and he planned on enjoying it.

"Meal you made looks good. What is?"

"My mom's Tater Tot surprise."

He raised a brow, having no idea what a Tater Tot was, and took the glasses of milk she'd poured for them, making his way to the rough wood table that sat in front of the windows looking out over the back gardens. Brightly colored pots decorated the cedar deck, illuminated by some artfully arranged and hidden lights. Beyond the edges of his manicured back lawn lay the darkness of the forest, and he wondered who was patrolling out there tonight. Jessica took care of the plants on the deck, but she left the rest of the half-acre garden to their staff.

He'd tried to give her a full-time chef and housekeeper, but she'd balked at the idea, eventually compromising to have a chef cook for them on the weekends and a maid service come in three times a week to clean the public areas of their nine thousand square foot home. It was a little big with just the two of them living in the main house, but they had plenty of company. Between the bodyguards, visiting friends, family, and business associates, there were always a number of people about. Jessica liked it that way, so he was more than happy to keep her surrounded by the people she enjoyed spending time with.

Oleg was at his home a little ways down the road with his family, close enough that it was only a ten-minute walk. When Alex decided to settle down in Ireland, Oleg had agreed to come along as long as he could bring his wife and daughters. Since Oleg's wife got along well with Jessica and their charming girls adored his fiancé, he was more than happy to agree. Alex had come home to the sound of feminine giggles filling the house more than once when Jessica played with the girls, doing things like braiding hair and painting nails.

She would make a good mother.

It made him want to see her swollen with his child in the worst way.

Jessica cleared her throat. "So what's the Northern Lights party?"

He took a bite of the cheesy potato and ham mixture then washed it down with milk before answering. "Is surprise, but you will like. Will need

379

new wardrobe."

"Alex, I don't need any more clothes! I already have more than I can wear in a lifetime."

He waved her complaint away. "You do not have gear warm enough for going as far north as we will be."

This intrigued her, and he couldn't help but smile as the excitement sparkling in her eyes grew brighter. "Where are we going?"

"Is near North Pole, best place for viewing the Aurora Borealis. You will have fun. Is big party, many of my friends will be there."

Suddenly, she stilled. "Will there be more of your ex-girlfriends there, trying to trample me to get to you?"

He winced, remembering the scene in Paris when one of his ex-mistresses had made a public play for him with Jessica standing right there at a gallery opening they'd attended. The woman had latched onto his arm, her hands rubbing his bicep. At the moment, he hadn't really been paying attention, too busy listening to Nico talk about an experimental vaccine he was working on, and if he was honest, he was used to having women paw at him. It was only when Jessica hissed for the other woman to get her damn hands off Alex before she cut them off that he paid attention to the woman clinging to him.

It had amused him to realize his sweet, gentle, delicate little Jessica had been ready to fight the other woman out of jealousy. That amusement had fled when he realized her feelings had been hurt, and that night they had a long discussion about their boundaries and what they both considered unacceptable. While the conversation hadn't been an easy one, it had been necessary. He understood now that while Jessica enjoyed selecting certain women to play with them, it was always a woman who loved her man and wasn't someone Jessica would consider a threat. The same rules applied for him. He didn't want any man who would try to steal her from him to touch her, and they'd ended that night making passionate love, the act itself so intense it had branded his soul forever.

While he continued to eat, she talked about work being done on their home, how she was volunteering at the local library, and which of her friends was coming to visit next.

"Tell Maks," she said in an irritated tone, "to stop fucking my friends. Debbie and Margo are about ready to come to blows over him, and I'm tired of their pleading phone calls that I talk to him to see if he likes them."

Laughing, Alex sat back and shook his head. "They are adults, and I am sure you let them know what a 'manwhore' you think he is."

That made her flush, and he knew it was because she'd been busted by Alex giving her friend a lecture about staying away from Maks. He could hardly blame the other man. Jessica's friends were attractive, sweet, and bubbly like her. They were the kind of women who filled a house with joy, and his men had been drawn to their light. He didn't want to discuss his men's sex lives, so he merely nodded along while she went off on one of her adorable tangents.

When she finally wound down, she looked at him then smoothed her hair back and sighed. "So as you can see, there is no way I can have both Margo and Debbie come over for Christmas. They'd end up in a cat fight over who got to warm Maks' bed."

He shrugged. "So they both share his bed. Is no big deal."

Her gaze locked on his. "My friends are not having a threesome with Maks! They aren't like that."

Yawning, he stood and tried not to flinch at the pain. "You never know, *prinsessa moya*. Maybe you tell them about the...filthy things you have done and discover they have done same."

The spark of lust flared in her gaze, and her nipples hardened beneath her top. Jessica loved being a filthy, dirty little girl. Loved it even more when he called her one, and he had to admit, he loved the fact she was so kinky once she overcame her natural shyness. Their sex life would never be boring because they trusted each other, because she knew when he was calling her his dirty girl he wasn't insulting her, but instead, complimenting her.

Her gaze went down his body, stopping at the bruising still visible on his ribs. "It must have been a bad accident."

"It was."

"I wish I was there to take care of you."

Touched by her generous spirit, he held his hand out to her. "Come, is time for sleep."

She slipped her hand into his, her trust in him filling him with warmth. "I'm so glad you're home. Our bed feels empty without you."

He switched off lights as they made their way to the stairs leading to their massive suite on the second level. "My heart feels empty when you are not near."

She turned her head as they took the stairs together, lifting his hand to her lips and kissing it. "Mine, too. Thanks for bringing the rest of my heart home. I love you."

"I love you, too, *prinsessa moya*."

Chapter Twenty-Four

J essica stared at the gigantic master bedroom made entirely of ice.

It was *insane*.

The walls and furniture were all made of carved blocks of ice that were illuminated by LED lights frozen into them, and it made the man-size slabs of cut ice glow like they had shifting fairy lights within the walls. The bed was a monstrous creation, large enough to sleep five adults, with silk sheets, a goose down comforter, and a gigantic fur blanket. According to the concierge who had shown them into their room, there was some kind insulation between the ice frame of the bed and the sheets that kept it the sleeping portion warm and dry. The whole thing was super lush, and she wondered what they did to keep the mattress from getting cold or the ice below them from melting. As she pondered this, Alex came up behind her, the fur of his jacket rubbing against her neck before he placed a kiss on her cheek.

"You like?"

She turned in his arms and glanced out the gorgeous windows. The snow had been carved into these lovely floral patterns that gave the illusion of looking through an ice garden to see the Northern Lights flashing overhead. Out there, somewhere in the cold of the North Pole, Krom and his men patrolled the area, no doubt freezing their balls off. She'd have to try and get Catrin to give Krom a blowjob as an apology. That thought made her giggle. She sighed in delight, resting her head against Alex's soft mink jacket, which had belonged to his grandfather. Evidently being big and broad was in his genetics because the coat fit perfectly on his frame.

She'd never considered a man in fur sexy before, she didn't like animals suffering, but the coats she and Alex wore were old, but in pristine condition. While he went with dark mink, she wore his mother's silver fox jacket.

To her surprise, and Alex's, a large box filled with his mother's fur coats had arrived yesterday from his father. She'd been a bit freaked out, especially when she saw it made Alex agitated, but he'd forced himself to smile at her and mutter something about his father knowing they were going on vacation. At first she'd been scared to even approach the box, but as she dug through the coats, she pulled out one and rubbed her face against the rabbit fur jacket. When she'd slipped her hand into the pocket, she'd found a small letter. It was a handwritten note from Alex's father, talking about one of the times his wife had worn this jacket, briefly describing the evening and how special she was to him without saying it directly.

Maks watched her curiously while she went through each coat, reading the notes one by one before putting them back in the jacket. She'd debated if she should mention these love letters —for lack of a better term—to Alex, but wasn't sure if he'd be happy or pissed. When she finally showed them to Alex, he was as baffled as she was. Later, he'd cuddled with her in bed, and draped across his body, she read the letters to him while he closed his eyes and mourned. It had been an intense, intimate moment with him that had drawn them together, closer than ever, and she couldn't help but squeeze Alex tight.

"This place is magical," she said with a sigh. "Very romantic."

The perfect place to tell him your news, her mind whispered, but she tried to ignore it.

He laughed softly as he smoothed down her hair. The air inside the hotel was chilly, but also strangely warm from the igloo effect. She wondered how much her butt was going to freeze when she used the bathroom and hoped they didn't expect her to sit on an ice toilet to do her business. Just the thought had her butt tightening beneath Alex's fingertips.

"What was that thought, *devushka milaya*?"

"I was wondering if the bathroom was going to be made out of ice as well. I don't want to get frostbite on my nether bits...or shower in an ice bath."

His deep chuckle ghosted over her skin, more felt than heard. "You have no idea how much I have missed you, Jessica."

She looked up into his silvery gaze, the odd lighting of the room giving his face an ethereal cast. There were dark shadows beneath his deep-set eyes, and his full lips looked so kissable. She wanted to taste him, to wrap herself around him and feel the proof that he'd returned to her, alive and somewhat well. He was still bruised, but not as stiff as he had been two days ago. She'd babied him, making him rest and sleep, cuddling in bed with him as he slept with his head on her lap and she read on her eReader. The memory of sifting her fingers through his hair had her rubbing a strand now.

There was something she needed to tell Alex, something important, but she chickened out.

"Your hair, it's a lot longer than when we met."

"You seem to like my hair longer, so I have been not getting it cut as much. Gives you something to grab onto while I fuck you."

She shivered, and he licked his lips. "Yes, yes, it does."

He closed his eyes, took a step back, and rubbed his knuckles over her cheeks. "Come, we have something we must do."

"Oh-uh...I thought we could stay here a bit and

talk."

An odd, frustrated look turned his lips down. His hair wasn't the only thing that was longer. His goatee had lengthened as well, and the look was strikingly good on him. She knew every line on his face, every scar on his body, and most of the ones on his soul as well. He was anxious about something, but also excited. At first, she thought he was looking forward to showing her how amazing the hotel was, but that wasn't it. There seemed to be more.

Putting aside her own worries for the moment, she cocked her head. "Alex, what's wrong?"

"Nothing, if we hurry."

"What?"

He grabbed her hand and dragged her behind him, out of the suite, and into the large hallway of the hotel wing housing the suites. Maks stood guard next to the door, his normally bland expression gone, replaced instead by a broad smile. She stared at him, but Alex was hauling her away before she could ask what the hell was going on. They went down three rooms, and Alex knocked on the one with a big cut-out heart above it, letting the sound of feminine voices and laughter spill out into the hall. As soon as they heard the knock, women began to scream with excitement, and Jessica wondered what the hell was going on.

Her answer came in the form of Kisha, her best friend from back home, grabbing her in a huge hug. "*Chica*! It's been so long. I've missed you."

As usual, when Kisha got excited, her Puerto Rican accent came out full force. They were polar opposites looks wise, Jessica was tall, fair, and beanpole skinny while Kisha was short, dark, and had the kind of curves that had been like a siren song to men since she hit puberty. Jessica was nearly speechless. Hugging her soft friend, Jessica said in a slightly stunned voice, "What are you doing here?"

Alex gently spun Jessica away from Kisha and smiled down at her. "I love you."

"I...uh...love you too."

"Good, because we're getting married today."

"What?"

To her shock, her aunts and female cousins dragged her into the suite, surrounding her with laughter and hugs as she spotted more of her friends from home along with her new friends from Alex's circle. Happiness filled her until she was sniffing back tears, getting so many hugs at once, so much love. She'd never felt anything like it. Everyone finally settled down, and Catrin clapped her hands loudly.

"Okay, we agreed before Jessica got here that our goal is to get her off and married in timely manner, which means I get to tell you what to do and you do it, or you get the hell out. Am I clear?"

Jessica giggled as all the women agreed, some with rather shocked expressions.

Catrin was wearing a pale gray, sheath dress with a necklace of pink diamonds and matching earrings, along with a pair of knee-high fur boots and a matching black fur jacket. She approached Jessica with a huge smile. "Ready to see your dress?"

"My dress?"

"We helped her pick it out." Kisha stood next to Jessica, and she, too, was beaming. "Girl, this thing is fabulous. It was custom made for you, and when I say Alex went all out, I mean he went *all* out."

Dazed, she accepted a glass of champagne passed to her. "Did he pick it out?"

"No." Aunt Mary smiled at Jessica. "He wants to be surprised."

Catrin turned Jessica slowly, and a few of her cousins stepped out of her line of sight, giving her an unobstructed view of the glorious lace creation displayed on a dress frame. It was white with pale blue undertones, practically glowing against the ice surrounding them. Soft music played from hidden speakers, a soothing melody with acoustic guitars and a woman's lovely soprano voice. Jessica began to walk slowly to her dress, her gaze devouring every detail. It would be tight on her breasts, but as it neared her waist, it flowed out into a skirt long enough to have a small train in the back. The top was long sleeved with a sweetheart neckline, and a white fur stole was draped over a nearby chair. To her amusement, she saw that she would be getting married in a pair of flat, white fur boots.

Little crystals had been stitched into the lace so it would almost appear like she was covered in snow, glittering with each subtle change of the lights. It was the most exquisite dress she'd ever seen, and Alex had done this for her. She reached out and gently ran her fingers over the thin blue silk ribbon that ran along the waist of the dress, scarcely believing this was real.

While she was still caught up in the beautiful gown, the women began to efficiently strip away her layers of clothing. She shivered when she was bare then flushed as everyone watched her put on her thigh high stockings along with a white lacy garter and bra ensemble. Surrounded by helpful hands, she slid into her gown, realizing after she had it was stretchy and warm with its long sleeves, even with the lower portion of the back cut out displaying a good amount of skin. While her hair was fussed with by a pair of hairdressers who seemed to appear out of thin air and a makeup artist did her face up, the other women laughed and joked with each other, everyone clearly in high spirits.

Her Aunt Mary studied her face, a slow smile curving her lips. She wore an elegant cashmere dress with black fur boots and a short black fur cape that flowed over her shoulders. Diamonds sparkled in her ears and on her fingers while she talked with Kisha about which set of jewelry to wear. Jessica was talking with one of her cousins when Catrin, appearing decidedly pale, came back holding a laptop. She examined Jessica then announced, "Everyone out."

Immediately, women began to protest, but Catrin swallowed and spoke in a firm voice. "I mean it, out. Jessica has to be out there soon, and I want to give her time to relax and for everyone here to get in their places. Now go."

Once the room was emptied, Catrin whipped around to face Jessica. "Your future father-in-law wishes to speak with you."

"What?"

Clutching her laptop, Catrin nodded. "Jorg Novikov is on Skype. He said he wishes to see you on your wedding day."

"Does Alex know?"

"No. Mr. Novikov demanded I go directly to you and forbid me to tell anyone." Catrin's lower lip quivered. "I-I can tell him I couldn't find you."

Catrin would obviously rather chop off her arm than tell Alex's father no, so Jessica took a deep breath. "It's okay. I'll talk to him. Better to face him now than later."

"I will stay with you," Catrin said in a determined voice.

"Thank you."

Moving to a table with cushion-covered chairs made of ice, she set out a placemat and placed the laptop on it. Catrin arrived a moment later with Jessica's stole. "Here. I don't think he's going to say anything mean. He seemed...happy? I don't know. I've never seen the man happy, so I could be crazy."

"Catrin, would you open the chat please?"

"Oh, yes, of course."

She leaned over and opened her laptop, and after a few clicks, an older, thinner version of Alex stared back at her, complete with the famous Novikov gray eyes. Jessica had seen him before and researched him extensively, but to actually be—virtually—face to face with him was another matter. She could feel the power rolling off the mature man in the elegant black suit. He was seated in what she would assume was some kind of library by the books lining the wall behind him. From off camera came the noise of someone moving around, and Jorg watched them before returning his attention to his computer.

She knew the moment her image came through because he gasped and said something in Russian before switching over to English, "Jessica. I see now why my son has fallen for you. Your beauty is enchanting."

Flushing, really wishing there was a mirror around, she smiled in relief that he hadn't started out with calling her a gold-digging whore. "Thank you. It's very nice to meet you, Mr. Novikov."

His gaze softened, turning to the familiar, affectionate light gray that she recognized from Alex's eyes.

"Americans. Interesting people, but your roots are Irish. My second wife, Dimitri's mother, was part Irish and had hair lighter than yours, a beautiful flame-red to your deep garnet. Alex always loved her hair and would sit with her while she brushed it before bed, telling my children stories before they fell asleep."

The look on his face became slightly confused for a second, "She'll be cross that we missed your wedding, but we must stay here and protect you from afar. Our enemies are everywhere, but we will not let them harm you."

Alarmed by his abrupt shift in attitude and angry tone, she darted a glance at Catrin who looked equally worried. Not wanting to upset the man, but needing to talk to Alex about him, she said in a soothing tone, "We'll miss you, but please know that you'll be here in our hearts."

"Kind girl," he murmured as he studied her through the computer screen. "That is why my spies have said about you. Kind, sweet, a good woman. You are too fragile for our world, *prinsessa moya*, and I fear my son cannot protect you from our enemies. My wife wants me to bring you here, to our home, where it would be safe for you and Alex."

"She does? That's...that's very kind of her."

From the other side of the computer screen, out of Jorg's sight, Catrin had gone as white as a sheet and had her fingertips pressed to her mouth, which was not helping Jessica keep her composure.

"Alex, of course, will not hear of it." He flapped his hands like it was the most ridiculous thing he'd ever heard. "No matter, we will work together to keep you safe."

"Thank you," she whispered again, not able to form any more words than that.

This was bad, really bad. She knew Alex's father had some mental issues, but she had no idea the man was delusional. He was talking as if Alex's mother was still alive, when she'd been dead for years. There was a knock on her door, but she needed to get more information from Jorg so she ignored it.

"When will you see your wife again?"

His brow twitched. Then he gave an almost puzzled from. "I don't know. She is busy with her social calendar."

Not wanting to agitate him, she smiled. "When you speak to her next, please extend my thanks and let her know I look forward to meeting her."

"She will like that." His frown deepened. "I must go. My headache is getting worse. Goodbye, sweet Jessica. Make my son happy."

"I will. Thank you."

She closed the laptop so hard it rocked on the table. When her gaze met Catrin's, she took a deep breath and let it out slowly. "He thinks his wife is still alive."

Catrin slowly nodded. "What do we do?"

"I don't know." The knock on the door came again, and she darted a glance at it. "We wait until after the wedding. I'm not letting his father ruin this."

"Agreed," Catrin said right away, her hands clasped nervously together. "You need to think happy thoughts."

"Why?"

"Because right now you look like you're about to throw up."

She felt that way too, but stood and forced herself to take some deep, calming breaths. "Okay, I can do this. Today is about Alex and I, not his father, not any of that bullshit."

The walk into the ice chapel was a blur, as was her walk down the aisle on Uncle Peter's arm. She was still trying to come to terms with the bombshell from Alex's father, and the surprise that she still had to reveal to him, when Alex took her hand. The instant he did, all her worries fled, and for the first time, she became aware of a lovely melody played by a piano and harp.

Beautiful and ethereal, the music wrapped around her while she lifted her face to look at Alex. When she smiled it was bright enough that the light reflected back at her in Alex's gaze. He wore a tux, with a navy tie and handkerchief in his breast pocket. His citrus and sandalwood scent filled her, warming her even as the air chilled her cheeks slightly. She was vaguely aware of the audience watching them, and more people standing out in the doorway, but her attention was focused solely on Alex.

The priest did his thing, reading in both Russian and English, binding them together forever in front of their friends and family.

Soft and slightly scratchy, Alex's goatee rubbed against her skin as he kissed her long and hard in front of the cheering crowd. When he finally let her up for a breath of fresh air, she placed a hand on his chest to steady herself, laughing at his totally satisfied grin and her pink lipstick smeared over his mouth. Still laughing, she tried to clean him up, only to have him kiss off the rest of her lipstick. Once they managed to tear themselves away from each other, they finally turned and walked down the aisle together, their gazes locked on each other. The minute they were outside of the chapel, they were both grabbed by their makeup team and cleaned up for photos. With her new husband at her side, she stood and thanked an endless parade of people who wished them well, never letting go of his hand tightly clutching hers.

By the time they made it into the actual reception, she'd almost forgotten about Alex's father, but she didn't forget about her surprise, especially when, during a round of toasts, someone handed her a shot glass of vodka. Panicked, she tried to figure out how to get rid of it without drinking it, but everyone was watching her. They were at a long, elevated table at the end of an enormous ice ballroom. The silver candelabras gleamed, and the scent of delicious food filled the air. Alex had done half a dozen shots by now, and she knew that he'd noticed her refusal to take one.

Then Dimitri offered a lovely toast, talking about

how happy he was to have her in his family, and held up his glass in expectation to her.

She raised her glass as well, trying not to wince when he boomed out, "To Jessica and Alex."

Everyone drank their shots, and she accidentally-on-purpose knocked hers over and drank from her water glass instead.

An older woman, wearing lots of jewels and a black fur jacket, took the microphone next and began to speak in Russian. While she was speaking, Alex leaned over and placed his hand high on her thigh, right below her hips. His gaze slowly traveled up her, and she was pretty sure he paid extra attention to her belly.

"Something you have to tell me?"

"Uh-yeah, but not here."

When his eyes met hers again, they shone with joy, and she knew he'd guessed. He raised his eyebrows, his gaze darting between her belly and face, before she slowly nodded. With shaking fingertips, he placed his hand on her lower belly. "My baby?"

Leaning closer to him, she gently held his face in her hands and finally shared the news that she'd been wanting to shout at him from the moment he returned home. "Yes, Alex, I'm pregnant."

From two seats away, a very drunk Kisha slammed down her wine glass then yelled, "Holy shit, Jessica, you're pregnant?"

In the silence that followed, Alex said in a loud voice, "*Radost moya. Moya krasivaya. Ya lyubb-lyu tebya vsem sertsem, vsey dushoyu. Ya budu vsegda lyubit tebya. Vsegda*"

Complete chaos erupted that ended with everyone giving them a standing ovation. Jessica was crying at the outpouring of love, and Alex had her clasped to him so tightly she was having trouble breathing. The clapping continued, and soon, the chiming of glasses filled the air.

"What is that?" Alex asked while he gently peppered her face with kisses.

"American tradition asking us to kiss."

"With pleasure, my wife."

Then he kissed her so well that she once again forgot where she was, and who was watching, as she kissed her husband back hard enough to make his knees weak. When they broke apart, soft music started to play from the band across the room and Alex smiled, holding out his hand. "Come with me."

She gladly slipped her hand in his, once again feeling like they were the only two people in the room. They passed tables full of friends and family, gazing into each other's eyes when they finally came to the dance floor. With a smile, she bent and gathered up her train, looping it around her wrist so she could dance without tripping on it. When he pulled them together, his erection pressed into her, and she had to stifle a giggle against his neck, being careful not to get her peachy pink lipstick on his collar.

"What is funny?" he whispered against her hair as he expertly led her around the dance floor. They often danced together at home when they were alone, and he taught her all the different moves to dances she didn't know people actually did anymore. To her surprise, she'd picked it up quickly and often sought him out for a dance when the mood struck her. She had no problem flowing in the steps of an old waltz, her amusement growing as his cock hardened further against her.

"Alex, you better get control of that thing. We're being videotaped, and I don't want our first dance to be something we can't show our children."

He laughed and held her closer. "We will just

keep dancing."

"People are going to want to eat the wedding cake."

"They can wait."

"For what? Your cock to go down?"

"No, for them to become drunk enough that they don't care. Get ready for wild night. They will go someplace away from your family, but Catrin is greedy as ever and wants to play with you. I told her that you are mine on our wedding night."

She laughed and rested her head on his shoulder. "My life is weird, but I love it."

To her surprise, he dipped her, and the crowd applauded as he followed that dip with a kiss. After pulling her back on her feet, he chuckled while she stumbled for a second, overcome by her desire. So far, for her at least, being pregnant was awesome. She was fourteen weeks and beginning to show a bump that wasn't super noticeable thanks to her long frame, but she had noticed her friends giving her belly a considering look when she was dressing.

Alex pressed his erection into her again, slowing their moves as they shifted into another style of dance, this one much more intimate. The band picked up on their mood and swung into a sexy style of American jazz, and their families joined them on the dance floor. Many of Alex's friends were already drunk, and she spotted Dimitri flirting with one of her younger aunts, a widow who was giving Dimitri cougar eyes.

"That is why I cannot stop my dick from getting hard. The thought that you are carrying my baby is very arousing. I cannot wait to see your body full and round. Your breasts are already bigger, and the bump of your belly that I thought was so cute is more than a bump."

She grinned. "That's what tipped me off. All of a

sudden it looked like I'd been blessed with a new set of boobs overnight. Then I got a pooch."

He rubbed his chest against hers in a sinuous move, stealing her breath. "I love your breasts and tiny belly. The thought of you growing round with our child arouses me unbearably. I cannot wait to get my mouth on you."

"Stop, everyone is watching us." She looked up into his eyes, her muscles relaxed as he gentled his touch, their bodies just swaying together now while she carefully studied him. "Are you really happy about the baby?"

He beamed at her then gave her a squeeze. "I am beyond happy. Is boy or girl?"

"I'm fourteen weeks pregnant, so we don't know yet, but we should be able to tell soon."

His grip on her tightened. "Healthy?"

"Very. I didn't know I was pregnant until three weeks ago, but you were…gone, and I wanted to tell you in person."

He closed his eyes and held her close, their bodies unmoving as everyone danced around them. "I am sorry, *prinsessa moya*, but I promise you that I am working hard to keep you safe. Will be worth it in the end."

"I know, Alex, I know."

She didn't admit that she was constantly stressing out about his safety, about someone doing something that hurt her baby. Already she didn't care if she lived or died, as long as the tiny life growing inside of her survived. The strength of her maternal instincts still caught her by surprise, but she'd had three weeks to become accustomed to her little passenger. The baby books said that she might begin to feel 'flutters' soon as the baby moved, and every time she felt anything in her stomach, she'd freeze and wait to see if she could tell if it was the baby or not.

That had also earned her some odd looks, but she'd ignored them.

"A baby," he whispered as he led her off the dance floor. "I'm going to be a father."

"You are."

He stopped abruptly and placed both of his hands on her shoulders, looking her straight in the eye in an unexpectedly serious way. "I swear to you, Jessica, that I will do everything I can to keep our child safe."

Wanting to ease the terrible worry in his gaze, she slid her arms around his waist. "And I'll do everything I can to keep our baby safe and comfy cozy inside of me."

Her teasing words did the trick, and once again there was more happiness than grief in his beautiful storm gray eyes. "I love you."

"I love you, too, Alex. So much."

Chapter Twenty-Five

arly the next morning, Alex could easily read the shock on Dimitri's face as they stood just inside the bedroom of the honeymoon suite and he laid out what Jessica had just told him and Catrin, via phone, had confirmed.

Shaking his head in disbelief, Dimitri stared at him. "Father actually said your mother was alive?"

"Yes," Alex replied in Russian, trying to keep his voice level and smooth. Jessica was watching them with weary eyes, having just told him of her conversation with Jorg before the wedding. He wanted to strangle Catrin for giving the laptop to Jessica, but he understood better than most that Catrin had no choice. If she defied Jorg, he would make her, and Nico, pay. That did not mean he liked that the women had hid it from him until now, and they would be having words about it later, but he understood.

Jessica was tucked safely beneath the warm blankets, cocooned by furs and looking tired. He'd kept her up most of the night, unable to keep his hands off of her as he took her again and again, celebrating their wedding and her pregnancy.

"Son of a bitch," Dimitri whispered in a rough voice. "I haven't been able to see father alone for many days now. Every time I try to make an appointment, he breaks it, and when I show up, he is surrounded by his cronies and nurses. I knew something was going on, but never suspected this."

"Something is wrong. I am coming to Moscow with you."

"No, no. I can handle this with Oleg's help. Enjoy your wife. If I need you, I will call you."

"Dimitri, I will not leave you to handle this alone." Alex tugged on a thick forest green and black sweater then ran his hands through his hair. "We have a doctor's appointment in three days to see baby. I will come out after it is done."

Dimitri rubbed his face, his eyes bloodshot and the reek of vodka coming off of him. With a groan, he stumbled to Alex's bed and collapsed with his head in Jessica's lap. "Your aunt Michelle is animal in bed. I think she broke my dick."

She gave a disgusted look that dissolved into laughter. "That is so nasty. Get off me, you pervert. She's like almost twenty years older than you!"

He chuckled then snaked his arm around her neck, drawing Jessica into a quick kiss. She jerked back and wiped her mouth with disgust. "Nasty!"

"Do not worry. I washed before coming here and brushed teeth. Even gargled."

Jessica looked ready to do violence to Dimitri. Alex hauled his brother up and snapped in Russian, "What are you doing?"

"I am distracting her. She is with child, should not be worried like this. Is not good for baby."

Forcing himself to relax, and ignore Jessica still going off on a tangent about how disgusting Dimitri was for fucking her aunt, Alex nodded then looked Dimitri directly in the eyes and spoke in Russian. "Something must be done about our father, now."

"I'm not a fool," Dimitri ground out. "I know something must be done, and I've been trying, but he's our father, and I cannot take him out."

"I'm not talking about killing him. I want to get him committed, his medicine adjusted. And I want him to see new doctors."

"I've already tried that. He refused."

"Refusing is no longer an option. Dimitri. He has access to weapons of mass destruction, biological weapons that could destroy Moscow—hell, the whole world if he orders their release. It must be dealt with, now." He glanced over at Jessica, hating the tension now radiating from her. Soon, he promised himself, soon he would be able to give her the life and the safety she and their child deserved.

Five weeks later

Alex held his phone tight to his ear, eager to hear Jessica's news as he froze his balls off on the outskirts of Moscow. He was getting rid of a body at a veterinarian's crematorium owned by the Novikov *Bratva*. He could have been inside, waiting with Maks as the grim job was done, but he welcomed the bite of the cold. His soul felt so dark right now, a month without Jessica's light to cleanse him. He missed her more than his next breath, but his world was falling down around him in Moscow, and he had to stop it before the violence spilled over onto her.

"Alex," Jessica said again, her excitement pulling a smile from him. "You there?"

"I'm here, *lyubov moya*. How did appointment go?"

"Great! We're going to have a big baby. Everything looks good."

"Jessica..."

"What?" Her giggle made his chest tight. "Oh, fine. I suppose you'd like to know what we're having."

"That would be nice."

"I should make you wait until you come home, but I'm not that mean. We're having a girl."

His knees gave out as his heart thumped hard enough to roar in his ears. "A girl?"

She picked up on his distress instantly. "Yes, a girl. Did you not want a girl?" Her tone was cautious, uncertain.

Of course he wanted a girl, but after the shit he'd seen this week, the things he'd had to do to keep a *Bratva*-wide territory war from breaking out, his paranoia was at an all-time high. He could not help but fear the Novikov Curse that had taken so many women from them. Having a son would be safer, but he could not be disappointed by the idea of his daughter growing in Jessica's belly. The biting wind numbed his face as he turned to the building he'd just left.

"Do not tell anyone until I come home. Is important."

"Don't tell anyone? What the hell are you talking about? Look, this is not the reaction I was hoping for."

Tears filled her voice, and he internally cursed himself. "No, no. Is not what I mean. I love that we are having baby girl. I pray she has your hair, has your everything. I just do not want to share with world yet, to have something to keep for ourselves. A secret only we know."

He held his breath, hoping his blatant and clumsy attempt at manipulating her worked. "That's so adorable. Of course I'll keep it our secret. I haven't told anyone else. I wanted you to be the first to know. It will be our special secret."

"Thank you." The door to the crematorium banged open, and Maks came out, his left eye starting to swell shut from where one of the now dead men had kicked him in the face. "I have to go. I love you."

"I love you, too. Oh, wait, Alex, what do you think of the name Tatiana?"

Even the hostile wind could not steal the warmth in his heart at that moment. "My mother's name."

"Yes. I was thinking Tatiana Kathleen."

"Is perfect."

Maks jerked his head in the direction of the car.

Their work for the night wasn't finished yet, unfortunately. They had to meet Dimitri and discuss what they'd learned from the two men who'd attacked them tonight. Someone had indeed tampered with Jorg's meds. It was evident in the blood tests they'd done as well as Nico's examination of the pills the *Pakhan* had been taking for at least three months. Placebos, all of them. Well-done fakes. The two nurses who had attended Jorg had fled, along with a doctor and pharmacist. Without them to question, they had no idea who had penetrated the ring of protection around Jorg, or how.

They walked back to the black Bentley together, each man scanning their surroundings uneasily. This far out of the city, the only light came from the building behind them, and the parking lot of the clinic, hidden behind an acre of forest from the road, was empty except for their car and the man's who'd run the crematorium for them.

"How is your wife," Maks asked in a voice rough from lack of sleep.

"She is well."

He sucked in a quick breath then let it out again, clearing his head as best he could.

His phone rang, and he glanced down at it, seeing Luka's name. "Hello?"

"Alex," Luka sounded out of breath as he said in a rush, "Nicolai Gilyov was behind the warehouse fires and the guys that were beating up our prostitutes. That fucker has been playing us. Can't talk, not safe."

And with that he hung up.

A stunned Alex relayed the information to Maks, who looked at him with wide eyes. Bits and pieces of information began to come together in a rush, and Alex saw his dawning realizations reflected in Maks' green eyes. If true, and he had no reason to believe it wasn't, the Novikov *Bratva*, for the first time in a decade, would be forced to go to war.

Nicolai Gilyov had signed his own death warrant.

"So someone would like for us to think the Boldins are the ones who are taking shots at our truce, but in reality, it might be Nicolai Gilyov's men. Fuck."

The Gilyov *Bratva*, up until this point, had been a pain in Alex's ass, but not a threat. At least, not on the surface. It turned out Nicolai had been a busy man behind closed doors, sabotaging the Novikov *Bratva* with information he learned through various spies within the *Bratva*. His gut clenched. Shit. Oleg's wife's sister was married to one of Nicolai's lieutenants, Matto...who was very close with his sister-in-law and visited often.

God, no.

Because of this, his first call was to Oleg. "My friend, brace yourself."

"Jessica," Oleg breathed out in a harsh voice.

"No, not Jessica. We have rats in our house, nibbling away at our stores, poisoning our food with their shit. Your house has probably been compromised, but not this phone. These traitors are conspiring to bring the Novikov and Boldin *Bratvas* to war while they sit back and reap the profits of war. One of them being Matto, your brother-in-law. Where is he? We need to talk with him."

There was dead silence before Oleg said in a rush, "He's staying with us in Ireland, visiting with my wife and girls."

Alex's heart seized in his chest, and he managed to croak out, "No."

"Yes. I'm getting off this train at the next stop and will get home as quickly as I can. An hour at most."

"Call Krom, tell him what is going on. Tell him to

isolate Matto by any means necessary. We have to question him. Do not kill the fucker, but make sure he goes nowhere." Alex's hand shook, and he tried to calm himself. "Do it, now."

Oleg didn't bother to reply, just hung up.

Next, he called Jessica and got nothing but her voicemail. This was not unusual. She forgot her phone everywhere, but he prayed she would hear it this time and pick up. When she didn't, he called Dimitri back.

Before he could speak, Dimitri said in an utterly shaken voice, "Thank God it's you. Our father has lost his mind and kidnaped the Boldin twins, killing a bunch of their guards. He has them in the winter manor. We have to get them out, right now. If we don't, the Boldin *Bratva* will burn us to the ground."

Ireland
7 hours later

Jessica was awakened from a deep sleep by a man clasping his hand over her mouth. She tried to fight and scream, but Krom whispered into her ear. "Listen fast. Alex's father has lost his mind. He has captured Alex on suspicion of treason, and your husband is being tortured for information he will never give. Jorg is demanding to talk to you on your computer. You need to be calm, rational, and you may save your husband's life and yours. Understood?"

She blinked up at him as her mind processed this information. Then she nodded her head, tears already prickling her eyes. A sense of foreboding, so huge it overwhelmed her, threatened to stun her into inaction, but she managed to shake it off.

Krom removed his hand, and she sat up quickly, grabbing her flannel robe and tugging it on before

looping the belt around her waist. Inside, she was
screaming, wailing, and, in general, having an epic
freak out. On the outside, she was calm and
composed, her mind focused only on one thing,
saving her family from a monster masquerading as a
man.

It took her less than thirty seconds to get up
from bed and go to the computer desk across her
large room, not caring that her hair was probably
sticking out all over the place from her braid or that
her face was pale with shock.

Someone was torturing Alex.

She blinked rapidly, fighting back her tears,
turning her mind from that thought which could
easily make her insane.

When the call connected, she flinched at the
sight of Alex's father, who was totally off-the-wall-
fucked-up on something. His gaze was heavily-lidded,
and he kept listing to the left. Someone must be there
with him, because they were propping him up. When
he focused on her, he smiled, and she noticed a drop
of blood on his cheek that had slowly dripped down,
leaving a dried trail behind it, and more dark
splatters on his shirt.

She wondered if it was Alex's blood, and if she
might just throw up all over the computer.

Krom placed his hand on her shoulder and gave
it a squeeze. "Here she is. Now let him go."

"Listen to me, Jessica," Jorg said in a wavering
voice. "They are putting me down now like an animal
that has gone crazed, but I must talk to you first.
Someone drugged me tonight, and some terrible
things have happened as a result. But I have also
learned that a miracle has occurred, that you carry
the future of the Novikov line in your belly."

She pressed her hands over her stomach as if she
could protect her unborn daughter from this

monster. "I-I do. Where is Alex?"

"Dimitri and Lady Death have him. He is safe."

"Lady Death?"

"Mimi Stefano, I believe you have met in Rome, but is not important." Jorg frowned then snarled something in Russian to someone off screen. "Alex told me you are having girl."

"He told you?"

"He also told me that he promised he wouldn't. Do not worry. I did not hurt him, merely a little persuasion with medications. In this case, to tell the truth. A truth he tried to hide because he knows it is your death sentence."

"What?"

Once again, his eyes cut to someone off screen, and he growled out something in a tone that indicated he was way-the-fuck pissed off.

His gaze shifted to the stoic Krom standing behind her, and he said in English, "Get her out of there. Boldin has men on the way to kidnap her, and Gilyov's man is unaccounted for."

"Wait, what?"

"Jessica," Jorg snapped, his gaze becoming more clear by the second as whatever drugs he was on were burned off by his anger. "Do you love your daughter?"

"Of course."

"Do you want her to live?"

"What!"

"If you want your daughter to live to see her first birthday, you will leave with Krom, now, and disappear."

Krom said something in a stunned voice behind her, but Jorg ignored him and focused on Jessica. "We will stage your death, set you up with a new life, and your daughter can grow up in safety without a bounty on her head."

Feeling like she'd been slapped, she slumped

back in her chair. "You're crazy."

"No," he roared. "Crazy is my world, where men are drugged and mind-washed, women are killed because of those they love, and you, gentle Jessica, would not survive it. You are dead if you stay with my son, or you could easily be the cause of his death. If you want your daughter to live, you have one option."

"But I'm safe here. My Uncle Peter—"

"Is no match for the Boldin *Bratva*," Jorg sneered. "They will kill him, and everyone he loves including the little girl from Belfast your aunt and uncle are about to adopt."

"What? The adoption went through?"

"Yes. Would be terrible if the Boldins decide to get their revenge by killing her once she finally found a loving family."

Hugging herself, she trembled. "You're serious."

"Yes, and you are out of time." He rattled off a long list of what almost sounded like instructions to Krom before telling her one last thing. "From this moment on, Jessica Venture is dead. Become whoever you want to be, but stay away from my son or your death will be on my soul."

With that, he signed off, and she was left staring at the screen. Krom gently lifted her into his arms, carrying her like an invalid. "I need your wedding ring."

"What?"

Tormented empathy filled his dark gaze. "For the scene of your death, we will need your ring."

"I...but my mother..."

He closed his eyes, then held her hand, and gently slid the gold bands off. "I swear to you, Jessica Novikov, that if there was any way out of this that would not result in you dying, I would take it. You have a way out, an opportunity that many, many wish they had, but never do."

"An opportunity?" she whispered, tears pouring down her face. "My husband is going to think I died!"

"Jorg Novikov will kill you if Alex finds out you are alive. That is guaranteed by him and witnessed by everyone in the room."

"What? He'd kill me?"

His eyes were filled with a grave, terrible seriousness. "To save his son? Yes."

"Krom, I can't leave Alex. He's my world. Please don't make me."

"Listen to me." He clasped her cold fingers in his own and lowered his voice. "If you do as Jorg wants and flee now, I promise you, I swear to you, when it is safe, I will find you and bring you back home to Alex, but only when it is safe."

A tiny flame of hope flickered in her bleeding heart. "Swear it."

He pressed her hands to his hard chest over his heart. "On my life."

There was a swift knock at the door followed by a voice she didn't recognize speaking in Russian. Krom stiffened, then set her on her feet, minus her wedding rings, which he put in his pocket. She frantically looked around the room, wanting to grab something, anything, to remember Alex by. Then Krom reached for her collar that she stored in a box next to her bed while sleeping.

"No!" she jerked it out of his hands. "Not this. I swear I will never show it to anyone, anywhere, but this is mine! You can have my ring, but not my collar."

More pounding from the door, and Krom threw up his hands. "You have two minutes to get dressed. Then we leave."

She put on her collar then frantically ripped off her nightgown, trying to keep her stomach from emptying all over the place. Those little flutters in her lower belly were going crazy, and she dimly hoped her baby wasn't being hurt by all the shocks her mother was suffering. She forced herself to put on her clean underwear, maternity jeans, and a loose white shirt with a thick black cardigan. Taking one more glance around her closet, she tried to burn everything into her memory, especially the neatly hung rows of Alex's suits. His scent filled the air, and before she could stop herself, she stole some of his cologne, shoving the slender bottle into her pocket and pulling her blowsy shirt and cardigan over it. She had no idea why she did it, just that she needed something of his.

When she returned, Krom and a man she didn't know eyed her up and down.

"Let's go," the older, slender man in the brown knit hat said and motioned to her.

"Krom?" She looked at her bodyguard, not trusting anyone but him at the moment.

"I am right behind you. Go, I will cover you. We must hurry. There is fighting at the gate."

She mimicked the movements of the man in front of her and crouched down, moving through her dimly lit house almost silently. It should have felt silly, but when a man like Krom acted tense, it was best to be alert. They moved through the house, and once again, she tried to commit every inch of it to memory as she reached out and touched objects as they passed. Instead of going out the front, they went out the back, and Krom placed his hand over her mouth when she found one of the perimeter guards unconscious, possibly dead.

"I knocked him out. He is fine," Krom said. "But no one can see you leave."

Nodding, she found herself at the bottom of the sloping, wooded side yard of the house and on one of the many footpaths that wound through the woods a short while later. Krom carried her most of the way, occasionally brushing away her tears with a soft murmur in Russian. He displayed an almost eerie ability to walk through the forest at night without stumbling once. The thin guy in the hat was a little loud, but not nearly as noisy as she was when she had to crawl over or under something. Suddenly, gunfire and men shouting came from behind them, and Jessica pressed her hands over her belly in an almost unconscious protective gesture.

Krom stopped, put her down, turned around, and pulled out two handguns. He glanced over his shoulder at her, his features nearly invisible in the darkness. "Go. I will hold off any that come this way."

"We can't leave you," she said in a low, panicky voice.

"Jessica, I promise you, once it is safe I will come for you and bring you back to Alex."

Hope blossomed in her and she clung to his arm. "Swear it!'

"I swear." More shouts came from closer than last time, and Krom snarled, "Go!"

With a muffled cry, she allowed the other man to lead her away from Krom, who quickly blended into the forest behind them. Thankfully, they didn't have much farther before they reached a luxurious black SUV hidden on a side road about five minutes from where Krom had left them. Her body ached with tension, and she flinched every time she stepped on a branch or made some noise. They were almost to the SUV when gunshots exploded, much closer than she expected. The tall man looked at her and pulled out his gun. "Time to run, lass."

She quickly clambered into the SUV, and the moment her door shut, the man started the engine and pulled out, not using any headlights, just driving what, to her, seemed blindly through a forest lit by a half-moon.

"Name's Shane O'Doyle," the man offered. "Mr. Novikov, Senior, contacted me an hour ago and made me an offer I couldn't refuse. Now, my mother Margo thinks fondly of you, but even I can't go against the will of Mr. Novikov. However, we're going to help you as much as we can. You're going in our private jet back to the United States. We'll take anywhere you want, set you up in a home of your choice, in the town of your choice, but you must be reclusive 'til after you've had your daughter."

"Why? What are you talking about?"

Her belly cramped, and she tried to slow her breathing.

Tatiana, hang in there, baby. Mommy's going to get her shit together and stop flooding your system with fear chemicals.

She actually had no idea if that was even possible, but it made sense in her head.

"You can't go out there lookin' like you, love. You're famous. Pictures of your wedding are all over the world. Someone'll spot you for sure. If you want a new life, you're gonna have ta change some things after the baby comes, at least at first."

"Seriously?"

"You don't do Internet searches for yourself or Alex?"

She sighed. "You have a point. Look, if I can't go out looking like myself, then who will I look like?"

"Just small changes, hair dye, contacts, breast implants—"

"Wait, what? I'm not getting a boob job."

He shrugged. "Well then, I guess it won't be long before someone finds you and kills you."

That thought absolutely took the fight out of her. "Do you think Krom is all right?"

"He'll be fine. He's resourceful. I'm worried about you. Tender young thing, pregnant at that, having to make a go of it alone. My sister is a single mum, and she said a nanny is the best thing you could possibly have, so we'll pay for any nanny that you might want to use as well. This life can be whatever you make of it, Jessica. In his own twisted way, Jorg Novikov has given you a great gift. He could have easily just killed you to end his son's divided loyalties. Instead, he's arranged your death, which is no easy thing, to the point where it will fool your husband."

At the mention of Alex, she burst into tears, and Shane awkwardly patted her back. "It'll be okay. Really, it will be. You'll have your little girl, and you'll be all right."

"But who will my husband have?" she whispered, and he jerked back with a guilty look. "Right. He is going to go insane. He's going to be all alone, his wife and daughter dead just like his mother, his stepmother, his sister. How much death can a man take? It will break him."

"He's strong. It won't be easy, but he'll survive. If he's any kind of man, you know he'd do anything to keep you safe, even if he is unknowingly doing it."

The car bumped onto a paved road, and she leaned her head against the window, exhausted and heartsick. "I don't want to talk anymore."

"It'll be a three hour drive, so you rest up."

Words were beyond her as she tried to face a future where her daughter would never know how much her father loved her.

Chapter Twenty-Six

Four months later

J essica moaned in pain, too exhausted to even cry, sure she was dying as her whole body tensed with the next contraction. The salt of her sweat stung her dry lips, but they wouldn't give her anything more than ice chips to suck on. Her throat was ragged from moaning, and she felt so damn alone, and scared. It hurt, more than she'd imagined by a million, and she was so tired she fell asleep between contractions. For two hours she'd been pushing, and her legs shivered uncontrollably in the stirrups.

"You can do this," Shannon, Jessica's motherly doula, said while the doctor stood between Jessica's legs, his gaze focused on her pelvic area.

People bustled about the lovely birthing suite with an ocean view, getting ready for Tatiana to make her appearance. This was the top hospital in Miami and one she'd probably have picked on her own, but she'd been forced to come here by Jorg. He'd paid in advance for every aspect of her pregnancy care, and allowed her to choose her own doctor from among those at the hospital. She'd sent him a note back begging him to reconsider taking her away from Alex. He hadn't responded, which was a response in itself.

A hard, body-clenching pain ripped through her, and she thrashed her head against the damp pillow, wanting to quit, but she couldn't. She'd given up her marriage for this baby, given up everything to keep her safe, and Jessica wasn't going to fail her child now. Her entire being was focused on the terrible pain, a pain so overwhelming that she couldn't think, couldn't do anything but operate on instinct. Sweat soaked the bed beneath her as she strained to keep from pushing, to listen to Shannon's instructions.

"Okay, sugar, let's do this."

With Shannon coaching her the entire time, Tatiana Kathleen St. Cloud made her appearance twenty minutes later into the world at eight pounds and six ounces, a big, healthy girl who cried loudly in protest at being taken so rudely from her safe cocoon.

Exhausted, Jessica watched them clean her daughter up, and her already broken heart shattered further as her tears fell unchecked. Alex should be here right now, holding her hand, telling her how beautiful their daughter was, how much he loved her. Her lower lip trembled as she bit back a sob, not wanting one of the first sounds her daughter heard to be her mother breaking down. Jessica had managed to keep herself somewhat together during the last part of her pregnancy, not wanting to risk damage to her daughter with her grief, but now, the loss of her husband, Tatiana's father, overwhelmed her. Their daughter would never get to know the man who would have lavished her with love, spoiled her with attention, and been the best father a little girl could ever want.

Shannon, dressed in a pair of scrubs with parrots all over her top, made a clucking noise then enveloped Jessica in a hug.

"Alex?" she asked in a low voice.

Unable to answer, Jessica nodded and hated the lies her life had become. Shannon, and everyone else, believed that Jessica's husband had died and left her a wealthy young widow with no family or friends. This was part of her new identity, as was her new name, Jessa St. Cloud, and her lovely new home outside of Miami. When given the choice to pick anywhere in the US to live, she'd selected Miami

416

because it was about as unlike Ireland as one could get and far away from her friends and family in the States. Warm weather, the ocean, and a vibrant culture had all seemed like the ideal location to raise her daughter. Unfortunately, her depression marred any possible enjoyment of the natural beauty and vibrancy of Miami, wrapping her in a suffocating blanket of indifference that only her daughter could pierce.

Nodding, Jessica returned the woman's hug even as she felt like the worst person in the world. "He...he would have been so happy."

"I'm sure he's here with you right now, and he's overjoyed."

Oh, the guilt was never ending, the pain so cruel she didn't know if she could survive it.

"I miss him so much."

The words came out in a harsh stutter, and she allowed herself the luxury of crying in Shannon's arms. It took her a few minutes to get herself together, but when she did, she sucked in a deep, hitching breath and let it out, trying to feel something other than heartache and pain. She missed Alex every minute of every day, and her soul was dying without him.

However bad she felt, it must be nothing compared to what he was going through, and that made it all the worse, the knowledge that her husband was suffering. She'd read all the articles she could on the Internet about her death, but there hadn't been much. Just that she'd died in a car accident and one lone picture from her funeral. She'd only seen Alex's profile as he stood in the cemetery next to Dimitri, along with her Uncle Peter and Aunt Mary. Dimitri and Peter had been holding Alex up in the photo as though they had caught him falling to his knees next to her flower-covered coffin. That one image had been enough to make her want to go to him, to somehow tell him they were okay, but Jorg had men watching her, and she knew what would happen if she was caught trying to contact Alex. Krom had promised he would find her when it was safe so she had to trust him and play by Jorg's insane rules.

If she didn't, they'd kill her and take her daughter.

"Here's your little girl," a sweet young nurse said with a bright smile, handing Jessica the warm, wiggly bundle. "She has quite a set of lungs on her."

Feeling the weight of her baby in her arms, she lost herself in the surreal fact that the little person she was touching had been in her belly less than fifteen minutes ago. The moment she saw Tatiana's squished up little face, her entire being melted, her battered and wounded heart picking up pace as she carefully pulled the blanket back, meeting her daughter's light blue eyes for the first time and instantly falling in love.

"She's so beautiful," she whispered in a raspy voice.

Shannon reached out and gently ran her fingertip over Tatiana's head before placing a small pink hat on the fussy newborn. "She has your hair."

Indeed she did, a fine patch of peach-colored down covered her baby's perfect little head. Not knowing why she did it, Jessica cradled her baby close and took a deep inhalation of her scent, and the warmth in her heart began to spread then melted away the ice. When she pulled back, she found that Tatiana had calmed and was looking at her with bright, curious eyes.

Placing dozens of soft kisses all over her daughter's face and head, Jessica whispered, "Hello, beautiful girl. I'm your mother, and I love you more than anything in this world."

A little over two years later

Jessica was on her lunch break when it happened.

As usual, her head was full of facts and figures as she mentally went over one of her accounts, not really paying attention to the world around her. It was another beautiful day in Miami, the sun was shining, delicious food smells mixed with the exhaust of cars from the nearby street, and everyone was bustling about the downtown area. Dressed in a light cream suit and black heels with a yellow bow at the back, Jessica blended in with the rest of humanity, going with the flow of the foot traffic as she made her way to her favorite Cuban restaurant to grab the lunch she'd already ordered.

When she'd first been set up with her new identity, she had no idea how extensive her new life was. Not only did she have a new name, but she also had a history that included a financial degree and an awesome credit score. At first, she felt guilty about the fake degree, but she was only three semesters away from having that kind of degree for real anyway. Her new background story was so solid she'd been able to get a job at a prominent local bank working in their fraud department. The irony that she was working in fraud detection while being a total fake wasn't lost on her, but she was managing to build a quiet, comfortable life for herself and her daughter while being able to work part-time two days a week.

As she stood waiting for a light to change, she turned her face up to the sun and let its warmth seep into her. She was feeling stronger than she had in a long time, thanks in no small part to her nanny, Gwen's, positive influence. Gwen was the daughter of her midwife, Shannon, and was amazing with Tatiana. The cute half-Dominican woman was two years younger than Jessica, but a total free spirit who managed to always look on the bright side of things.

In what felt like her past life, Jessica had viewed herself as an optimist, but since being forced to leave Alex, her view of the world had become very jaded. Now, she suspected everyone of nefarious intentions, and her ability to trust had been almost completely destroyed. Whenever she met someone new, she always wondered if they were one of Jorg's spies or if they were somehow involved in criminal dealings. Paranoia was her new normal, and she had to work hard against it to keep from becoming a complete shut-in. Had she been alone, she might have sequestered herself from the world with only her memories to keep her company, but Tatiana deserved better.

Jessica was daydreaming about taking her daughter to the Miami Zoo this weekend when someone walking behind her pushed her, hard. Before she could fall, another man was there, catching her then shoving her into the backseat of a waiting limo. Her scream was muffled by another man, this one probably in his fifties with a thick head of gray hair, clasping his hand over her mouth. She tried to kick, to claw, to scratch, but the limo was already pulling out into traffic. In less than fifteen seconds, she'd been snatched off the street.

The man removed his hand, but before she could draw in a breath, a white cloth was placed over her mouth and the acrid fumes knocked her out.

As she slowly shook off the drugs enough to wake fully, she had no idea how much time had passed, only that she was tied to a somewhat comfortable chair in an empty room with pale wood floors and deep green walls illuminated by a bare bulb overhead. A large television was set up in front of her, but other than that, the room was bare. There was a single window, but it only looked out over a nondescript, darkened expanse of what was probably the back yard. She took a deep breath and managed to keep her panic at bay. It was imperative that she keep her cool. Tatiana was counting on her so she had to think, had to find a way out.

She'd obviously been kidnapped, but not harmed other than being tied to this chair. All of her clothes were still in place, but her shoes were missing. Flexing her hands, she attempted to wiggle out of the ropes but there was absolutely no give to them. Fear made a harsh, stinging sweat break out over her body as she wondered if one of the Novikov's enemies had found her.

The door opened, and the same man who'd drugged her walked in, his expression completely closed down, his dark eyes lifeless.

"I see you are awake."

His English was good, but the Russian accent immediately sent her into a panic. "Please, please, let me go."

He frowned, and another man entered the room, this one also older with a balding head and a dark gray suit.

His smooth, uninflected voice filled the room. "Ms. Venture, or should I say Ms. St. Cloud, there is no need for hysterics. We will let you go, unharmed, after we have delivered Mr. Novikov's message. You will not be hurt. You have my word."

All the strength left her body, and she sagged back into the chair. Shit, had Jorg somehow known that she'd been considering contacting Alex? Had he sensed the chains he'd put on her to keep her from her husband were weakening? Her love for Alex hadn't faded, not in the least, and she dreamed about him every night. The longer she was away the more she questioned her decision, wondering if she'd played right into Jorg's hands. The only thing that had held her back was the knowledge that Krom, who she'd seen with Alex in some recent pictures on-line, hadn't contacted her.

She licked her dry lips. "What is his message?"

Instead of answering, he took a remote control out of his pocket.

Her breath came out in harsh pants, the sound filling the room while the TV was turned on and the video started. At first, she had trouble making sense of it. The video was shot from a distance, and the photographer kept shifting around, the jerky motions making her head hurt. When he finally settled and zoomed in, she stopped breathing all together. Oleg stood before a white, closed coffin covered in flowers with his sobbing wife on one arm and his youngest daughter on the other. They looked to be in a funeral home of some kind, and massive amounts of elaborate floral arrangements surrounded the casket. The camera panned to the left, and she saw a huge picture of Oleg's sixteen-year-old daughter, also draped in flowers and wreathed in black silk.

"Oh my God," Jessica whispered, her nose burning as tears fell. "Kia's dead?"

She remembered hanging out with Oleg's two giggling, light-hearted daughters and their equally happy mother in Ireland. Kia had been the quieter of the two girls, more apt to have her nose buried in a book than her active sister. The bittersweet memory of the young girl shyly asking Jessica if she could feel the baby move ripped through her, and she looked away from the screen, unable to handle witnessing the grief twisting Oleg's face as he led his hysterical wife and wailing daughter away from the coffin.

"I don't understand. What happened?"

The American glanced at her then back at the screen. "Two weeks ago, Kia was killed in a drive-by shooting that was meant for Oleg."

"That's terrible," she gasped.

"It is. Mr. Novikov wanted you to see this to remind you how important it is for you to stay away from Alexandr, and not just for your own sake."

"I have been!" she shouted, trying not to see the screen playing out the funeral from the corner of her eye as she held the American man's gaze.

"If you do not," he continued like she'd never spoken, "if Mr. Novikov feels that you are trying to contact Alexandr in any way, Tatiana will be taken from you and given to someone who can keep her safe, and you will never see her again."

"No." Her words came out in a whisper, the fear she felt now eclipsing everything. "No, please, please, no. I haven't contacted him. I'll never contact him. I promise, I swear. Please don't take my daughter."

He held up his hand, cutting off her begging, his face an impassive mask as if he was doing a particularly boring chore, not threatening her child. "Then you have nothing to worry about."

With that he turned and left, ignoring her sobs as she cursed Jorg Novikov bitterly, hating him more than she'd ever hated anyone as Kia's funeral played in the background.

Chapter Twenty-Seven

Siberia

D imitri squinted his eyes against the glare of the bleak winter landscape, looking for his brother, out there somewhere, training his men.

With the wind stirring up the snow and slapping it against his face in little stinging pellets, Dimitri braved the elements to stalk his way across the open field. Since a few months after Jessica's death, Alex had sequestered himself at the Novikov's Siberian training outpost, isolating himself from a world he could no longer endure. The loss of his wife and unborn daughter had almost entirely killed his heart, and their father ground out whatever life that might've remained with his heel.

Rage flashed through Dimitri, warming him as he slogged through the calf-high snow. The sight of Alex, beaten bloody, replayed on a loop Dimitri couldn't stop. Their father's men, on his delusional orders, had tried to torture the whereabouts of the Boldin twins from his brother. Alex didn't know. He'd only rescued them and delivered the girls to his uncle Petrov. Alex wasn't part of the planning for the next step, so he couldn't confess anything.

Luckily, Mimi Stefano, known in some circles as Lady Death, had been staying with Jorg at the time and had managed to track Alex down and free him before killing his torturers and contacting Dimitri.

He had gotten his brother to a private clinic where he was eventually stabilized enough to know the truth about what had happened while he was unconscious. Dimitri was at the clinic with him when

Alex found out the terrible news that Jessica, along with their unborn child, had died in a car bombing in Ireland. It had been one of the worst moments of his life, and Dimitri still winced at the memory of Alex's inhuman roars of grief.

Just the recollection of Oleg's voice breaking as he relayed the news had caused Dimitri's throat to burn while he'd looked at his brother sleeping in his hospital bed, knowing that when Alex found out his reason for living was gone he was going to lose his mind.

Dimitri had not been wrong.

After burying his family and spending a great deal of time and effort trying to track down those responsible for their deaths, Alex had left for Siberia a broken man. He didn't answer anyone's calls, including their father's. On some level, Dimitri understood that their father had been acting under the influence of someone messing with his medications, but he couldn't help but hate the old man for his role in Jessica's death.

He wished he could let his brother mourn up here forever, but Dimitri needed him desperately. The Novikov *Bratva* had gained a lot of new territory when they took over what the Gilyov *Bratva* used to own. Alex had embarked on a path of vengeance, and his men had followed, eager to avenge Jessica's death on anyone who might be involved in any way. The men took her loss hard, especially Oleg, Maks, and Krom. Krom had been shot in the head during the Boldin's attempt on Alex's old home in Ireland, but the injury had only affected his memory a bit and hadn't done permanent damage to his body. Emotionally, Krom had been devastated that Jessica had died during his watch, and Dimitri knew it tore his friend apart that he couldn't remember what happened.

As if summoned by the thought, Krom stepped from behind a tree, quiet as a ghost but obviously letting Dimitri see him. "Welcome to hell."

With a grimace, Dimitri nodded. "Don't worry. I came to drag him back to the land of the living. I need him."

"You've tried it before."

"I know, but this is different."

"He won't leave willingly."

"He will when he hears what I have to say."

Krom shrugged then motioned to a trail leading through the thick forest to the left. "He's down there, making his men suffer."

Following the trail, Dimitri came to a small clearing, drawn by the retches of someone throwing up.

When he walked up next to Alex, he made a disgusted sound as he stepped around a steaming mound of puke. The men before him were doing pushups in the snow, their grunts of pain loud in the silence of the forest. Having done pushups many times during his own training, Dimitri grimaced at the memory of the agony of his hands being frozen by the cold. This was a punishment, and he wondered what they'd done to piss Alex off. These days it could be anything. His brother was easy to anger.

"What do you want?" Alex's voice was low, cold, and dead.

Dimitri studied his brother's profile, taking in the new scars on his face he'd gained during his torture. The one on his upper lip was the largest visible one, but Dimitri would never forget the crinkly, tough skin of the scar shaped like a clothing iron on his brother's lower ribs. He forced his gaze back to Alex's face, knowing he hated it when Dimitri felt guilty about what had happened to him.

If only he'd managed to find Alex sooner, he

427

could have spared him the pain.

"Did you come here to moon over me or say something?"

"I need you to come back."

"No."

"I need you."

"You are doing fine on your own."

Months of frustration from trying to do his and Alex's job filled his voice. "No, I am not."

For the first time in what seemed like forever Alex really looked at Dimitri, his tired eyes distant and unfocused. "Maks can help."

"No, he can't." Running his hands through his hair, Dimitri jerked his head in the direction of the men still doing pushups. "Get rid of them."

Displaying no emotion, Alex curtly dismissed them, and the men ran off like their backs were on fire.

Beginning to pace, Dimitri glared at Alex. "Yesterday, a nuclear warhead almost made it off the black market through a broker associated with us. A fucking *nuclear bomb* was almost on the way to the Middle East to who-the-fuck knows, and we would have been responsible for it. It was only because of one of our men's quick thinking that we avoided a catastrophe. It's too much. I can't do it alone. Please, Alex, I need you."

"I can't." Alex stared down at the snow, not moving. "I don't know how to live without her. Do you know why I stay out here? There is nothing to distract me from thinking about her, from remembering our time together. If I think hard enough, it is almost like her touch is real, and for a brief moment, I no longer feel dead inside. Yet no matter how much I think about her, no matter how hard I try, I know I'm slowly forgetting things. I can't remember if she was left- or right-handed, what she wore on our second night in Rome, and a thousand other things. I can't forget anymore, can't let any more of her memories go."

His heart breaking for his brother, Dimitri blew out a hot breath that instantly turned to vapor. "But Alex, you aren't dead. You're alive."

Slowly shaking his head, Alex gave Dimitri a look filled with such grief that he wondered if he was going to lose his brother to his mourning like he'd lost his father. "Many times I wish I wasn't."

"Do not say that. Ever."

With a sigh, Alex stared out into the woods. "Do not worry. I will not be ending my life. I have tried, many times, but I cannot do it."

Fear made Dimitri step forward and grab his brother by the shoulders and shake him—hard. "Have you lost your mind? Do you really think Jessica would want you to do that?"

His face was expressionless as he held Dimitri's gaze. "No, I don't. I think, if she is watching me from heaven, it would hurt her."

"Alex, please, don't leave me alone." He pulled his brother into a hard hug. "You are the only family I have left."

His brother let him hug him for a moment, but he stiffened before he broke away. "I will not desert you."

"Swear it."

"Do not be so worried." He stroked the hilt of the hunting knife strapped to his upper thigh with his gloved fingertips. "I decided that God has me here for a reason, and if I do whatever his task is for me, I will get to go to heaven as my reward. See my wife and child again."

"Alex, you can't go on like this. You sound like a mad man."

Instead of being offended, or laughing, Alex

returned his unseeing gaze to the forest, "I'm not sure how to live anymore. How to want to be anywhere but lost in my memories."

He closed the distance between them and stood by his brother's side. "I will help. You have friends that love you, people that want nothing more than to help you deal with your loss."

"I do not want to forget anything about her. I want to remember her forever."

"And you will. Your location won't change that." He switched tactics, worried his balls might freeze off soon. "Your people need you. You cannot abandon them like this."

They stood out there long enough that Dimitri was sure he was going to get frostbite despite his cold weather gear. The sky began to darken, and Alex finally let out a shuddering sigh. "I will come back. I will help protect our people, but I never want to see our father again."

Relief swept over Dimitri, so profound it almost brought him to his knees. He'd tried dozens of times to get his brother to return to Moscow, only to be turned away over and over again. "You don't have to. He knows what happened to you, knows he witnessed and ordered it. Even if he can't remember it clearly, he feels guilt. He will not force his presence on you."

Alex turned to the direction of the massive house with its barracks and began to walk. Snow crunched beneath their boots, and the wind had calmed down, pushing now at their backs as they walked the trail. Dimitri moved next to his brother, where he belonged, vowing to try and bring Alex back to life.

.

Epilogue

Nearly Two Years Later

Jessica tried to smile through her tears as she read the perfectly timed letter from a headhunter interested in hiring her for some overseas contract work. Goosebumps broke out over her skin at how perfectly everything was working out, and she wondered if her luck might finally change. She managed to stifle a sob while her live-in nanny and best friend, Gwen, went to check on Tatiana before coming back to Jessica's in home office. She partially shut the door behind her then headed over to Jessica's desk, her midnight black hair hanging in a long braid down her back with a red ribbon woven through it.

The woman was a godsend, and more friend than employee, so she didn't take offense when Gwen said in her sweet, smooth voice, "What the hell is going on with you? First, you're late and you don't call. Then when you do come home you look like a zombie. You're scaring me. What's wrong?"

"What's wrong? Where do I begin?" A watery laugh burst out of Jessica, and she wiped at her cheeks, knowing her makeup was long gone after her frequent crying bouts during her humiliating afternoon. "I've been fired, and it sucked so bad."

"Oh, oh no! Sweetheart, that's terrible."

Gwen gathered her close in a hug, her curvy body soft and comforting. Even though the cute Latina was around Jessica's age, she had this mothering instinct that was bone-deep, and she tried to take care of everyone. Unable to have any children of her own, Gwen treated Tatiana like the most special thing in

431

the world, and Jessica's daughter adored the woman. Giving her back a brisk pat, Gwen began to swear up a storm that eventually made Jessica laugh. Then she dried her face off on the sleeve of her discarded suit coat.

"Fuck them," Gwen declared. "Fortunately for you, *chica*, you have a big fat trust fund to fall back on. I know, I know, you don't like to touch it, want it all for Tatiana, but it's worth dipping into the money your husband left you rather than work for such faithless bastards. I cannot believe they thought you were stealing from them! Like you need it!"

The usual guilt nagged at Jessica as she heard Gwen repeat the lies she'd told her about her past. Gwen had no idea where the small fortune in Tatiana's trust fund and Jessica's bank accounts came from, that it wasn't her daughter's inheritance from her fictional dead father but blood money from the child's grandfather. Gwen knew the state of Jessica's finances because she paid the bills and kept the house bank account, often teasing Jessica about living like a miserly old woman when she had over six million dollars in liquid assets. While Jessica had used Jorg's money to buy her small, lush beachfront home outside of Miami and had invested some of it as well, she tried to use it as little as possible, and then only for things that Tatiana needed.

Waving her hands in front of Jessica's face, her silver bangles clattering, Gwen yelled, "Hello? Earth to Jessica?"

When Jessica had run all those years ago, she'd taken the advice of the man handling the forging of her documents and stuck with her first name since it was so common, but picked a new last one. So now she was Jessica St. Cloud, single mother and unemployed forensic accountant. Well, maybe not unemployed for long.

"Yeah, they fired me. Well, let me put it this way, they said I could quit and they won't press charges."

"Jeeze, what did they say you did?"

"Embezzled a bunch of Colombian drug money! But I totally did not. Someone pulled one on them, and they set me up to take the blame. I was the scapegoat, paraded through the office with my box of things and security following me as I did the walk of shame out of the building. It was horrible. Everyone was whispering, and those bitches in marketing were so damn smug looking I wanted to drop my box and kick their butts just so I had the satisfaction of being fired for something I'd actually done! I'm innocent."

"Well duh. You're the most honest woman I know."

Once again, there was the internal wince of shame at how little Gwen actually knew about the real Jessica. Forcing herself to bury that feeling, something she had a lot of practice doing, she took a deep breath, her anger deflating as reality set in. "I quit, gave them some humiliating and tearful rant, then packed up my shit, and left."

"Wow, that is a shitty day."

Giggling, somewhat hysterically, Jessica nodded. "It was...really, really shitty."

She would have suspected Jorg was somehow behind her being fired, but that didn't make any sense. He hadn't bothered her since he'd had her kidnapped and had his goons show her Kia's funeral, a day that still caused her nightmares. She'd wake in the middle of the night, convinced Jorg had finally come to take Tatiana from her, dripping in sweat. Those dreams always made her run to her daughter's room just to see her little sleeping form in her princess-like canopy bed, to touch her soft red hair, to kiss her little freckled nose and breathe in her sweet scent. More often than not, she'd climb into

433

bed with her daughter and fall asleep holding her close.

"We need to go on a cruise." Gwen clapped her hands together. "Another Disney one. Tatiana had a blast on the last one, and we can ask hunky Mark if he wants to come. I'm sure, with your free time now, you can finally date him. Nothing better to do while unemployed than hook up with your rich, hot, single neighbor."

Mark was their good-looking, charismatic neighbor who'd been after Jessica for as long as they'd lived next to each other. Never pushy, never overly aggressive, but always there and letting her know that he would take their friendship further if she desired. She was tempted—hell, she was human—and she hadn't been with anyone since Alex, but she couldn't get involved with Mark. If shit ever hit the fan, he'd be target number one as her boyfriend, and she had no doubt that is what he would become.

Plus, she had this weird feeling that he was submissive in the bedroom, and that would not work.

The whole situation with the man formerly known as her husband had messed her up so bad she hadn't even considered dating since she left him to save their daughter. A decision she never regretted from the moment she held Tatiana in her arms. Well, she may not have regretted it, but that didn't mean she didn't hurt every moment of every day in those first years. Ached inside of her heart in a way that wouldn't heal. At least she had her love for Tatiana to keep her strong...and over the last few years he had his hundreds of women.

Panic hit her as she realized she was doing the forbidden, thinking about him. No, the only way she survived was by not thinking about him. She quickly cleared her mind, irrationally fearful that even thinking about *him* would somehow call Jorg down on her, on Tatiana. Her heart raced at the memory of the feel of *his* lips on hers, of his scent filling her as he held her so securely in his arms. No matter how much she tried to keep *him* from her mind, *he* haunted her as surely as any ghost.

"Jessica?"

Her hands trembled so she crossed her arms like she was cold. "What?"

"Want me to book that cruise?"

She blinked for a moment then remembered their conversation. "No, no. I won't have the free time. I've been head-hunted."

Putting her hands on her ample hips, Gwen pursed her lips. "I don't get what you're saying. Explain."

"It means that I've been given a crazy good job offer on the very day I got fired. I'm to fly out to Spain to meet the owners of a technology firm who need my expertise in American fraud schemes. And they're giving me a generous signing bonus along with an amazing five-bedroom home right on the Mediterranean."

Gwen collapsed in the comfy, floral padded chair across from Jessica's desk, her dark eyes wide. "Shut the front door! You're lying."

"No, I'm serious! Look!"

As Gwen scanned the documents and websites, Jessica pulled up a couple different screens on her computer. "See, I've researched them and everything. They're legit. And they want me. I need to get them to sign me before the word gets out that I've been let go for suspected theft."

"Gossip travels fast," Gwen muttered before looking back up at Jessica. "Well, you best pack your bags, beautiful. You're on your way to Spain, and if you get this job, you know I'm coming with you. I loooove European men, and I can take some sculpting classes while I'm over there, maybe look into some gallery showings if I can get them. I'll book you on the next flight out."

Springing into motion, Jessica couldn't help the excitement filling her. A new place, somewhere she'd never been, someplace she could explore with her daughter. For a moment, a bit of apprehension bit at her stomach at the possibility of being closer to he-who-shall-not–be-named, but she dismissed her fear. It had been almost five years. He-of-no-name had moved on, repeatedly, and she'd seen it all on the Internet. She'd managed not to do a search on him for ten months now, and it was slowly getting easier to push back the clawing urge to make sure he was still all right, that he was still alive.

Maybe someday she would finally be ready to move on from the memory of the woman she used to be.

Gathering four of her suits and stuffing them into a travel bag, she then quickly filled two suitcases with everything she'd need. Gwen would call for a car service both to and from the airport, so all Jessica would have to do was get on and off the plane. When she was in her bathroom chucking her makeup and perfume into a bag, Gwen came in holding up a piece of paper with kittens printed on it.

"Your itinerary, and a car is on the way to take you to the airport."

Snatching up the decorative note, she scanned it quickly before sighing. "You are a miracle worker."

"You know it!" She took Jessica's hands in her own and met her friend's gaze. "Deep breath, you can do this. I have faith in you, and I just know your luck is changing."

Wishing with all her might that was true, Jessica lifted her shoulders and nodded. "Right. You have my number. Let Tatiana know I'll Skype with her as soon as I get settled in."

"I will." She gave Jessica a big hug. "Bigger and better things, my friend."

Closing her eyes, Jessica prayed that was true.

Madrid, Spain

Alex stared off into the distance, a storm rolling over the Mediterranean Sea far enough away that it was nothing more than dark clouds and flashes of lighting on the horizon. He gripped the warm wrought iron railing of his balcony facing water and wished he could enjoy the sunset. It was getting harder and harder for him to give a shit about things lately. Seeing his brother's love with Rya, witnessing their joy first hand, made him ache for someone to love him like that, but no woman he'd met could compare to his Jessica.

In a way, her death had cursed him to never love again.

He was snapped out of his trance by a man clearing his throat then speaking with a thick Irish brogue. "Been a long time, Alex."

Disbelief filled Alex as he turned and stared at a man he'd threatened to kill if he ever came near him again. At the sight of an older Peter standing there with more white in his hair than he'd had at Jessica's funeral, something in Alex slipped, some delicate grip he'd had on his rage snapped, and he snarled with anger before launching himself at Jessica's Uncle Peter. The bastard had delivered Rya to his father, even knowing what kind of monster he was. That was unforgivable.

Before he could get a grip on the other man who'd failed to protect Jessica, who'd endangered Alex's beloved sister-in-law, he was grabbed by his own damn bodyguards. Glaring at Krom and Oleg, he was shocked to see tears, god-be-damned tears in their eyes. His men never cried, ever. What the hell was going on?

Taking a firm step forward, Peter thrust a manila envelope to Alex. "Take this and sit down."

"Fuck you. I should shoot you in the face right now."

"Alex, be calm." Krom growled into Alex's ear. "You need to see this. Is most important thing that will ever happen to you."

Puzzled more than anything else by now, Alex snatched the envelope from Peter then, and in a useless act of defiance, stood instead of sitting on the long, brown couch that took up a wall in the master bedroom of his vacation home in Madrid.

After pulling out the contents of the envelope, he wished he'd listened to Krom, because with just the briefest glimpse at the pictures inside, he found himself falling like an invalid and landing hard on the soft cushions, almost sliding off the couch. He'd lost the ability to feel anything beyond overwhelming confusion and a shock so profound he found himself unable to think. It couldn't be...there was no way. He held up the photograph and stared at it, hard, examining a woman who almost looked like his Jessica with deep brown hair and a little girl that had the Novikov gray ringed with black eyes and auburn hair that matched Peter's. Except her eyes had a feline tilt to them that matched her mother's now brown eyes.

With his hands shaking, hell, his whole body trembling, he looked at the next picture, this one causing black spots to dance around the edges of his vision. Her feline blue eyes, a little older now, smiled at him as she posed for a picture with the little girl. This one, he assumed, had been taken a few years ago. She must have forgotten to put her fake contacts in and the sight of her brilliant blue eyes made black dots dance around the edges of his vision before he gasped in a strangled breath.

He saw his eye color and her shape blended perfectly in their daughter's round little face.

Something lurched in his chest, and he pulled in another tortured gasp of air. It couldn't be. They were dead. And yet the females in this picture glowed with life and happiness. Then again, he could see differences in Jessica now that he studied her image closer. Small lines around her eyes and the baby fat all gone from her face now, revealing the stunning beauty he'd seen from the moment their gaze met across a busy pub in Dublin all those years ago.

The memory assaulted him, his recollection of that moment perfect down to the scent of the pub mixing with his damp wool jacket.

Jessica.

Alive?

He didn't realize he'd spoken those words aloud until Peter said in an urgent voice. "I know this is a lot to take in, but time is of the essence. She'll be here in an hour. Thinks she's gettin' a job over here, and the house comes with it as a perk. There are some things you need to know before she arrives. Things that you'll hate, but must be said in order for you to understand why she left. And I need you to keep it together. If you can't handle yourself, Krom'll sit on ya."

Utterly dazed, he looked up to Krom. The scarred, stern man didn't remember that night because of his head injury and blamed himself for Jessica's death. He'd never gotten over it.

"It is Jessica. She is alive," Krom confirmed, then closed his eyes, "I made Peter show me the evidence before it was revealed to you. If he was wrong, I did

439

not want to have you endure the pain of false hope. She is alive. Somehow, I did not fail her."

"You did not fail her," Alex replied on a whisper. He felt a mighty load began to lift from his soul. "I need to know what happened."

"Your father." Peter held up his hand when Alex began to growl. "Control yourself. Your father convinced Jessica that if she stayed, her baby would die...or you would. Though I don't know exactly what was said, he easily manipulated Jessica into going into hiding. New name, new life, new everything back in the United States. Under strict orders from Jorg to never contact you again."

The need to rage, to destroy, to roar with anger tore at him, but he did not have the luxury of indulging his anger if Jessica was indeed truly on her way here. Yet the thought that his father did this to him, that somehow that vile old monster had taken Jessica away, sank inside of his heart like poison. Jorg knew how much Alex had suffered and had never said anything.

He couldn't die soon enough to pay for his sins.

"Relax, Alex," Krom murmured. "Do not meet her again with murder in your heart. God takes away blessings from those who do not appreciate it. Yes?"

Forcing himself to calm down, to appreciate the miracle that was really happening and wasn't some twisted dream he liked to torture himself with, Alex stared at the pictures, lovingly setting each one on the brass and glass table before the couch with a shaking hand. The third image was of an exhausted and melancholy looking Jessica smiling at the camera with a newborn Tatiana in her arms. His daughter had been born with a patch of peach-colored fuzz on her tiny head. The next one was of Jessica sleeping with the baby curled up on her chest. Jessica had her hand on the baby's little rump, holding their daughter close even in her sleep. A kind looking, young woman with long, dark hair held back in a braid with a pink ribbon through it was captured in the photo pulling the blanket up around them, no doubt tucking his exhausted woman in for a well-deserved nap.

He wished with all his heart he had been there.

The enormity of what he'd been missing in his life stared back him in the last picture. It was more recent, and he knew his daughter should be a over four years old right now. Mother and daughter were curled up together in a hammock. The nicely rounded woman with light brown skin and black hair held back in a single braid who had been in the hospital picture now blew bubbles at them in the new picture. Jessica was laughing, her fingertips reached out as though to touch a bubble, and he could see more of his Jessica in this photo. Despite her artificially dark hair, which looked good on her, she couldn't get rid of her freckles and his fingers trembled as he touched the image of her face.

The thought that soon he'd be able to touch her in the flesh almost destroyed him.

Sucking in a hard breath through his nose, he said in a low, furious voice, "My father was behind this?"

"Easy," Peter warned. "Your father thought, in his own psychotic way, he was protecting her from your enemies. When he was lucid enough to realize what he'd done, he decided it was better for her to be out of your life, and his, forever. Out of the reach of those who would kill Tatiana, so he set them up with new identities, money, and forbid her to ever see you again."

Giving a cry of pure rage, Alex exploded off the couch then began to throw anything he could get his hands on, needing some outlet for the emotions rampaging through him. His frenzy went on for a while until he stood there, sweating and panting, his right hand bleeding where he'd cut it on something. The room was utterly destroyed, but he'd calmed enough to think.

Peter said in a dry voice, "You now have half an hour until she's here."

Glaring at the other man, Alex strode past Peter and into his bathroom, stripping down and washing up as best he could in less than five minutes. He didn't give a fuck as his hand bled or that the water pouring off his face was more from tears than shower spray. Once he got out, Krom was there with a change of clothes and a med kit while Maks and Peter were cleaning up the room behind him. The scarred man silently bandaged Alex's hand then left so Alex could get dressed. He shrugged on his shirt and froze while looking in the mirror.

There, inked into his flesh, was the memorial to his wife and daughter...who were not dead.

Two perfect roses that lived on, taken from him by his father.

If his father wasn't dead by the time he returned home, Alex was going to personally kill him and smile while he did it.

He buttoned his shirt as best he could with his shaking, injured hand, which had begun to throb, before finishing getting ready in less than seven minutes.

Krom held up a black suit coat for Alex, which he shrugged on. Sudden elation filled him at the thought that he was getting ready to see Jessica again. His most fervent prayers had been answered. On the heels of that came crushing disbelief, and he wondered if he was losing his mind like his father had. These intense emotions were coming out of nowhere, hammering at his self-control, making him

442

feel for the first time in years.

"Alex," Peter said in a low voice, "Listen to me. I believe she is going to try to run away from you. She probably still believes that, if she returns, Jorg will kill her and take Tatiana away. No one has approached her yet. You will be the first, but this will be a great shock to her. You must control yourself."

"Control myself? *Control* myself?" He trembled with the need for violence, the anger coming hard and fast that this man would dare imply Alex would ever hurt her. "If I did not control myself, you would have been dead the moment I laid eyes on you, and I would *never* abuse my wife."

Peter shifted uncomfortably. "I'm not sayin' ya would. Just go easy on her."

"I do not care if I have to chain her to our bed for the next twenty years, she will never escape from me again." He pulled out his phone and began to dial his brother's number. "We do not have much time. Peter, is she bringing our daughter with her?"

"No. She's back in the States with her nanny."

"I want my daughter brought to me in Moscow. We will leave here tomorrow so that should give them time to pack whatever they want to bring with them. Only a few clothes, I will provide everything they need so only personal items and mementos. And they bring the nanny as well. Persuade her."

"Maybe we should wait for Jessica—"

"I have lived with the belief that my daughter was *dead.* You will bring her to me, now!"

"It will be done," Krom said in a low voice.

Peter threw up his hands. "You're just gonna piss her off."

Something occurred to Alex, and he paused as he left a text for his brother to call him as soon as possible. "Peter, why aren't you with her? Where's Mary?"

"Mary is back home with April. She's got pneumonia, and we didn't want to leave her without a parent." He ran a hand through his thinning hair. "Jessica doesn't know she's been found yet, and if she sees me, she'll know you aren't far behind. I know how you've suffered without her and wished I could do something to help you. Now I can. You need to talk to her before I do, but rest assured, I'll be having words with my niece about not coming to me for help. You have an uphill battle, Alex. I hope you realize this. From what I've seen, Jessica is a different woman now, not the one you used to know."

"Do you not understand? It does not matter. Nothing matters. As long as she is alive, I have chance to win her heart."

Peter shifted, his tired eyes searching Alex's. "What are you going to do about your father?"

"I will take care of it."

Alex's phone rang, and he let it go to voice mail since it was from his latest mistress, who he would no longer need. He would see that she was paid off most generously and make his plane available to take her anywhere in the world she wished—as long as her destination was away from him. The only women he'd have in his life now were his wife and daughter, and he couldn't be happier. No more sex without love, no more fucking just to try to feel some kind of connection to another human being, no more being alone.

Tears threatened again, but he would not cry in front of his men. His men had seen him broken when he buried her, but it had been raining that day so his tears had been hidden. No matter what, men did not cry.

The call that came in a few seconds later was from Dimitri. "Alex, Maks said I need to call you right away. What is wrong?"

444

"Sit down."

"What?"

An American woman's voice— Dimitri's wife, Rya—came from the background. "Is everything okay?"

Alex had to force the words out, words he'd never dreamed of saying. "Jessica and my daughter are alive and living in the States. I'm bringing them back to Moscow with me, and I need you to get some things ready for their arrival."

"What!" Dimitri roared. "I do not believe it."

"It is true...our father..."—his voice broke with rage—"took her from me."

"How?"

"I do not have time to explain. She is almost here. I need Rya to prepare my apartment in your building for Jessica and Tatiana. Tell her to make one of the spare bedrooms for Tatiana."

"Tatiana," Dimitri breathed. "Your daughter lived?"

"Yes. I have seen pictures. Hair like her mother's, but our eyes and her smile. Beautiful."

His phone beeped, and he saw his Uncle Petrov's name. "Dimitri, I have to go. It's Petrov."

"Of course. Everything will be done. A room is needed for Jessica—"

"No, it will be our room. I will not sleep another night without her at my side."

"Rya is asking how old Tatiana is."

"Almost five. Raised in America. I have to go."

With that, he switched over to Petrov's call, "Hello?"

His uncle's voice was vibrating with suppressed emotion as he said, "I hear you are having a visit from a ghost?"

No surprise that Petrov knew what had happened. Alex's heart galloped in his chest, and he wondered if maybe he would die of a heart attack right before she walked through the door. Bitter irony at its finest. "Yes."

"Alive?"

"Yes."

"Both of them?"

Alex had to force the words out, overcome by his feelings to the point where he'd be embarrassed if anyone but the men in this room saw him in such a state. Even now, they turned their backs, giving him what privacy they could in a show of respect. "Yes."

"God is merciful. What happened?"

"I don't know the specifics. Call Peter. He can fill you in on the details. My father was involved, that is of a certainty."

The silence coming through the phone was heavy, just the faint whisper of Petrov breathing. "Is she harmed?"

"I do not think so. The pictures I saw, and some had to be recent, show that she has changed her hair and wears colored contacts to try to blend in. Maybe some minor surgery on her face? Or maybe she is just older. Fuck, five years, Petrov. Five years of *hell*."

The command in his uncle's voice came through loud and clear, "Alex, listen to me. Now is a time when you must be strong. Now is a time when you will be a man and care for your family. It will not be easy, trust me—I have to keep three women happy—but it will be worth it. Her emotions will be intense. She may hate you. She may be scared of you. She may run as far away from you as she can. Somehow, she has managed to cut herself out of your life all of these years, and she may have done that by demonizing you in her mind." He sighed. "Or she may love you and cannot wait to be in your arms again. From all that I have heard from you about her...that kind of love does not die. Even your father could not destroy it."

446

Calm settled over Alex, the voice of his trusted mentor soothing him as he listened to Petrov and thought about the older man's words. He'd been given a second chance, a miracle, and he was not going to screw it up. While he wasn't a religious man, he realized he owed God some good deeds because of this. He'd offered God everything over and over again for another chance with his Jessica.

He heard the knock on the door to the suite.

And that opportunity, that miracle, had finally happened.

"She's here. I must go."

"Good luck."

It didn't matter anymore what Petrov had to say, because the door was opening and her voice, her *voice*, filled the air. Real, not imagined, not a fantasy born of his mind almost breaking beneath the weight of their deaths. With his soul starving for just a glimpse, he watched her enter the room, her gaze going first to Krom then the smile dropping from her lips as she paled.

Yes, she looked different now, but still as beautiful. With age, her cheeks had hollowed out, giving her tilted eyes an even more exotic look above her sharp cheekbones that would bring any man to his knees. She wore brown contacts, and her hair was still long, but it was a deep mahogany that flattered her pale skin. Her lips were the same, as was the way she placed her hand over her mouth when she was shocked by something.

Her desperate gaze scanned the room, her body shaking as she saw Peter, then Maks, then Oleg, and finally, she found him.

Stalking toward her, he ignored everything Petrov had said to him as irrational fury mingled with relief filled him. "How nice to see you again, Jessica. Care to tell me where the hell you have been for the

447

last five *years*?"

Immediate regret pierced through him like a sharp knife as her eyes rolled back and she began to collapse into a dead faint. Fuck, he was an asshole. He caught her just before every other male in the room sprinted to her aid, all of them glaring at Alex. Guilt replaced his anger, and he struggled to get hold of himself, entirely overwhelmed by the events of the last hour. Closing his eyes, he cradled her to his chest, her body fuller now, more womanly. Possibly curves given to her by motherhood. She felt divine, and he sank to the floor with her in his arms, leaning against the side of the couch while staring at her, his eyes burning as he refused to blink and miss even one second.

"Alex," Maks said in a strained voice,

"Get out."

"But—" Peter began.

"Out. Everyone except Krom."

Maks and Peter glared at him for a moment, but mainly kept their eyes on Jessica like they were starving for a glimpse of her.

The moment the door closed, Alex said to Krom, "I'm trusting you to assemble a team and go get my daughter. I'll have Jessica call and let her nanny know arrangements have been made to fly her and Tatiana out on a private jet. Follow my earlier instructions and update Dimitri with every detail. I will be unavailable for a while."

"It will be done."

He jerked his head to the door, the fact that his Jessica was in his arms tearing at the barriers between his controlled mask and the tempest raging inside of him. "Call my personal assistant and tell him to help Rya with anything she needs to ready the apartment for us. Let Ivan know as well. Gia can help. I want all my clothes brought from my townhome to the apartment. Contact Luka and tell him to activate a Black Tier for my family. Make sure it includes females and that they speak English. No ex-lovers of mine."

Krom nodded and turned to leave, then paused and looked back, his still stunned gaze firmly on Jessica. "Alex, she was terrified of us. Absolutely petrified by fear the moment she saw us, and you alarmed her so much she passed out. Be gentle."

"Fuck you," he snarled, pissed at everyone telling him to calm down like he was some raving lunatic. Yes, so he had lost his mind for a while after he thought she had died. Great, empty expanses of time were missing from his memory when he drank himself into oblivion night after night in the empty darkness of Siberia. If Dimitri hadn't come when he did, Alex was sure he would have drunk himself to death, but that was the past. Now his wife and daughter were back, and he would do whatever was necessary to keep them there.

Jessica stirred in his arms, and he leaned down, smelling her hair. Her perfume was different now, more sophisticated, but it still held a strong hint of apples, deluging him in beautiful memories. He shook as he touched the warm, soft skin of her neck, her pulse beating strong and sure beneath his fingertip. She still had the scar beneath her chin she'd gotten falling out of a tree when she was a child. A tear fell down the cheek bearing the scar his father's torture master had given him, then another, as he held his wife and reverently kissed her delicate face and began to plan his strategy to heal the damage his father had done to them and win her love back.

449

Dear Beloved Reader,

Please put away the pitchforks and torches. I can't write the next book if I've been beaten by a wet noodle for having a cliffhanger-ish. ;) I'm working hard now on 'Alexandr's Reluctant Submissive' (Submissive's Wish, #4), the conclusion of Jessica and Alex's story, with an expected publication date of early Fall 2015. You can check for more information on ARS on either my website, www.annmayburn.com or at www.fatedesires.com . Thank you once again for giving me the chance to entertain you, and for spending some time with my hot Russian Doms and the women who love them.

Ann

About the Author

With over forty published books, Ann is Queen of the Castle to her husband and three sons in the mountains of West Virginia. In her past lives she's been an Import Broker, a Communications Specialist, a US Navy Civilian Contractor, a Bartender/Waitress, and an actor at the Michigan Renaissance Festival. She also spent a summer touring with the Grateful Dead-though she will deny to her children that it ever happened.

From a young Ann has had a love affair with books would read everything she could get her hands on. As Ann grew older, and her hormones kicked in, she discovered bodice ripping Fabio-esque romance novels. They were great at first, but she soon grew tired of the endless stories with a big wonderful emotional buildup to really short and crappy sex. Never a big fan of purple prose, throbbing spears of fleshy pleasure and wet honey pots make her giggle, she sought out books that gave the sex scenes in the story just as much detail and plot as everything else-without using cringe worthy euphemisms. This led her to the wonderful world of Erotic Romance, and she's never looked back.

Now Ann spends her days trying to tune out cartoons playing in the background to get into her 'sexy space' and has accepted that her Muse has a severe case of ADD.

Ann loves to talk with her fans, as long as they realize she's weird and that sarcasm doesn't translate well via text. You can find her at:

Website
http://www.annmayburn.com/

Facebook
https://www.facebook.com/ann.mayburn.5

Pintrest
http://pinterest.com/annmayburn/

Twitter
https://twitter.com/AnnMayburn

Book List

Prides of the Moon Series
Amber Moon
Emerald Moon
Onyx Moon
Amethyst Moon
Opal Moon

Club Wicked Series
My Wicked Valentine
My Wicked Nanny
My Wicked Devil
My Wicked Trainers
My Wicked Masters

Virtual Seduction Series
Sodom and Detroit
Sodom and the Phoenix

Submissives Wish Series
Ivan's Captive Submissive
Dimitri's Forbidden Submissive
Alexandr's Cherished Submissive
Alexandr's Reluctant Submissive

Long Slow Tease Series (FemDom)
Still
Penance

Emma's Arabian Nights (FemDom)
First Kiss
Second Touch
Third Chance
Fourth Embrace(Coming Soon)

Bondmates Series
Casey's Warriors
Jaz's Warriors(Novella Coming Soon)
Paige's Warriors(Novel Coming Soon)

Iron Horse MC Series
Exquisite Trouble
Exquisite Danger

For the Love of Evil Series
Daughter of the Abyss
Princess of the Abyss

Sam and Cody
Want
Cherish
Adore

Chosen by the Gods
Cursed
Blessed
Dreamer

Single Titles
Blushing Violet
Bound for Pleasure (FemDom)
Sensation Play
Peppermint Passion
The Breaker's Concubine
Guarding Hope
Scandalous Wish
Pursued by the Prisoner
The Bodyguard's Princess
Summer's Need
Wild Lilly
Diamond Heart

Made in the USA
San Bernardino, CA
19 September 2015